SAM EASTLAND

The Red Coffin

faber and faber

First published in 2011
by Faber and Faber Limited
Bloomsbury House,
74–77 Great Russell Street,
London WC1B 3DA

Typeset by RefineCatch Limited, Bungay, Suffolk
Printed in England by CPI Mackays, Chatham

All rights reserved
© Sam Eastland, 2011

The right of Sam Eastland to be identified as author of this work
has been asserted in accordance with Section 77 of the Copyright,
Designs and Patents Act 1988

This book is sold subject to the condition that it shall not,
by way of trade or otherwise, be lent, resold, hired out or otherwise circulated
without the publisher's prior consent in any form of binding or cover
other than that in which it is published and without a similar condition
including this condition being imposed on the subsequent purchaser

A CIP record for this book
is available from the British Library

ISBN 978–0–571–24530–7

2 4 6 8 10 9 7 5 3 1

The Red Coffin

Sam Eastland lives in the US and the UK. He is the grandson of a London police detective.

by the same author

EYE OF THE RED TSAR

THE RED COFFIN

As the motorcycle crested the hill, sunlight winked off the goggles of the rider. Against the chill of early spring, he wore a double-breasted leather coat and a leather flying cap which buckled under his chin.

He had been on the road for three days, stopping only to buy fuel along the way. His saddlebags were filled with tins of food he'd brought from home.

At night, he did not stay in any town, but wheeled his motorcycle in amongst the trees. It was a new machine, a Zundapp K500, with a pressed-steel frame and girder forks. Normally he could never have afforded it, but this trip alone would pay for everything, and more besides. He thought about that as he sat there alone in the woods, eating cold soup from a can.

Before camouflaging the motorcycle with fallen branches, he wiped the dust from its sprung leather seat and the large teardrop-shaped fuel tank. He spat on every scratch he found and rubbed them with his sleeve.

The man slept on the ground, wrapped in an oilcloth sheet, without the comfort of a fire or even a cigarette. The smell of smoke might have given away his location, and he could not afford to take the risk.

Sometimes, he was woken by the rumble of Polish Army trucks passing by on the road. None of them stopped.

Once he heard a crashing in among the trees. He drew a revolver from his coat and sat up, just as a stag passed a few paces away, barely visible, as if the shadows themselves had come to life. For the rest of the night, the man did not sleep. Tormented by childhood nightmares of human shapes with antlers sprouting from their heads, he wanted only to be gone from this country. Ever since he crossed the German border into Poland, he had been afraid, although no one who saw him would ever have realised it. This was not the first time he had been on such a journey, and the man knew from experience that his fear would not leave him until he was back among his own people again.

On the third day, he crossed into the Soviet Union at a lonely border checkpoint manned by one Polish soldier and one Russian soldier, neither of whom could speak the other's language. Both men came out to admire his motorcycle. 'Zundapp,' they crooned softly, as if saying the name of a loved one and the man gritted his teeth while they ran their hands over the chrome.

A few minutes after leaving the checkpoint, he pulled over to the side of the road and raised the goggles to his forehead, revealing two pale moons of skin where the road dust had not settled on his face. Shielding his eyes with one hand, he looked out over the rolling countryside. The fields were ploughed and muddy, seeds of rye and barley still sleeping in the ground. Thin feathers of smoke rose from the chimneys of solitary farmhouses, their slate roofs patched with luminous green moss.

The man wondered what the inhabitants of those houses might do if they knew their way of life would soon be ending.

Even if they did know, he told himself, they would probably just carry on as they had always done, placing their faith in miracles. That, he thought, is precisely why they deserve to be extinct. The task he had come here to accomplish would bring that moment closer. After today, there would be nothing they could do to stop it. Then he wiped the fingerprints of the border guards off his handlebars and continued on his way.

He was close to the rendezvous point, racing along deserted roads, through patches of mist which clung to the hollows like ink diffusing in water. The words of half-remembered songs escaped his lips. Otherwise he did not speak, as if he were alone upon the earth. Driving out across that empty countryside, that was how he felt himself to be.

At last he came to the place he had been looking for. It was an abandoned farmhouse, roof sagging like the back of an old horse. Turning off the road, he drove the Zundapp through an opening in the stone wall which ringed the farmyard. Over-grown trees ringed the farmhouse, their thick trunks sheathed with ivy. A flock of crows scattered from their branches, their ghostly shapes reflected in the puddles of the farmyard.

When he cut the engine, silence descended upon him. Removing his gauntlets, he scratched at the dried mud which had spattered on his chin. It flaked away like scabs, revealing a week's growth of stubble beneath.

Shutters hung loose and rotten on the windows of the farmhouse. The door had been kicked in and lay flat on the floor inside the house. Dandelions grew between cracks in the floorboards.

He set the Zundapp on its kick stand, drew his gun and stepped cautiously into the house. Holding the revolver down by his side, he trod across the creaking floorboards. Grey light filtered through the slits between the shutters. In the fire-place, a pair of dragon-headed andirons scowled at him as he walked by.

'There you are,' said a voice.

The Zundapp rider flinched, but he did not raise the gun. He stood still, scanning the shadows. Then he spotted a man, sitting at a table in the next room, which had once been a kitchen. The stranger smiled, raised one hand and moved it slowly back and forth. 'Nice motorcycle,' he said.

The rider put away his gun and stepped into the kitchen.

'Right on time,' said the man. Set on the table in front of him was a Tokarev automatic pistol, two small metal cups, each one not bigger than an eggshell. Beside the cups stood an unopened bottle of Georgian Ustashi vodka, a blue-green colour from the steppe grass used to flavour it. The man had placed a second chair on the other side of the table, so that the rider would have a place to sit. 'How was your trip?' asked the man.

'Do you have it?' said the rider.

'Of course.' The man reached into his coat and pulled out a bundle of documents which had been rolled up like a news-paper. He let them fall with a slap on to the table, raising a tiny cloud of dust from the dirty wooden surface.

'That's everything?' asked the rider.

The man patted the bundle reassuringly. 'Full operational schematics for the entire Konstantin Project.'

The Zundapp rider put one foot on the chair and rolled up his trouser leg. Taped to his calf was a leather envelope. The man removed the tape, swearing quietly as it tore away the hair on his leg. Then he removed a stack of money from the envelope and laid it on the table. 'Count it,' he said.

Obligingly, the man counted the money, walking the tips of his fingers through the bills.

Somewhere above them, in the rafters of the house, starlings trilled and clicked their beaks.

When the man had finished counting, he filled the two small cups with vodka and lifted one of them. 'On behalf of the White Guild, I would like to thank you. A toast to the Guild and to the downfall of Communism!'

The man did not reach for his cup. 'Are we finished here?' he asked.

'Yes!' The man knocked back his vodka, then reached for the second cup, raised it in salute and drank that too. 'I think we are finished.'

The rider reached across and picked up the documents. As he tucked the bundle into the inside pocket of his coat, he paused to look around the room. He studied the canopies of spider webs, the puckered wallpaper and the cracks which had crazed the ceiling like the growth lines on a skull. You will be home soon, he thought to himself. Then you can forget this ever happened.

'Would you care for a smoke?' asked the man. He laid a cigarette case on the table and set a brass lighter on top.

The rider stared at him, almost as if he knew this man from someplace before but could not remember where. 'I should be going,' said the rider.

'Maybe next time.' The man smiled.

The rider turned away and started walking back towards his motorcycle.

He had gone only three paces when the man snatched up his Tokarev pistol, squinted down the line of his outstretched arm and, without getting up from the table, shot the rider in the back of the head. The bullet tore through the rider's skull and a piece of his forehead skittered away across the floor. He dropped to the ground like a puppet whose strings had been cut.

Now the man rose to his feet. He came out from behind the table and rolled the corpse over with his boot. The rider's arm swung out and his knuckles struck against the floor. The man bent down and removed the documents from the rider's pocket.

'You'll drink now, you fascist son of a bitch,' he said. Then he took the bottle of vodka and emptied it out over the rider, soaking his head and shoulders and pouring a stream along the length of his legs. When the bottle was empty, he threw it away across the room. The heavy glass slammed against a rotten wall but did not break.

The man stashed the money and the documents in his pocket. Then he gathered up his gun, his little cups and his box of cigarettes. On his way out of the house, he spun the metal wheel of his lighter and when the fire jumped up from the wick, he dropped the lighter on top of the dead man. The alcohol burst into flames with a sound like a curtain billowing in the wind.

The man walked out into the farmyard and stood before the motorcycle, trailing his fingers over the Zundapp name emblazoned on the fuel tank. Then he straddled the motorcycle and lifted the helmet and goggles from where they hung on the handlebars. He put on the helmet and settled the goggles over his eyes. The heat of the dead man's body was still in the leather eye pads. Kick-starting the motorcycle, he drove out on to the road and the Zundapp snarled as he shifted through the gears.

Behind him, already in the distance, a mushroom cloud of smoke rose from the blazing ruins of the farmhouse.

Officially, the Borodino restaurant, located in a quiet street just off the Bolotnia Square in Moscow, was open to the public. Unofficially, the owner and head waiter, a gaunt-faced man named Chicherin, would size up whoever came through the front door, its frosted glass panes decorated with a pattern of ivy leaves. Then Chicherin would either offer the patrons a table or would direct them down a narrow unlit corridor to what they assumed was a second dining room on the other side of the door. This would take them directly into an alley at the side of the restaurant. By the time they realised what had happened, the door would have locked automatically behind them. If the patrons still refused to take the hint and chose to come back into the restaurant, they would be confronted by the bartender, a former Greek wrestler named Niarchos, and ejected from the premises.

On a dreary afternoon in March, with clumps of dirty snow still clinging to the sunless corners of the city, a young man in a military uniform entered the restaurant. He was tall, with a narrow face, rosy cheeks and a look of permanent curiosity. His smartly tailored *gymnastiorka* tunic fitted closely to his shoulders and his waist. He wore blue dress trousers with a red line of piping down the outside and knee-length black boots which glowed with a fresh coat of polish.

Chicherin scanned the uniform for any sign of elevated rank. Anything below the rank of captain was enough to qualify a soldier for a trip down the corridor to what Chicherin called The Enchanted Grotto. Not only did this young man have no rank, he was not even wearing any insignia to denote his branch of service.

Chicherin was disgusted, but he smiled and said, 'Good day,' lowering his head slightly but not taking his eyes off the young man.

'Good day to you,' came the reply. The man looked around at the full tables, admiring the plates of food. 'Ah,' he sighed. 'Shashlik.' He gestured towards a plate of fluffy white rice, on which a waiter was placing cubes of roast lamb, onions and green peppers, carefully sliding them from the skewer on which they had been grilled. 'Has the lamb been soaked in red wine,' he sniffed at the steam which drifted past his face, 'or is it pomegranate juice?'

Chicherin narrowed his eyes. 'Are you looking for a table?'

The young man did not seem to hear. 'And there,' he pointed. 'Salmon with dill and horseradish sauce.'

'Yes, that's right,' Chicherin took him gently by the arm and steered him down the corridor. 'This way, please.'

'Down there?' the young man squinted into the dark tunnel of the corridor.

'Yes, yes,' Chicherin reassured him. 'The Enchanted Grotto.'

Obediently, the young man disappeared into the alley.

A moment later, Chicherin heard the reassuring clunk of the metal door locking shut. Then came the helpless rattle of the door knob as the young man tried to get back in.

Usually, people took the hint, and Chicherin never saw them again. This time, however, when the young man reappeared less than a minute later, still smiling innocently, Chicherin nodded to Niarchos.

Niarchos was smearing a grubby-looking rag inside glasses used for serving tea. When Niarchos caught Chicherin's eye, he raised his head with a short, abrupt movement, like a horse trying to shake off its bridle. Then, very carefully, he set down the glass he had been polishing and came out from behind the bar.

'There seems to be some kind of mistake,' said the young man. 'My name is Kirov, and . . .'

'You should go,' Niarchos interrupted. He resented having to come out from behind the bar, and lose the pleasant flow of daydreams as he mindlessly polished the glasses.

'I think . . .' Kirov attempted once more to explain.

'Yes, yes,' hissed Chicherin, appearing suddenly beside him, the smile having evaporated from his face. 'Some kind of mistake, you say. But the only mistake is your coming in here. Can't you see that this is not the place for you?' He glanced out over the tables, populated mostly by jowly, red-faced men with grizzled grey hair. Some wore olive-brown gaberdine tunics bearing the ranks of senior commissars. Others had civilian clothes, of European cut and good-quality wool, so finely woven that it seemed to shimmer beneath the orchid-shaped light fixtures. Sitting among these officers and politicians were beautiful but bored-looking women, sipping smoke from cork-tipped cigarettes. 'Listen,' said Chicherin, 'even if you could get a table here, I doubt you could afford the meal.'

'But I have not come to eat,' protested Kirov. 'Besides, I do my own cooking, and it looks to me as if your chef relies too heavily on his sauces.'

Chicherin's forehead crumpled in confusion. 'So you are looking for a job?'

'No,' replied the young man. 'I am looking for Colonel Nagorski.'

Chicherin's eyes widened. He glanced towards a table in the corner of the room where two men were eating lunch. Both of the men wore suits. One was shaved bald, and the great dome of his head looked like a sphere of pink granite resting on the starched white pedestal of his shirt collar. The other man had thick black hair combed straight back on his head. The sharp angle of his cheekbones was offset by a slightly pointed beard cut close against his chin. This made him look as if his face had been stretched over an inverted triangle of wood, and so tightly that even the slightest expression might tear the flesh from his bones.

'You want Colonel Nagorski?' asked Chicherin. He nodded towards the man with the thick black hair. 'Well, there he is, but . . .'

'Thank you.' Kirov took one step towards the table.

Chicherin gripped his arm. 'Listen my young friend, do yourself a favour and go home. Whoever sent you on this errand is just trying to get you killed. Do you have any idea what you are doing? Or who you are dealing with?'

Patiently, Kirov reached inside his jacket and removed a telegram, the fragile yellow paper banded with a line of red across the top, indicating that it had come from an office of the government. 'You should take a look at this.'

Chicherin snatched the telegram from his hand.

All this time, the bartender Niarchos had been looming over the young man, his dark eyes narrowed into slits. But now, at the sight of this telegram, which looked to him so frail that it might at any moment evaporate into smoke, Niarchos began to grow nervous.

By now, Chicherin had finished reading the telegram.

'I need that back,' said the young man.

Chicherin did not reply. He continued to stare at the telegram, as if expecting more words to materialise.

Kirov slipped the flimsy paper from between Chicherin's fingers and set off across the dining room.

This time, Chicherin did nothing to stop him.

Niarchos stepped out of the way, his huge body swinging to the side as if he were on some kind of hinge.

On his way to the table of Colonel Nagorski, Kirov paused to stare at various meals, breathing in the smells and sighing with contentment or making soft grunts of disapproval at the heavy-handed use of cream and parsley. Arriving at last beside Nagorski's table, the young man cleared his throat.

Nagorski looked up. The skin stretched over his cheekbones looked like polished wax. 'More blinis for the caviar!' he slapped his hand down on the table.

'Comrade Nagorski,' said Kirov.

Nagorski had turned back to his meal, but at the mention of his name he froze. 'How do you know my name?' he asked quietly.

'Your presence is required, Comrade Nagorski.'

Nagorski glanced towards the bar, hoping to catch the eye of Niarchos. But Niarchos's attention seemed completely focused on polishing tea glasses. Now Nagorski looked around for Chicherin, but the manager was nowhere to be seen. Finally, he turned to the young man. 'Exactly where is my presence required?' he asked.

'That will be explained on the way,' said Kirov.

Nagorski's companion sat with arms folded, gaze fixed, his thoughts unreadable.

Kirov couldn't help noticing that although Nagorski's plate was loaded with food, the only thing set in front of the bald giant was a small salad made of pickled cabbages and beets.

'What makes you think,' began Nagorski, 'that I am just going to get up and walk out of here with you?'

'If you don't come willingly, Comrade Nagorski, I have orders to arrest you.' Kirov held out the telegram.

Nagorski brushed the piece of paper aside. 'Arrest me?' he shouted.

A sudden silence descended upon the restaurant.

Nagorski dabbed a napkin against his thin lips. Then he threw the cloth down on top of his food and stood up.

By now, all eyes had turned to the table in the corner.

Nagorski smiled broadly, but his eyes remained cold and hostile. Digging one hand into the pockets of his coat, he withdrew a small automatic pistol.

A gasp went up from the nearby tables. Knives and forks clattered on to plates.

Kirov blinked at the gun.

'You look a little jumpy,' smiled Nagorski. Then he turned the weapon in his palm so that the butt was facing outwards and handed it to the other man at the table.

His companion reached out and took it.

'Take good care of that,' said Nagorski. 'I'll be wanting it back very soon.'

'Yes, Colonel,' replied the man. He set the gun beside his plate, as if it were another piece of cutlery.

Now Nagorski slapped the young man on the back. 'Let's see what this is all about, shall we?'

Kirov almost lost his balance from the jolt of Nagorski's palm. 'A car is waiting.'

'Good!' Nagorski announced in a loud voice. 'Why walk when we can ride?' He laughed and looked around.

Faint smiles passed across the faces of the other customers.

The two men made their way outside.

As Nagorski walked by the kitchen, he saw Chicherin's face framed in one of the little round windows of the double swinging doors.

Outside the Borodino, sleet lay like frog spawn on the pavement.

As soon as the door had closed behind them, Nagorski grabbed the young man by his collar and threw him up against the brick wall of the restaurant.

The young man did not resist. He looked as if he'd been expecting this.

'Nobody disturbs me when I am eating!' growled Nagorski, lifting the young man up on to the tips of his toes. 'Nobody survives that kind of stupidity!'

Kirov nodded towards a black car, its engine running, pulled up at the kerbside. 'He is waiting, Comrade Nagorski.'

Nagorski glanced over his shoulder. He noticed the shape of someone sitting in the back seat. He could not make out a face. Then he turned back to the young man. 'Who are you?' he asked.

'My name is Kirov. Major Kirov.'

'Major?' Nagorski let go of him suddenly. 'Why didn't you say so?' Now he stood back and brushed at Kirov's crumpled lapel. 'We might have avoided this unpleasantness.' He strode across to the car and climbed into the rear seat.

Major Kirov got in behind the wheel.

Nagorski settled back into his seat. Only then did he look at the person sitting beside him. 'You!' he shouted.

'Good afternoon,' said Pekkala.

'Oh, shit,' replied Colonel Nagorski.

Inspector Pekkala was a tall, powerful-looking man with broad shoulders and slightly narrowed eyes the colour of mahogany. He had been born in Lappeenranta, Finland, at a time when it was still a Russian colony. His mother was a Laplander, from Rovaniemi in the north.

At the age of eighteen, on the wishes of his father, Pekkala travelled to Petrograd in order to enlist in the Tsar's elite Finnish Legion. There, early in his training, he had been singled out by the Tsar for duty as his own Special Investigator. It was a position which had never existed before and which would one day give Pekkala powers considered unimaginable before the Tsar chose to create them.

In preparation for this, he was given over to the Police, then to the State Police – the Gendarmerie – and after that to the Tsar's Secret Police, who were known as the Okhrana. In those long months, doors were opened to him which few men even knew existed. At the completion of Pekkala's training, the Tsar presented him with the only badge of office he would ever wear – a heavy gold disc, as wide across as the length of his little finger. Across the centre was a stripe of white enamel inlay, which began at a point, widened until it took up half the disc and narrowed again to a point on the other side. Embedded in the middle of the white enamel was a large, round emerald. Together, these elements formed the unmistakable shape of an eye. Pekkala never forgot the first time he held the disc in his hand, and the way he had traced his fingertip over the eye, feeling the smooth bump of the jewel, like a blind man reading Braille.

It was because of this badge that Pekkala became known as the Emerald Eye. The public knew little else about him. His photograph could not be published or even taken. In the absence of facts, legends grew up around Pekkala, including rumours that he was not even human, but rather some demon conjured into life through the black arts of an arctic shaman.

Throughout his years of service, Pekkala answered only to the Tsar. In that time he learned the secrets of an empire, and when that empire fell, and those who shared those secrets had taken them to their graves, Pekkala was surprised to find himself still breathing.

Captured during the Revolution, he was sent to the Siberian labour camp of Borodok, where he tried to forget the world he'd left behind.

But the world he left behind had not forgotten him.

After seven years alone in the forest of Krasnagolyana, during which time he lived more like a wild animal than as a man, Pekkala was brought back to Moscow on the orders of Stalin himself.

Since that time, maintaining an uneasy truce with his former enemies, Pekkala had continued in his role as Special Investigator.

Deep beneath the streets of Moscow, Colonel Rolan Nagorski sat on a metal chair in a cramped cell of the Lubyanka prison. The walls were painted white. A single light bulb, protected by a dusty metal cage, lit the room.

Nagorski had taken off his jacket and hung it on the back of the chair. Braces stretched tight over his shoulders. As he spoke, he rolled up his sleeves, as if preparing for a brawl. 'Before you start firing questions at me, Inspector Pekkala, let me ask one of you.'

'Go ahead,' said Pekkala. He sat opposite the man, on the same kind of metal chair. The room was so small that their knees were almost touching.

Even though it was stifling in the room, Pekkala had not taken off his coat. It was cut in the old style: black and knee length, with a short collar and concealed buttons which fastened on the left side of his chest. He sat unnaturally straight, like a man with an injured back. This was caused by the gun which he kept strapped across his chest.

The gun was a Webley .455 revolver, with solid brass handles and a pin-sized hole drilled into the barrel just behind the forward sight to stop the pistol from bucking when it fired. The modification had been made not for Pekkala but for the Tsar, who received it as a gift from his cousin King George V. The Tsar then issued the Webley to

Pekkala. 'I have no use for such a weapon,' the Tsar had told him. 'If my enemies get close enough for me to need this, it will already be too late to do me any good.'

'The question I wanted to ask you,' said Nagorski, 'is why you think I would give away the secret of my own invention to the same people we might have to use it against?'

Pekkala opened his mouth to reply, but he did not get the chance.

'You see, I know why I'm here,' continued Nagorski. 'You think I am responsible for breaches of security in the Konstantin Project. I am neither so naive, nor so uninformed that I don't know what's going on around me. That's why every stage of development has taken place in a secure facility. The entire base is under permanent lockdown and under my own personal control. Everyone who works there has been cleared by me. Nothing happens at the facility without my knowing about it.'

'Which brings us back to your reason for being here today.'

Now Nagorski leaned forward. 'Yes, Inspector Pekkala. Yes, it does, and I could have saved you some time and myself a very expensive meal if you had simply let me tell your errand boy . . .'

'That "errand boy", as you call him, is a major of Internal Security.'

'Even NKVD officers can be errand boys, Inspector, if their bosses are running the country. What I could have told your major is the same thing I'm going to tell you now, which is that there has been no breach of security.'

'The weapon you are calling the T-34 is known to our enemies,' said Pekkala. 'I'm afraid that is a fact you can't deny.'

'Of course, its existence is known. You can't design, build and field-test a machine weighing thirty tons, and expect it to remain invisible. But its existence is not what I'm talking about. The secret lies in what it can do. I admit it's true that there are members of my design team who could tell you pieces of this puzzle, but only one person knows its full potential.' Nagorski sat back and folded his arms. Sweat was running down his polished face. 'That would be me, Inspector Pekkala.'

'There is something I don't understand,' said Pekkala. 'What is so special about your invention? Don't we already have tanks?'

Nagorski coughed out a laugh. 'Certainly! There is the T-26.' He let one hand fall open, as if a miniature tank were resting on his palm. 'But it is too slow.' The hand closed up into a fist. 'Then there is the BT series.' The other hand fell open. 'But it doesn't have enough armour. You might as well ask me why we are building weapons at all when there are plenty of stones lying around to throw at our enemies when they invade.'

'You sound very confident, Comrade Nagorski.'

'I am more than confident!' Nagorski barked in his face. 'I am certain, and it is not merely because I invented the T-34. It is because I have faced tanks in battle. Only when you have watched them lumbering towards you, and you know you are helpless to stop them, do you understand why tanks can win not only a battle but a war.'

'When did you face tanks?' asked Pekkala.

'In the war we fought against Germany, and God help us if we ever have to fight another. When the war broke out in the summer of 1914, I was in Lyon, competing in the French Grand Prix. Back then, racing automobiles was my entire life. I won that race, you know, the only automobile race our country has ever won. It was the happiest day of my life, and it would have been perfect if my chief mechanic hadn't been struck by one of the other race cars, which skidded off the track.'

'Was he killed?' asked Pekkala.

'No,' replied Nagorski, 'but he was badly injured. You see, racing is a dangerous game, Inspector, even if you're not behind the wheel.'

'When did you first become interested in these machines?'

As the topic turned to engines, Nagorski began to relax. 'I got my first look at an automobile in 1907. It was a Rolls-Royce Silver Ghost, which had been brought into Russia by the Grand Duke Mikhail. My father and he used to go hunting each year, for Merganser ducks up in the Pripet Marshes. Once, when the Grand Duke had stopped by our house in his car, father asked to see the inner workings of the machine.' Nagorski laughed. 'That's what he called them. The inner workings. As if it was some kind of mantel clock. When the Grand Duke lifted the hood, my life changed in an instant. My father just stared at it. To him, it was nothing more than a baffling collection of metal pipes and bolts. But to me that engine made sense. It was as if I had seen it before. I have never been able to explain it properly. All I knew for certain was that my future lay with these engines. It wasn't long before I had built one for myself. Over the next ten years, I won more than twenty races. If the war hadn't come along, that's what

I'd still be doing. But everybody has a story which begins that way, don't they, Inspector? If the war hadn't come along . . .'

'What did happen to you in the war?' interrupted Pekkala.

'I couldn't get back to Russia, so I enlisted in the French Foreign Legion. There were men from all over the world, caught in the wrong country when the war broke out and with no way to return home. I had been with the Legion almost two years when we came up against tanks near the French village of Flers. We had all heard about these machines. The British first used them against the Germans at the battle of Cambrai in 1917. By the following year, the Germans had designed their own. I had never even seen one until we went into action against them. My first thought was how slowly they moved. Six kilometres an hour. That's a walking pace. And nothing graceful about them. It was like being attacked by giant metal cockroaches. Three of the five broke down before they even reached us, one was knocked out with artillery and the last managed to escape, although we found it two days later burned out by the side of the road, apparently from engine malfunction.'

'That does not sound like an impressive introduction.'

'No, but as I watched those iron hulks being destroyed, or grinding to a halt of their own accord, I realised that the future of warfare lay in these machines. Tanks are not merely some passing fad of butchery, like the crossbow or the trebuchet. I saw at once what needed to be done to improve the design. I glimpsed technologies that had not even been invented yet, but which, in the months ahead, I created in my head and on any scrap of paper I could find. When the war ended, those scraps were what I brought back with me to this country.'

Pekkala knew the rest of that story; how one day Nagorski had walked into the newly formed Soviet Patent Office in Moscow with over twenty different designs which ultimately earned him the directorship of the T-34 project. Until that time, he had been eking out a living on the streets of Moscow, polishing the boots of men he would later command.

'Do you know the limits of my development budget?' asked Nagorski.

'I do not,' replied Pekkala.

'That's because there aren't any,' said Nagorski. 'Comrade Stalin knows exactly how important this machine is to the safety of our country. So I can spend whatever I want, take whatever I want, order whomever I choose to do whatever I decide. You accuse me of taking risks with the safety of this country, but the blame for that belongs with the man who sent you here. You can tell Comrade Stalin from me that if he continues arresting members of the Soviet armed forces at the rate he is doing, there will be no one left to drive my tanks even if he does let me finish my work!'

Pekkala knew that the true measure of Nagorski's power was not in the money he could spend, but in the fact that he could say what he'd just said without fear of a bullet in the brain. And Pekkala himself said nothing in reply, not because he feared Nagorski, but because he knew that Nagorski was right.

Afraid that he was losing control of the government, Stalin had ordered mass arrests. In the past year and a half, over a million people had been taken into custody. Among them were most of the Soviet high command, who had then either been shot or sent out to the Gulags.

'Perhaps,' suggested Pekkala, 'you have had a change of heart about this tank of yours. It might occur to someone in that situation to try to undo what they have done.'

'By giving its secrets to the enemy, you mean?'

Pekkala nodded slowly. 'That is one possibility.'

'Do you know why it is called the Konstantin Project?'

'No, Comrade Nagorski.'

'Konstantin is the name of my son, my only child. You see, Inspector, this project is as sacred to me as my own family. There is nothing I would do to harm it. Some people cannot understand that. They write me off as some kind of Dr Frankenstein, obsessed only with bringing a monster to life. They don't understand the price I have to pay for my accomplishments. Success can be as harmful as failure when you are just trying to get on with your life. My wife and son have suffered greatly.'

'I understand,' said Pekkala.

'Do you?' asked Nagorski, almost pleading. 'Do you really?'

'We have both made difficult choices,' said Pekkala.

Nagorski nodded, staring away into the corner of the room, lost in thought. Then suddenly he faced Pekkala. 'Then you should know that everything I've told you is the truth.'

'Excuse me, Colonel Nagorski,' said Pekkala. He got up, left the room and walked down the corridor, which was lined with metal doors. His footsteps made no sound on the grey industrial carpeting. All sound had been removed, as if the air had been sucked out of this place. At the end of the corridor, one door remained slightly ajar. Pekkala knocked once and walked in to a room so filled with smoke that his first breath felt like a mouthful of ashes.

'Well, Pekkala?' said a voice. Sitting by himself in a chair in the corner of the otherwise empty room was a man of medium height and stocky build, with a pock-marked face and withered left hand. His hair was thick and dark, combed straight back on his head. A moustache sewn with threads of grey bunched beneath his nose. He was smoking a cigarette, of which so little remained that one more puff would have touched the embers to his skin.

'Very well, Comrade Stalin,' said Pekkala.

The man stubbed out his cigarette on the sole of his shoe and blew the last grey breath in two streams from his nose. 'What do you think of our Colonel Nagorski?' he asked.

'I think he is telling the truth,' replied Pekkala.

'I don't believe it,' replied Stalin. 'Perhaps your assistant should be questioning him.'

'Major Kirov,' said Pekkala.

'I know who he is!' Stalin's voice rose in anger.

Pekkala understood. It was the mention of Kirov's name which unnerved Stalin, since Kirov was also the name of the former Leningrad Party Chief, who had been assassinated five years earlier. The death of Kirov had weighed upon Stalin, not because of any lasting affection for the man, but because it showed that if a person like Kirov could be killed, then Stalin himself might be next. Since Kirov's death, Stalin had never walked out into the streets among the people whom he ruled but did not trust.

Stalin kneaded his hands together, cracking his knuckles one after the other. 'The Konstantin Project has been compromised, and I believe Nagorski is responsible.'

'I have yet to see the proof of that,' said Pekkala. 'Is there something you're not telling me, Comrade Stalin? Is there some proof that you can show? Or is this just another arrest, in which case you have plenty of other investigators you could use.'

Stalin rolled the stub of his cigarette between his fingers. 'Do you know how many people I allow to speak to me that way?'

'Not many, I imagine,' said Pekkala. Every time he met with Stalin, he became aware of an emotional blankness that seemed to hover around the man. It was something about Stalin's eyes. The look on his face would change, but the expression in his eyes never did. When Stalin laughed, cajoled and, if that didn't work, threatened, it was, for Pekkala, like watching an exchange of masks in a Japanese Kabuki play. There were moments, as one mask transformed into another, when it seemed to Pekkala that he could glimpse what lay behind. And what he found there filled him with dread. His only defence was to pretend he could not see it.

Stalin smiled, and suddenly the mask had changed again. 'Not many is right. None would be more correct. You are right that I do have other investigators, but this case is too important.' Then he put the cigarette butt in his pocket.

Pekkala had watched him do this before. It was a strange habit in a place where even the poorest people threw their cigarette butts on the ground and left them there. Strange, too, for a man who would never run short of the forty cigarettes he smoked each day. Perhaps there was some story in it, perhaps dating back to his days as a bank robber in

Tblisi. Pekkala wondered if Stalin, like some beggar in the street, removed the remaining tobacco from the stubs and rolled it into fresh cigarettes. Whatever the reason, Stalin kept it to himself.

'I admire your audacity, Pekkala. I like a person who is not afraid to speak his mind. That's one of the reasons I trust you.'

'All I ask is that you let me do my job,' said Pekkala. 'That was our agreement.'

Stalin let his hands fall with an impatient slap against his knees. 'Do you know, Pekkala, that my pen once touched the paper of your death sentence? I was that close.' He pinched the air, as if he were still holding that pen, and traced the air with the ghost of his own signature. 'I never regretted my choice. And how many years have we been working together now?'

'Six. Almost seven.'

'In all that time, have I ever interfered with one of your investigations?'

'No,' admitted Pekkala.

'And have I ever threatened you, simply because you disagreed with me?'

'No, Comrade Stalin.'

'And that,' Stalin aimed a finger at Pekkala, as if taking aim down the barrel of a gun, 'is more than you can say about your former boss, or his meddling wife, Alexandra.'

In that moment, Pekkala was hurled back through time.

Like a man snapping out of a trance, he found himself in the Alexander Palace, hand poised to knock upon the Tsar's study door.

It was the day he finally tracked down the killer Grodek.

Grodek and his fiancée, a woman named Maria Balka, had been found hiding in an apartment near the Moika Canal. When agents of the Tsar's secret service, the Okhrana, stormed the building, Grodek set off an explosive which destroyed the house and killed everyone inside, including the agents who had gone in to arrest him. Meanwhile, Grodek and Balka fled out the back, where Pekkala was waiting in case they tried to escape. Pekkala pursued them along the icy cobbled street until Grodek tried to cross the river on the Potsuleyev bridge. But Okhrana men had stationed themselves on the other side of the bridge, and the two criminals found themselves with nowhere left to run. It was at this moment that Grodek had shot his fiancée, rather than let her fall into the hands of the police. Balka's body tumbled into the canal and disappeared among the plates of ice which drifted out towards the sea like rafts loaded with diamonds. Grodek, afraid to jump, had tried to shoot himself, only to discover that his gun was empty. He was immediately taken into custody.

The Tsar had ordered Pekkala to arrive at the Alexander Palace no later than 4 p.m. that day, in order to make his report.

The Tsar did not like to be kept waiting, and Pekkala had raced the whole way from Petrograd, arriving with only minutes to spare. He dashed up the front steps of the Palace and straight to the Tsar's study.

There was no answer, so Pekkala knocked again and still there was no answer. Cautiously, he opened the door, but found the room empty.

Pekkala sighed with annoyance.

Although the Tsar did not like to be kept waiting, he had no trouble making others wait for him.

Just then, Pekkala heard the Tsar's voice coming from the room across the hall. It belonged to the Tsarina Alexandra and was known as the Mauve Boudoir. Of the hundred rooms in the Alexander Palace, it had become the most famous, because of how ugly people found it. Pekkala was forced to agree. To his eye, everything in that room was the colour of boiled liver.

Pekkala stopped outside the room, trying to catch his breath from all the rushing he had done to be on time. Then he heard the voice of the Tsarina and the Tsar's furious reply. As their words filtered into his brain, he realised they were talking about him.

'I am not going to dismiss Pekkala!' said the Tsar.

Pekkala heard the faint creak of the Tsar's riding boots upon the floor. He knew exactly which pair of boots they were — they had been specially ordered from England and had arrived the week before. The Tsar was trying to break them in, although his feet were suffering in the meantime. He had confided to Pekkala that he had even resorted to the old peasant trick of softening new boots, which was to urinate in them and leave them standing overnight.

Now Pekkala heard the Tsarina speaking in her usual soft tone. He had never heard her shout. The Tsarina's low pitch always sounded to him like a person uttering threats. 'Our friend has urged us,' she said.

At the mention of 'our friend', Pekkala felt his jaw muscles clench. That was the phrase the Tsar and the Tsarina used among themselves to describe the self-proclaimed holy man Rasputin.

Since his first appearance in the court of the Tsar, Rasputin's hold upon the Imperial Family had grown so strong that he was now consulted on all matters, whether about the war, which was now in its second year and moving from one catastrophe to the next, or about appointments to the Royal Court, or about the illness of the Tsar's youngest child, Alexei. Although it was officially denied, the young man had been diagnosed with haemophilia. Injuries which would have been laughed off by any healthy boy confined Alexei to his bed for days at a time. Often, he had to be carried wherever he went by his personal servant, a sailor named Derevenko.

The Tsarina soon came to believe that Rasputin held the cure to Alexei's disease.

Disturbed by the power Rasputin held over the royal family, the prime minister, Peter Stolypin, had ordered an investigation. The report he delivered to the Tsar was filled with stories of debauchery in Rasputin's Petrograd apartment and secret meetings between the Tsarina and Rasputin at the house of her best friend Anna Vyrubova.

The Tsarina was not well-liked among the Russian people. They called her Nemka, the German Woman, and now that the country was at war with Germany, they wondered where her own loyalties lay.

After reading the report, the Tsar ordered Stolypin never to speak to him again about Rasputin. When Stolypin was shot by an assassin named Dimitri Bogrov at an opera house in Kiev, dying five days later, the lack of concern shown by the Tsar and Alexandra was enough to cause a scandal in the Russian court.

When the assassin Bogrov was arrested, he turned out to be a paid informant of the Okhrana. Lawyers at Bogrov's trial were not permitted to ask whether there had been any connection between Bogrov and the Romanov family. Less than a week after Stolypin's death, Bogrov himself was executed.

From then on, Rasputin's meetings with the Tsarina continued unopposed. Rumours of infidelity spread. Although Pekkala himself did not believe that they were true, he knew many who did.

What Pekkala did believe was that the Tsarina's anxiety over her son's precarious health had pushed her to the brink of her own sanity. In spite of all the riches of the Romanovs, there was no cure their money could have bought. So the Tsarina had turned to the superstitions which now so governed her life that she existed in a world seen only through a lens of fear. And somehow, through that lens, Rasputin had taken on the presence of a god.

The Tsar himself was not so easily convinced, and Rasputin's influence might have faded if not for one event which secured for him the loyalty of the entire royal family, and also sealed his fate.

At the Romanovs' dreary hunting lodge of Spala, the young Tsarevich slipped getting out of the bath and suffered a haemorrhage so severe that the doctors told his parents to make preparations for a funeral.

Then a telegram arrived from Rasputin, assuring the Tsarina that her son would not die.

What happened next, even Rasputin's harshest critics were unable to deny.

After the arrival of the telegram, Alexei began, quite suddenly, to recover.

From that point on, no matter what Rasputin did, he became almost untouchable.

Almost.

Rasputin's excesses continued, and Pekkala had quietly dreaded the day when he might be summoned by the Tsar to investigate the Siberian. One way or the other, it would have been the end of Pekkala's career, or even of his life, just as it was for Stolypin. Perhaps for that very reason, or because he preferred not to know the truth, the Tsar had never placed upon Pekkala the burden of handling such a case.

'Our friend,' snapped the Tsar, 'would do well to keep in mind that I myself appointed Pekkala.'

'Now, my darling,' said the Tsarina, and there was the rustle of a dress as she moved across the floor, 'no one is suggesting that you were wrong to have appointed him. Your loyalty to Pekkala is beyond reproach. It is Pekkala's loyalty to you that has come into question.'

Hearing this, Pekkala felt a burning in his chest. He had never done anything remotely disloyal. He knew this and the Tsar knew this. But in that moment, Pekkala felt the bile rise in his throat, because he knew that the Tsar could be persuaded. The Tsar liked to think of himself as a decisive man, and in some things he was, but he could be made to believe almost anything if his wife had decided to convince him.

'Sunny, don't you understand?' protested the Tsar. 'Pekkala's loyalty is not to me.'

'Well, don't you think it should be?'

'Pekkala's duty is to the task I gave him,' replied the Tsar, 'and that is where his loyalty belongs.'

'His duty . . .' began the Tsarina.

The Tsar cut her off. 'Is to find out the truth of whatever matter I place before him, however unpleasant it might be to hear it. Such a man strikes fear into the hearts of those who are sheltering lies. And I wonder, Sunny, if our friend is not more worried for himself than he is for the wellbeing of the court.'

'You cannot say that, my love! Our friend wishes only for the good of our family, and of our country. He has even sent you a gift.' There was a rustling of paper.

'What on earth is that?'

'It is a comb,' she replied. 'One of his own, and he has suggested that it would bring you good fortune to run it through your hair before you attend your daily meetings with the generals.'

Pekkala shuddered at the thought of Rasputin's greasy hair.

The Tsar was thinking the same thing. 'I will not take part in another one of Rasputin's disgusting rituals!' he shouted, then strode out of the room and into the hallway.

There was nowhere for Pekkala to go. He only had one choice and that was to stay where he was.

The Tsar was startled.

For a moment, the two men stared at each other.

Pekkala broke the silence, saying the first thing that came into his mind. 'How are your boots, Majesty?'

The Tsar blinked in surprise. Then he smiled. 'The English make wonderful shoes,' he said, 'only not for human beings.'

Now the Tsarina appeared in the doorway. She wore a plain, white floor-length dress, with sleeves which stopped at the elbows and a collar that covered her throat. Tied around her waist was a belt made of black cloth, which had tassels at the end. Around her neck, suspended on a gold chain, she wore a crucifix made of bone which had been carved by Rasputin himself. She was a severe-looking woman, with a thin mouth downturned at the edges, deep-set eyes and a smooth, broad forehead. Pekkala had seen pictures of her just after she was married to the Tsar. She had seemed much happier then. Now, when her face was relaxed, lines of worry fell into place, like cracks in a pottery glaze. 'What do you want?' she demanded of Pekkala.

'His Majesty asked me to report to him at four p.m. precisely.'

'Then you are late,' she snapped.

'No, Majesty,' replied Pekkala. 'I was on time.'

Then the Tsarina realised he must have heard every word she said.

'What news of Grodek?' asked the Tsar, hurriedly moving to a new topic.

'We have him, Majesty,' answered Pekkala.

The Tsar's face brightened. 'Well done!' The Tsar slapped him gently on the shoulder. Then he turned to walk away down the hall. As he passed by his wife, he paused and whispered in her ear. 'You go and tell that to your friend.'

Then it was just Pekkala and the Tsarina.

Her lips were dry, the result of the barbiturate Veronal, which she had been taking in order to help her sleep. The Veronal upset her stomach, so she had resorted to taking cocaine. One drug led to another. Over time, the cocaine had given her heart trouble, so she began taking small doses of arsenic. This had tinted the skin

beneath her eyes a brownish green and also caused her sleepless-
ness, which put her right back where she started. 'I suffer from
nightmares,' she told him, 'and you, Pekkala, are in them.'

'I do not doubt it, Majesty,' he replied.

For a moment, the Tsarina's mouth hung slightly open as she
tried to grasp the meaning of his words. Then her teeth came
together with a crack. She walked into her room and closed the
door.

'You ask for proof that the T-34 has been compromised?' asked Stalin. 'All right, Pekkala. I will give you proof. Two days ago, a German agent tried to purchase design specifications of the entire Konstantin Project.'

'Purchase them?' asked Pekkala. 'From whom?'

'The White Guild,' replied Stalin.

'The Guild!' Pekkala had not heard that name in a long time.

Some years before, Stalin had ordered the formation of a secret organisation, to be known as the White Guild, made up of former soldiers who had remained loyal to the Tsar long after his death and were committed to overthrowing the Communists. The idea that Stalin would create an organisation whose sole purpose was to topple himself from power was so unthinkable that none of its members ever dreamed that the whole operation had been controlled from the start by the NKVD's Bureau of Special Operations. It was a trick Stalin had learned from the Okhrana; to lure enemies out of hiding, persuade them that they were taking part in actions against the state, and then, before the acts of violence could take place, to arrest them. Since the White Guild came into existence, hundreds of anti-Communist agents had met their deaths by firing squad against the stone wall of the Lubyanka courtyard. 'But if that's who they were dealing with,' said Pekkala, 'then you have nothing to worry about because you control the Guild. It is your own invention, after all.'

'You are missing the point, Pekkala.' Stalin scratched at the back of his neck, fingernails rustling over the smallpox scars embedded in his skin. 'What worries me is that they even know the T-34 exists. The only time a secret is safe is when no one knows there is even a secret being kept.'

'What happened to the German agent?' asked Pekkala. 'May I question him?'

'You could,' replied Stalin, 'but I think you would find it a very one-sided conversation.'

'All right,' said Pekkala, 'but at least we were successful in preventing the enemy from acquiring the information.'

'That success is only temporary. They will come looking again.'

'If they are looking,' said Pekkala, 'then perhaps you should let them find what they think they're searching for.'

'That has already been arranged,' said Stalin, as he fitted a fresh cigarette between his lips. 'Now go back and question Nagorski again.'

In the forest of Rusalka, on the Polish–Russian border, a dirt road wandered drunkenly among the pines. It had been raining, but now bolts of sunlight angled through the misty air. On either side of the road, tall pine trees grew so thickly that no daylight could penetrate. Only mushrooms sprouted from the brown pine needles carpeting the ground – the white speckled red of Fly Agaric and the greasy white of the Avenging Angel, so poisonous that one small bite would kill a man.

The sound of hoofbeats startled a pheasant from its hiding place. With a loud, croaking squawk, the bird took to the air and vanished into the fog.

From around a bend in the road appeared a rider on a horse. He wore a uniform whose cloth was the same greyish brown as the fur of a deer in the winter. His riding boots glowed with a fresh coating of neat's-foot oil and the brass buttons of his tunic were emblazoned with the Polish eagle crest. In his left hand, the man carried a lance. Its short, pigsticker blade shone brightly as it passed through the pillars of sunlight. Both horse and horseman looked like ghosts from a time long before the one in which they had materialised. Then more men appeared – a troop of cavalry – and these had rifles slung across their backs. They moved in beautiful formation, two columns wide and seven deep.

The men belonged to the Pomorske Cavalry Brigade and were on a routine patrol. The road on which they travelled snaked back and forth across the Polish–Russian border, but since it was the only road, and since the forest was so seldom visited except by woodcutters and soldiers patrolling the border, Soviet and Polish troops sometimes crossed paths in the Rusalka.

As the point rider moved around another bend in the road, he was lost in thoughts of how uneventful these patrols were and what a dreary place the Rusalka was and how unnaturally quiet it always seemed here.

Suddenly his horse reared up, almost throwing him. He struggled to stay in the saddle. Then he saw, blocking the path ahead of him, the huge, squat shape of a tank unlike any he had ever seen before. The barrel of its cannon pointed straight at him, and the opening at the end of the barrel seemed to glare like the eye of a cyclops. Its rotten-apple green paint made it seem as if the machine had sprouted from the dirt on which it stood.

As the other troopers came around the bend, both men and animals were startled. The clean lines of their riding formation broke apart. The lancers snapped commands and tugged at reins, trying to bring their mounts under control.

Awakened from its iron sleep, the tank engine gave a sudden, bestial roar. Two columns of bluish smoke belched from its twin exhaust pipes, rising like cobras into the damp air.

One of the Polish horses reared up on its hind legs. Its rider toppled off into the mud. The officer in charge of the troop, identifiable only by the fact that he wore a revolver on his belt, shouted at the man who had fallen. The trooper, his whole side painted with mud, scrambled back up into the saddle.

The tank did not move, but its engine continued to bellow. All around the huge machine, the khaki-silted puddles trembled.

The lancers exchanged glances, unable to hide their fear.

One trooper unshouldered his rifle.

Seeing this, the officer spurred his horse towards the man, knocking the gun from his grasp.

Just when it seemed that the lancers were about to withdraw in confusion, the tank's engine clattered and died.

The echo faded away through the trees. Except for the heavy breathing of the horses, silence returned to the forest. Then a hatch opened on the turret of the tank and a man climbed out. He wore the black leather double-breasted jacket of a Soviet tank officer. At first, he gave no sign of realising that the Poles were even there. As soon as he had cleared the turret hatch, he swung his legs to the side and clambered down to the ground. Only then did he acknowledge the presence of the horsemen. Awkwardly, he raised one hand in greeting.

The Poles looked at each other. They did not wave back.

'Tank bust!' said the tank officer, speaking in broken Polish. He threw up his hands in a gesture of helplessness.

In an instant, all fear vanished from the Polish lancers. Now they began to laugh and talk amongst themselves.

Two more soldiers emerged from the tank, one through the turret and another through a forward hatch which flopped open like the lazy blinking of an eyelid. The men who climbed out wore stone-grey overalls and padded-cloth helmets. They glanced at the Poles, who were still laughing, then went around to the back of the tank. One man opened the engine compartment and the other looked inside.

The black-jacketed Soviet commander seemed unaffected by the laughter of the cavalrymen. He only shrugged and said again, 'Tank bust!'

The Polish officer gave a sharp command to his men, who immediately began to form up in their original columns. As soon as this had been done, the officer snapped his hand forward and the troop advanced. The two columns divided around the hulk of the tank, like the flow of water around a stone set in a stream.

The Poles could not hide their contempt for the broken

machine. The point rider dipped the tip of his lance and dragged the blade along the metal hull, scraping up a curl of white paint from a large number 4 painted on its side.

The Soviets did nothing to stop them. Instead they busied themselves with repairing the engine.

As the last Polish lancer rode by, he leaned in his saddle until he could have touched the tank commander. 'Machine bust!' he mocked.

The officer nodded and grinned, but as soon as the horses had passed, the smile sheared off his face.

The two crewmen, who had been stooped over the engine compartment, both straightened up and watched the swinging rear ends of the horses as they rounded the next bend in the road and disappeared.

'That's right, Polak,' said one of the crewmen, in a voice barely above a whisper. 'Laugh it up.'

'And we'll laugh, too,' said the other, 'when we are pissing on your Polish graves.'

The tank commander spun one finger in a circle; the signal for the engine to be started up again.

The crewmen nodded. They closed the engine cover and climbed back inside the tank.

Once more, the T-34 thundered into life and the machine jolted forward, gouging the road and kicking up a spray of mud as it rolled onwards. When it came to an unmarked trail, the driver locked one of the tracks. The tank slewed sideways and then both tracks began to move again. The T-34 crashed into the undergrowth, splintering trees as it went. Soon, it had vanished from sight and there was only the sound of its engine, fading into the distance.

In a dark, narrow side street two blocks from the Kremlin, Pekkala inserted a long brass key into the lock of a battered door. The door was plated with iron which had once been painted a cheerful yellow, as if to lure in more light than the few minutes a day when the sun shone directly overhead. Now, most of the paint was gone and what remained had faded to the colour of old varnish.

As Pekkala made his way up to the third floor, treading heavily upon the scuffed wooden stairs, his fingers trailed along the black metal banister. The only light came from a single bulb, fringed with dusty cobwebs. In a dark corner, an old grey cat with matted fur lounged on a broken chair. Empty zinc coal buckets were stacked outside a doorway and coal dust glittered on the carpeting.

But at the third floor, everything changed. Here, the walls were freshly painted. A wooden coat rack stood at one end of the hallway, an umbrella hanging from one crooked peg. On the door, stencilled in black letters, was Pekkala's name and under it, the word Investigator. Beneath it, in smaller letters, was 'Kirov, assistant to Inspector Pekkala'.

Every time Pekkala reached the third floor, he silently gave thanks to his fastidious assistant.

There were times when, entering his office, Pekkala wondered if he had got lost and wandered instead into some strange arboretum. Plants sat on every surface – the sweet, musty smell of tomatoes, the pursed lips of orchid blossoms, the orange and purple beak-shaped bloom of the Bird of Paradise. The dust was swept daily from their leaves, the soil kept damp but not wet, showing marks where Kirov regularly pressed the earth down with his fingers, as if tucking an infant into bed.

The air felt heavy in here, almost jungly, Pekkala thought, and seeing his desk almost hidden among the foliage, he had the impression that this was how his office might look if all humans suddenly vanished from the world and plants took over, swallowing the world of men.

Today, the office smelled of cooking and Pekkala remembered it was Friday, the one day of the week when Kirov prepared him a meal. Pekkala breathed a sigh of contentment at the odour of boiled ham, cloves and gravy.

Kirov, still in his uniform, hunched over the stove, which took up one corner of the room. He was stirring the contents of a cast-iron pot with a wooden spoon and humming quietly to himself.

When Pekkala shut the door, the young man wheeled around, spoon raised like a magic wand. 'Inspector! Just in time.'

'You know you don't have to go to all this trouble,' said Pekkala, trying to sound convincing.

'If it was up to you,' replied Kirov, 'we would be eating army-issue cans of Tushonka meat three times a day. My taste buds would commit suicide.'

Pekkala took a pair of earthenware bowls from the shelf and carried them over to the window sill. Then, from the drawer of his desk, he brought out two metal spoons. 'What have you got for us today?' he asked, peering over Kirov's shoulder into the pot. He saw a dark sauce, a knot of ham, potatoes, boiled chestnuts and a bundle of what looked like yellow twigs.

'*Boujenina*,' replied Kirov, tasting the end of the steaming wooden spoon.

'What's that?' asked Pekkala, pointing at the twigs. 'It looks like grass.'

'Not grass,' explained Kirov. 'Hay.'

Pekkala brought his face closer to the bubbling mixture in the pot. 'People can eat hay?'

'It's just for seasoning.' Kirov picked up a chipped red and white enamelled ladle and scooped some of the stew into Pekkala's bowl.

Pekkala sat down in the creaky wooden chair behind his desk and peered suspiciously at his lunch. 'Hay,' he repeated, and sniffed at the steam as it rose from his stew.

Kirov perched on the window sill, among his potted plants. His long legs dangled almost to the floor.

Pekkala opened his mouth to ask another question. Several questions, actually. What kind of hay was it? Where had it come from? Who thought this up? What does *boujenina* mean? But Kirov silenced him before he had a chance to speak.

'Don't talk, Inspector. Eat!'

Obediently, Pekkala spooned the *boujenina* into his mouth. The salty warmth spread through his body. The taste of cloves sparked in his brain, like electricity. And the taste of the hay reached him now; a mellow earthiness which summoned memories of childhood from the darkened corners of his mind.

They ate in comfortable silence.

A minute later, when Pekkala's spoon was scraping the bottom of the bowl, Kirov loudly cleared his throat. 'Have you finished already?'

'Yes,' replied Pekkala. 'Is there any more?'

'There is more, but that's not the point! How can you eat so quickly?'

Pekkala shrugged. 'It's what I do.'

'What I mean,' explained Kirov, 'is that you should learn to savour your food. Food is like dreams, Inspector.'

Pekkala held out his bowl. 'Could I have some more while you explain this to me?'

Sighing with exasperation, Kirov took the bowl from Pekkala's hand, refilled it and handed it back. 'There are three kinds of dream,' he began. 'The first is just a scribble in your mind. It means nothing. It's just your brain unwinding like a clock spring. The second kind does mean something. Your unconscious mind is trying to tell you something, but you have to interpret what it means.'

'And the third?' asked Pekkala, his mouth full of stew.

'The third,' said Kirov, 'is what the mystics call *Barakka*. It is a waking dream, a vision, when you glimpse the workings of the universe.'

'Like Saint Paul,' said Pekkala, 'on the road to Damascus.'

'What?'

'Never mind.' Pekkala waved his spoon. 'Keep going. What does this have to do with food?'

'There is the meal you eat simply to fill your stomach.'

'Like a can of meat,' suggested Pekkala.

Kirov shuddered. 'Yes, like those cans of meat you put away. And then there are the meals you buy at the café where you eat your lunch, which are not much better except that you don't have to clean up after yourself.'

'And then?'

'And then there are meals which elevate food to an art.'

Pekkala, who had been eating all this time, dropped his spoon into the empty bowl.

Hearing this, Kirov shook his head in amazement. 'You have no idea what I'm talking about, do you, Inspector?'

'No,' agreed Pekkala, 'but I've had some excellent dreams. I don't know why you didn't become a professional chef.'

'I cook because I want to,' replied Kirov, 'not because I have to.'

'Is there a difference?' asked Pekkala.

'All the difference in the world,' said Kirov. 'If I had to cook all day for men like Nagorski, it would take all the pleasure out of cooking. Do you know what he was eating when I went into that restaurant? Blinis. With Caspian Sevruga, each morsel like a perfect black pearl. He was just stuffing it into his face. The art of food was lost on him completely.'

Self-consciously, Pekkala glanced into his already empty bowl. He had done his best to eat at a dignified pace, but the truth was that if Kirov hadn't been there, he would have set aside the bowl and would be eating right out of the pot by now.

'Any luck with Nagorski?' asked Kirov.

'Depends,' sighed Pekkala, 'on what you call luck.'

'That machine he built,' said Kirov. 'I hear it weighs more than ten tons.'

'Thirty, to be precise,' replied Pekkala. 'To hear him speak of it, you'd think that tank was a member of his family.'

'You think he's guilty?'

Pekkala shook his head. 'Unpleasant maybe, but not guilty, as far as I can tell. I released him. He is now back at the facility where his tank is being designed.' It was then he noticed a large box placed just inside the door. 'What is that?'

'Ah,' Kirov began.

'Whenever you say "Ah", I know it's something I'm not going to like.'

'Not at all!' Kirov laughed nervously. 'It's a present for you.'

'It's not my birthday.'

'Well, it's *sort* of a present. Actually it's more of a . . .'

'So it's not really a present.'

'No,' admitted Kirov. 'It's really more of a suggestion.'

'A suggestion,' repeated Pekkala.

'Open it!' said Kirov, brandishing his spoon.

Pekkala got out of his chair and fetched the box. He placed it on his desk and lifted the lid. Inside was a neatly folded coat. Several other garments lay underneath.

'I thought it was time you had a new outfit,' said Kirov.

'New?' Pekkala looked down at the clothes he was wearing. 'But these are new. Almost, anyway. I bought them just last year.'

Kirov made a sound in his throat. 'Well, when I say new, what I mean is up to date.'

'I am up to date!' Pekkala protested. 'I bought these clothes right here in Moscow. They were very expensive.' And he was just about to go on about the prices he'd been forced to pay when Kirov cut him off.

'All right,' Kirov said patiently, trying another angle. 'Where did you buy your clothes?'

'Linsky's, over by the Bolshoi Theatre. Linsky makes durable stuff!' said Pekkala, patting the chest of his coat. 'He told me himself that when you buy a coat from him, it's the last one you will ever need to wear. That's his personal motto, you know.'

'Yes,' Kirov brought his hands together in a silent clap, 'but do you know what people call his shop? Clothes for Dead Men.'

'Well, that seems a little dramatic.'

'For goodness' sake, Inspector, Linsky sells clothes to funeral homes!'

'So what if he does?' Pekkala protested. 'Funeral directors need something to wear, you know. They can't all walk around naked. My father was a funeral director . . .'

Kirov was finally losing his patience. 'Linsky doesn't sell clothes to the directors! Linsky makes the clothes that go on bodies when they are laid out for a viewing. That's why his clothes are the last ones you'll ever wear. Because you'll be buried in them!'

Pekkala frowned. He inspected his lapels. 'But I've always worn this style of coat.'

'That's the problem, Inspector,' Kirov reasoned with him. 'There is such a thing as fashion, even for people like you. Now look.' Kirov walked across the room and removed the coat from the box. Carefully, he unfolded it. Then, holding it by the shoulders, he lifted it up for Pekkala to see. 'Look at this. This is the latest style. Try it on. That's all I'm asking.'

Reluctantly, Pekkala put on the jacket.

Kirov helped him into it. 'There!' he announced. 'How does it feel?'

Pekkala raised his arms and lowered them again. 'All right, I suppose.'

'You see! I told you! And there's a shirt there and a new pair of trousers as well. No one will be able to call you a fossil now.'

Pekkala frowned. 'I didn't realise anyone called me a fossil.'

Kirov patted him on the shoulder. 'It's just an expression. And now I have something else for you. A real present this time.' He held his arm out towards the windowsill, where a small plant sagged under the weight of bright orange fruits.

'Tangerines?' asked Pekkala.

'Kumquats,' Kirov corrected him. 'It took me months to find one of these plants and more than a year to get it to bear fruit. Are you ready?'

'Kumquats,' said Pekkala, still trying out the word.

Kirov reached out and took hold of a fruit between his thumb and first two fingers. Gently he twisted until the ball came away from its stem, then held it out to Pekkala.

Pekkala plucked the kumquat from Kirov's fingers and sniffed at it.

'Eat!' said Kirov, his cheeks flushing red. 'That's an order!'

Pekkala raised his eyebrows. 'An order, Kirov?'

'I do outrank you.'

'But I don't have a rank!'

'Exactly.' Kirov flapped his hand at Pekkala as if he were shooing a fly. 'Don't make me ask you again!'

Pekkala took a small bite, tearing through the thin glowing skin of the kumquat and into the yellowy segments beneath. His eyes closed tightly as the sour taste flooded his mouth. 'It's inedible!'

'It's perfect,' said Kirov. Then he went back to the windowsill and traced one finger lovingly over the deep green, shiny leaves.

'You need a girlfriend, Kirov. Or a wife. You're spending too much time with these kumquats. Now please go down and bring the car around front.'

'Where are we going?'

'We have a rendezvous with thirty tons of Russian steel. Nagorski has offered to give us a tour of the place where the tank is being designed. He is anxious to prove to us that the facility is secure.'

'Yes, Inspector.' Kirov picked up his keys and headed out the door.

'Did you remember your gun?' Pekkala called to him.

Kirov groaned. His footsteps came to a halt.

'You forgot again, didn't you?'

'I don't need it this time,' Kirov protested.

'You never know when you will need it. That's why there are regulations, Kirov!'

Kirov trudged back up the stairs and into the office. Then he began rifling through the drawers of his desk.

'Have you lost it?' asked Pekkala.

'It's in here somewhere,' muttered Kirov.

Pekkala shook his head and sighed.

'Ah!' shouted Kirov. 'Here it is!' He held up a Tokarev automatic; standard issue for army officers and members of state security.

'Now go and get the car,' Pekkala told him.

'On my way!' Kirov swept past and clattered down the stairs.

Before Pekkala left the office, he removed the new jacket, replaced it in the box, and put his old coat on again. As he fastened the buttons, he went over to the window and looked out over the rooftops of Moscow. Late-afternoon sunlight shone weak and silvery upon the slates. Crows and pigeons shared the chimney pots. His gaze returned to the plants on the windowsill. Glancing back to see if Kirov had returned, Pekkala reached out and plucked another kumquat. He put the whole thing in his mouth and bit down. The bitter juice exploded in his mouth. He swallowed and let out a gasp. Then he made his way down to the street.

A gentle rain was falling.

Kirov stood beside the car. It was a model 1935 Emka, with a squared-off roof, a large front grille and headlights mounted on the wide and sweeping cowlings, giving it a haughty look.

Kirov held open the passenger door, waiting for Pekkala. The engine was running. The Emka's wipers twitched jerkily back and forth, like the antennae of an insect.

As Pekkala shut the battered yellow door behind him, he turned and almost barged into two women who were walking past.

The women were bundled in scarves and bulky coats. They chattered happily, breath condensing into halos about their heads.

'Excuse me,' said Pekkala, rocking back on his heels so as not to collide with the women.

The women did not break their stride. They merely glanced at him, then returned to their conversation.

Pekkala watched them go, staring at the woman on the left. He had only caught a glimpse of her – pale eyes and a wisp of blonde hair trailing across her cheek – but now the blood drained out of his face.

Kirov noticed. 'Pekkala,' he said quietly.

Pekkala did not seem to hear. He walked quickly after the women. Just before they turned the corner, reaching out, he touched the shoulder of the pale-eyed woman.

She wheeled about. 'What is it?' she asked, suddenly afraid. 'What do you want?'

Pekkala jerked his hand away as if he'd just been shocked. 'I'm sorry,' he stammered. 'I thought you were somebody else.'

Kirov was walking towards them.

Pekkala swallowed, barely able to speak. 'I'm so sorry,' he told her.

'Who did you think I was?' she asked.

Kirov came to a stop beside them. 'Excuse us, ladies,' he said cheerfully. 'We were just going in the opposite direction.'

'Well, I hope you find who you are looking for,' the woman told Pekkala.

Then she and her friend walked on down the street, while Kirov and Pekkala returned to the car.

'You didn't have to come after me like that,' said Pekkala. 'I'm perfectly capable of getting myself out of embarrassing situations.'

'Not as capable as you are of getting into them,' replied Kirov. 'How many times are you going to go galloping after strange women?'

'I thought it was . . .'

'I know who you thought it was, and I also know as well as you do that she's not in Moscow. She's not even in the country! And even if she was here, right in front of you, it wouldn't matter because she has another life now. Or have you forgotten all that?'

'No,' sighed Pekkala, 'I have not forgotten.'

'Come on, Inspector, let's go have a look at this tank. Maybe they will let us take one home.'

'We wouldn't have to worry about someone taking our parking spot,' said Pekkala, as he climbed into the rear seat of the Emka. 'We'd just park on top of them.'

As Kirov pulled out into the stream of cars, he did not see Pekkala look back at the empty road where he had stood with the women, as if to see some ghost of his old self among the shadows.

Her name was Ilya Simonova. She had been a teacher at the Tsarskoye Primary school, just outside the grounds of the Tsar's estate. Most of the Palace staff sent their children to the Tsarskoye school, and Ilya often led groups of students on walks across the Catherine and Alexander Parks. That was how Pekkala had met her; at a garden party to mark the beginning of the new school year. He had not actually gone to the party, but saw it on his way home from the station. He stopped at the wall of the school and looked in.

Of that moment in time, Pekkala had no recollection of anything else except the sight of her, standing just outside a white marquee set up for the occasion. Ilya was wearing a pale green dress. She did not have a hat, so he could see her face clearly – high cheekbones and eyes a dusty blue.

At first, he thought he must know her from somewhere before. Something in his mind made her seem familiar to him. But that wasn't it. And whatever it was, this sudden lurching of his senses towards something it couldn't explain, stopped him in his tracks and kept him there. The next thing he knew, a woman on the other side of the wall had come up and asked him if he was looking for somebody. She was tall and dignified, her grey hair knotted at the back.

'Who is that?' asked Pekkala, nodding towards the woman in the green dress.

'That's the new teacher, Ilya Simonova. I am the head-mistress, Rada Obolenskaya. And you are the Tsar's new detective.'

'Inspector Pekkala.' He bowed his head in greeting.

'Would you like me to introduce you?'

'Yes!' Pekkala blurted out. 'I just . . . she looks like someone I know. At least, I think she does.'

'I see,' said Madame Obolenskaya.

'I might be wrong,' explained Pekkala.

'I don't suppose you are,' she replied.

He proposed to Ilya Simonova exactly one year later.

A date was set, but they were never married. They never got the chance. Instead, on the eve of the Revolution, Ilya boarded the last train heading west. It was bound for Paris, where Pekkala promised to meet her as soon as the Tsar had granted him permission to get out of the country. But Pekkala never did get out. Some months later, he was arrested by Bolshevik militia men while attempting to cross into Finland. From there, his journey to Siberia began, and it would be many years before he had another chance to leave the country.

'You are free to go now if you wish,' said Stalin, 'but before you make your decision, there is something you should know.'

'What?' asked Pekkala nervously. 'What do I need to know?'

Stalin was watching him closely, as if the two men were playing cards. Now he opened a drawer on his side of the desk, the dry wood squeaking as he pulled. He withdrew a photograph. For a moment, he studied it. He laid the picture down, placed one finger on top of it and slid the photograph towards Pekkala.

It was Ilya. He recognised her instantly. She was sitting at a small café table. Behind her, printed on the awning of the café, Pekkala saw the words Les Deux Magots. She was smiling as she watched something to the left of where the camera had been placed. He could see her strong, white teeth. Now, reluctantly, Pekkala's gaze shifted to the man who was sitting beside her. He was thin, with dark hair combed straight back. He wore a jacket and tie and the stub of a cigarette was pinched between his thumb and second finger. He held the cigarette in the Russian manner, with the burning end balanced over his palm as if to catch the falling ash. Like Ilya, the man was smiling. Both of them were watching something just to the left of the camera. On the other side of the table was an object which at first Pekkala almost failed to recognise, since it had been so long since he had seen one. It was a baby carriage, its hood pulled up to shelter the infant from the sun.

Pekkala realised he wasn't breathing. He had to force himself to fill his lungs.

Quietly, Stalin cleared his throat. 'You must not hold it against her. She waited, Pekkala. She waited a very long time. Over ten years. But a person cannot wait forever, can they?'

Pekkala stared at the baby carriage. He wondered if the child had her eyes.

'As you see,' Stalin gestured towards the picture, 'Ilya is happy now. She has a family. She is a teacher, of Russian of course, at the prestigious École Stanislas. She has tried to put the past behind her. That is something all of us must do at some point in our lives.'

Slowly, Pekkala raised his head, until he was looking Stalin in the eye. 'Why did you show this to me?'

Stalin's lips twitched. 'Would you rather have arrived in Paris, ready to start a new life, only to find that it was once more out of reach?'

'Out of reach?' Pekkala felt dizzy. His mind seemed to rush from one end of his skull to the other, like fish trapped in a net.

'You could still go to her, of course.' Stalin shrugged. 'But whatever peace of mind she might have won for herself in these past years would be gone in an instant. And let us say, for the sake of argument, that you might persuade her to leave the man she married. Let us say that she even leaves behind her child . . .'

'Stop,' said Pekkala.

'You are not that kind of man,' continued Stalin. 'You are not the monster that your enemies once believed you to be. If you *were, you would never have been such a formidable opponent for people like myself. Monsters are easy to defeat. With such people, it is merely a question of blood and time, since their only weapon is fear. But you, Pekkala, you won the hearts of the people and the respect of your enemies. I do not believe you understand how rare a thing that is. Those whom you once served are out there still.' Stalin brushed his hand towards the window of his study, and out across the pale blue autumn sky. 'They have not forgotten you, Pekkala, and I don't believe you have forgotten them.'*

'No,' whispered Pekkala, 'I have not forgotten.'

'What I am trying to tell you, Pekkala, is that you can leave this country if you want to. I'll put you on the next train to Paris if that's really what you want. Or you can stay here, where you are truly needed and where you still have a place if you want it.'

Until that moment, the thought of staying on in Russia had not occurred to him. But now Pekkala realised that his last gesture of affection for the woman he'd once thought would be his wife must be to let her believe he was dead.

They were out in open country now, the Emka's engine roaring contentedly as Kirov raced along the dusty Moscow Highway.

'Do you think I have made a mistake?' asked Pekkala.

'A mistake with what, Inspector?' asked Kirov, glancing at Pekkala in the rear-view mirror before turning his eyes back to the road.

'Staying here. In Russia. I had a chance to leave and turned it down.'

'Your work here is important,' said Kirov. 'Why do you think I asked to work with you, Inspector?'

'I judged that to be your own business.'

'It's because every night when I lie down to sleep, I know I have done something that really matters. How many people can honestly say that?'

Pekkala did not reply. He wondered if Kirov was right, or whether, in agreeing to work for Stalin, he had compromised every ideal for which he'd ever stood.

Grey clouds hung just above the treetops.

As they neared the Nagorski facility, Pekkala looked out at a tall metal fence which stretched along one side of the road. The fence seemed to go on forever. It was twice the height of a man, topped by a second stage of fencing which jutted out at an angle towards the road and was lined with four strands of barbed wire. Beyond the wire grew an unkempt tangle of forest, rising from the poor and marshy soil.

The monotony of this structure was broken only by occasional black metal signs which had been bolted to the fence. Stencilled on each sign, in dull yellow paint, was a jawless skull and crossbones.

'Seems pretty secure so far,' remarked Kirov.

But Pekkala wasn't so certain. One intimidating sign and a layer of wire which could have been cut through with a set of household pliers did not fill him with confidence.

Finally, they came to a gate. A wooden guard shack, barely big enough for one person, stood on the other side of the wire. It was raining now, and droplets lay like silver coins upon the shack's tar-paper roof.

Kirov brought the car to a stop. He sounded the horn.

Immediately, a man came tumbling out of the shack. He wore a rough-cut army tunic and was strapping on a plain leather belt, weighed down by a heavy leather holster. Hurriedly, he unlocked the gate, sliding back a metal bolt as thick as his wrist, and swung it open.

Kirov rolled the car forward, until it stood adjacent with the guard shack.

Pekkala rolled down his window.

'Are you the doctors?' asked the man in a breathless voice. 'I wasn't expecting you so soon.'

'Doctors?' asked Pekkala.

The man's dull eyes grew suddenly sharp. 'If you aren't doctors, then what do you want here?'

Pekkala reached inside his pocket for his ID.

The guard drew his revolver and aimed it at Pekkala's face. Pekkala froze.

'Slowly,' said the guard.

Pekkala withdrew his pass book.

'Hold it up so I can see it,' said the guard.

Pekkala did as he was told.

The pass book was the size of a man's outstretched hand, dull red in colour, with an outer cover made from fabric-covered cardboard in the manner of an old school text book. The Soviet state seal, cradled in its two bound sheaves of wheat, had been emblazoned on the front. Inside, in the top left-hand corner, a photograph of Pekkala had been attached with a heat seal, cracking the emulsion of the photograph. Beneath that, in pale bluish-green letters, were the letters NKVD and a second stamp indicating that Pekkala was on Special Assignment for the government. The particulars of his birth, his blood group, and his state identification number filled up the right-hand page.

Most government pass books contained only those two pages, but in Pekkala's, a third page had been inserted. Printed on canary yellow paper with a red border around the edge, were the following words:

THE PERSON IDENTIFIED IN THIS DOCUMENT IS ACTING UNDER THE DIRECT ORDERS OF COMRADE STALIN.

DO NOT QUESTION OR DETAIN HIM.

HE IS AUTHORISED TO WEAR CIVILIAN CLOTHES, TO CARRY WEAPONS, TO TRANSPORT PROHIBITED ITEMS, INCLUDING POISON, EXPLOSIVES AND

FOREIGN CURRENCY. HE MAY PASS INTO RE-
STRICTED AREAS AND MAY REQUISITION EQUIP-
MENT OF ALL TYPES, INCLUDING WEAPONS AND
VEHICLES.

IF HE IS KILLED OR INJURED, NOTIFY THE
BUREAU OF SPECIAL OPERATIONS IMMEDIATELY.

Although this special insert was known officially as a
Classified Operations Permit, it was more commonly referred
to as a Shadow Pass. With it, a man could appear and disappear
at will within the wilderness of regulations that controlled the
state. Fewer than a dozen of these Shadow Passes were known
to exist. Even within the ranks of the NKVD, most people
had never seen one.

Rain flicked at the pass book, darkening the paper.

The guard squinted to read the words. It took a moment
for him to grasp what he was looking at. Then he looked at
the gun in his hand as if he had no idea how he had come to
be holding it. 'I'm sorry,' he mumbled, hurriedly replacing
the weapon in its holster.

'Why would you think we were doctors?' asked Pekkala.

'There has been an accident,' explained the guard.

'What happened?'

The guard shrugged. 'I couldn't tell you. When the facility
called me here at the guard house about half an hour ago, all
they said was that a doctor would be arriving soon and to let
him through without delay. Whatever it is, I'm sure Colonel
Nagorski has the situation under control.' The guard paused.
'Listen, are you really Inspector Pekkala?'

'Why wouldn't I be?' asked Pekkala.

'It's just . . .' The guard smiled awkwardly, scratching his forehead with his thumbnail, 'I wasn't sure you really existed.'

'Do we have your permission to proceed?' asked Pekkala.

'Of course!' The guard stood back and waved them forward with a sweep of his arm, like a man clearing breadcrumbs off a table.

Kirov put the car in gear and drove on.

For several minutes, the Emka travelled on the long, straight road with the facility nowhere in sight.

'This place really is in the middle of nowhere,' muttered Kirov.

Pekkala grunted in agreement. He squinted up at the trees, which seemed to stoop over the car as if curious to see who was inside.

Then, up ahead, they saw where the woods had been cut back around a group of hunched and flat-roofed brick buildings.

As they pulled into a dirt courtyard, the door to one of the smaller buildings swung open and a man dashed out, making straight towards them. Like the guard, he wore a military uniform. By the time he reached the Emka, he was already out of breath.

Pekkala and Kirov got out of the car.

'I am Captain Samarin,' wheezed the NKVD man. He had black, Asiatic-looking hair, thin lips and deep-set eyes. 'It's this way, Doctor,' he panted. 'You'll need your medical bag.'

'We are not doctors,' explained Pekkala.

Samarin was flustered. 'I don't understand,' he said. 'What is your business here?'

'I am Inspector Pekkala, of the Bureau of Special Operations, and this is Major Kirov. Colonel Nagorski was kind enough to offer us a tour of the facility.'

'I'm afraid that a tour is out of the question, Inspector,' replied Samarin, 'but I would be glad to show you why.'

Samarin led them to the edge of what looked at first glance to be a huge half-drained lake filled with large puddles of dirty water. In the middle of it, sunk almost to the top of its tracks in the mud, lay one of Nagorski's tanks, a large white number 3 painted on its side. Two men stood beside the tank, their shoulders hunched against the rain.

'So that is the T-34,' said Pekkala.

'It is,' confirmed Samarin, 'and this place,' he waved his hand across the sea of mud, 'is what we call the proving ground. This is where the machines are tested.'

The rain was falling harder now, pattering on the dead leaves in the nearby woods so that the air filled with a hissing sound. The smell of the damp earth hung heavy in the air and the solid mass of clouds, like a blind man's eye rolled around to white, encased the dome of sky above them.

'Where is Nagorski?' asked Pekkala.

Samarin pointed at the men beside the tank.

The huddled figures were too far away for Pekkala to be able to see which one of them was the Colonel.

Pekkala turned to Kirov. 'Wait here,' he said. Then, without another word, he stepped forward and slid down the steep embankment. He arrived at the end of the slope on his back, his clothes and hands plastered with slime. The brownish-yellow ooze stood out sharply against the black of his coat. As

Pekkala rose to his feet, dirty water poured out of his sleeves. He took one step towards the tank before realising that one of his shoes had come off. Gouging it out of the clay, Pekkala perched on one leg like a heron and jammed his foot back into the shoe before continuing on his way.

After several minutes of wading from one flooded crater to the next, Pekkala arrived at the tank. The closer he came, the larger the machine appeared, until at last he stood before the tank. Even though it was half buried in the mud, the T-34 still towered over him.

Pekkala glanced at the two dishevelled men. Both were as plastered in filth as he was. One wore what had once been a white lab coat. The other had a brown wool coat with a fur collar which was also painted with mud. But neither of them was Nagorski.

'Are you the doctor?' asked the man in the filthy lab coat. He had a big, square face, with a thick crop of bristly grey hair.

Pekkala explained who he was.

'Well, Inspector Pekkala,' said the grey-haired man, spreading his arms wide, 'welcome to the mad house.'

'An investigator already,' quipped the other, a short, frail-looking man with a complexion so pale that his skin looked like mother-of-pearl. 'You people don't waste any time.'

'Where is the Colonel?' asked Pekkala. 'Is he hurt?'

'No, Inspector,' the grey-haired man replied. 'Colonel Nagorski is dead.'

'Dead?' shouted Pekkala. 'How?'

The men exchanged glances. They seemed reluctant to speak.

'Where is he?' demanded Pekkala. 'In the tank?'

It was the grey-haired man who finally explained. 'Colonel Nagorski is not in the tank. Colonel Nagorski is under the tank.'

His companion pointed at the ground. 'See for yourself.'

Now, just beside the T-34's track, Pekkala noticed a cluster of fingertips; pale dimples rising just above the surface of the water. As his eyes struggled to see into the murky water, he spotted a leg, visible only from the knee down. At the end of this limb, which seemed to have been partially torn from the body, Pekkala could make out a distorted black shoe. It appeared to have split at all its seams, as if forced on someone with a foot much too large for the shoe. 'That is Nagorski?' he asked.

'What's left of him,' replied the grey-haired man.

No matter how many times Pekkala looked down upon the dead, the first sight of a corpse always stunned him. It was as if his mind could not bear to carry the burden of this moment and so, time after time, erased it from his brain. As a result, the initial shock never lessened in intensity.

What struck Pekkala was not how different the dead appeared but how much alike bodies became, no matter if they were man or woman, old or young, when the life had left their bodies. The same terrible stillness surrounded them, the same dull eyes and, eventually, the same piercing sweet smell. Some nights, he would wake with the stench of the dead flooding his nostrils. Staggering to the sink, he would wash his face and scrub his hands until the knuckles bled but still the smell remained, as if those corpses lay about the floor beside his bed.

Pekkala crouched down. Reaching out, he touched Nagorski's fingertips, his own hand forming a reflection of the one which lay submerged beneath the muddy water. The image of Nagorski returned to him, blustery and sweating in the interrogation room of the Lubyanka jail. There had seemed to be something indestructible about him. Now Pekkala felt the cold skin of the dead man radiating up through his arm, as if his own life were being drained out through his pores. He pulled his hand away and rose to his feet, thoughts already turning to the work that lay ahead. 'Who are you two?' he asked the men.

'I am Professor Ushinsky,' explained the one with the grey hair, 'responsible for developing armaments here at the facility. And this,' he gestured to the man in the brown coat, 'is Professor Gorenko.'

'I am the drive train specialist,' explained Gorenko. He kept his hands inside his pockets. His shoulders were trembling with the cold.

'How did this happen?' asked Pekkala.

'We aren't sure.' Gorenko tried to wipe some of the mud from his coat but succeeded only in smearing it into the wool. 'This morning, when we reported for work, Nagorski said he would be working on Number 3.' With knuckles blue from cold, he rapped on the side of the tank. 'This is Number 3,' he said.

'The Colonel said he would be working by himself,' added Ushinsky.

'Was that unusual?'

'No,' replied Ushinsky. 'The Colonel often carried out tests on his own.'

'Tests? You mean the tank is not finished yet?'

Both men shook their heads.

66

'There are seven complete machines at the facility. Each one has been equipped with slightly different mechanisms, engine configurations and so on. They are constantly being tested and compared to each other. Eventually, we will standardise the pattern. Then the T-34 will go into mass production. Until then, the Colonel wanted to keep everything as secret as possible.'

'Even from you?'

'From everyone, Inspector,' replied Gorenko. 'Without exception.'

'At what point did you realise that something had gone wrong?'

'When I stepped outside the main assembly plant.' Ushinsky nodded towards the largest of the facility buildings. 'We call it the Iron House. It's where all the parts for the tanks are stored. There's so much metal in there, I'm surprised the whole structure hasn't sunk beneath the ground. Before I went outside, I'd been working on the final drive mechanism. The single straight reduction gears have armoured mountings at each side of the tail . . .'

As if he could not help himself, Gorenko's hands drifted up to the chest of his coat and began scraping once more at the mud embedded in the cloth.

'Will you stop that!' shouted Ushinsky.

'It's a brand-new coat,' muttered Gorenko. 'I only bought it yesterday.'

'The boss is dead!' Ushinsky grabbed Gorenko by the wrists and pulled his hands away. 'Can't you get that into your thick skull?'

Both men appeared to be in shock. Pekkala had seen behaviour like this many times before. 'When did you realise that something had gone wrong?' he asked patiently, trying to steer them back on track.

'I was out smoking my cigarette . . .' said Ushinsky.

'No smoking in the factory,' interrupted Gorenko.

'I can do this by myself!' shouted Ushinsky, jabbing a finger against Gorenko's chest.

Gorenko staggered backwards, and almost lost his footing. 'You don't have to be like that!' he snapped.

'And I noticed that Number 3 was half sunk in the mud,' continued Ushinsky. 'I thought – look what the Colonel's gone and done. He's buried the machine. I assumed he had got it stuck on purpose, just to see what would happen. That's exactly the kind of thing he would do. I waited to see if he could get it out of there, but then I began to think that something might have gone wrong.'

'What gave you that idea?' asked Pekkala.

'To begin with, the engine wasn't running. Nagorski wouldn't have cut power to the motor under those circumstances, not even for an experiment. The whole tank could sink into this mud. If water flooded the engine compartment, the entire drive train could be ruined. Even Nagorski wouldn't take a chance like that.'

'Anything else?'

'Yes. The turret hatch was open, and it was pouring with rain. He would have closed the hatch. And, finally, there was no sign of Colonel Nagorski.'

'What did you do then?

'I went in and fetched Gorenko,' said Ushinsky.

Gorenko took this as a sign that he could speak at last. 'We both went out to take a look,' he explained.

'First we checked inside the tank,' said Ushinsky. 'It was empty.'

'Then I spotted the body lying under the tracks,' added Gorenko. 'We ran and found Captain Samarin, the head of security. We all came back to the tank and Samarin told us to stay here.'

'Not to touch anything.'

'Then he ran to call the ambulance.'

'And we've been here ever since,' said Gorenko, hugging his arms against his chest.

'Shouldn't we get him out from under there?' Ushinsky was staring at the Colonel's hand, which seemed to tremble in the wind-stirred puddle at their feet.

'Not just yet,' replied Pekkala. 'Until I have examined the area, no evidence can be disturbed.'

'It's hard to think of him like that,' muttered Gorenko. 'As evidence.'

The time would come, Pekkala knew, when Nagorski's body would receive the respect it deserved. For now, the dead man was part of an equation, along with the mud in which he lay and the iron which had crushed out his life. 'If Nagorski was out here by himself,' asked Pekkala, 'do you have any idea how he could have ended up beneath the machine?'

'We've been asking ourselves the same question,' said Ushinsky.

'It just doesn't seem possible,' Gorenko chimed in.

'Have you been inside the tank since you got here?' asked Pekkala.

'Only to see that it was empty.'

'Can you show me the driver's compartment?'

'Of course,' replied Gorenko.

At the opposite end of the tank from where Nagorski's body had been pinned, Pekkala set his foot on one of the wheels and tried to lift himself up on the side of the tank. He lost his balance and with a groan of frustration fell back spread-eagled into the water. By the time he emerged, Gorenko had gone around to the front of the tank and put his foot up on the fender. 'Always board from the front, Inspector. Like this!' He scrambled up on to the turret, opened the hatch and dropped down inside.

Pekkala followed, his soaked coat weighing on his back and ruined shoes slipping on the smooth metal surfaces. His fingers clawed for a grip as he moved from one hand hold to another. When he finally reached the turret hatch, he peered down into the cramped space of the compartment.

'How many people fit in here?' he asked.

'Five,' replied Gorenko, looking up at him.

To Pekkala, it didn't look as if there was even enough room for himself and Gorenko, let alone three other men.

'Are you all right, Inspector?'

'Yes. Why?'

'You look a little pale.'

'I'm fine,' Pekkala lied.

'Well, then,' said Gorenko. 'Down you come, Inspector.'

Pekkala sighed heavily. Then he clambered down into the tank.

The first thing he noticed, as his eyes grew accustomed to the gloom, was the smell of new paint mixing with the odour of diesel fuel. Cramped as it had appeared from above, the interior space seemed even smaller now that he was inside it.

Pekkala felt as if he had entered a tomb. Sweat beaded on his forehead. He had struggled with claustrophobia ever since he was a child, when his brother Anton, for a joke, had locked him in the crematorium oven belonging to their father's undertaking business.

'This is the fighting compartment,' said Gorenko, perched on a seat in the far right corner. The seat was fixed into the metal wall and had a separate back support which wrapped around in a semicircle, following the contours of the walls. Gorenko gestured to an identical seat on the left of the compartment. 'Please,' he said, with the cordiality of a man inviting someone into his living room.

Hunched almost double, Pekkala took his place in the seat.

'You are now in the loader's position,' explained Gorenko. 'I am where the commander sits.' He stretched out one leg and rested his heel on a rack of huge cannon shells which stretched along the side of the compartment. Each shell was fastened with a quick-release clasp.

'You say the engine wasn't running when you found it.'

'That's right.'

'Does that mean someone had switched it off?'

'I would assume so.'

'Is there any way to check?'

Gorenko peered into the driver's area, an even smaller space located just ahead of the main fighting compartment. His eyes narrowed as he deciphered the confusion of steering levers, gear sticks and pedals. 'Ah,' he said. 'I was wrong. It's still in forward. First gear. The engine must have stalled out.'

'So someone else was driving it?'

'Probably,' replied Gorenko, 'but I couldn't guarantee it. The clutch may have slipped while he was outside the machine.'

'I've heard of clutches popping out of gear,' said Pekkala, 'but never popping in.'

'These machines have not yet been perfected, Inspector. Sometimes they do things they aren't supposed to do.'

Pekkala's instincts begged him to get out. He forced himself to remain calm. 'Do you see anything else in here which looks out of place?'

Gorenko glanced around. 'Everything is as it should be.'

Pekkala had seen what he needed to see. Now it was time to retrieve Nagorski's body. 'Can you drive this machine?' he asked.

'Of course,' replied Gorenko, 'but whether it can get out of this crater without being towed is another question. That's probably what Nagorski was trying to discover.'

Pekkala nodded. 'Will you try?'

'Certainly, Inspector. You had better wait outside. It's hard to tell what will happen once I move the tracks. It could sink even deeper and if that happens, this compartment is going to flood. Give me a minute to check the controls, and make sure you are standing well clear when I start the engine.'

While Gorenko squeezed into the tiny driver's compartment, Pekkala clambered out of the tank. His broad shoulders caught painfully on the rim of the turret hatch. As his hands gripped the metal holding bar on the outside of the hatch, the cold solidity of the machine seemed to radiate through his skin. Pekkala was glad to get out into the open air, even if it was only to stand in the rain once again.

Outside the tank, Ushinsky was puffing on a cigarette, his hand cupped over the burning tip to shield it from the wind and rain.

'Gorenko says the engine was in gear,' said Pekkala, as he splashed down into the mud beside Ushinsky.

'So it wasn't an accident.'

'Possibly not,' replied Pekkala. 'Did Nagorski have enemies here?'

'Let me put it this way, Inspector,' he replied. 'The hard part would be finding someone around here who didn't have a grudge against him. The bastard worked us like slaves. Our names were never even mentioned on the design reports. He took all the credit for himself. Comrade Stalin probably thinks Nagorski built this entire machine by himself.'

'Is there anyone who felt strongly enough to want him dead?'

Ushinsky brushed aside the words, like a man swatting cobwebs from his face. 'None of us would ever think of hurting him.'

'And why is that?' asked Pekkala.

'Because even if we did not like the way Nagorski treated us, the Konstantin Project has become the purpose of our lives. Without Nagorski, the project would never have been possible. I know it might be hard to understand, but what might look like hell to you,' he raised his arms, as if to encompass the T-34, along with the vast and filthy basin of its proving ground, 'is paradise to us.'

73

Pekkala breathed out. 'How can men work inside those things? What happens if something goes wrong? How can they get out?'

Ushinsky's lips twitched, as if it was a subject he did not feel safe discussing. 'You are not the only one to have considered this, Inspector. Once inside, the tank crew are well protected, but if the hull is breached, say by an anti-tank round, it is extremely difficult to exit.'

'Can't you change that? Can't you make it easier for the tank crew to escape?'

'Oh, yes. It can be done, but Nagorski designed the T-34 with regard to the optimum performance of the machine. The equation is very simple, Inspector. When the T-34 is functioning, it is important to protect those who are inside. But if the machine is disabled in combat, its life, effectively, is over. And those who operate it are no longer considered necessary. The test drivers have already coined a name for the tank.'

'And what is that?'

'They call it the Red Coffin, Inspector.' Ushinsky's voice was drowned out by the tank, as Gorenko fired up the engine.

Pekkala and Ushinsky stood back as the tracks spun, spraying a sheet of muddy water out the back of the tank. Then the treads found their grip and the T-34 began to crawl up the sides of the crater. For a moment, it seemed as if the whole machine might slide backwards, but then there was a crash of gears and the tank lurched out of the hole. When it reached level ground, Gorenko set the motor in neutral, then switched off the engine.

The silence which followed, as the cloud of exhaust smoke

unravelled into the sky, was almost as deafening as the sound of the engine itself.

Gorenko climbed out. His mud-smeared coat flapped behind him like a pair of broken wings as he jumped down to the ground. He joined Pekkala and Ushinsky at the edge of the pit. In silence, the three men stared down into the trough of churned-up water.

The crater's surface was goose-fleshed with raindrops, obscuring the surface of the water. At first, they could not see the body. Then, like a ghost appearing through the mist, the corpse of Colonel Nagorski floated slowly into view. Rain pattered on his heavy canvas coat, which appeared to be the only thing holding his body together. The broken legs trailed like snakes from his misshapen torso. With the bones snapped in so many places, the limbs seemed to ripple, as if they were reflections of his body instead of the actual flesh. His hands had swollen obscenely, the weight of the tracks having forced the fluids of his body into its extremities. The pressure had split his fingertips wide open, like a pair of worn-out gloves. Some curvature of the soft ground had preserved half of Nagorski's face, but the rest had been crushed by the tracks.

Ushinsky stared at the corpse, paralysed by what he saw. 'It's all ruined,' he said. 'Everything we worked for.'

It was Gorenko who moved first, sliding down into the crater to retrieve the body. The water came up to his chest. He lifted Nagorski in his arms. Staggering under the weight, Gorenko returned to the edge of the pit.

Pekkala grabbed Gorenko by the shoulders and helped him out. Gently, Gorenko laid the Colonel's body on the ground.

With the body stretched out before him, Ushinsky seemed to wake from his trance. In spite of the cold, he took off his coat and laid it over Nagorski. The drenched material moulded to the dead man's face.

Now Pekkala caught sight of a tall man standing at the edge of the proving ground, half obscured by veils of rain which swept across the space between them. At first, he thought it might be Kirov, but on second glance he realised the man was much taller than his assistant.

'That's Maximov,' said Ushinsky. 'Nagorski's chauffeur and bodyguard.'

'We call him the T-33,' said Gorenko.

'Why is that?' asked Pekkala.

'Before Nagorski decided to build himself a tank,' explained Ushinsky, 'we say, he built himself a Maximov.'

Just then, from somewhere among the drab buildings of the facility, they heard a shout.

Captain Samarin ran to the edge of the proving ground.

Kirov was close behind him. He yelled to Pekkala, but his words were lost in the rain.

As suddenly as they had arrived, Samarin and Kirov disappeared from view, followed by Maximov.

'What's happened now?' muttered Ushinsky.

Pekkala did not reply. He had already set off through the mud, heading towards the facility. Along the way, he sank up to his knees in craters of water, lost his footing and stumbled with arms outstretched beneath the surface. For a moment, it seemed as if he might not reappear, but then he rose up, gasping, hair matted by silt, mud streaked across his face, like a creature forced into existence by some chemical reaction in the dirt. Having scrabbled up the slope, Pekkala paused to catch his breath at the edge of the proving ground. He glanced back towards the tank and saw the two scientists still standing by the body of Nagorski, as if they did not know where else to go. They reminded Pekkala of cavalry horses, standing on the battle-field beside their fallen riders.

He caught up with Kirov and the others on the road which led out of the facility.

'I saw someone,' explained Samarin, 'hiding in one of the supply buildings, where they keep spare parts for the vehicles. I chased him out on to the road. Then he just vanished.'

'Where are the other security guards?' asked Pekkala.

'There's one stationed out at the gate. You saw him when you came in. There are only four others and they're guarding the buildings. That is the protocol Colonel Nagorski put in place. In the event of an emergency, all buildings are locked and guarded.'

'If this work is so important, why are there so few of you guarding this place?'

'This isn't a jewellery shop, Inspector,' replied Samarin de-fensively. 'The things we guard here are as big as houses and weigh about as much. You can't just put one in your pocket and make off with it. Colonel Nagorski could have had a hundred people patrolling this place if he'd wanted it, but he said he didn't need them. What worried the Colonel was that someone might run away with the plans for these inventions. Because of that, the fewer people wandering around this facil-ity, the better. That's the way he saw it.'

'All right,' said Pekkala, 'the buildings are sealed. What other steps have been taken?'

'I put in a call to NKVD headquarters in Moscow and asked for assistance. As soon as I confirmed that Colonel Nagorski had been killed, they said they would dispatch a squad of soldiers. After I sent you out into the proving ground, I received a call that the doctors had been intercepted and ordered to return to Moscow. The soldiers will be here soon, but for now it's just us. That's why I fetched these two,' he gestured towards Kirov and Maximov. 'I need all the help I can get.'

Pekkala turned to Maximov, ready to introduce himself. 'I am . . .' he began.

'I know who you are,' interrupted Maximov. His voice was deep and resonant, as if it emerged not from his mouth but in vibrations through his chest. As he spoke to Pekkala, he removed his cap, revealing a clean-shaven head and a wide forehead which looked as solid as the armour of Nagorski's tank.

'This man you saw,' began Pekkala, turning back to Samarin. He was curious as to why they had not decided to pursue him.

'He's gone into the woods,' said Samarin, 'but he won't last long in there.'

'Why not?' asked Pekkala.

'Traps,' replied Samarin. 'During the construction of the facility Colonel Nagorski disappeared into those woods almost every day. No one was allowed to follow him. He dragged in slats of wood, metal pipes, rolls of wire, shovels, boxes nailed shut so that no one could see what was in them. No one knows how many traps he built.

Dozens. Maybe hundreds. Or what kind of traps, exactly. And where they are, nobody knows that either, except Colonel Nagorski.'

'Why go to all that trouble?' asked Kirov. 'Surely . . .'

'You did not know Colonel Nagorski,' interrupted Samarin.

'Is there really no map of where these traps were placed?' asked Pekkala.

'None that I've ever seen,' replied Samarin. 'Nagorski hammered small coloured discs into some of the trees. Some are blue, others red or yellow. What they mean, if they mean anything at all, only Nagorski knows.'

Squinting into the depths of the forest, Pekkala could make out some of these coloured discs, glimmering like eyes from the shadows.

A sound made them turn their heads – a series of muffled thumping sounds, somewhere lost among the trees.

'There!' shouted Samarin, drawing his revolver.

Something was running through the woods.

The figure moved so quickly that at first Pekkala thought it must be some kind of animal. No human could move that fast, he thought. The shape appeared and disappeared, bounding like a deer through the brambled thickets which grew between the trees. Then, as it leaped across a clearing, Pekkala realised it was a man.

In that moment, something snapped inside him. Pekkala knew that if they didn't catch him now, they'd never find him in this wilderness. He had not forgotten about Nagorski's traps, but some instinct had woken in him, overriding thoughts of his own safety. Without a word to the others, Pekkala set off running through the woods.

'Wait!' screamed Samarin.

Pekkala raced among the trees, drawing his gun as he sprinted.

'Have you gone completely mad?' shouted Samarin.

Kirov too had joined the chase, hurdling the thickets as he struggled to catch up with Pekkala.

'This is insane!' roared Samarin. Then, with a shout, he lunged after them.

Brambles tore at their legs as the three men raced through the dying light.

'There he is!' shouted Samarin.

Pekkala's lungs were burning. The weight of the coat hung on his shoulders and dragged against his thighs.

Samarin had overtaken him now, picking up speed as he gained on the running man. Then, suddenly, he skidded to a halt, one hand raised in warning.

Barely in time to avoid crashing into Samarin, Pekkala managed to stop. He bent double, hands on his knees, his throat raw and painful as he struggled for breath.

With twitching fingertips, Samarin pointed to a strand of wire strung across the path. It threaded through a bent nail which had been hammered into the trunk of a nearby stump. From there the wire stretched up through the leaves of a tree beside the path until at last Pekkala's straining eyes could see where it wrapped around the handle of a Type 33 grenade, bound with threads of dried grass to a branch directly above their heads. A tug on the wire would bring it down. This movement would arm the grenade, since Type 33s – like iron soup cans attached to a short heavy stem and wrapped with a gridded fragmentation sleeve – were normally activated by the movement of throwing them through the air.

'We'll keep after him,' said Samarin, as he bent down to untie the string, 'as soon as I've disarmed this thing.'

As Pekkala moved forward, he glanced up once more at the grenade. It was then he noticed that the slide cover at the top of the grenade, which should have contained the cigarette-shaped detonator, was empty. The thought that this might, somehow, have been intentional was only half-born in his mind when he heard a loud rustle in the branches above him.

He had just enough time to turn his head to look at Samarin.

Their eyes met.

A shape flashed in front of Pekkala. The speed of it brushed cold against his cheek. Then came a dull and heavy thump. Leaves flickered down around him.

Pekkala had not moved, paralysed by the closeness of whatever had swept past him, but now he forced himself to turn and look at Samarin.

At first glance, Samarin appeared to be crouched against a tree stump. His arms were thrown out to the sides, as if to steady himself. A shape, some tangling of earth and wood and weather-beaten steel, obscured his body.

It took Pekkala a moment to understand that this object was an iron pipe. It had been sawn through on a diagonal so that the end was like the needle of a huge syringe. The pipe had then been bound with vines to the trunk of a bent sapling and had been released by the weight of Samarin's foot.

The grenade was only a diversion, drawing their gaze away from the real danger hidden in the leaves.

The sharpened pipe had struck Samarin square in the chest. Its force had thrown him back against the stump. The rotten wood had exploded and now, from that throne of dust, a rabble of shiny black ants, pincer-tailed earwigs and wood lice streamed out in confusion. The insects swarmed over Samarin's shoulders, migrating down his arms and out along the walkways of his fingers.

Samarin was still alive. He stared straight ahead, a look of resignation on his face. Then something happened to his eyes. They became like those of a cat. And suddenly he was dead.

The rain had stopped. Through shredded clouds, beams of sunlight slanted through the trees so that the air itself appeared like molten copper.

'Where the hell is Maximov?' asked Kirov. 'Why didn't he help?'

'Too late now,' replied Pekkala. 'Whoever that man was, we have lost him.' As he stared once more at the place where the man had disappeared, it occurred to him that they might not have been chasing a human at all, but something supernatural, a creature that could drift above the ground, oblivious to the traps, drawing around itself the million tangled branches of the trees to vanish in the air.

The two men walked over to Samarin.

There was no gentle way to pry him loose. Pekkala set his boot against the dead man's shoulder and wrenched the bar out of his chest.

Together, Kirov and Pekkala carried Samarin's body back to the road. There, they found Maximov waiting just where they had left him.

Maximov stared at the body of Samarin. Then he raised his head and looked Pekkala in the eye, but he did not say a word.

Kirov could not contain his anger. He stalked over to Maximov, so that the two men were only an arm's length apart. 'Why didn't you help us?' he raged.

'I know what's out there in those woods,' replied Maximov. His voice betrayed no emotion.

'*He* knew!' Kirov pointed at the body of Captain Samarin. 'He knew and still he came with us.'

Maximov's head turned slowly, until he was looking at Samarin's corpse. 'Yes, he did,' said Maximov.

'What's the matter with you?' yelled Kirov. 'Were you afraid to take the risk?'

At this insult, Maximov seemed to shudder, as if the ground were trembling beneath his feet. 'There are better ways to serve your country, Comrade Commissar, than by throwing your life away at the first opportunity.'

'You can settle this later,' said Pekkala. 'Right now, we have company.'

An army truck with NKVD licence plates was coming down the road. The canvas covers were battened down. As it passed, the driver glanced out the side window, caught sight of Samarin, then turned to say something to someone in the passenger seat.

The truck pulled up in front of the facility. Armed men, wearing the blue-and-red peaked caps of NKVD Security troops, jumped down on to the muddy ground and took up positions around the buildings.

An officer emerged from the cab of the truck. It was only when the officer began walking towards them that Pekkala realised it was a woman, since she wore the same clothes and cap as the men, hiding the curve of her hips and her chest.

The woman stopped in front of them, surveying the filthy disarray of their clothes. She was of medium height, with a round face and wide green eyes. 'I am Commissar Major Lysenkova of NKVD Internal Affairs.'

As soon as her name reached his ears, Pekkala realised he had heard about this woman. She was famous for her work within the NKVD, for which most of her colleagues despised her. Commissar Lysenkova had the unenviable task of investigating crimes inside her own branch of service. In the past two years, over thirty NKVD men had gone to their deaths after being convicted of crimes investigated by Lysenkova. Within the close-knit ranks of the NKVD, Pekkala had never heard a kind word said about her. He had even heard a rumour that she denounced her own parents to the authorities, and that her whole family ended up in Siberia as a result.

Given the reputation that preceded her, Pekkala was surprised at how Lysenkova appeared in person. Her tough reputation did not seem to match the gentle angles of her face and the clothes she wore would have been too small for him by the time he was twelve years old.

'Which one of you is Pekkala?' she asked.

'I am.' Pekkala felt the stare of her luminous green eyes.

'What has happened here?' demanded Lysenkova, flicking a finger towards Samarin's corpse.

Pekkala explained.

'And you failed to catch this person?'

'That is correct,' admitted Pekkala.

'I am curious to know,' she continued, 'how you managed to arrive at the crime scene before me, Inspector.'

'When we set out for this place,' replied Pekkala, 'the crime had not yet been committed. But now that you are here, Commissar Lysenkova, I would appreciate whatever help you can give us.'

The green eyes blinked at him. 'You seem to be confused, Inspector, about who is in charge of this investigation. This facility is under NKVD control.'

'Very well,' said Pekkala. 'What do you intend to do now?'

'I will examine Colonel Nagorski's body myself,' replied Lysenkova, 'to see if I can determine the exact circumstances of his death. In the meantime, I will send guards out to patrol the main road, in case this runner makes it through the woods.'

'What about Nagorski's family?' asked Pekkala.

'His wife and son live here on the compound,' said Maximov.

'Do they know what has happened?' Lysenkova asked.

'Not yet,' replied the bodyguard. 'There is no phone at the house and no one has been out there since the accident.'

'I will break the news to them,' said Pekkala, but even as he spoke, he wondered where he'd find the words. His trade was with the dead and those who brought them to that place, not with those who had to go on living in the wake of such disaster.

Lysenkova considered this for a moment. 'All right,' she replied, 'and report back to me when you're done. But first,' she nodded towards Samarin, 'you can bury that.'

'Here?' Kirov stared at her. 'Now?'

'This is a secret facility,' she answered. 'Everything that happens here is classified, including who works here and who has the misfortune of dying in this place. Have you ever heard of the White Sea Canal, Major?'

'Of course,' replied Kirov.

Designed to link the White Sea and the Baltic, a distance of over 200 kilometres, the canal had been dug in the early 1930s almost entirely by convict labourers using primitive tools in some of the harshest conditions on earth. Thousands had perished. In the end, the canal proved too narrow for the cargo ships it had been designed to carry.

'Do you know what they did with the prisoners who died on that project?' Without waiting for a reply, Lysenkova went on. 'Their corpses were sunk into the wet cement which made up the walls of the canal. That's what happens to secrets in this country, Major. They get buried. So do as I tell you and put him under ground.'

'Where?' asked Kirov, still unable to believe what he was hearing.

'Here in the road, for all I care,' snapped Lysenkova, 'but wherever it is, do it now.' Then she spun on her heel and left them.

'I guess the rumours are true about her,' said Kirov, watching Lysenkova as she strode back to the truck.

Maximov turned his head away and spat.

'Why didn't you pull rank on her, Inspector?' Kirov asked Pekkala.

'I have a bad feeling about this,' replied Pekkala. 'The fact that she is here at all means there is more going on than we realise. For now, let's just see where she leads us.' He turned to Maximov. 'Can you take me to Nagorski's wife?'

Maximov nodded. 'First we'll bury Samarin, and then I'll take you there.'

The three men carried the body a short distance into the woods. Lacking a shovel, they used their hands to claw a grave out of the soft, dark earth. Half an arm's length from the surface, the hole filled with black liquid seeping from the peaty ground. They had no choice but to lay Samarin in it, arms folded across his chest, as if to hide the tunnel through his heart. The black water swallowed him up. Then they packed the spongy earth on top of his body. When it was done and they climbed to their feet, picking the dirt from under their fingernails, there was barely a trace to indicate that a man had just been buried there.

When Maximov went off to fetch his car, Kirov turned to Pekkala. 'Why don't we start by arresting that bastard?'

'Arrest him?' asked Pekkala. 'On what charges?'

'I don't know!' spluttered Kirov. 'What about cowardice?'

'You seem to have made up your mind about him very quickly.'

'Sometimes a moment is all it takes,' insisted Kirov. 'I've seen him before, you know. He was sitting at the table, that day I went into Chicherin's restaurant to find Nagorski. I didn't like the look of him then and I like him even less now.'

'Did you stop to think that maybe he was right?'

'Right about what?'

'About not running into those woods. After all, why did you run?'

Kirov frowned, confused. 'I ran because you ran, Inspector.'

'And do you know why I ran,' asked Pekkala, 'in spite of the warning Samarin had given us?'

'No,' shrugged Kirov, 'I suppose I don't.'

'Neither do I,' replied Pekkala, 'so it is only luck that we are standing here instead of lying in the ground.'

Maximov's car appeared from behind one of the buildings and made its way towards them.

'I need you to keep an eye on Lysenkova,' Pekkala told Kirov. 'Whatever you learn, keep it to yourself for now. And keep your temper, too.'

'That,' muttered the young Major, 'I cannot promise you.'

With Pekkala in the front passenger seat, Maximov drove along a narrow road leading away from the dreary facility.

'I am sorry about my assistant,' said Pekkala. 'Sometimes he does things without thinking.'

'Seems to me,' replied Maximov, 'that he is not the only one. But if you are worried about my feelings, Comrade Inspector, you can save yourself the trouble.'

'Where are you from, Maximov?'

'I have lived in many places,' he replied. 'I am not from anywhere.'

'And what did you do before the Revolution?'

'The same as you, Inspector. I made a living for myself and I managed to survive.'

Pekkala studied the blur of trees flickering past. 'That's two questions you have avoided.'

Maximov hit the brakes. The tyres locked and skidded. For a moment, it looked as if they were going to end up in the ditch, but they came to a stop just before the car left the road. Maximov cut the engine. Then he turned to face Pekkala. 'If you don't like me avoiding your questions, maybe you should stop asking them.'

'It's my job to ask questions,' said Pekkala, 'and, sooner or later, you will need to answer them.'

Maximov glared at Pekkala but, as the seconds passed, the anger went out of his eyes. 'I'm sorry,' he said at last. 'The only reason I've survived as long as I have is by keeping my mouth shut. Old habits die hard, Inspector.'

'Survival has been difficult for all of us,' said Pekkala.

'That's not what I hear about you. People say you've lived a charmed life.'

'Those are merely stories, Maximov.'

'Are they? I just saw you walk out of those woods without so much as a scratch.'

'I was not the only one.'

'I'm sure Captain Samarin would take comfort in that, if he was still alive. You know, when I was a child, I heard that if a Russian goes into the woods, he becomes lost. But when a Finn steps into the forest,' he touched his fingertips together and then let them drift apart, like someone releasing a dove, 'he simply disappears.'

'Like I told you. Just stories.'

'No, Inspector,' he replied. 'There's more to it than that. I have seen it for myself.'

'What have you seen?' asked Pekkala.

'I was there, that day on the Nevski Prospekt, where I know for a fact you should have died.'

It was a summer evening. Pekkala had spent the day trying to find a birthday present for Ilya, wandering up and down the arcade of shops in the Passazh – a glass-roofed corridor, lined with expensive jewellers, tailors and vendors of antiques.

For hours, he had paced back and forth in front of the Passazh windows, steeling himself to enter the cramped shops where he knew he would immediately be set upon by sales attendants.

Three times, he had abandoned the arcade and fled across the Nevski Prospekt to the huge produce market known as the Gostiny Dvor. The floors were strewn with sawdust, wilted cabbage leaves and discarded sales receipts scribbled on cheap grey notepad paper. Trucks pulled up on to the wide, cobblestoned delivery area and porters in blue tunics with silver buttons, their hands bound with scraps of cloth as protection against the splintery wooden crates, unloaded vegetables and fruit.

Inside the vast, cold, echoing hall of the Gostiny Dvor, surrounded by vendors chanting out their lists of goods and the soft murmur of footsteps shuffling through the sawdust, Pekkala sat on a barrel in a café frequented by the porters, sipping a glass of tea and feeling his heart unclench after the stuffiness of the Passazh.

The last train to Tsarskoye Selo would be leaving in half an hour. Knowing that he could not go home empty-handed, he steeled himself for another trip to the Passazh. It's now or never, Pekkala thought.

A minute later, on his way out of the hall, he noticed a man standing by one of the pillars at the exit. The man was watching him and trying not to make it obvious. But Pekkala could always tell when he was being watched, even if he could not see who was doing the watching. He felt it like a static in the air.

Pekkala glanced at the man as he walked past, noting the stranger's clothing – the knee-length coat made of wool, grey like the feathers of a dove, the slightly out-of-fashion Homburg hat, rounded at the top and with an oval brim that sheltered his eyes so that Pekkala could not see them. He had an impressive moustache, which grew down to the line of his jaw, and a small, nervous-looking mouth.

But Pekkala was too preoccupied with Ilya's birthday present to think much more about it.

Outside, the evening sky, which would not darken until midnight at this time of year, shimmered like an abalone shell.

He had almost reached the exit when he felt something nudge him in the back.

Pekkala spun around.

The man in the Homburg hat was standing there. He was holding a gun in his right hand. It was a poorly made automatic pistol, of a type manufactured in Bulgaria, which often showed up at crime scenes, since it was cheap and easy to purchase on the black market.

'Are you who I think you are?' asked the man.

Before Pekkala could come up with a reply, he heard a loud clapping sound.

Sparks erupted from the cylinder of the gun. The air became hazy with smoke.

Pekkala realised he must have been shot, but he felt neither the impact of the bullet, nor the burning, stinging pain which, he knew, would quickly change to a numbness radiating out through his whole body. Astonishingly, he felt nothing at all.

The man was staring at him.

Only then did Pekkala notice that everything around him had come to a standstill. There were people everywhere, porters, shoppers with string bags, vendors behind their barricades of produce. And all of them were staring at him.

'Why?' he asked the man.

There was no reply. A look of terror spread across the man's face. He set the gun against his own temple and pulled the trigger.

With the sound of that gunshot still ringing in Pekkala's ears, the man fell in a heap on to the ground.

Then, where there had been silence only a second before, a wall of noise surrounded him. He heard the guttural cries of panicked men, shouting useless commands. A woman grabbed him by the shoulders. 'It's Pekkala!' she shrieked. 'They've killed the Emerald Eye!'

Carefully, Pekkala began to undo his coat. The act of unfastening the buttons felt suddenly unfamiliar, as if this was the first time he had ever done such a thing. He opened his coat, then his waistcoat and finally his shirt. He prepared himself for the sight of the wound, the terrible whiteness of punctured flesh, the pulsing flow of blood from an arterial break. But the skin was smooth and unbroken. Not trusting his eyes, Pekkala ran his hands over his chest, certain that the wound must be there.

'He's not hurt!' shouted a porter. 'The bullet did not even touch him.'

'But I saw it!' shouted the woman who had grabbed Pekkala's shoulders.

'There is no way he could have missed!' said the porter.

'Perhaps the gun wasn't working!' said another man, a fish-monger in an apron splashed with guts and scales. He bent down and picked up the weapon.

'Of course it works!' The porter gestured at the dead man. 'There is the proof!'

Around the head of the corpse grew a halo of blood. The Homburg lay upturned beside him, like a bird's nest knocked out of a tree. Pekkala's eyes fixed on the tiny bow of silk used to join the two ends of the leather sweatband.

'Let me see that,' the porter tried to take the gun from the fishmonger.

'Be careful!' snapped the fishmonger.

As their fingers closed on the gun, it went off. The bullet smacked into a pyramid of potatoes.

The two men yelped and dropped the gun.

'Enough!' growled Pekkala.

They stared at him with bulging eyes, as if he were a statue come to life.

Pekkala picked up the gun and put it in his pocket. 'Go find me the police,' he said quietly.

The two men, released from his freezing stare, scattered in opposite directions.

Later that night, having made his report to the Petrograd police, Pekkala found himself in the Tsar's study.

The Tsar sat behind his desk. He had been going through papers all evening reading by the light of a candle set into a bronze holder in the shape of a croaking frog. He insisted on reading all official documents himself and used a blue pencil to make notes in the margin. It slowed down the process by which any matters of the state could be accomplished, but the Tsar preferred to handle these things personally. Now he had set aside his documents. He rested his elbows on the desk and settled his chin upon his folded hands. With his soft blue eyes, the Tsar regarded Pekkala. 'Are you sure you are all right?'

'Yes, Majesty,' replied Pekkala.

'Well, I'm not, I don't mind telling you,' replied the Tsar. 'What the hell happened, Pekkala? I heard some madman shot you in the chest, but the bullet vanished in mid-air. The police checked out the gun. Their report indicates that it is functioning perfectly. The whole city is talking about this. You should hear the absurdities they're uttering. They believe you're supernatural. By tomorrow, it will be all over the country. Any idea who this man was, or why he was trying to kill you?'

'No, Majesty. He was carrying no identification. His body had no distinctive marks, no tattoos, scars or moles. All the labels had been removed from his clothes. Nor does he match the description of anyone currently wanted by the police. It is likely we will never know who he was, or why he attempted to kill me.'

'I was afraid you were going to say that,' said the Tsar. He sat back in his chair, letting his eyes wander across the gold-leafed titles of the books upon his shelves. 'So we've got no answers at all.'

'We do have one,' replied Pekkala, placing something on the desk before the Tsar – a crumpled knot of grey the size of a robin's egg.

The Tsar picked it up. 'What's this? Feels heavy.'

'Lead.' The candle flame trembled. A thread of molten wax poured into the frog's open mouth.

'Is this the bullet?' He studied it with one eye closed, like a jeweller appraising a diamond.

'Two bullets fused together,' replied Pekkala.

'Two?' asked the Tsar. 'And where did you get them?'

'I removed them from the skull of the dead man.'

The Tsar dropped the bullets back on to the desk. 'You could have told me that before.' He took out a handkerchief and wiped his fingers.

'While the police were examining the gun,' explained Pekkala, 'I decided to examine the body. It was not the gun that malfunctioned, Majesty. It was the bullet.'

'I don't understand,' the Tsar frowned. 'How does a bullet malfunction?'

'The bullet he fired at me contained the wrong amount of gunpowder. The weapon was of poor quality, as was the ammunition that came with it. When the gun discharged, the cartridge ejected, but it only drove the bullet into the barrel, where it became stuck. Then next time he pulled the trigger, a second bullet smashed into the first . . .'

'And both bullets went into his head at the same time.'

'Precisely.'

'Meanwhile, the world thinks you're some kind of sorcerer.' The Tsar brushed his fingers through his beard. 'Have you informed the police about this discovery of yours?'

'Not yet. It was late by the time I had finished my investigation. I will inform the Petrograd chief first thing in the morning. He can then make an announcement to the public.'

'Now, Pekkala.' The Tsar rested his fingertips on the desk top, like a man about to begin playing a piano. 'I want you to do something for me.'

'And what is that, Majesty?'

'Nothing.'

'I beg your pardon?'

'I want you to do nothing.' He gestured towards the door, beyond which lay the vast expanse of Russia. 'Let them believe what they want to believe.'

'That the bullet disappeared?'

The Tsar picked up the piece of lead and dropped it in the pocket of his waistcoat. 'It has disappeared,' he said.

'You were there?' asked Pekkala.

'I happened to be passing through the market place,' replied Maximov. 'I saw the whole thing. I've always wondered how you managed to survive.'

'Later on,' replied Pekkala, 'when you have answered some of my questions, perhaps I can answer some of yours.'

The cottage belonging to Nagorski was of the type known as a dacha. Built in the traditional style, with a thatched roof and shuttered windows, it had clearly been here many years longer than the facility itself.

Perched at the edge of a small lake, the dacha was the only building in sight. Except for a clearing around the cottage itself, dense forest crowded down to the water's edge.

It was still and peaceful here. Now that the clouds had cleared away, the surface of the lake glowed softly in the fading sunlight. Out on the water, a man sat in a rowboat. In his right hand, he held a fishing rod. His arm waved gently back and forth. The long fly line, burning silver as it caught the rays of sunset, stretched out from the tip of the rod, curving back upon itself and stretching out again until the speck of the fly touched down upon the surface of the lake. Around the man, tiny insects swirled like bubbles in champagne.

Pekkala was so focused on this image that he did not see a woman come around from the back of the house until she stood in front of him.

The woman looked beautiful but tired. An air of quiet desperation hung about her. Tight curls waved across her short, dark hair. Her chin was small and her eyes so dark that the blackness of her irises seemed to have flooded out into her pupils.

Ignoring Pekkala, the woman turned to Maximov, who was getting out of the car. 'Who is this man,' she asked, 'and why is he so filthy dirty, as well as being dressed like an undertaker?'

'This is Inspector Pekkala,' Maximov answered, 'from the Bureau of Special Operations.'

'Pekkala,' she echoed. The dark eyes raked his face. 'Oh, yes. You arrested my husband in the middle of his lunch.'

'Detained,' replied Pekkala, 'not arrested.'

'I thought that was all cleared up.'

'It was, Mrs Nagorski.'

'So why are you here?' she asked. She spat out the words as if her mouth was filled with shards of glass.

Pekkala could tell that a part of her already knew. It was as if she had been expecting this news, not just today but for a very long time.

'He's dead, isn't he?' she asked.

Pekkala nodded.

Maximov reached out to lay his hand upon her shoulder.

Angrily she brushed his touch away. Then her hand flew back, catching Maximov across the face. 'You were supposed to take care of him!' she shrieked, raising her fists and bringing them down hard against his chest with a sound like muffled drumbeats.

Maximov staggered back, too stunned by her fury to resist.

'That was your job!' she shouted. 'He took you in. He gave you a chance when no one else would. And now this! This is how you repay him?'

'Mrs Nagorski,' whispered Maximov. 'I did everything I could for him.'

Mrs Nagorski stared at the man as if she did not even know who he was. 'If you had done everything,' she sneered, 'my husband would still be alive.'

The figure in the boat turned his head to see where the shouting had come from.

Pekkala could see now that it was a young man, and he knew it must be the Nagorskis' son, Konstantin.

The young man reeled in his line, set the fishing rod aside and took up the oars. Slowly, he made his way towards the shore, oars creaking in the brass wishbones of the oarlocks, water dripping from the blades like a stream of mercury.

Mrs Nagorski turned and walked back towards the dacha. As she climbed the first step to the porch, she stumbled. One arm reached out to brace herself against the planks. Her hands were shaking. She sank down on the steps.

By then, Pekkala had caught up with her.

She glanced at him, then looked away again. 'I always said this project would destroy him, one way or another. I must see my husband,' she said.

'I would not advise that,' replied Pekkala.

'I will see him, Inspector. Immediately.'

Hearing the finality in the widow's voice, Pekkala realised there was no point trying to dissuade her.

The rowing boat ground up against the shore. The boy hauled in his oars with the unconscious precision of a bird folding its wings, then stepped out of the tippy boat. Konstantin was head and shoulders taller than his mother, with dark eyes and short, unkempt hair that needed washing. His heavy canvas trousers were patched at the knees and looked as if they had belonged to someone else before they came to him. He wore a sweater with holes in the elbows and his bare feet were speckled with bug bites, although he did not seem to notice them.

Konstantin looked from face to face, waiting for someone to explain.

It was Maximov who went to him. He put his arm around the boy, speaking in a voice too low for anyone else to hear.

Konstantin's face turned pale. He seemed to be staring at something no one else could see, as if the ghost of his father were standing right in front of him.

Pekkala watched this, feeling a weight settle in his heart, like a man whose blood had turned to sand.

While Maximov drove Mrs Nagorski to the facility, Pekkala sat with her son at the dining table in the dacha.

The walls were covered with dozens of blueprints. Some were exploded engine diagrams. Others showed the inner workings of guns or traced the crooked path of exhaust systems. On shelves around the room lay pieces of twisted metal, fan blades, a slab of wood into which different-sized screws had been drilled. A single link of tank track lay upon the stone mantelpiece. The room did not smell like a home – of fires and cooking and soap. Instead, it reeked of machine oil and the sharply pungent ink used on the blueprints.

The furniture was of the highest quality – walnut cabinets with diamond-paned glass fronts, leather chairs with brass nails running like machine-gun belts along the seams. The dining table at which they sat was far too big for the cramped space of the dacha.

Pekkala knew that the Nagorski family had probably belonged to the old aristocracy. Most of these families had either fled the country during the Revolution, or been swallowed up in labour camps. Only a few remained, and fewer still had held on to the relics of their former status in society. Only those who had proved themselves valuable to the government were permitted such luxuries.

Nagorski may have earned that right, but Pekkala wondered what would become of the rest of his family, now that he was gone.

Pekkala knew that there was nothing he could say. Sometimes, the best that could be done was just to keep a person company.

Konstantin stared fiercely out the window as the last purpling twilight bled into the solid black of night.

Seeing the young man so locked away inside his head, Pekkala remembered the last time he had seen his own father, that freezing January morning when he left home to enlist in the Tsar's Finnish Legion.

He was leaning out of the window of a train as it pulled

out of the station. On the platform stood his father, in a long black coat and wide-brimmed hat set squarely on his head. His mother had been too upset to accompany them to the station. His father held up one hand in a gesture of farewell. Above him, bent back like the teeth of eels, icicles hung from the station-house roof.

Two years later, left to run the funeral parlour alone, the old man suffered a heart attack while dragging a body on a sledge to the crematorium that he maintained some distance into the woods behind their house. The horse that usually hauled the sledge had slipped on the ice that winter and was lame, so Pekkala's father had tried to do the work himself.

The old man was found on his knees in front of the sledge, hands resting on his thighs, chin sunk on to his chest. Slung across his shoulders were the leather traces normally worn by the horse for inching the sledge along the narrow forest path. The way he knelt gave the impression that he had just stopped for a moment to rest and would, at any moment, rise to his feet and go back to hauling his burden.

Although it had been his father's wish that Pekkala enlist in the Legion, rather than remain at home to help with the family business, Pekkala had never forgiven himself for not having been there to pick up the old man when he stumbled and fell.

Now Pekkala saw that same emotion on the face of this young man.

Suddenly, Konstantin spoke. 'Are you going to find who murdered my father?'

'I am not certain he was murdered, but if he was, I will track down whoever is responsible.'

'Find them,' said Konstantin. 'Find them and put them to death.'

At that moment, headlights swept through the room as Maximov's car pulled up beside the house. A moment later, the front door opened. 'Why is it so dark in here?' asked Mrs Nagorski, as she hurried to light a kerosene lamp.

Konstantin rose sharply to his feet. 'Did you see him? Is it true? Is he really dead?'

'Yes,' she replied, tears coming at last to her eyes. 'It is true.'

Pekkala left them alone to grieve. He went out and stood on the porch with Maximov, who was smoking a cigarette.

'Today is his birthday,' said Maximov. 'That boy deserves a better life than this.'

Pekkala did not reply.

The smell of burning tobacco lingered in the damp night air.

Pekkala returned to the assembly building; the flat-roofed brick structure which Ushinsky had christened the Iron House. Engines hung in wooden cradles against one wall. Against the other wall, the bare metal shells of tanks balanced on iron rails, rust already forming on the welding joints, as if the steel had been sprinkled with cinnamon powder. Elsewhere, like islands in this vast warehouse, machine guns had been laid out in a row. Arching high above the work floor, metal girders held the ceiling in place. To Pekkala, an air of lifelessness hung about this place. It was as if these tanks were not pieces of the future but fragments from the distant past, like the bones of once-formidable dinosaurs waiting to be reassembled by archaeologists.

A table had been cleared off. Engine parts were strewn across the floor where NKVD men had hurriedly set them aside. On the table lay the remains of Colonel Nagorski. The terrible whiteness of torn and bled-out flesh seemed to glow under the work lights. Lysenkova was spreading an army rain cape over Nagorski's head, having just examined the body.

Beside her stood Kirov, the muscles drawn tight in his face. He had seen bodies before, but nothing like this, Pekkala knew.

Even Lysenkova looked upset, although she was trying hard to conceal it. 'It's impossible to say for sure,' the commissar told Pekkala, 'but everything points towards an engine malfunction. Nagorski was out testing the machine on his own. He put the engine in neutral, got out to check something, and the tank must have popped into gear. He lost his footing and the tank ran over him before the engine stalled. It was an accident. That much is obvious.'

Kirov, standing behind her, slowly shook his head.

'Have you spoken to the staff here at the facility?' Pekkala asked Lysenkova.

'Yes,' she replied. 'All of them are accounted for and none of them were with Nagorski at the time of his death.'

'What about the man we chased through the woods?'

'Well, whoever he is, he doesn't work here at the facility. Given the fact that Nagorski's death is an accident, the man you chased was likely just a hunter who had made his way into the grounds of the facility.'

'Then why did he run when he was ordered to stop?'

'If men with guns were chasing you, Inspector Pekkala, wouldn't you run away, too?'

Pekkala ignored the question. 'Would you mind if I examine the body?'

'Fine,' she said, irritably, 'but be quick. I am heading back to Moscow to file my report. Nagorski's body will remain here for now. Guards will be arriving soon to make sure the corpse is not disturbed. I expect you to be gone when they arrive.'

The two men waited until Major Lysenkova had left the building.

'What did you find out?' Pekkala asked Kirov.

'What she said about the scientists is correct. They have all been accounted for by the guards at the time Nagorski died. During work hours, guards are stationed inside each of the facility buildings, which means that the scientists were also able to account for the whereabouts of the security personnel. Samarin was on his usual rounds this morning. He was seen by all of the staff at one time or another.'

'Is anyone missing?'

'No, and no one seems to have been anywhere near Nagorski when he died.' Kirov turned his attention to the rain cape, whose dips and folds crudely matched the contours of a human body. 'But she's wrong about this being an accident.'

'I agree,' replied Pekkala, 'but how have you reached that conclusion?'

'You had better see for yourself, Inspector,' replied Kirov.

Grasping the edge of the cape, Pekkala slowly drew it back until Nagorski's head and shoulders were revealed. What he saw made him draw in his breath through clenched teeth.

Only a leathery mask remained of Nagorski's face, behind which the shattered skull looked more like broken crockery than bone. He had never encountered a body as traumatised as the one which lay before him now.

'There.' Kirov pointed to a place where the inside of Nagorski's skull had been exposed.

Gently taking hold of the dead man's jaw, Pekkala tilted the head to one side. In the glare of the work light, a tiny splash of silver winked at him.

Pekkala reached into his pocket and brought out a bone-handled switch blade. He sprung the blade and touched the tip of the stiletto against the silver object. Lifting it from the rippled plate of bone, he eased the fleck of metal on to his palm. Now that he could see it clearly, Pekkala realised that the metal wasn't silver. It was lead.

'What is it?' asked Kirov.

'Bullet fragment.'

'That rules out an accident.'

Removing a handkerchief from his pocket, Pekkala placed the sliver of lead in the middle and then folded the handkerchief into a bundle before returning it to his pocket.

'Could it have been suicide?' asked Kirov.

'We'll see.' Pekkala's focus returned to the wreckage of Nagorski's face. He searched for an entry wound. Reaching under the head, fingers sifting through the matted hair, his fingertip snagged on a jagged edge at the base of the skull where the bullet had impacted the bone. Pressing his finger into the wound, he followed its trajectory to an exit point on the right side of the dead man's face, where the flesh had been torn away. 'This was no suicide,' said Pekkala.

'How can you be sure?' asked Kirov.

'A man who commits suicide with a pistol, will hold the gun against his right temple if he is right-handed or against his left temple if he is left-handed. Or, if he knows what he is doing, he will put the gun between his teeth and shoot himself through the roof of the mouth. That will take out the dura oblongata, killing him instantly.' He pulled the rain cape back over Nagorski's body, then wiped the gore from his hands on a corner of the cape.

'How do you get used to it?' asked Kirov, as he watched Pekkala scrape the blood out from under his finger nails.

'You can get used to almost anything.'

They left the warehouse, just as three NKVD guards arrived to take charge of Nagorski's corpse. Standing in the dark, the two men turned up the collars of their coats against a spitting rain.

'Are you certain Major Lysenkova didn't spot the bullet wound in Nagorski's skull?' asked Pekkala.

'She barely glanced at the remains,' replied Kirov. 'It seemed to me that she just wants this case to go away as fast as possible.'

Just then, a figure appeared from the darkness. It was Maximov. He had been waiting for them. 'I need to know,' he said. 'What happened to Colonel Nagorski?'

Kirov glanced at Pekkala.

Almost imperceptibly, Pekkala nodded.

'He was shot,' replied the Major.

The muscles twitched along Maximov's jaw. 'This is my fault,' he muttered.

'Why do you say that?' asked Pekkala.

'Yelena – Mrs Nagorski – she was right. It was my job to protect him.'

'If I understand things correctly,' replied Pekkala, 'he sent you away just before he was killed.'

Maximov nodded. 'That's true, but still, it was my job . . .'

'You can't protect a man who refuses to be protected,' said Pekkala.

If Maximov took comfort in Pekkala's words, he gave no sign of it. 'What will happen to them now?' he asked. 'To Yelena? To the boy?'

'I don't know,' replied Pekkala.

'They won't be looked after,' said Maximov, 'not now that he is gone.'

'And what about you?' asked Pekkala. 'What will you do now?'

Maximov shook his head, as if the thought had not occurred to him. 'Just make sure they are looked after,' he said.

A cold wind blew through the trees, with a sound like the slithering of snakes.

'We'll do what we can, Maximov,' replied Pekkala. 'Now go home and get some rest.'

'That man makes me nervous,' said Kirov, after Maximov had vanished back into the dark.

'That's part of his job,' replied Pekkala. 'When we get back to the office, I want you to find out everything you can about him. I asked Maximov some questions and he avoided every one of them.'

'We could bring him in for questioning at the Lubyanka.'

Pekkala shook his head. 'I don't think we'd get much out of him that way. The only time a man like that will talk is if he wants to. Just find out what you can from the police files.'

'Very well, Inspector. Shall we head back to Moscow?'

'We can't leave yet. Now that we know a gun was used, we have to search the pit where Nagorski's body was found.'

'Can't it wait until morning?' moaned Kirov, clutching his collar to his throat.

Pekkala's silence was the answer.

'I didn't think so,' mumbled Kirov.

Pekkala woke to the sound of someone banging on the door.

At first, he thought one of the shutters must have been dislodged by the wind. There was a snowstorm blowing. Pekkala knew that, in the morning, he would have to dig his way out of the house.

The banging came again, and this time Pekkala realised someone was outside and asking to come in.

He lit a match and set the oil lamp burning by his bed.

Once more he heard the pounding on the door.

'All right!' shouted Pekkala. He fetched his pocket watch from the bedside table and squinted at the hands. It was two in the morning. Beside him, he heard a sigh. Ilya's long hair covered her face and she brushed it aside with a half-conscious sweep of her hand. 'What's going on?' she asked.

'Someone's at the door,' Pekkala replied in a whisper, as he pulled on his clothes, working the braces over his shoulders.

Ilya propped herself up on one elbow. 'It's the middle of the night!'

Pekkala did not reply. After doing up the buttons of his shirt he walked into the front room, carrying the lamp. Reaching out to the brass door knob, he suddenly paused, remembering that he had left his revolver on the chest of drawers in the bedroom. Now he thought about going to fetch it. No good news ever came knocking at two o'clock in the morning.

The heavy fist smashed against the wood. 'Please!' said a voice.

Pekkala opened the door. A gust of freezing air blew in, along with a cloud of snow which glittered like fish scales in the lamplight.

Before him stood a man wearing a heavy sable coat. He had long, greasy hair, piercing eyes and a scruffy beard which gave him a slightly pointed chin. In spite of the cold, he was sweating. 'Pekkala!' wailed the man.

'Rasputin,' growled Pekkala.

The man stepped forward and fell into Pekkala's arms.

Pekkala caught the stench of onions and salmon caviar on Rasputin's breath. A few of the tiny fish eggs, like beads of amber, were even lodged in the man's frozen beard. The sour reek of alcohol oozed from his pores. 'You must save me!' moaned Rasputin.

'Save you from what?'

Rasputin mumbled incoherently, his nose buried in Pekkala's shirt.

'From what?' repeated Pekkala.

Rasputin stood back and spread his arms. 'From myself!'

'Tell me what you are doing out here,' demanded Pekkala.

'I was at the church of Kazan,' said Rasputin, unbuttoning his coat to reveal a blood-red tunic and baggy black breeches tucked into a pair of knee-length boots. 'At least I was until they threw me out.'

'What did you do this time?' asked Pekkala.

'Nothing!' shouted Rasputin. 'For once, all I did was sit there. And then that damned politician Rodzianko told me to leave. He called me a vile heathen!' He clenched his fist and waved it in the air. 'I'll have his job for that!' Then he slumped down into Pekkala's chair.

'What did you do after they threw you out?'

'I went straight to the Villa Rode!'

'Oh, no,' muttered Pekkala. 'Not that place.'

The Villa Rode was a drinking club in Petrograd. Rasputin went there almost every night, because he did not have to pay his bills there. They were covered by an anonymous numbered account which, Pekkala knew, had actually been set up by the Tsarina. In addition, the owner of the Villa Rode had been paid to build an addition on to the back of the club, a room which was available only to Rasputin. It was, in effect, his own private club. The Tsarina had been persuaded to arrange this by members of the Secret Service, who were tasked with following Rasputin wherever he went and making sure he stayed out of trouble. This had proved to be impossible, so a safe house, in which he could drink as much as he wanted for free, meant at least that the Secret Service could protect him from those who had sworn to kill him if they could. There had already been two attempts on his life: in Pokrovsky in 1914 and again in Tsaritsin the following year. Instead of frightening him into seclusion, these events had only served to convince Rasputin that he was indestructible. Even if the Secret Service could protect him from these would-be killers, the one person they could not protect him from was himself.

'When I was at the Villa,' continued Rasputin, 'I decided I should file a complaint about Rodzianko. And then I thought – No! I'll go straight to the Tsarina and tell her about it myself.'

'The Villa Rode is in Petrograd,' said Pekkala. 'That's nowhere near this place.'

'I drove here in my car.'

Pekkala remembered now that the Tsarina had given Rasputin a car, a beautiful Hispano-Suiza, although she had forgotten to give him any lessons on how to drive it.

'And you think she would allow you in at this time of night?'

'Of course,' replied Rasputin. 'Why not?'

'Well, what happened? Did you speak to her?'

'I never got the chance. That damned automobile went wrong.'

'Went wrong?'

'It drove into a wall,' he gestured vaguely at the world outside, 'somewhere out there.'

'You crashed your car,' said Pekkala, shaking his head at the thought of that beautiful machine smashed to pieces.

'I set out on foot for the palace, but I got lost. Then I saw your place and here I am, Pekkala. At your mercy. A poor man begging for a drink.'

'Someone else has already granted your request,' replied Pekkala. 'Several times.'

Rasputin was no longer listening. He had discovered one of the salmon eggs in his beard. He plucked it out and popped it in his mouth. His lips puckered as he chased the egg around the inside of his cheek. Then suddenly his face brightened. 'Ah! I see you already have company. Good evening, teacher lady.'

Pekkala turned to see Ilya standing at the doorway to the bedroom. She was wearing one of his dark grey shirts, the kind he wore when he was on duty. Her arms were folded across her chest. The sleeves, without their cufflinks, trailed down over her hands.

'Such a beauty!' sighed Rasputin. 'If your students could only see you now.'

'My students are six years old,' Ilya replied.

He waggled his fingers, then let them subside on to the arms of the chair, like the tentacles of some pale ocean creature. 'They are never too young to learn the ways of the world.'

'Every time I feel like defending you in public,' said Ilya, 'you go and say something like that.'

Rasputin sighed again. 'Let the rumours fly.'

'Have you really crashed your car, Grigori?' she asked.

'My car crashed by itself,' replied Rasputin.

'How,' asked Ilya, 'do you manage to stay drunk so much of the time?'

'It helps me to understand the world. It helps the world to understand me as well. Some people make sense when they're sober. Some people make sense when they're not.'

'Always speaking in riddles.' Ilya smiled at him.

'Not riddles, beautiful lady. Merely the unfortunate truth.' His eyelids fluttered. He was falling asleep.

'Oh, no, you don't,' said Pekkala. He grasped the chair and jerked it around, so the two men were facing each other.

Rasputin gasped, his eyes shut tight.

'What's this I hear,' asked Pekkala, 'about you advising the Tsarina to get rid of me?'

'What?' Rasputin opened one eye.

'You heard me,' said Pekkala.

'Who told you that?'

'Never mind who told me.'

'It is the Tsarina who wants you dismissed,' said Rasputin, and suddenly the drunkenness had peeled away from him. 'I like you, Pekkala, but there is nothing I can do.'

'And why not?'

'Here is how it works,' explained Rasputin. 'The Tsarina asks me a question. And I can tell from the way she asks it whether she wants me to say yes or no. And when I tell her what she wants to hear, it makes her happy. And then this idea of hers becomes my idea, and she runs off to the Tsar, or to her friend Vyrubova or to whomever she pleases, and she tells them I have said this thing. But what she never says, Pekkala, is that it was her idea to begin with. You see, Pekkala, the reason I am loved by the Tsarina is that I am exactly what she needs me to be, in the same way that you are needed by the Tsar. She needs me to make her feel she is right, and he needs you to make him feel safe. Sadly, both of those things are illusions. And there are many others like us, each one entrusted to a different task – investigators, lovers, assassins, each one a stranger to the other. Only the Tsar knows us all. So if you have been told that I wish you to be sent away, then yes. It is true.' He climbed unsteadily out of the chair and stood weaving in front of Pekkala. 'But it is only true, because the Tsarina desired it first.'

'I think you've preached enough for one night, Grigori.'

Rasputin smiled lazily. 'Good night, Pekkala.' Then he waved at Ilya, as if she were standing in the distance and not just on the other side of the room. As he moved his hand back and forth, a bracelet gleamed on his wrist. It was made of platinum, and engraved with the Royal crest: another gift from the Tsarina. 'And good night, beautiful lady whose name I have forgotten.'

'Ilya,' she said, more with pity than with indignation.

'Then good night, beautiful Ilya.' Rasputin spread his arms and bowed extravagantly, his greasy hair falling in a curtain over his face.

'You can't go out there now,' Pekkala told him. 'The storm has not let up.'

'But I must,' replied Rasputin. 'I have another party to attend. Prince Yusupov invited me. He promised cakes and wine.'

Then he was gone, leaving a stench of sweat and pickled onions hanging in the air.

Ilya stepped into the front room, her bare feet avoiding the slushy puddles which had oozed out of Rasputin's boots. 'Every time I've seen that man, he has been drunk,' she said, wrapping her arms around Pekkala.

'But he's never as drunk as he appears,' replied Pekkala.

Two days later, Pekkala arrived in Petrograd just in time to see Rasputin fished out of the Malaya Neva River, near a place called the Krestovsky Island. His corpse had been rolled in a carpet and shoved beneath the ice.

Soon after, Pekkala arrested Prince Yusupov, who readily confessed to murdering Rasputin. In the company of an army doctor named Lazovert and the Grand Duke Dimitri Pavlovitch, first cousin of the Tsar, Yusupov had attempted to murder Rasputin with cakes laced with arsenic. Each cake contained enough poison to finish off half a dozen men, but Rasputin ate three of them and appeared to suffer no effects. Then Yusupov poured arsenic into a glass of Hungarian wine and served that to Rasputin. Rasputin drank it and then asked for another glass. At that point, Yusupov panicked. He took the Browning revolver belonging to the Grand Duke and shot Rasputin in the back. No sooner had Dr Lazovert declared Rasputin dead than Rasputin sat up and grabbed Yusupov by the throat. Yusupov, by now hysterical, fled to the second floor of his palace, followed by Rasputin, who crawled after him up the stairs. Eventually, *after shooting Rasputin several more times, the murderers rolled him in the carpet, tied it with rope and dumped him in the boot of Dr Lazovert's car. They drove to the Petrovsky bridge and threw his body into the Neva. An autopsy showed that, even with everything that had been done to him, Rasputin died by drowning.*

In spite of Pekkala's work on the case, and the proven guilt of the participants, none of his investigation was ever made public and none of the killers ever went to prison.

When Pekkala thought back on that night when Rasputin had appeared out of the storm, he wished he'd shown more kindness to a man so clearly marked for death.

Under the glare of an electric light powered by a rattling portable generator, Pekkala and Kirov stood in the pit. At first, the freezing, muddy water had come up to their waists but, with the help of buckets, they had managed to bail out most of it. Now they used a mine detector to search for the missing gun. The detector consisted of a long metal stem, bent into a handle at one end, with a plate-shaped disc at the other. In the centre of the stem an oblong box held the batteries, volume control and dials for the various settings.

After being shown Pekkala's Shadow Pass, the NKVD guards had supplied them with everything they needed. They had even helped to wheel the generator out across the proving ground.

Slowly, Pekkala moved the disc of the mine detector back and forth over the ground, listening for the sound that would indicate the presence of metal. His hands had grown so numb that he could barely feel the metal handle of the detector.

The generator droned and clattered, filling the air with exhaust fumes.

On hands and knees, Kirov sifted his fingers through the mud. 'Why wouldn't the killer have held on to the gun?'

'He might have,' replied Pekkala, 'assuming it's a "he". More likely, he threw it away as soon as he could, in case he was caught and searched. Without a gun, he might have been able to talk his way out of it. But with a gun on him, there'd be no chance of that.'

'And he wouldn't be expecting us to search through all this mud,' said Kirov, his lips turned drowned-man blue, 'because that would be insane, wouldn't it?'

'Precisely!' said Pekkala.

Just then, they heard a beep: very faint and only one.

'What was that?' asked Kirov.

'I don't know,' replied Pekkala. 'I've never used one of these things before.'

Kirov flapped his arm at the detector. 'Well, do it again!'

'I'm trying!' replied Pekkala, swinging the disc back and forth over the ground.

'Slowly!' shouted Kirov. As he climbed up off his knees, mud sucked at his waterlogged boots. 'Let me try.'

Pekkala gave him the detector. His half-frozen hands remained curled around the memory of the handle.

Kirov skimmed the disc just above the surface of the mud. Nothing.

Kirov swore. 'This ridiculous contraption isn't even . . .'

Then the sound came again.

'There!' shouted Pekkala.

Carefully, Kirov moved the disc back over the spot.

The detector beeped once more, and then again and finally, as Kirov held it over the place, the sound became a constant drone.

Pekkala dropped to his knees and began to dig, squeezing through handfuls of mud as if he were a baker kneading dough. 'It's not here,' he muttered. 'There's no gun.'

'I told you this thing didn't work,' complained Kirov.

Just then, Pekkala's fist closed on something hard. A stone, he thought. He nearly tossed it aside, but then, in the glare of the generator light, he caught a glimpse of metal. Working his fingers through the mud, his fingers snagged on what Pekkala now realised was a bullet cartridge. Pinching it between his thumb and forefinger, he held it up to Kirov and smiled as if he'd been a gold digger who had found the nugget that would set him up for life. Pekkala rubbed away the dirt at the end of the casing until he could see the markings stamped into the brass. '7.62 mm,' he said.

'It could be a Nagent.'

'No, the cartridge is too short. This did not come from a Russian gun.'

After hunting for another hour, and finding nothing, Pekkala called an end to the search. They clambered out of the pit, switched off the generator and stumbled back through the dark towards the buildings.

The guard hut was closed and the guards were nowhere in sight.

By that time, both Pekkala and Kirov were shuddering uncontrollably from the cold. They needed to warm up before driving back to the city.

They tried to get into the other buildings, but all of them were locked.

In desperation, the two men heaped up several broken wooden pallets which they found stacked behind the Iron House. Using a spare fuel can from their car, they soon had the pallets burning.

Like sleepwalkers, they reached their hands towards the blaze. Sitting down upon the ground, they removed their boots and emptied out thin streams of dirty water. Then they held their pasty feet against the flames until their flesh began to steam. Darkness swirled around them, as if what lay beneath the ground had risen in a tide and drowned the world.

'What I don't understand,' said Kirov, when his teeth had finally stopped chattering, 'is why Major Lysenkova is here at all. NKVD has dozens of investigators. Why send one who only investigates crimes within the NKVD?'

'There's only one possibility,' answered Pekkala. 'NKVD must think one of their own people is responsible.'

'But that doesn't explain why Major Lysenkova would be in such a hurry to wrap up the investigation.'

Pekkala balanced the gun cartridge on his palm, examining it in the firelight. 'This ought to slow things down a bit.'

'I don't know how you can do it, Inspector.'

'Do what?'

'Work so calmly with the dead,' replied Kirov, 'especially when they have been so . . . so broken up.'

'I'm used to it now,' said Pekkala, and he thought back to the times when his father would be called out to collect bodies which had been discovered in the wilderness. Sometimes the bodies belonged to hunters who had gone missing in the winter. They fell through thin ice out on the lakes and did not reappear until spring, their bodies pale as alabaster, tangled among the sticks and branches. Sometimes they were old people, who had wandered off into the forest, gotten lost and died of exposure. What remained of them was often scarcely recognisable beyond the scaffolding of bones they left behind. Pekkala and his father always brought a coffin with them, the rough pine box still smelling of sap. They wrapped the remains in a thick canvas tarpaulin.

There had been many such trips, none of which plagued him with nightmares. Only one stuck clearly in his mind.

It was the day the dead Jew came riding into town.

His horse trotted down the main street of Lappeenranta in the middle of a blizzard. The Jew sat in the saddle in his black coat and wide brimmed hat. He appeared to have frozen to death, his beard a twisted mass of icicles. The horse stopped outside the blacksmith's shop, as if it knew where it was going, although the blacksmith swore he'd never seen the animal before.

No one knew where the Jew had come from. Messages sent to the nearby villages of Joutseno, Lemi and Taipalsaari turned up nothing. His saddlebags contained no clues, only spare clothing, a few scraps of food, and a book written in his language, which no one in Lappeenranta could decipher. He had probably come in from Russia, whose unmarked border was only a few kilometres away. Then he got lost in the woods, and died before he could find shelter.

The Jew had been dead for a long time – five or six days, thought Pekkala's father. They had to remove the saddle just to get him off the horse. The hands of the Jew were twisted around the bridle. Pekkala, who was twelve years old at the time, tried to untangle the leather from the brittle fingers, but without success, so his father cut the leather. Since the Jew's body was frozen, they could not fit him in a coffin. They did their best to cover him up for the ride back to Pekkala's house.

That evening, they left him on the undertaking slab to thaw, so that Pekkala's father could begin the work of preparing the corpse for burial.

'I need you to do something for me,' his father told Pekkala. 'I need you to see him out.'

'See him out?' asked Pekkala. 'He's already out.'

Pekkala's father shook his head. 'His faith holds that the spirit lingers by the body until it is buried. The spirit is afraid. It is their custom to have someone sit by the body, to keep it company until the spirit finally departs.'

'And how long is that?' asked Pekkala, staring at the corpse, whose legs remained pincered, as if still around the body of the horse. Water dripped from the thawing clothes, its sound like the ticking of a clock.

'Just until morning,' said his father.

His father's preparation room was in the basement. That was where Pekkala spent the night, sitting on a chair, back against the wall. A paraffin lamp burned with a steady flame upon the table where his father kept tools for preparing the dead – rubber gloves, knives, tubes, needles, waxed linen thread and a box containing rouges for restoring colour to the skin.

Pekkala had forgotten to ask his father if he was allowed to fall asleep, but now it was too late because his parents and his brother had all gone to bed hours ago. To keep himself busy, Pekkala thumbed through the pages of the book they had found in the Jew's saddlebag. The letters seemed to have been fashioned out of tiny wisps of smoke.

Pekkala set the book aside and went over to the body. Staring at the man's pinched face, his waxy skin and reddish beard, Pekkala thought about the spirit of the Jew, pacing about the room, not knowing where it was or where it was supposed to be. He imagined it standing by the brass-coloured flame of the lamp, like a moth drawn to the light. But maybe, he thought, only the living care about a thing like that. Then he went back and sat in his chair.

He did not mean to fall asleep, but suddenly it was morning. He heard the sound of the basement door opening and his father coming down the stairs. Pekkala's father did not ask if he had slept.

The Jew's body had thawed. One leg hung off the preparation table. His father lifted it and gently set it straight beside the other. Then he uncoiled the leather bridle from around the Jew's hands.

Later that day, they buried him in a clearing on the side of a hill, which looked out over a lake. His father had picked out the place. There was no path, so they had to drag the coffin up between the trees, using ropes and pushing the wooden box until their fingertips were raw from splinters.

'We had better make it deep,' his father said as he handed Pekkala a shovel, 'or else the wolves might dig him up.'

The two of them scraped through the layers of pine needles and then used pickaxes to dig into the grey clay beneath. When at last the coffin had been laid and the hole filled in, they set aside their shovels. Knowing only the prayers of a different god, they stood for a moment in silence before heading back down the hill.

'What did you do with his book?' asked Pekkala.

'His head is resting on it,' replied his father.

In the years since then, Pekkala had seen so many lifeless bodies that they seemed to merge in his mind. But the face of the Jew remained clear, and the smoke-trail writing spoke to him in dreams.

'I don't know how you do it,' Kirov said again.

Pekkala did not reply, because he did not know either.

Flames snapped, flicking sparks into the blue-black sky.

The two men huddled together, like swimmers in a shark-infested sea.

As Kirov drove the Emka through the Kremlin's Spassky Gate, with its ornamental battlements and gold and black clock tower above, Pekkala began to do up the buttons on his coat in preparation for the meeting with Stalin. The Emka's tyres popped over the cobblestones of Ivanovsky Square until they reached a dead end on the far side.

'I'll walk home,' he told Kirov. 'This might take a while.'

At a plain, unmarked door, a soldier stood at attention. As Pekkala approached, the soldier slammed his heels to-gether with a sound that echoed around the high brick walls and gave the traditional greeting of 'Good health to you, Comrade Pekkala.' This was not only a greeting, but also a sign that Pekkala had been recognised by the soldier and did not need to present his pass book.

Pekkala made his way up to the second floor of the build-ing. Here, he walked down a long, wide corridor with tall ceilings. The floors were covered with red carpeting. It was, Pekkala could not help noticing, the same colour as arterial blood. His footsteps made no sound except when the floor-boards creaked beneath the carpet. Tall doors lined the walls of this corridor on either side. Sometimes, these doors were open and he could see people at work in side large offices. Today all the doors were closed.

At the end of the corridor, another soldier greeted him and opened the double doors to Stalin's reception room. It was a huge space, with eggshell-white walls and wooden floors. In the centre of the room stood three desks, like life rafts in the middle of a flat calm sea. At each desk sat a man, wearing a collarless olive-green tunic in the same style as that worn by Stalin himself. Only one man rose to greet Pekkala. It was Poskrebyshev, Stalin's chief secretary: a short, flabby man with round glasses almost flush against his eyeballs. Poskrebyshev appeared to be the exact opposite of the stripped-to-the-waist, muscle-armoured workers whose statues could be found in almost every square in Moscow. The only thing exceptional about Poskrebyshev was his complete lack of emotion as he escorted Pekkala across the room to Stalin's study.

Poskrebyshev knocked once and did not wait for a reply. He swung the door open, nodded for Pekkala to enter. As soon as Pekkala walked into the room, the secretary shut the door behind him.

Pekkala found himself alone in a large room with red velvet curtains and a red carpet which lined only the outer third of the floor. The centre was the same mosaic of wood as in the waiting room. The walls had been papered dark red, with caramel coloured wooden dividers separating the panels. Hanging on these walls were portraits of Marx, Engels and Lenin, each one the same size and apparently painted by the same artist.

Close to one wall stood Stalin's desk, which had eight legs, two at each corner. On the desk lay several files, each one aligned perfectly beside the others. Stalin's chair had a wide back, padded with burgundy-coloured leather brass-tacked against the frame.

Apart from Stalin's desk, and a table covered with a green cloth, the space was spartanly furnished. In the corner stood a large and very old grandfather clock which had been allowed to wind down and was silent now, the full yellow moon of its pendulum at rest behind the rippled glass window of its case.

Comrade Stalin often kept him waiting, and today was no exception.

Pekkala had not slept, having arrived back in the city only an hour before. He had reached that point of fatigue where sounds reached him as if down the length of a long cardboard tube. His only nourishment in the past fifteen hours had been a mug of kvass, a drink made from fermented rye bread, which he'd bought from a street vendor on his way to the meeting.

The vendor had handed Pekkala a battered metal cup filled with the sudsy brown drink, scooped from a cauldron kept warm by coals glowing in a grate beneath. As Pekkala raised the drink to his lips, he breathed in its smell like burnt toast. When he had finished, he turned the mug upside down, as was customary, emptying out the last drops and handed it back. Just as he was doing so, he noticed a small stamp on the bottom of the cup. Looking closer, he saw it was the double-headed eagle of the Romanovs, a sign that it had once been in the inventory of the royal family. The Tsar himself used to drink from a cup like this, and Pekkala thought how strange it was to see this fragment of the old empire washed up outside the Kremlin like the flotsam of a shipwreck.

The Tsar was sitting at his desk.

The dark velvet curtains of his study, drawn back to let in the light, gleamed softly around the edge, like the feathers on a starling's back.

Lifting the heavy mug to his lips, the Tsar drank, his Adam's apple bobbing as he swallowed. Then he set the mug down with a satisfied grunt, picked up his blue pencil and began to tap out a rhythm on a stack of unread documents.

It was the autumn of 1916. After taking over command of the military, the Tsar had been spending most of his time behind the stockade fence of Army Headquarters at Mogilev.

In spite of the Tsar's having taken command, the Russian Army continued to suffer more and more devastating defeats on the battlefield.

The blame for this had fallen as heavily on the Tsarina as it had done on the Tsar. A rumour had even surfaced that the Tsarina, without consulting the Russian High Command, had begun secret peace negotiations with Germany using one of her German relatives as an intermediary. The rumour spread, threatening the Tsar's credibility as commander of the military.

On a rare visit to Petrograd, the Tsar had summoned Pekkala to the palace and ordered him to conduct an investigation to determine whether the rumour was legitimate.

Pekkala had known from the start that something was not right. Although the details of the investigation itself were to be kept secret, the Tsar had widely publicised the fact that he had ordered the investigation. News of Pekkala's work even appeared in the papers, a thing the Tsar rarely allowed.

It did not take Pekkala long to discover that the rumour was, in fact, true. The Tsarina had, through an intermediary in Sweden, made contact with her brother, the Grand Duke of Hesse, who was then serving as a high-ranking officer in the German Army. A visit by the Grand Duke had taken place, as near as Pekkala could reckon, some time in February of 1916.

Pekkala was not surprised to learn of the Tsarina's meddling. She had kept up a constant barrage of letters to the Tsar while her husband was in Mogilev, insisting that Rasputin's advice on military affairs should be followed, and that anyone who disagreed with it should be sacked.

What did surprise Pekkala was to learn that the Tsar had known about the Grand Duke's visit all along. Nicholas had even met with the Tsarina's brother, probably in the very room where Pekkala and the Tsar were meeting now.

Once he had concluded the investigation, Pekkala made his report. He left nothing out, even those facts of the case which incriminated the Tsar himself. Immediately afterwards, Pekkala unfastened the emerald eye from the underside of his lapel and laid it on the Tsar's desk. Then he drew his Webley revolver and set it down beside the badge.

'What's this?' demanded the Tsar.

'I am offering my resignation.'

'Oh, come now, Pekkala!' growled the Tsar, flipping his pencil into the air and catching it. 'Try to see this from my point of view. Yes, I admit we discussed the possibility of a truce. And yes, I admit this was done in secret, without the knowledge of the Russian High Command. But damn it all, Pekkala, there is no truce! The negotiations fell apart. I knew the Russian people wanted answers about whether these rumours were true. That's why I put you on the case – to set their minds at ease. The thing is, Pekkala, the answers they wanted were not the ones I knew you'd find.'

'And what would you have me do now, Majesty, with the information I have uncovered?'

'What I would have you do,' replied the Tsar, tapping the point of his pencil against Pekkala's revolver, 'is get back to work and forget about this whole investigation.'

'Majesty,' said Pekkala, struggling to remain calm, 'you do not employ me to provide you with illusions.'

'Quite right, Pekkala. You provide me with the truth, and I decide how much of it the Russian people need to hear.'

Pekkala was beginning to wonder if Stalin might keep him waiting there all day. To pass the time, he rocked gently back and forth on the balls of his feet, scanning the wall behind Stalin's desk. From previous visits, Pekkala knew that hidden somewhere in those wood panels was a secret door, impossible to see until it opened. Behind the opening stretched a low and narrow passageway, lit with tiny light bulbs no bigger than a man's thumb. The floor of this passageway was thickly carpeted, so that a person could move without making any sound. Where it led to, Pekkala had no idea, but he had been told that this whole building was honeycombed with secret passageways.

Finally, Pekkala heard the familiar click of the panel's lock releasing. The wooden slab swung outward and Stalin emerged from the wall. At first, he did not speak to Pekkala, or even look at him. His habit was to stare into every corner of the room, searching for anything that might be out of place. Finally, his gaze turned to Pekkala. 'Nagorski died in an accident?' he snapped. 'Do you expect me to believe that?'

'No, Comrade Stalin,' replied Pekkala.

This seemed to catch him by surprise. 'You don't? But that's what I read in the report!'

'Not my report, Comrade Stalin.'

Muttering curses under his breath, Stalin sat down at his desk and immediately fished his pipe out of the pocket of his tunic.

Pekkala had noticed that Stalin tended to smoke cigarettes when not in his office, but normally stuck to smoking a pipe when he was in the Kremlin. The pipe was shaped like a check mark, with the bowl at the bottom of the check and curved over at the top. It had already been stuffed with honey-coloured shreds of tobacco. Each time Pekkala saw Stalin smoking his pipe, the pipe itself looked new and Pekkala suspected that he did not keep them long before replacing them.

From a small cardboard box, Stalin fished out a wooden match, the splintery sticks rustling together as he pinched one from the box. Stalin had a way of lighting these matches which Pekkala had never seen before. Grasping the match between his thumb and first two fingers, Stalin would flick the match with his ring finger across the sandpaper strip. This never failed to light the match. It was such an unusual method that Pekkala, who did not smoke, had once bought a box of matches and spent an hour over his kitchen sink, trying to master the technique, but succeeded only in burning his fingers.

In the stillness of the room, Pekkala heard the hiss of the match, the tiny crackle of the tobacco catching fire and the soft popping sound as Stalin puffed on the end of the pipe. Stalin shook out the match, dropped it in a small brass ashtray, then sat back in his chair. 'No accident, you say?'

Pekkala shook his head. Removing a handkerchief from his pocket, he stepped forward to the desk, laid the cloth in front of Stalin and carefully unfolded it.

There, in the centre of the black handkerchief, lay the tiny sliver of lead which Pekkala had removed from Nagorski's skull.

Stalin bent forward, until his nose was almost touching the desk top, and peered intently at the fragment. 'What am I looking at, Pekkala?'

'Part of a bullet.'

'Ah!' Stalin gave a satisfied growl and sat back in his chair. 'Where did you find it?'

'In Colonel Nagorski's brain.'

Stalin nudged at the fragment with the stem of his pipe. 'In his brain,' he repeated.

Now, from his pocket, Pekkala removed the empty gun cartridge that he and Kirov had found in the pit the night before. He placed it before Stalin as if he were moving a pawn in a chess game. 'We also recovered this from the scene. It is from the same gun, I am almost certain.'

Stalin nodded with approval. 'This is why I need you, Pekkala!' He opened the grey file and plucked out the single sheet of paper it contained. 'The NKVD investigator who filed this report said that the body had been thoroughly examined. It says so right here.' He held the paper out at arm's length so he could read it. 'No sign of injury prior to being crushed by the tank. How could they have missed a bullet in his head?'

'The damage to the body was considerable,' offered Pekkala.

'That's a reason, not an excuse.'

'You should also know, Comrade Stalin, that the bullet did not come from a Russian-made gun.'

Almost before the words had left Pekkala's mouth, Stalin smashed his fist down on the desk. The little cartridge jumped and then rolled in a circle. 'I was right!' he shouted.

'Right about what, Comrade Stalin?'

'Foreigners carried out this murder.'

'That may be so,' replied Pekkala, 'but I doubt they could have done so without help from inside the country.'

'They did have help,' replied Stalin, 'and I believe the White Guild is responsible.'

Pekkala's eyes narrowed in confusion. 'Comrade Stalin, we have spoken about this before. The White Guild is a front. It is controlled by your own Bureau of Special Operations. How could the White Guild be responsible when you are the one who created it, unless you are the one who ordered Nagorski's death?'

'I know perfectly well,' replied Stalin coldly, 'who summoned the White Guild into being, and no, I gave no command for Nagorski to be liquidated.'

'Then surely the Guild poses no threat to us.'

'There have been some new developments,' muttered Stalin.

'And what are they?' asked Pekkala.

'All you need to know, Pekkala, is that our enemies are attempting to destroy the Konstantin Project. They know that the T-34 is our only chance of surviving the time that is coming.'

'I don't understand, Comrade Stalin. What do you mean by "the time that is coming"?'

'War, Pekkala. War with Germany. Hitler has retaken the Rhineland. He has forged a pact with Japan and Italy. My sources tell me he is planning to occupy parts of Czecho-slovakia and Austria. And he won't stop there, no matter what he tells the rest of the world. I have received reports from

Soviet agents in England that the British are aware of German plans to invade their country. They know that their only chance of preventing that is if the Germans become involved in a war against us. Germany would be tied down in a war to the east as well as to the west, in which case they might not have the resources to invade Britain at all. British Intelligence has been spreading rumours that we are planning to launch a pre-emptive strike against Germany through southern Poland.'

'And are we?'

Stalin got up from his desk and began to pace around the room, the report still clenched in his fist. The soft soles of his calfskin leather of his boots swished across the wooden floor. 'We have no such plan, but the Germans are taking these British rumours seriously. This means they are watching us for any signs of provocation. The slightest hostile gesture by us could bring about a full-scale war and Hitler has made no secret of what he would like to do with the Soviet Union. If he has his way, our culture will be annihilated, our people enslaved and this entire country turned into a living space for German colonists. The T-34 is not simply a machine. It is our only hope for survival. If we lose the advantage this tank can give us, we will lose everything. As of now, Pekkala, you are in charge of the investigation. You will replace this,' he squinted at the name on the report. 'Major Lysenkova.'

'If I could ask, Comrade Stalin . . .'

'What?'

'Why did you assign her to the case at all?' asked Pekkala.

'I didn't,' replied Stalin. 'The guard in charge of security at Nagorski's facility put in a call to her directly.'

'That would be Captain Samarin,' said Pekkala.

'He had to call NKVD,' continued Stalin. 'He couldn't have called the regular police, because secret facilities are out of their jurisdiction. It had to be handled by Internal Security.'

'I realise that,' continued Pekkala, 'but my understanding is that Samarin specifically requested Major Lysenkova.'

'Maybe he did,' replied Stalin. 'Just ask him yourself.'

'Captain Samarin is dead, Comrade Stalin.'

'What? How?'

Pekkala explained what had happened in the woods.

Stalin sat quietly for a moment. His back seemed unnaturally straight, as if he wore a metal brace beneath his clothing. 'And this fugitive, the one you chased through the woods, has still not been located?'

'Since the death has been declared an accident, Comrade Stalin, I assume they have called off the search.'

'Called it off,' muttered Stalin. He picked up Lysenkova's report. 'Then it may already be too late. For this major's sake, I hope not.' He let the paper fall on to the desk.

'I will speak to the Major,' said Pekkala. 'Perhaps she can help us with some answers.'

'Suit yourself, Pekkala. I don't care how you do it, but I want the man who shot Nagorski before he goes and kills somebody else I cannot do without. In the meantime, no one must know about this. I do not want our enemies to think that we have faltered. They are waiting for us to make mistakes, Pekkala. They are looking out for any sign of weakness.'

Pekkala sat on the end of his bed.

In front of him, on a small collapsible table, lay his dinner – three slices of black rye bread, a small bowl of Tvorok cheese, and a mug of carbonated water.

Pekkala's coat and shoulder holster lay draped over his bed rail. He wore a pair of heavy corduroy trousers, their colour the same deep brown as a horse chestnut, and a sweater of undyed wool, the colour of oatmeal, whose shawl collar fastened across the neck.

His residence was a boarding house on Tverskaia street – not a particularly safe or beautiful part of town. In spite of this, over the past few years, the building had become over-crowded. Workers had flooded out of the countryside, looking for jobs in the city. These days, it was not unusual to find a dozen people crammed into a space which, under normal circumstances, would barely have suited half that number.

His one-room apartment was sparsely furnished, with a fold-up army cot, which took up one corner of the room, and a collapsible table at which he ate his meals and wrote up his reports. There was also a china cabinet, slathered with many layers of paint – its current incarnation being chalky white. Pekkala had no china, only enamelled cups and saucers, and only a couple each of those since he rarely had any guests. The remainder of the cabinet was taken up with several dozen cardboard boxes of .455 calibre bullets belonging to the brass-handled Webley he wore when he was on duty and for which ammunition was difficult to come by in this country.

Pekkala had survived on so little for so long that he could not get used to doing otherwise. He lived like a man who expected, at any moment, to be given half an hour's notice to vacate the premises.

Tucking a handkerchief into his collar, Pekkala brushed his hands against his chest and was about to begin his meal when a floorboard creaked in the hallway. He turned and saw the shadow of a pair of feet out in the hallway. A moment later, as Pekkala heard a knocking on his door, an old memory flickered to life in his head.

He stood outside the Tsarina's Mauve Boudoir, fist raised to rap his knuckles on the door.

To the Alexander Palace maids, who passed by with bundles of laundry, or trays of breakfast china or with feather dusters clasped like strange bouquets of flowers, he seemed to be frozen in place.

At last, as if the strength required for knocking on that door was more than he possessed, Pekkala sighed and lowered his hand.

Ever since the Tsarina sent for him that morning, Pekkala had been filled with uneasiness. She usually stayed as far away from him as she could get.

Pekkala did not know why she disliked him so intensely. He only knew that she did, and that she made no secret of it, his only consolation being that he was far from alone in finding himself out of favour with the Tsarina.

The Tsarina was a proud and stubborn woman, who made up her mind very quickly about people and rarely changed her opinion about them afterwards. Even among those whom she tolerated, very few could count themselves as friends. Aside from Rasputin, the Tsarina's only confidante was the pouty, moonfaced Anna Vyrubova. For both of them, remaining in good graces with the Tsarina had become a full-time job.

Now she had summoned Pekkala, and he had no idea what

she wanted. Pekkala wished he could have turned and walked away, but he had no choice except to obey.

As he raised his hand again to knock upon the door, he caught sight of a sun wheel carved into the top of the door frame. This crooked cross, its arms bent leftwards until it almost, but not quite, formed a circle, was the symbol the Tsarina had chosen as her own. It could be found carved into the door frames of any place she had stayed for any length of time. Her life was filled with superstitions, and this was only one of them.

Knowing there was nothing to be gained by postponing this meeting any longer, Pekkala finally knocked.

'Come in,' said a muffled voice.

The Mauve Boudoir smelled of cigarettes and the dense fragrance of pink hyacinth flowers, which grew in planters on the window sills. The lace curtains, a mauve colour like everything else in the room, had been drawn, turning the light which filtered into the room into the colour of diluted blood. The dreary uniformity of its furnishings and the fact that she never seemed to open the windows combined to make the space unbearably stifling to Pekkala.

Adding to his discomfort was the presence of an entire miniature circus made out of thin strands of glass, gold filigree and pearls. There were more than a hundred pieces in all. The circus had been specially commissioned by the Tsar from the workshops of Karl Fabergé and was rumoured to be worth the lifetime salaries of more than a dozen Russian factory workers.

The fragile figures – elephants, tigers, clowns, fire eaters and tightrope walkers – were balanced precariously on the edge of every flat surface in the room. Pekkala felt as if all he had to do was sigh and everything would come crashing to the floor.

The Tsarina lay on an overstuffed day bed, legs covered by a blanket, wearing the grey and white uniform of a nurse of the Russian Red Cross. It was the second year of the war and ever since casualties had first started pouring back from the front, the Great Hall of the Catherine Palace had been turned into a hospital ward and the Tsarina and her daughters had taken on the role of nurses to the wounded.

Soldiers who had grown up in thatch-roofed, dirt-floored Izhba huts now woke each day in a room of golden pillars, walked across a polished marble floor and rested in linen-sheeted beds. In spite of the level of comfort, the soldiers Pekkala had seen there did not look comfortable at all. Most would have preferred the more familiar surroundings of an army hospital, instead of being showcased like these glass circus animals, as the Tsarina's contribution to the war.

There were times when, in spite of her hostility towards him, Pekkala felt sorry for the Tsarina, particularly since war had broken out. No matter how hard she worked, her German background had made it almost impossible to make any gesture of loyalty to Russia without the gesture recoiling upon her. In trying to ease the suffering of others, she had only succeeded in prolonging it for herself.

But Pekkala had come to realise that this might not have been entirely by accident. The Tsarina was drawn towards suffering. A particular nervous energy surrounded her whenever the topic turned to misfortune. Attending to the wounded had given new purpose to her life.

Now, with Pekkala standing before her, the Tsarina gestured towards a fragile-looking wicker chair. 'Sit,' she told Pekkala.

Hesitantly, Pekkala settled on to the chair, afraid that its legs would collapse under his weight.

'Pekkala,' said the Tsarina, 'I believe we have got off to a bad start, you and I, but it is simply a matter of trust. I would like to trust you, Pekkala.'

'Yes, Majesty.'

'With that in mind,' she said, her clasped hands pressing into her lap as if she had a cramp in her stomach, 'I would like for us to work together on a matter of great importance. I require you to conduct an investigation.'

'Of course,' answered Pekkala. 'What do you need me to investigate?'

She paused for a moment. 'The Tsar.'

Pekkala breathed in sharply. 'I beg your pardon, Majesty?' The wicker seat creaked underneath him.

'I need you,' she continued, 'to look into whether my husband is keeping a mistress.'

'A mistress,' repeated Pekkala.

'Yes.' She watched him closely, her lips formed into an awkward smile, 'You know what that is, don't you?'

'I do know, Majesty,' replied Pekkala. He also knew that the Tsar did, in fact, have a mistress. Or, at least, there was a woman who had been his mistress. Her name was Mathilde Kschessin-ska and she was the lead dancer of the Russian Imperial Ballet. The Tsar had known her for years, since before his marriage to the Tsarina, and had even bought her a mansion in Petrograd. Officially, he had broken off ties with her. Unofficially, Pekkala knew, the Tsar kept in contact with this woman. Although the full extent of their relationship was unknown to him, he knew for certain that the Tsar continued to visit her, even using a secret door located at the back of the Petrograd Mansion, so that he could enter undetected.

Pekkala had always assumed that the Tsarina knew everything about this other woman. The reason for this was that he did not believe the Tsar to be capable of keeping any secret from his wife. He lacked the necessary guile, and the Tsarina was far too suspicious to allow an affair to continue undetected.

'I regret,' said Pekkala, rising to his feet, 'that I cannot investigate the Tsar.'

The Tsarina appeared to have been waiting for this moment. 'You can investigate the Tsar,' she told him as her eyes lit up. 'The Tsar himself gave you the right to investigate anyone you choose. That is by Imperial Decree. And, what is more, I have the right to order this investigation.'

'I understand, Majesty, that technically I am permitted . . .'

'Not permitted, Pekkala. Obliged.'

'I understand,' he continued.

She cut him off again. 'Then it is settled.'

'Majesty,' pleaded Pekkala, 'what you ask, I must not do.'

'Then you refuse?' she asked.

Pekkala felt a trap closing around him. To refuse an order from the Tsarina would amount to treason, the penalty for which was death. The Tsar was at army headquarters in Mogilev, halfway across the country. If the Tsarina wished it, Pekkala could be executed before the Tsar even found out what was wrong.

'You refuse?' she asked again.

'No, Majesty.' The words fell likes stones from his mouth.

'Good. I am glad we are finally able to see –' the Tsarina held out her hand towards the door – 'eye to emerald eye.'

The knocking came again, but there was something un-usual about it. The knuckles were striking halfway down the door.

At first, Pekkala could make no sense of it, but then he smiled. He stepped over to the door and opened it just as the little girl on the other side was about to knock again. 'Good evening, Talia.'

'Good evening, Comrade Pekkala.'

Before Pekkala stood a girl about seven years old, with plump cheeks and a dimple in her chin, wearing a khaki shirt and dress, and the red scarf of a Young Pioneer around her neck. In a fashion popular among girls in the Communist Youth Movement, her short hair had been cut in a straight line across her forehead. Smiling, she gave him the Pioneer salute: the knife edge of her outstretched hand held at an angle in front of her face, as if to fend off an attack.

Conscious of how much he towered over the girl, Pekkala got down on one knee so they were looking each other in the face. 'And what has brought you here this evening?'

'Babayaga says you are lonely.'

'And how does she know that?'

The child shrugged. 'She just does.'

Pekkala glanced back at his dinner laid out on the table – the lumps of bread and bowl of watery cheese. He sighed.

'Well, Talia, it just so happens that I could use a little company right now.'

Talia stepped back into the hall and held out her hand for him to take. 'Come along then,' she said.

'One moment,' said Pekkala. He pulled on his coat which, although it had been cleaned, still looked the worse for wear after his journey across the proving ground.

Joining Talia out in the corridor, Pekkala caught the smell of evening meals – the fug of boiled potatoes, fried sausages and cabbage.

The two held hands as they walked down the pale green hallway with its ratty carpet to the apartment where Talia lived with her grandmother.

Until six months ago, Talia had lived with her parents in a large apartment in what had once been called the Sparrow Hills district of the city but had since been renamed Lenin Hills.

Then, one night, NKVD men arrived at their door, searched the house and arrested the parents. Until the time of their arrest, both had been model Communists, but now they were classed as Type 58. This fell under the general heading of 'Threat to National Security' and earned them each a sentence of fifteen years at the Solovetsky Labour Camp.

The only reason Talia and her grandmother even knew this much was because Pekkala, having been their neighbour for several years, had made inquiries on their behalf. As for the precise nature of the parents' crime, even the NKVD records office could not tell him. Stalin had confided in Pekkala that even if only 2 per cent of the arrests turned out to be warranted, he would still say it had been worth arresting all the others. So many people had been brought in this past year, over a million according to the records office, that it was not possible to keep track of them all. What Pekkala knew, and what he could not bring himself to tell the grandmother, was that more than half of those people arrested were shot before they ever boarded the trains bound for Siberia.

Their family had once been farmers in the fertile Black Earth region of the Altay mountains. In 1930, the Communist party had ordered the farm to be merged with others in their village. They called it 'collectivisation'. The running of this collectivised farm, or Kolkhoz, had then been given over to a party official who, with no farming experience of his own, ran the collective into the ground in under two years. The collective broke up and Talia's family had drifted, like so many others, to the city.

They began working for the Mos-Prov plant, which supplied most of the electricity to Moscow. The husband-and-wife team immediately joined the Communist Party and rose quickly through its ranks. Before their arrest, they had been rewarded with special rations like extra sugar, tea and cigarettes, tickets to the Bolshoi Theatre and trips to the Astafievo resort outside the city.

According to Babayaga, the father had often spoken about the merits of 'perekovka'; the remoulding of the human soul through forced labour in the Gulag system. Pekkala wondered what the father thought now that he was in one. Like many good Communists, the man probably believed that he and his wife were simply victims of some bureaucratic error, which would soon be corrected, at which time they could return to their old lives; any suffering he endured now would be rewarded on some distant day of reckoning, when errors were set straight.

Although the parents might have been innocent of any charges brought against them, it did not mean that they had been arrested by mistake. They might have been denounced by someone who wanted their apartment, or who envied their marriage or whose seat they had taken on the bus which brought them to work. The accusations were seldom investigated and even the most preposterous stories served as justification for arrest. One man had been arrested for blowing smoke rings which, in the eyes of his accuser, seemed to bear a resemblance to the outline of Stalin's face.

Pekkala suspected that the reason for their imprisonment had nothing to do with them at all and was only the result of quotas imposed upon NKVD, ordering them to arrest so many people in each district per month.

It was after the parents went away that Talia came to live with her grandmother. The old woman's real name was Elizaveta, although she never used it and had chosen for herself instead the name of a witch from an old Russian fairy tale. The witch lived in the forest, in a house which turned round in circles at the top of two giant chicken legs. In the fairy tale, the witch was cruel to children, but Pekkala knew the little girl was lucky to have a woman as kind as Babayaga looking after her. Talia seemed to know it, too, and the name became a joke they shared between them.

The thing Pekkala noticed when he first walked into their apartment was what Babayaga called a Patriotic Corner. Here, small portraits of Stalin, as well as pictures of Lenin and Marx, were on display. Other pictures, of men like

Zinoviev, Kamenev, Radek and Piatakov had been re-moved after the men in question were accused of Counter Revolutionary Activity and liquidated.

The Stalin corner was always on display, but in a closet by the bathroom, the grandmother kept small wooden paint-ings of saints. Each icon had little wooden doors which could be opened so that the icons could stand on their own. The wooden doors were inlaid with pieces of mother-of-pearl and curls of silver wire which looked like musical notes in the black wood.

Following their arrests, Talia's parents had been dismissed from the Communist Party and her membership in the Young Pioneers revoked. In spite of this, she continued to wear her uniform, although only inside the building where she lived.

'Here he is, Babayaga,' said the little girl, swinging wide the door to their apartment.

Babayaga sat at a bare wood table. In one hand, she held an outdated copy of Rabotnitsa, the Women's Journal of the Communist Party. In her other hand, she clasped a tiny pair of nail scissors. Her eyes squinting with concentration, the old woman cut out pieces of the paper. In front of her, strewn across the table, were dozens of tiny clippings. 'Now then, Pekkala,' she said.

'What are you cutting?'

Babayaga nodded at the clippings. 'See for yourself.'

Pekkala glanced at the neat rectangles. On each one he saw the name of Stalin, some in large print, others in letters almost too small to read. Nothing else had been cut out – only that one word. 'Are you making a collage?' he asked.

'She's making toilet paper!' announced Talia.

The woman put down her scissors. Neatly, she folded the paper. Then, with crooked fingers, she gathered up the clippings. Rising from the table, she went over to a wooden trunk in the corner. It was the kind of trunk which might have stored blankets in the summer months, but when Babayaga opened the lid, Pekkala realised that it was entirely filled with paper clippings of Stalin's name.

'I heard a story,' said Babayaga, as she tossed in the clippings, letting them fall like confetti from her fingertips. 'A man was arrested when the police came to search his house and found a newspaper in the toilet. Stalin's name was in the paper, of course. It is on every page of every paper every day. But because Stalin's name was on the paper, and because . . .' she twisted her hand in the air, 'of the purpose of the paper, they arrested him. Sent him to Kolyma for ten years.' She smiled at Pekkala, folds of skin crimping her cheeks. 'They won't get a hold of me that way! But just in case –' Babayaga pointed at a laminated cardboard suitcase by the door – 'I always keep a bag packed. If they do find a reason, at least I'll be ready to go.'

What saddened Pekkala about this was not that Babayaga kept the suitcase ready, but that she believed she would live long enough in custody to make use of whatever it contained.

'I understand,' said Pekkala, 'why you might want to cut Stalin's name from the paper, but why are you saving all the clippings?'

'If I throw them away, I could get arrested for that, too,' she replied.

Talia sat between them, doing her best to follow the conversation. She looked from Babayaga, to Pekkala and then back to Babayaga again.

Once or twice a week, the old woman sent for Pekkala, knowing that he lived alone.

Babayaga was lonely, too, but less for human contact than for those days before the revolution, when the world had made more sense to her. Now she lived like an overlapping image seen through a pair of broken binoculars, half in the present, half in the past, unable to bring either into focus.

'Off you go now.' Babayaga rested her hand on Talia's forehead. 'Time for bed.'

When the little girl had gone, Pekkala sat back in his chair. 'I have a present for you, Babayaga,' he said. Reaching into his pocket, he pulled out two small, votive candles and set them down in front of her. He had picked up the candles at the Yeliseyev store on his way home that day, knowing that she liked to burn them when she prayed beside her icons.

Babayaga picked one up, smelled it and closed her eyes. 'Beeswax,' she said. 'You have brought me the good ones. And now I have a present for you.' She went into the kitchen, which was separated from the living room only by a curtain of wooden beads, and reappeared a moment later with a battered brass samovar. Steam puffed from the top as if from the smokestack of a miniature train. She returned to fetch one glass in an ornate brass holder and a small, chipped mug, which Pekkala recognised from its pattern of interwoven birds and flowers to have been made by the old firm of Gardner's. The firm had been founded in Russia by an Englishman, and Pekkala had not seen or heard anything of the firm since the Bolsheviks took over. It was quite likely, he imagined, Babayaga's most treasured possession. She laid before him a dish of rock sugar and another dish in which lay the twisted black grains of smoked tea. Laying out the tea was done as a gesture of politeness, allowing the guest to strengthen the tea if he thought it was not brewed correctly. But, out of politeness, Pekkala did not touch it. He merely bent down and breathed in the slightly tar-like scent of pine-smoked tea, which he doubted Babayaga could afford.

She poured him a cup, taking the strong-brewed tea from the pot at the top of the samovar and diluting it with the water stored in the lower section. Then she handed it over to him. 'That glass belonged to my husband,' she said.

She told him that every time, and every time Pekkala took the glass from her with the reverence it deserved.

Babayaga produced a lemon from the pocket of her apron, and a small silver knife, with which she carved a slice and held it out to him, thumb pressing the sliver to the blade. And when he had taken it, she held the blade in the steam coming out of the samovar, so that the silver would not tarnish from the lemon juice.

'The Tsar was very fond of pine-smoked tea,' said Pekkala, squeezing the lemon into his drink.

'Do you know what people say, Inspector? Those of us who can still remember the way things used to be? They say the spirit of the Tsar sees through that emerald eye of yours.'

Pekkala reached up to his collar. Slowly, he folded it back. The eye came into view like that of a sleeper awakening. 'Then he must be looking at you now.'

'I should have worn a nicer dress.' She smiled and her face turned red. 'I miss him. I miss what he meant to our people.' Then her smile suddenly vanished. 'But not her! Not the Nemka! She has much to answer for.'

Pekkala travelled to the mansion of Mathilde Kschessinska. He did not present himself at the front door, which might have drawn attention. Instead, he went around to the quiet street at the back of the mansion and let himself in through the gate that the Tsar himself used when he came to visit Madame Kschessinska.

The private door, just beyond the gate, was overgrown with ivy, making it difficult to spot. Even the brass doorbell had been overpainted green to camouflage it.

Pekkala glanced back into the street, to see if anyone had seen him come in, but the street was empty. A rain shower had passed through about an hour before. Now a pale blue sky stretched overhead. He pressed the doorbell and waited.

It was only a few seconds before Madame Kschessinska appeared. She was short and very slight, with a softly rounded face and bright, inquisitive eyes. Her hair was wrapped in a towel in the manner of a turban and she wore a man's silk-brocaded smoking jacket, which probably belonged to the Tsar. 'I heard the gate creak,' she began, but then she breathed in sharply, realising it was not the Tsar. 'I thought you were somebody else.'

'Madame Kschessinska,' he said, 'I am Inspector Pekkala, the Tsar's personal investigator.' He reached up to his lapel and turned it over, revealing the badge of his service.

'The Emerald Eye. Nicky has often spoken about you.' Suddenly she looked afraid. 'Oh, no. Has something happened? Is he all right?'

'He is perfectly well.'

'Then what brings you here, Inspector?'

'May I come in?'

She hesitated for a moment, then swung the door wide and stood back.

Pekkala followed her into a well-lit house, on whose walls hung numerous framed programmes and posters from the Imperial Ballet. In the front hall, peacock feathers sprouted from a brass umbrella holder like a strange bouquet of flowers. Tucked in among the feathers, Pekkala noticed one of the Tsar's walking sticks, throated with a band of gold engraved with the Imperial crest.

They sat in her kitchen, which looked out on to a small garden where a willow tree draped its leaves over a wooden bench.

She served him coffee and toast with apricot jam.

'Madame Kschessinska,' Pekkala began, but then words failed him and he gave her a desperate look.

'Inspector,' she said, reaching across the table and touching the tips of her fingers against the gnarled bumps of his knuckles, 'whatever this is, I am not in the habit of killing messengers who bring bad news.'

'I am glad to hear you say it,' replied Pekkala. Then he explained why he had come. When he got to the end of his story, he pulled out a handkerchief and wiped drops of sweat off his forehead. 'I am so sorry,' he said. 'I would never have troubled you with this if I could have found a way to refuse.'

'I don't understand,' said Kschessinska. 'She knows about me. She has known about me for years.'

'Yes, I believe she does. It is also a mystery to me.'

For a moment, Kschessinska seemed lost in thought. Then she brushed her hand across her mouth as an idea occurred to her. 'How well do you get along with the Tsarina?'

'Not well at all.'

'Then I think, Inspector Pekkala, that this investigation really has nothing to do with me.'

'I beg your pardon?'

'It is about you, Inspector Pekkala.' She got up and walked to the open window. Outside, in the garden, a breeze rustled the willow branches. 'What do you think the Tsar will do when he finds out you have been investigating him, especially on a matter such as this?'

'He will be furious,' answered Pekkala, 'but the Tsarina has ordered the investigation. I cannot refuse the order, so the Tsar can hardly blame me for coming here to speak with you.'

She turned and looked at him. 'But he will blame you, Pekkala, for the simple reason that he cannot blame his wife. He will forgive her anything, no matter what she does, but what about you, Pekkala?'

'Now I am worried for both of us.'

'You shouldn't be,' she replied. 'I will not be hurt by this, Inspector. If the Tsarina had wanted me out of the way, she would have seen to that a long time ago. It is you she is after, I'm afraid.'

Her words settled on him like a layer of dust. Everything she said was true.

During the course of their conversation, it became clear to Pekkala that Madame Kschessinska was, in almost every way, the polar opposite of the Tsarina. For the Tsar to have fallen in love with a woman like Kschessinska seemed not only plausible, but inevitable.

'Thank you, Madame Kschessinska,' he said as she walked him to the door.

'You must not worry, Inspector,' she replied. 'The Tsarina may try to feed you to the wolves, but from what I know about you, you may be the one who ends up eating the wolf.'

One week later, Pekkala presented himself once again at the Tsarina's study door.

He found the Tsarina exactly as he had left her, lying on the daybed. It was almost as if she had not moved since they'd last parted company. She was knitting a sweater, the needles clicking rhythmically.

'I have concluded my investigation,' he told her.

'Yes?' The Tsarina kept her eyes on her knitting. 'And what have you discovered, Inspector?'

'Nothing, Majesty.'

The click of the knitting needles came abruptly to a stop. 'What?'

'I have discovered no irregularities.'

'I see.' She pressed her lips together, draining the blood from the flesh.

'In my opinion, Majesty,' he continued, 'everything is as it should be.'

Her eyes filled with hate as she took in the meaning of his words. 'You listen to me, Pekkala,' she said through clenched teeth. 'Before he died, my friend Grigori made clear that there is a time of judgement coming. All secrets will be laid bare and for those who have not followed a path of righteousness, there will be no one to whom they can turn. And I wonder what will happen to you on that day.'

Pekkala thought about Rasputin after the police had pulled him from the river. Pekkala wondered what the Tsarina would have said about the day of judgement if she could have seen her friend that day, lying on the quayside with a bullet in his head.

The Tsarina turned away. With a swipe of her hand, she dismissed him.

After that, Pekkala sometimes came across Madame Kschessinska, buying food in the Gostiny Dvor market or shopping on the Passazh. They never spoke again, but they always remembered to smile.

As often happened, by the time Pekkala had finished his tea, Babayaga had already fallen asleep, chin resting on her chest and breathing heavily.

He left the room, closing the door quietly behind him. In the hallway, he took off his shoes and carried them, so as not to wake the others on his floor.

The next morning, when Pekkala walked into his office, Kirov was already there.

So was Major Lysenkova.

Kirov stood beside her, holding out his kumquat plant in its rust-coloured earthenware pot. 'You should try one!' he urged.

'No, really,' replied Lysenkova, 'I would rather not.'

Neither of them had seen Pekkala come in.

'You may never see another,' persisted Kirov. Sunlight through the dusty window glinted off the waxy green leaves.

'I wouldn't mind that at all,' answered Lysenkova.

Pekkala shut the door more loudly than usual.

Kirov jumped. 'Inspector! There you are!' He hugged the plant to his chest as if trying to take cover behind it.

'What can we do for you, Major Lysenkova?' asked Pekkala, taking off his coat and hanging it on the peg beside the door.

'I came here to ask for your help,' said Lysenkova. 'As you might have heard, the Nagorski case has been reopened, and I am no longer in charge.'

'I did hear that,' said Pekkala.

'In fact, I have been told that you and Major Kirov will be running the investigation from now on.'

'We are?' asked Kirov, as he replaced the plant on the windowsill.

'I was just about to tell you,' explained Pekkala.

'The truth is,' said Lysenkova, 'I never wanted it in the first place.'

'Why is that?' asked Pekkala. 'You seemed pretty certain before.'

'I was certain about a number of things,' replied Lysenkova, 'and it turned out I was wrong about all of them. That's why I need your help now.'

Pekkala nodded, slightly confused.

'I need to keep working on the case,' she said.

Pekkala sat down in his chair and put his feet up on his desk. 'But you just said you didn't want to be working on it in the first place.'

Lysenkova swallowed. 'I can explain,' she said.

Pekkala held open his hand. 'Please do.'

'Until yesterday,' she began, 'I'd never even heard of Project Konstantin. Then, when Captain Samarin called, informing me that Colonel Nagorski had been killed, I told him he must have dialled the wrong number.'

'Why did you think that?'

'I am, as you know, an internal investigator. My task is to pursue crimes committed inside the NKVD. I was explaining that to Samarin when he told me he believed someone in the NKVD might actually be responsible for Nagorski's death.'

Pekkala's focus sharpened. 'Did he say why?'

'The location of the facility is a state secret,' continued Lysenkova. 'According to Samarin, the only people who had access to that information and who might have been able to infiltrate the facility were NKVD. We didn't have time to discuss it any further. He told me to get out there as quickly as I could. At that point, I realised I didn't have any choice, even though this was nothing like the cases I normally handle. I deal in cases of corruption, extortion, bribery, blackmail. Not murders, Inspector Pekkala. Not bodies that have been ground up by tank tracks! That's why I didn't spot the bullet fragment you pulled out of his skull.'

'I don't understand, Major. You say you never wanted the case, and it sounds to me as if you got your wish, but now you want to keep working on it?'

'I don't want to, Inspector, I *have* to. It's only a matter of time before I'm accused of counter-revolutionary activity for coming to the wrong conclusion about Nagorski's death. The only chance I've got is to remain on the case until it is solved, and the only person who can make that happen is you.'

Pekkala was silent for a while. 'I understand,' he said finally, 'but I will have to speak with Major Kirov here before making any decision.'

'I realise we did not get off to a good start, but I could be useful to you.' Her voice had taken on a tone of pleading. 'I know how the NKVD works, inside and out. Once you start investigating them, they will close ranks and you'll never get a word out of them. But I can and I will, if you'll let me.'

'Very well.' Pekkala took his feet off the desk and stood up. 'We will let you know our decision as soon as we can. Before you go, Major, I do have one question to ask you.'

'Of course, Inspector. Anything.'

'What do you know about the White Guild?' asked Pekkala, as he walked her out into the hall.

'Not a great deal, I'm afraid. It's some kind of top secret department in the Bureau of Special Operations.'

'Have you heard them mentioned recently?'

'Special Operations is a tribe of phantoms, Inspector. You ought to know that, since you're one of them. Where I come from nobody even speaks their name.'

'Thank you, Major,' sighed Pekkala.

'Oh, I almost forgot.' From her pocket, Lysenkova removed a stained and tattered piece of paper. 'Consider this a peace offering.'

Pekkala squinted at the document. At first glance, what he saw looked to him like Arabic writing on the page. Then he realised it was actually scientific equations, dozens of them, completely covering the paper. 'Where did this come from?' he asked.

'I found it in Nagorski's pocket.'

'Do you have any idea what it means?'

'None,' she told him.

'Does anyone else know about this?'

She shook her head.

He folded up the page. 'I appreciate this, Major.'

'Then I will hear from you?'

'Yes.'

She paused, as if there might be something else to say, but then she turned away and walked back down the stairs.

Kirov came and stood beside Pekkala. They listened to her footsteps fading away.

'I never thought I would feel sorry for that woman,' said Kirov.

'But you do.'

'A little.'

'From the way you were talking to her, I'd say you felt a little more than sorry.'

Back inside the office, Pekkala busied himself straightening piles of papers which had slid in miniature avalanches across the surface of his desk.

'What's bothering you, Inspector?' asked Kirov. 'You never tidy up your desk unless something is bothering you.'

'I am not certain about taking her on,' replied Pekkala.

'I don't think we have a choice,' replied Kirov. 'If Captain Samarin was right that the NKVD were involved, we'll never get to the bottom of this without her working on the case.'

'Your willingness to work with Major Lysenkova wouldn't have anything to do with . . .'

'With those eyes?' asked Kirov. 'Those . . .'

'Exactly.'

'I don't know what you're talking about, Inspector.'

'No,' muttered Pekkala. 'Of course you don't.'

'Besides,' continued Kirov, 'if we don't give Major Lysenkova a chance to set things straight with Comrade Stalin, you know what will happen to her.'

Pekkala did know, because the same thing had happened to him during the Revolution, when he was arrested by

Bolshevik Guards on his way out of the country. He thought back to the months he had spent in a solitary confinement cell, the endless interrogations and his sanity wearing so thin he no longer knew what remained of it. And then came the winter's night when he was delivered, still wearing his flimsy beige prison pyjamas, to a railroad siding on the outskirts of Moscow. There, he boarded a train bound for Siberia.

The thing he would always remember was the way people died standing up.

As convict transport ETAP-61 made its way east towards the Borodok Labour Camp, Pekkala abandoned hope of ever seeing home again. The train was over fifty wagons long. Each one contained eighty men, crammed into a space designed to hold forty.

It was too crowded for anyone to sit. Prisoners took turns in the middle, where there was body heat to share. The rest stood at the edges. Dressed only in dirty beige pyjamas, a few of them froze every night. There was no room for them to fall, so the corpses remained on their feet while their lips turned blue and spider webs of ice glazed their eyes. By morning, they were cloaked in white crystals.

With his face pressed to a tiny opening criss-crossed with barbed wire, Pekkala looked out at the cities of Sverdlovsk, Petropavlovsk and Omsk. Until he saw their names spelled out on blue-and-white enamel signs above the station platforms, those places had never seemed real. They had existed as locations destined to remain always beyond the horizon, reachable only in dreams. Like Zanzibar or Timbuktu.

The train passed through these cities after dark, in order to hide its contents from the people living there. At Novosibirsk, Pekkala spotted two men illuminated by a glow cast through the open doorway of a tavern. He thought he heard them singing. Snow fell around the men like a cascade of diamonds. Beyond, silhouetted against the blue-black sky, rose the onion-shaped domes of orthodox churches. Afterwards, as the train pressed on into darkness so complete it was as if they'd left Earth and were now hurtling through space, the singing of those two men haunted him.

Hour after hour, the wheels clanked lazily along the tracks, their sound like a monstrous sharpening of knives.

Only in open country did the engines ever come to a halt. Then the guards jumped down and beat against the outsides of the wagons with their rifle butts, in order to dislodge those who had become frozen to the inner walls. Usually the corpses had to be prised free, leaving behind the imprints of their faces, complete with eyelashes and shreds of beard, in the wagon's icy plating.

Beside the tracks lay skeletons from previous convict transports. Rib cages jutted from rags of clothing and silver teeth glinted in their skulls.

Pekkala smoothed a hand across his face, fingertips rustling over the razor stubble on his chin. Knowing the fate that lay in store for Major Lysenkova, Pekkala realised he could not simply stand by and do nothing to help. 'All right,' he sighed.

'Good!' Kirov clapped his hands and rubbed his palms together. 'Shall I fetch her back?'

Pekkala nodded. 'But before you go, tell me what you found out about Nagorski's bodyguard, Maximov.'

'Nothing, Inspector.'

'You mean you didn't look?'

'Oh, I looked,' replied Kirov. 'I searched the police files. I even checked Gendarmerie and Okhrana files from before the Revolution, those that still exist. There's nothing. As far as I can tell, the first record of Maximov's existence is the day he was hired by Nagorski. Do you want me to bring him in for questioning?'

'No,' replied Pekkala. 'He may be hiding something, but I doubt it has anything to do with our case. I was just curious.'

'Inspector,' said Kirov, 'if you want me to catch up with Major Lysenkova . . .'

Pekkala breathed in sharply. 'Yes. Go. When you find her, make sure you let her know that, from this point on, our primary suspect must be that man who escaped through the woods. We've already ruled out the regular staff at the facility, and since Samarin believed NKVD were involved somehow, it seems likely that the man who escaped was working for them. Anything Lysenkova can find out will be useful, but tell her she is not to pursue or arrest any suspects without informing us first.'

'You don't have to worry about her cooperating, Inspector. You just saved her life, after all.'

While Kirov struggled into his coat, Pekkala took another look at the piece of paper Lysenkova had given him. The writing was blurred from having been soaked while Nagorski lay beneath the tank. It was still legible, but only to someone who could decipher the impossible tangle of equations and Pekkala was not one of those.

Knowing that Kirov might not be back any time soon, Pekkala went across the road to the Café Tilsit, where he always ate lunch when he was in town.

The Café Tilsit never closed.

There wasn't even a lock on the front door.

By night it was the haunt of those who, during the hours of darkness, managed the great engine of the city. There were watchmen and museum guards, soldiers passing through on leave and policemen coming off their shifts. Those were the ones who had jobs. But there were also those who had no place to live, or who were afraid to go home, for reasons known only to themselves. There were the broken-hearted and those who stood upon the precipice of madness and those whose sanity had folded up like paper aeroplanes.

By day, the clientele was mostly taxi drivers, truckers and construction workers, ghostly pale under their layers of concrete dust.

Pekkala liked the bustle of the place, the condensation-misted windows and the long, bare wood tables where strangers sat elbow to elbow. It was the strange communion of being alone and not being alone which suited him.

There was no choice of meal and the food was always simple, served by a man named Bruno, who wrote the menu each day on a double-sided chalk board which he propped up on the pavement outside the café. Inside, Bruno shuffled from table to table in worn-out felt *valenki* boots.

Today, Bruno had made breaded cutlets, chick peas and boiled carrots, served in wooden bowls, which were his only tableware.

Pekkala ate his meal and read through the headlines of *Pravda*.

The off-duty taxi driver sitting next to him was trying to read Pekkala's paper, straining to see it from the corner of his eye. To make it easier for the taxi driver, Pekkala lowered the paper to the table. As he did this, he realised that the man opposite was staring at him.

The stranger had a heavy jaw, a broad, unwrinkled forehead and once-blond hair which was beginning to turn grey. He wore the typical clothing of a worker in this city – a short-brimmed wool cap and double-breasted coat whose sleeves were panelled with leather to make the garment more durable.

To catch a person's eye in a place like this meant that you either smiled and said hello or looked away, but this man just kept on staring.

'Do I know you?' asked Pekkala.

'You do.' The man smiled. 'From a long time ago.'

'I know many people from a long time ago,' Pekkala replied, 'and most of them are dead.'

'Then I am happy to be the exception,' said the man. 'My name is Alexander Kropotkin.'

Pekkala sat back, almost tipping off the bench. 'Kropotkin!'

The last time they had seen each other was far from here, in the city of Ekaterinburg, where Kropotkin was Chief of Police. Pekkala had travelled there to investigate the discovery of bodies believed to be those of the Tsar and his family. Kropotkin had worked closely with Pekkala during the course of the investigation, which had nearly cost both of them their lives. Kropotkin had been in charge of the Ekaterinburg police department before the Revolution and when Pekkala first met him, after the Communists had come to power, he was still managing to hold on to his job. Pekkala had wondered how long that would last, since Kropotkin, an honest but short-tempered man, had little patience for the labyrinth of Soviet bureaucracy and the people who enforced it.

Kropotkin reached across to shake Pekkala's hand.

'What brings you to Moscow?' asked Pekkala.

'Well, as you can see,' he gave an awkward laugh, 'I am no longer a chief of police.'

The taxi driver was still trying to read Pekkala's paper.

Pekkala could feel the man's breath on his cheek. He picked up the paper and handed it to him.

The taxi driver grunted thanks, took the paper and resumed slurping his soup.

Pekkala turned back to Kropotkin. 'What happened? Were you reassigned? Did you quit?'

'Dismissed,' answered Kropotkin, 'for striking the District Commissar.'

'Ah,' Pekkala nodded slowly, not entirely surprised that Kropotkin would do such a thing. He seemed the type to dispense justice with a truncheon rather than with a court case.

'I'm better off now,' said Kropotkin. 'No more petty officials to deal with! I came here and trained as a heavy machinery operator at the Moscow Technical Institute. I can operate pretty much anything now. Heavy transport vehicles. Tractors. Bulldozers. Cranes.'

'And which one did you choose?' asked Pekkala.

'I drive a Hanomag from one end of this country to the other.'

Pekkala had heard about the Hanomags. These German-made trucks were capable of moving vast amounts of cargo. In the past few years, with huge road-building projects under way, trucking routes had opened up all the way from the Baltic to the Black Sea and from the Polish border to Siberia.

'Most of the highways in this country are still made out of dirt. As long as there's a road, I'll drive on it. But this is where I come when I'm in town,' said Kropotkin, glancing warily into his bowl, 'no matter what Bruno serves up.'

'This was one of the Tsarina's favourite meals,' said Pekkala.

'This!' Kropotkin held up his fork, on which he had speared a chunk of meat whose origin appeared suspicious. 'Well, I find that hard to believe.'

'She once ate chicken cutlets twice a day for a month,' said Pekkala.

Kropotkin stared at him for a moment. Then he laughed. 'With all the beluga in the world to choose from, you are telling me she ate chicken cutlets all day long?'

Pekkala nodded.

Kropotkin shook his head. 'No, Pekkala. That cannot be true.'

Like many others, Kropotkin had created for himself an image of the Romanovs which existed only in his head.

Pekkala wondered what Kropotkin would have thought of the drearily furnished rooms in the Alexander Palace, where the Romanovs lived at Tsarskoye Selo. Or of the Tsar's four daughters, dressed as they always were in identical clothes – one day in striped sailor's shirts, another day in blue-and-white polka-dot dresses – or of the Tsarevich Alexei, who once ordered a company of soldiers to march into the sea? Which would have offended him more: the behaviour of the little prince or that of the soldiers, who strode into the waves with the obedience of clockwork toys?

For the new generation of Russians, Nicholas Romanov had been transformed into a ghoul. But for men like Kropotkin, whose loyalties belonged to a time before the Revolution, the Tsar and his family were the subject of a fairy tale. The truth, if there even was such a thing any more, lay somewhere in between.

'The last time we spoke,' Kropotkin said with a smile, 'you said you were leaving the country.'

'Yes,' said Pekkala, 'that had been my intention.'

'There was a woman, wasn't there?' asked Kropotkin.

Pekkala nodded. 'She is in Paris. I am in Moscow. Many years have passed.'

Kropotkin pushed away his half-finished bowl of food. 'It's stuffy in here. Will you walk outside with me?'

Pekkala, too, had lost his appetite.

As they stood up from the table, the taxi driver reached across, hooked one dirty thumb over the lip of Kropotkin's bowl and dragged it towards himself.

The two men stepped out into the street. A fine rain was falling. They turned up the collars of their coats.

'Still working for them?' asked Kropotkin.

'Them?'

He jerked his chin towards the domes of the Kremlin, visible above the rooftops in the distance. 'Special Operations.'

'I do the same work as I have always done,' replied Pekkala,

'No regrets?' asked Kropotkin, walking with his hands shoved in his pockets.

'About what?'

'About staying here in this country. About not leaving when you could.'

'This is where I belong,' replied Pekkala.

'Let me ask you, Pekkala. Do you stay because you want to or because you have to?'

'Well, if you are asking me whether I could simply depart on the next train out of Russia, I admit that might prove complicated.'

'Listen to you!' laughed Kropotkin. 'Listen to the language you are using. You couldn't get out of here, even if you wanted to.' Now he stopped and turned to face Pekkala. 'You and I are the last of the old guard. This world will never see the likes of us again. We owe it to ourselves to stick together.'

'What are you trying to say, Kropotkin?'

'What if I told you I could help you escape?'

'I don't understand.'

'Yes, you do, Pekkala. You understand exactly what I'm saying. I drive my truck all over Russia. I know the highways of this country like the creases in my palm. I know roads that aren't even on the map, roads that wind back and forth across borders because they are centuries older than the borders themselves. I know where there are checkpoints and where there aren't.' Removing one hand from the pocket of his coat, he clasped Pekkala by the arm. 'I can get you out of here, old friend. The time must come when you will have to choose between the actions that your job requires and what your conscience will allow.'

'So far,' said Pekkala, 'I have been able to live with myself.'

'But when you do come up against that wall, remember your old friend Kropotkin. With my help, you can start your life over and never look back.'

In that moment, Pekkala did not feel Kropotkin's grip upon his arm. Instead, it seemed to him as if a hand were clasped around his throat. He had resigned himself to staying here. At least, he thought he had. But now, with Kropotkin's words ringing in his ears, Pekkala realised that the notion of escape was still alive in him. He knew that Kropotkin's offer was genuine, and that the man could do what he promised. All Pekkala had to do was say the words.

'Are you all right, brother?' asked Kropotkin. 'Your hands are shaking.'

'What would I do?' asked Pekkala, as much to himself as to Kropotkin. 'I can't just start all over.'

Kropotkin smiled. 'Of course you could! People do it all the time. And as for what you would do, there isn't a police force in the world that would turn down the chance to have you work for them. If you ask me, Pekkala, the people who are running this country don't deserve the loyalty of a man like you.'

'The people I investigate would be criminals no matter who was in charge of this country.'

Kropotkin stopped. He turned and faced Pekkala, eyes narrowed against the spitting rain. 'But what if the people who are running the country are the greatest criminals of all?'

Pekkala heard the aggression in Kropotkin's voice. From anyone else, it might have come as a surprise. But Kropotkin was in the habit of speaking his mind, with little thought to how his opinions were received, and Pekkala felt glad that there was no one else around. Words like that, in a place like this, could get a man in trouble.

'Ask yourself, Pekkala, how can a man do good when he is surrounded by those who do not?'

'That,' replied Pekkala, 'is when good men are needed the most.'

A look of sadness passed across Kropotkin's face. 'So your mind is made up?'

'I am grateful for your offer, Kropotkin, but my answer will have to be no.'

'If you change your mind,' smiled Kropotkin, 'look for me at the café where we ate our lunch.'

'I will,' said Pekkala, 'and thank you.'

Kropotkin hooked his thumb under the watch chain attached to his waistcoat button. He lifted the watch from his pocket, glanced at it and let it slip back into the pocket. 'Time to hit the road,' he said.

'I hope we will meet again soon.'

'We will. And in the meantime, Inspector, God protect us both.'

At the mention of those words, Pekkala tumbled into the past, like a man falling backwards off a cliff.

'God protect us!' wept the Tsarina. 'God protect us. God protect us.'

Early one morning in January 1917, in the crypt of the private Fyodorov chapel, the body of Rasputin was laid to rest.

The only people present were the Tsar, the Tsarina, their children, a priest and Pekkala, who was there for security, since the service was being held in secret.

After the discovery of Rasputin's corpse in the Neva river, the Tsarina had ordered that Rasputin should be buried in his home village of Pokrovskoye, in Siberia. The Minister of the Interior, Alexander Protopopov, persuaded her that the hostility towards Rasputin, even in death, would guarantee that his body would never reach its destination, so she decided to bury him in secret on the grounds of the Tsarskoye Selo estate.

It was an open-coffin service, but Rasputin's face had been covered with a white cloth. This was to hide the bullet hole in the middle of his forehead, which no amount of undertaker's skill could obscure.

This bullet hole had been made by a different weapon from the other three found in his body. It was Chief Inspector Vassileyev who had alerted Pekkala to the discrepancy. 'We have a big problem,' he said.

'That Rasputin was shot by more than one gun?' asked Pekkala. They already had two men in temporary custody. Prince

Felix Yusupov had immediately confessed to the crime, along with Lazovert, the army doctor. There were other suspects, including the Grand Duke Dimitri Pavlovitch, but it was the Tsar himself who made clear to theOkhrana investigators, Pekkala included, that none of these men would ever be brought to trial. Given this fact, the number of bullet holes in Rasputin's body hardly seemed to matter.

'It's not simply that two weapons were used,' Vassileyev told Pekkala. 'It is the type of gun which caused this.' He pressed a finger to his forehead, where the bullet had entered Rasputin's skull. 'Our chief medical examiner has determined that the head wound was made by a soft-sided bullet. Every type of gun firing that calibre of bullet uses a hard copper casing. Every type except one.' Now Vassileyev pointed at Pekkala's chest, where his revolver rested in its shoulder holster. 'Fetch it out.'

Confused, Pekkala did as he was told.

Vassileyev took the gun, opened the chamber and emptied the large .455 calibre bullets out on to the table.

'Do you mean somebody thinks I played a part in this?' asked Pekkala.

'No!' growled Vassileyev. 'Look at the bullets! Soft-sided. The only weapon commonly available in this size and with this kind of ammunition is the British Webley revolver, the same kind the Tsar gave to you as a present, and which he received from his cousin King George the Fifth of England.'

'The British murdered Rasputin?'

Vassileyev shrugged. 'They had a hand in it, Pekkala. That much is almost certain.'

'But why?'

'They were not fond of Rasputin. It was on that lunatic's

insistence that several British advisers were sent home in disgrace.'

'Is that why the investigation has been halted?'

'Halted?' laughed Vassileyev. 'The investigation was never begun. What I've just told you will never be written in the history books. In the future, Pekkala, they will not squabble over who killed Rasputin. Instead, they will be asking who didn't.'

Throughout the short burial service, Pekkala stood by the half-open door of the church, looking out across the grounds of Tsarskoye Selo. The smell of sandalwood incense blew past him and out into the freezing air.

It was cold in the chapel. No fires had been lit. The Romanovs stood in fur coats while the priest read the eulogy. Throughout this, the Tsarina wept, a lace handkerchief clenched in her fist and pressed against her mouth to hide her sobbing.

Glancing back from the door, Pekkala watched the daughters lay a painted icon on Rasputin's chest. The Tsar and Alexei stood off to one side, grim faced but detached.

'Where is the justice in this?' shrieked the Tsarina, as the lid of the coffin was closed.

The priest stepped back in alarm.

The Tsar took hold of his wife's arm. 'It's over,' he told her. 'There is nothing more we can do.'

She collapsed into his arms and sobbed against his chest. She began her chant again. 'God protect us. God protect us.'

Pekkala wondered what that meant for the man in the box, whose brains had been blown through his skull.

As the Romanovs left the church, Pekkala stood outside the door to let them pass.

The Tsarina swept past him, then stopped and turned. 'I've

been meaning to thank you,' she whispered, 'for keeping us safe here on earth. Now I have two guardians. One here and one who's up above.'

Looking into the Tsarina's bloodshot eyes, Pekkala remembered what Rasputin had told him, that night he came in from the cold.

'You see, Pekkala,' he had said, 'the reason I am loved by the Tsarina is that I am exactly what she wants me to be. Just as she needs me now to be beside her, the time will come when she will need me to be gone.'

Once more, the Tsar took hold of his wife's arm. 'Our friend is gone now,' he murmured in her ear. 'We should be going too.'

There was an expression on his face which Pekkala had never seen before — some blur of fear and resignation — as if the Tsar had glimpsed, through some tear in the fabric of time, the spectre of his own fast-approaching doom.

Pekkala watched as Kropotkin crossed the road, disappearing in the misty veils of rain.

Then he went back to the office.

An hour later, when Kirov had still not returned, he began to grow nervous. There had been so many arrests this past year that no one could feel safe, no matter what rank they held or how innocent they were. The way Pekkala saw it, the same idealism that made Kirov a good upholder of the law also made the young man vulnerable to how randomly enforced that law could be. Pekkala had seen it before – the stronger the convictions, the greater the distance between the world as these people envisaged it and the world as it really was.

At the same time, Pekkala knew that Kirov might take it as a lack of confidence if he went searching for him now.

So Pekkala continued to wait in the office, as evening shadows crept about the room. Before long, he found himself in total darkness. By now, there was no point heading home for the night, so he put his feet up on the desk, folded his hands across his stomach, and tried to fall asleep.

But he couldn't.

Instead, Pekkala paced around the room, studying Kirov's potted plants. Now and then, he paused to pick a cherry tomato or to chew on a basil leaf.

Finally, with an hour still to go before the sun came up, Pekkala put on his coat and left the building, on his way to Kirov's apartment.

It was a long walk, almost an hour through the winding streets. He could have made the journey in ten minutes by taking the subway, but Pekkala preferred to remain above ground in spite of the fact that there were no reliable maps of the city. The only charts available for Moscow showed either what the city had looked like before the Revolution or what the city was supposed to look like when all of the new construction projects had been finished. Most of these had not even begun, and there were whole city blocks which, on these maps, bore no resemblance to what actually stood on the ground. Many streets had been renamed, as had entire cities around the country. Petrograd was Leningrad, Tsaritsin was Stalingrad. As the locals said in Moscow – everything is different but nothing has really changed.

Pekkala was walking along the edge of Gorki Park when a car pulled up alongside him. Before the car, a black GAZ-M1 saloon, had even stopped, the passenger side door flew open and a man jumped out.

Without thinking about it, Pekkala drew his gun.

By the time the man's feet were on the ground, he was already looking down the blue-eyed barrel of Pekkala's revolver.

The man wore round glasses, balanced on a long, thin nose. Beard stubble made a blue haze under his pasty skin.

To Pekkala, he looked a like a big, pink rat.

The expression of angry determination on the man's face gave way to stunned disbelief. Slowly, he raised his hands. 'You are going to wish you hadn't done that, Comrade,' he said quietly.

It was only now that Pekkala got a good look at him. Even though he wore plain clothes, Pekkala knew immediately that the man was NKVD. It was the way he carried himself and his look of perpetual disdain. Pekkala had been so worried about Kirov being hauled in on some random charge that he had not stopped to consider the same thing might happen to him. 'What do you want?' he asked.

'Put that down!' snapped the man.

'Give me an answer,' replied Pekkala calmly, 'if you want to keep your brains in your head.'

'Are you licensed to carry that antique?'

Pekkala set his thumb on the hammer and pulled it back until it cocked. 'I'm licensed to use it as well,' he said.

Now the man shrugged his right shoulder, revealing a gun in a holster tucked under his armpit. 'You're not the only person with a gun.'

'Go ahead,' replied Pekkala, 'and let's see what happens next.'

'Why don't you just show me your papers!'

Without lowering the Webley, Pekkala reached inside his coat, removed his pass book and held it out.

'You're NKVD?' asked the man.

'See for yourself.'

Slowly, the rat man took it from his hand and opened it.

'What's taking so long?' said a voice. Then the driver of the car climbed out. '*Svoloch!*' he shouted when he saw Pekkala's revolver, and struggled to draw his own gun.

'Don't,' said Pekkala.

But it was too late. The man's Tokarev was now aimed squarely at Pekkala.

Pekkala kept his own weapon pointed at the rat man.

For a moment, the three men just stood there.

'Let's just all of us calm down and see what we've got here,' said the rat man, as he opened Pekkala's identification book.

A long period of silence followed.

'What's the matter?' demanded the driver, his gun still aimed at Pekkala. 'What the hell is going on?'

The rat-faced man cleared his throat. 'He's got a Shadow Pass.'

The driver looked suddenly lost, like a sleepwalker who had woken up in a different part of town.

'It's Pekkala,' said the rat-faced man.

'What?'

'Inspector Pekkala, you idiot! From Special Operations.'

'It was your idea to stop!' complained the driver. Uttering another curse, he stuffed his gun back into its holster as if the weapon had drawn itself against his wishes.

The rat-faced man closed Pekkala's ID book. 'Our apologies, Inspector,' he said as he handed it back.

Only now did Pekkala lower his gun. 'I'm taking this car,' he told them.

'Our car?' asked the driver, his face turning pale.

'Yes,' replied Pekkala. 'I am requisitioning your vehicle.' He walked around to the driver's side.

'You can't do that!' said the driver. 'This car belongs to us!'

'Be quiet, you idiot!' shouted the rat man. 'Didn't you hear me? I said he had a Shadow Pass. We can't detain him. We can't question him. We can't even ask him the bloody time of day! He is licensed to shoot you and no one's even allowed to ask him why he did it. He's also permitted to requisition anything he chooses – our weapons, our car. He can leave you standing naked in the street if he wants to.'

'It pulls a little to the left,' said the driver. 'The carburettor needs adjusting.'

'Shut up and get out of his way!' the rat-faced man yelled again.

As if jolted by an electric shock, the driver tossed Pekkala the keys.

Pekkala got behind the wheel. The last he saw of the two men, they were standing on the pavement, arguing. He drove the rest of the way to Kirov's apartment on Prechistenka street. Then he just sat in the car for a while, hands still on the wheel, trying to stop breathing so hard.

'When guns are drawn,' said Chief Inspector Vassileyev, 'you must never show fear. A man with a gun aimed at you is more likely to pull the trigger if he sees you are afraid.'

At the end of every day of his training with the Okhrana, the Tsar's Secret Police, Pekkala would report to Vassileyev. The procedures Pekkala learned from other agents transformed him into an investigator, but what he learned from Vassileyev saved his life.

'Surely,' argued Pekkala, 'if I show I am afraid, I would be less of a threat to someone with a gun.'

'I am not talking about what should happen,' replied Vassileyev, 'I am talking about what will happen.'

Even though the Chief Inspector always seemed to talk in riddles, Pekkala looked forward to the time he spent with Vassileyev. His office was small and comfortable, with lithographs of hunting scenes and antique weaponry hung on the walls. Vassileyev spent most of his time here, poring over reports and receiving visitors. As a younger man, he had gained a reputation for going about the city on foot, often in disguise. It was said that no one could hide from Vassileyev in Petrograd, because he knew every corner of the city. Those days came to an end one day as he was walking down the steps of the police building in order to meet the head of the Moscow Okhrana, who had just arrived by car. Vassileyev had almost reached the vehicle when a bomb, thrown through the window on the other side, exploded. The

Moscow chief was killed instantly and Vassileyev sustained injuries that put him behind a desk for the rest of his career.

'The person who lives without fear,' continued Vassileyev, 'does not have long to live. Fear sharpens the senses. Fear can keep you alive. But learn to hide it, Pekkala. Bury the fear deep someplace inside you, so your enemies can't see it in your eyes.'

When, at last, his breathing had returned to normal, Pekkala left the keys in the glove compartment, got out of the car and walked across the street to Kirov's building.

It had been freshly painted in a cheerful shade of orange. Large windows, trimmed in white, looked down the tree-lined avenue.

Pekkala knocked on the door to Kirov's apartment, then took two steps back and waited.

After a minute, the door opened a crack and Kirov peered from inside. His eyes were squinty and his hair stuck up in tufts. Behind him, on the walls, were dozens of awards and certificates from various Communist Youth Organisations. Kirov had been collecting these certificates of merit since he was five years old, when he had won a prize for a week of community service in the Young Pioneers. After this, he had gone on to win awards for best orienteering, best science experiment, best tent-pitching. Each certificate bore a hammer and sickle, nestled between two sheaves of wheat. Some of the certificates had been ornately hand-lettered. Others were no more than scrawls. But all of them had been framed and they hung from every vertical surface in his apartment. 'What are you doing here?' asked Kirov.

'Good morning to you, too,' replied Pekkala. 'Get dressed. We have to go.'

'Where ?'

Pekkala held up the piece of paper Lysenkova had given him. 'To talk to the scientists at the facility. Maybe they can decipher this. There may be a link between the equation and the man who escaped, but we won't know until we understand what's written here.'

'Who is that?' asked a woman's voice from inside the apartment. 'Is that Inspector Pekkala?'

Kirov sighed heavily. 'Yes.'

'So that's why you didn't come back!' spluttered Pekkala. 'Damn it, Kirov, I thought you'd been arrested!'

'Arrested for what?' asked Kirov.

'Never mind that now!'

'Aren't you going to let him in?' asked the woman.

Pekkala peered into the room. 'Major Lysenkova?'

'Good morning, Inspector.' She was sitting at the kitchen table, wrapped in a blanket.

Pekkala gave Kirov a withering stare.

Lysenkova got up from the table and walked towards them, bare feet padding on the floor. As she approached, Pekkala realised she wasn't wearing anything beneath the blanket. 'Major Kirov told me the good news,' she said.

'Good news?' asked Pekkala.

'That you've allowed me to keep working on the case,' she explained. 'I've already got down to work.'

Pekkala mumbled something unintelligible.

'I found some more information on the White Guild,' said Lysenkova.

'You did? What did you find out?'

'That they're gone.'

'Gone?' asked Pekkala.

'Finished. They were closed down a few weeks ago. All their agents got reassigned.'

'Do you think you might be able to find out where they are now?'

'I can try,' she said. 'I'll start on it as soon as I get back to NKVD headquarters.'

Ten minutes later, the Emka pulled up to the kerb. Kirov sat behind the wheel. His hair was wet and neatly combed.

Pekkala climbed in and slammed the door. 'Kremlin,' he said.

'But I thought we were going to talk to those scientists out at the facility.'

'There's something I need to do first,' replied Pekkala.

Kirov pulled out into the road. 'I made us some lunch,' he said, 'in case we're gone all day.'

Pekkala stared out the window. Sunlight flickered on his face.

'I take it you disapprove, Inspector,' said Kirov.

'Of what?'

'Of me. And Major Lysenkova.'

'As long as the investigation is not obstructed, Kirov, it's not for me to say one thing or another. After all, my own adventures in that field would not stand up to any test of sanity.'

'But you do disapprove. I can tell.'

'The only advice I have for you is to do what you can live with. The further you go beyond that point, the harder it is to return.'

'And how far have you gone, Inspector?'

'If I ever get back,' replied Pekkala, 'I will be sure to let you know.'

*

'I can't talk now, Pekkala,' growled Stalin, as he stood up from his desk. 'I'm on my way to the daily briefing. The Germans have moved into Czechoslovakia, just as I told you they would. It has begun, and we still don't have the T-34.'

'Comrade Stalin, what I need to ask you is also important.'

Stalin pressed his hand against a panel in the wall and the trap door clicked open. 'Well, come on, then!'

'In there?' asked Pekkala, the dread of confinement twisting in his guts.

'Yes! In here. Hurry up!'

He followed Stalin into the secret passageway, his stomach knotting as he ducked into the shadows.

When they were both inside, Stalin turned a metal lever in the wall and the door swung silently shut.

A line of weak electric bulbs lit the way, trailing into the darkness.

As soon as the trap door shut, Stalin set off through the tunnel.

Pekkala had to struggle to keep up, painfully stooped so as not to bang his head on wooden spacer beams which crossed the ceiling at regular intervals.

Doors appeared out of the gloom, each with its own opening-and-closing lever. The rooms to which they led were marked in yellow paint. It smelled dusty in the passageway. Now and then, he heard the murmur of voices on the other side of the wall.

By now, he was fighting against panic. The low ceiling seemed to be collapsing in on him. He had to remind himself to breathe. Each time they came to a door, he had to struggle against the urge to open it and escape from this rat tunnel.

They came to an intersection.

Pekkala looked down the other passageways, the pearl necklace of bulbs illuminating dingy tunnels leading deep into the heart of the Kremlin.

Stalin swung to his right and immediately began to climb a flight of stairs. He paused halfway up to catch his breath.

Pekkala almost ran into him.

'Well, Pekkala,' Stalin wheezed, 'are you going to ask me this question of yours or are you just keeping me company?'

'The White Guild is finished,' said Pekkala.

'That does not sound like a question.'

'Is it true? Has the White Guild been shut down?'

Standing above him on the stairs, Stalin loomed over Pekkala. 'The operation has been terminated.'

'And its agents have been reassigned?'

'Officially, yes.'

'Officially? What do you mean?'

This time Stalin did not reply. He turned and continued up the stairs. Reaching the top, he set out along another passageway. The floor was lined with dark green carpet, the centre of which had been worn down to the ridging underneath.

'Where are those agents?' asked Pekkala.

'Dead,' replied Stalin.

'What? All of them?' The sound of water gurgling in pipes rushed past Pekkala's ears.

'Last month, over the course of a single night, the six agents were tracked down to their lodgings in various parts of the city. It was a professional job. Each one was executed with a shot to the back of the head.'

'Do you have any suspects?'

Stalin shook his head. 'In his final report, one of those agents stated that he had been approached by some people wishing to join the Guild. One week later, the agents turned up dead. The names these people used turned out to be fake.'

'Whoever these people were,' said Pekkala, 'they must have discovered that Special Operations controlled the White Guild. They found out who the Special Operations agents were and killed them.'

'Correct.'

'What I don't understand, Comrade Stalin, is why you think the Guild might be involved in the Nagorski killing, when you have just told me you closed it down before he died.'

'I did close down the Guild,' said Stalin, 'but I am afraid it has come back to life. The Guild was once a trap for luring in enemy agents, but these people, whoever they are, have now turned it against us. I think you'll find they are the ones who killed Nagorski.'

'Why didn't you tell me any of this, Comrade Stalin?'

Stalin threw the lever which lay flush against the wall. The door swung open.

Beyond lay a room with a huge map of the Soviet Union on the wall. The heavy red velvet curtains had been drawn. Pekkala had never seen this place before. Men in a variety of military uniforms sat around a table. At the head of the table was one empty seat. There had been a murmur of talk in the room, but as soon as the door opened, it fell silent. Now all of the men were watching the space from which Stalin was about to emerge.

Before entering, Stalin turned to Pekkala. 'I did not tell you,' he said quietly, 'because I hoped I might be wrong. That does not seem to be the case, and it's why I am telling you now.' Then he stepped into the room and, a moment later, the door closed softly behind him.

Pekkala found himself alone in the passageway, with no idea where he was.

He retraced his steps to the stairs, then went down to the intersection. Before he reached it, all the lights went out. He realised they must have been on a timer, but where the switch was for that timer, Pekkala had no idea. At first, it was so dark inside the corridor that he felt as if he might as well have been struck blind. But slowly, as his eyes grew used to the blackness, he realised he could make out thin grey bands of light seeping under the bottoms of the trap doors spaced out along the passageway.

He could not read the yellow writing on the doors, so, sliding along with his back to the wall, he picked the first door he came to. Groping about on the wall, he found the lever and pulled.

The trap door clicked open.

Pekkala heard the sound of heels upon a marble floor and knew instantly he had emerged on to one of the main corridors of the Palace of Congresses, which adjoined the Kremlin Palace where Stalin's office was located. He stepped through the opening and almost collided with a woman wearing the mouse-grey skirt and black tunic of a Kremlin secretary. She was carrying a bundle of papers, but when she saw Pekkala appear like a ghost out of the wall, she screamed and the papers went straight up into the air.

'Well, I should be going,' said Pekkala, as the documents fluttered down around them. He smiled and nodded good-bye, then walked quickly away down the corridor.

'You forgot your gun again, didn't you?' asked Pekkala, as they drove towards the Nagorski facility.

'No, I didn't forget,' replied Kirov. 'I left it behind on purpose. We're only going to talk to those scientists. They won't give us any trouble.'

'You should always bring your gun with you!' shouted Pekkala. 'Pull over here!'

Obediently, Kirov brought the car to a halt. Then he turned in his seat to face Pekkala. 'What's up, Inspector?'

'Where is that lunch you made us?'

'In the boot. Why?'

'Follow me,' said Pekkala, as he got out of the car. From the boot, Pekkala removed the canvas satchel containing two sandwiches and some apples. Then he set off into a field beside the road, pausing to snap off a dead branch, about the size of a walking stick, from a tree beside the road.

'Where are you going with our food?'

'Stay there,' Pekkala called back. After he had gone a short way into the field, he stopped, jammed the branch into the ground, then removed an apple from the lunch bag and skewered it on to the end of the branch.

'We were going to eat that!' shouted Kirov.

Pekkala ignored him. He returned to where Kirov was standing, drew his Webley from its holster and handed it, butt first, to Kirov. He turned and pointed towards the apple. 'What we will be doing . . .' he began, then he flinched as the gun went off in Kirov's hand. 'For goodness' sake, Kirov! You must be careful. Take time to aim properly. There are many steps involved. Breathing. Stance. The way you grip the gun. It's going to take some time.'

'Yes, Inspector,' replied Kirov, meekly.

'Now,' said Pekkala, returning his attention to the apple. 'What? Where's it gone? Oh, damn! It's fallen off.' He strode back towards the stake, but had only gone a few paces when he noticed shreds of apple peel scattered across the ground. The apple appeared to have exploded, and it was a few more seconds before Pekkala finally got it into his head that Kirov had hit the apple with his first shot. He spun around and stared at Kirov.

'Sorry,' said Kirov. 'Did you have something else in mind?'

'Well,' growled Pekkala, 'that was a good start. But you mustn't get your hopes up. What we want is to be able to hit the target not just once, but every time. Or almost every time.' He fished another apple from the bag and stuck it on the end of the stick.

'What do you expect us to eat?' asked Kirov.

'Now don't go blasting away until I get back there,' ordered Pekkala as he strode towards Kirov. 'It is important to make a firm platform with your feet, and to grip the gun tightly but not too tightly. Now, the Webley is a well-balanced weapon, but it's got a hard kick, much greater than the Tokarev.'

Casually, Kirov raised the Webley and fired.

'Damn it, Kirov!' raged Pekkala. 'You've got to wait until you're ready!'

'I was ready,' replied Kirov.

Pekkala squinted at the stake. All that remained of the second apple was a cloud of white juice, diffusing in the air. Pekkala's mouth twitched. 'Stay there!' he said and went back into the field. This time he pulled up the branch, walked several paces further back and stuck it into the ground. Then he took a sandwich wrapped in brown wax paper from the bag and jammed it on to the stick.

'I'm not shooting my sandwich!' shouted Kirov.

Pekkala wheeled about. 'You won't? Or you *can't*?'

'If I hit that,' said Kirov, 'will you stop bothering me?'

'I certainly will,' agreed Pekkala.

'And you will admit that I'm a good shot?'

'Don't push your luck, Comrade Kirov.'

Three minutes later, the Emka was back on the road.

Pekkala slumped in the back, arms folded across his chest, feeling the warmth of the gun's cylinder radiating through his leather holster.

'You know,' said Kirov cheerfully, 'I have a certificate of merit from the Komsomol for target practice. It's hanging on my wall at home.'

'I must have missed that one,' mumbled Pekkala.

'It's in the living room,' said Kirov, 'right next to my music award.'

'You got an award for music?'

'For my rendition of "Farewell, Slavianka",' replied Kirov. He breathed in, stuck out his chest and began to sing, glancing in the mirror at his audience. 'Farewell, the land of the fathers . . .'

One raised eyebrow from Pekkala shut him up.

Machine gun fire echoed around the buildings of the Nagorski facility.

In the confined space of the Iron House, the percussion of each shell merged into a continuous, deafening snarl. To Pekkala, standing at the entrance, it was as if the air itself were being torn apart. Beside him stood Kirov, the two men waiting while the metal snake of bullets uncoiled from its green ammunition box, spitting a shower of flickering brass from the ejection port of the machine gun. Just when it seemed as if the sound would never end, the belt ran out and the gunfire ceased abruptly. Spent cartridges rang musically as they tumbled to the concrete floor.

Gorenko and Ushinsky set the gun aside, climbed to their feet and removed the cup-shaped noise protectors from their ears. A hazy wreath of gunsmoke hung about their heads.

The weapon was aimed at a pyramid of 100-litre metal barrels. The diesel fuel these barrels once contained had been replaced with sand to absorb the impact of the bullets. Now gaping tears showed in the metal and sand poured in streams from the holes, forming cones upon the floor like time marked in an hourglass.

Ushinsky held up a stop watch. 'Thirty-three seconds.'

'Better,' said Gorenko.

'Still not good enough,' replied Ushinsky. 'Nagorski would have been breathing down our necks . . .'

'Gentlemen,' said Pekkala, his voice resonating through the girders which supported the corrugated-iron roof.

Surprised, both scientists wheeled about to see where the voices had come from.

'Inspector!' exclaimed Ushinsky. 'Welcome back to the mad house.'

'What are you working on here?' asked Kirov.

'We are testing the rate of fire of the T-34's machine guns,' replied Ushinsky. 'It's not right yet.'

'It's close enough,' said Gorenko.

'If the Colonel was alive,' insisted Ushinsky, 'he'd never let you say a thing like that.'

Pekkala walked over to where the scientists were standing. He removed the paper from his pocket, unfolded it and held it out towards the two men. 'Can either of you tell me what this means?'

Both of them peered at the page.

'That's the Colonel's writing,' said Ushinsky.

Gorenko nodded. 'It's a formula.'

'A formula for what?' asked Pekkala.

Ushinsky shook his head. 'We're not chemists, Inspector.'

'That kind of thing is not our speciality,' agreed Gorenko.

'Is there anyone here who could tell us?' asked Kirov.

The scientists shook their heads.

Pekkala sighed with annoyance, thinking that they had come all this way for nothing. 'Let's go,' he said to Kirov.

As they turned to leave, the scientists began a whispered conversation.

Pekkala stopped. 'What is it, gentlemen?'

'Well . . .' began Ushinsky.

'Keep your mouth shut,' ordered Gorenko. 'Colonel Nagorski may be dead, but this is still his project and his rules should be obeyed!'

'It doesn't matter now!' yelled Ushinsky. He kicked an empty bullet cartridge across the floor. It skipped over the concrete, spinning away among the sleeping hulks of half-assembled tanks. 'None of it matters now! Can't you see?'

'Nagorski said . . .'

'Nagorski is gone!' bellowed Ushinsky. 'Everything we've done has been for nothing.'

'I thought the Konstantin Project was almost finished,' said Pekkala.

'Almost!' replied Ushinsky. 'Almost is not good enough.' He waved his arm across the assembly area. 'We might as well just throw these monsters on the junk heap!'

'One of these days,' Gorenko warned him, 'you're going to say something you'll regret.'

Ignoring his colleague, Ushinsky turned to the investigators. 'You'll need to speak with a man named Lev Zalka.'

Gorenko looked at the ground and shook his head. 'If the Colonel heard you say that name . . .'

'Zalka was part of the original team,' continued Ushinsky. 'He designed the V2 diesel. That's what we use in the tanks. But he's been gone for months. Nagorski fired him. They got into an argument.'

'An argument?' muttered Gorenko. 'Is that what you call it? Nagorski attacked him with a 40-millimetre wrench! The Colonel would have killed Zalka if he hadn't ducked. After that, Nagorski said that if anyone so much as mentioned Zalka's name, they would be thrown off the project.'

'What was this fight about?' asked Pekkala.

Both scientists shrugged uneasily.

'Zalka had wanted to install bigger turret hatches, as well as hatches underneath the hull.'

'Why?' asked Kirov. 'Wouldn't that make the tank more vulnerable?'

'Yes, it would,' replied Gorenko.

'But bigger hatches,' interrupted Ushinsky, 'would mean that the tank crew had a better chance of escaping if the engine caught fire or if the hull was breached.'

'Colonel Nagorski refused to consider it. For him, the machine came first.'

'And that's why your test drivers have been calling it the Red Coffin,' said Pekkala.

Gorenko shot an angry glance towards Ushinsky. 'I see that someone has been talking.'

'What does it matter now?' growled Ushinsky.

'Are you certain this is what Nagorski and Zalka were arguing about on that day?' asked Pekkala, anxious to avoid another argument between the two men.

'All I can tell you,' replied Gorenko, 'is that Zalka left the facility that day and he never came back.'

'Do you have any idea where we could find this man?' asked Kirov.

'He used to have an apartment on Prechistenka Street,' said Ushinsky, 'but that was back when he worked here. He may have moved since then. If anybody knows what that formula means, it's him.'

When Pekkala and Kirov left the building, Gorenko followed them out. 'I'm sorry, Inspectors,' he said. 'You'll have to forgive my colleague. He loses his temper a lot. He says things he doesn't mean.'

'It sounds like he meant them to me,' remarked Kirov.

'It's just that we had some bad news today.'

'What news is that?' asked Pekkala.

'Come. Let me show you.' He led them around to the back of the assembly building to where a T-34 had been parked at the edge of the trees. The machine had a large number 4 painted on the side of its turret. Pekkala's eye was drawn to a long, narrow scrape, which had cut down to the bare metal. The silver stripe passed along the length of the turret, neatly bisecting the number. 'They brought it back this morning.'

'Who did?' asked Pekkala.

'The Army,' Gorenko replied. 'They had it out on some secret field trial. We weren't allowed to know anything about it. And now it's ruined.'

'Ruined?' asked Kirov. 'It looks the same as all the others.'

Gorenko climbed up on to the flat section at the back of the tank and opened up the engine grille. He reached his hand into the engine and when he drew it out, his fingertips were smeared with what looked like grease. 'You know what this is?'

Pekkala shook his head.

'It's fuel,' explained Gorenko. 'Ordinary diesel fuel. At least that's what it is supposed to be. But it has been contaminated.'

'With what?'

'Bleach. It has destroyed the inner workings of the engine. The whole thing will have to be refitted, the fuel system drained, all hoses and feeds replaced. It needs a complete rebuild. Number 4 was Ushinksy's own special project. Each of us here had a favourite. We sort of adopted them. And Ushinsky is taking this hard.'

'Perhaps it was an accident,' suggested Kirov.

Gorenko shook his head. 'Whoever did this knew exactly how to wreck an engine. Not just damage it, you understand. *Destroy* it. There's no doubt in my mind, Inspectors. This was a deliberate act.' He jumped down from the tank, pulled a handkerchief from his pocket and wiped the fuel from his fingers. 'If you knew how hard he worked on this machine, you'd understand how he feels.'

'Is he right?' asked Pekkala. 'Is the whole project ruined?'

'No!' replied Gorenko. 'In a few months, as long as we can keep working on it, the T-34 should be ready. Even with Nagorski gone, the T-34 will still be an excellent machine, but there's a difference between excellence and perfection. The trouble with Ushinsky is that he needs everything to be perfect. As far as he's concerned, now that the Colonel is gone, any hope of perfection is out of reach. And I'll tell you what I've been telling Ushinsky since we first began this project. It would never have been perfect. There will always be something, like the rate of fire in those machine guns, which will just have to be good enough.'

'I understand,' said Pekkala. 'Tell him we took no offence.'

'If you could tell him yourself,' pleaded Gorenko. 'If you could just talk to him, tell him to choose his words more carefully, I think it would really help.'

'We don't have time now,' said Kirov.

'Call us at the office later,' suggested Pekkala. 'Right now, we need to find Zalka.'

'Maybe Ushinsky was right after all,' said Gorenko. 'Now that Nagorski is gone, we could use all the help we can get.'

One hour later, Kirov dropped Pekkala at the office.

'I'll put in a call to Lysenkova,' said Pekkala. 'I need to tell her she can stop searching for those White Guild agents. As of now, all our efforts should be focused on locating Zalka. Get down to the records office and see if you can find out where he lives. But don't try to bring him in on your own. We should assume that Zalka was the man in the woods. It looks like he had the motive for killing Nagorski, and the fact, that he would have known his way around the facility would explain why Samarin thought someone on the inside was responsible for the murder.'

While Kirov drove to the public records office, Pekkala went up to the office and called Lysenkova. Worried that NKVD might be listening in, he told her they needed to meet in person.

As soon as she arrived, Pekkala explained about the White Guild agents.

'Did you have any luck deciphering the formula, Inspector?' asked Lysenkova.

'That's the other reason for tracking down Zalka,' replied Pekkala. 'If he's still alive, he may be the only one who can help us.'

Lysenkova stood. 'I'll get started right away. And thank you for trusting me, Inspector. There are many who don't. I'm sure you've heard the rumours.'

'There are always rumours.'

'Well, you should know that some of them are true.'

Pekkala raised his head and looked her in the eye. 'I heard that you denounced your own parents.'

Lysenkova nodded. 'Yes, I did.'

'Why?'

'Because my father told me to. It was my only way out.'

'Out of where?'

'A place you know well, Inspector. I am talking about Siberia.'

Pekkala stared at her. 'But I thought they were sent to Siberia because you denounced them. You mean you were already there?'

'That's right. My mother had already been sentenced to twenty years as a class 59 criminal.'

'Your mother? What did she do?'

'My mother,' explained Lysenkova, 'was the only female supervisor on the production staff of the Leningrad Steam Turbine Factory. The factory was to be one of the great industrial triumphs of the 1920s, a place where foreign dignitaries could be brought to show the efficiency of the Soviet Union. Stalin himself had arranged to visit the factory on its opening day. The trouble was that construction had fallen behind schedule, but Stalin still refused to change the date of his visit. So at a time when the factory should have been operational, they had not yet produced a single tractor. In fact, the main construction floor didn't even have a roof yet. And that was exactly where Stalin had announced he would meet the workers of the factory. So, roof or no roof, that's where the meeting was held. It was raining the day he arrived. My mother ordered a podium to be built so that Stalin could stand above the crowd and look out over the heads of the workers.

There was also a tarpaulin to shield him from the rain. The day before his visit, political advisers had arrived at the factory. Above the podium, they hung a banner.' Lysenkova spread her arms above her head, as if to frame the text between her hands. '"Long Live Stalin, The Best Friend Of All Soviet Workers". But there was no way to shelter the workers from the rain, so they all stood there getting wet. They stood for an hour and a half before Stalin even arrived. By then, the letters of the banner had started to run. Red ink was dripping off the banner. It made puddles on the concrete floor. When Stalin walked up to the podium, everybody clapped, as the political advisers had instructed them to do. The trouble was, nobody knew when to stop. They all assumed that Stalin would make some gesture, or start talking, or something, anything, to indicate when the clapping should cease. But when the applause started, Stalin just stood there. Of course, it was obvious he must have been furious that the factory was only half built, but he showed no anger. He just smiled at everybody getting soaked. Red droplets fell from the banner. The clapping continued. The workers were too afraid to quit.

'This went on for twenty minutes. My mother was in charge of the floor. That was her job. Nobody else was doing anything. She began to think it might be her responsibility to get the meeting started. The longer this clapping went on, the more convinced she became that, since no one else was prepared to act, she ought to be the one.'

Lysenkova brought her hands slowly together and then drew them apart and kept them there. 'So she stopped clapping. That was the moment Stalin had been waiting for, but not so that he could start the meeting. He looked at my mother. That's all. Just looked at her. Then he got down from the podium, and he and his entourage drove away. No one had said a word. It was still pouring. The letters on the banner had completely washed away. One week later, my mother, my father and I were all shipped out to the Special Settlement of Dalstroy-Seven.'

'The settlement,' whispered Pekkala. And then he went blind as an image of that place exploded behind his eyes.

Dalstroy-Seven was a collection of half a dozen log houses, poorly and hurriedly built, bunched at the edge of a stream in the valley of Krasnagolyana.

The site was less than ten kilometres from Pekkala's camp. He had arrived in the valley five years before. It was early summer then, which gave him plenty of time to work on the cabin before the first snow of autumn appeared. His cabin had been solidly constructed in the style known as zemlyanka, *in which half of the living space was underground and the gaps between the logs caulked with mud and grass.*

But the inhabitants of Dalstroy-Seven had shown up just after the first frost and there had been no time to build adequate shelters before the winter set in.

Special Settlement people were a subsection of the Gulag camp system, in which husbands and wives might all be shipped off to different camps, and the children sent to orphanages if they were too young to work. Special Settlements were shipped out to Siberia as complete families, dumped in the forest or out on the tundra and left to fend for themselves until such time as they might be required as labour in the Gulag camps. Until then, the settlements were nothing more than prisons without walls. Sometimes these settlements lasted. More often, when guards arrived to take away the prisoners, all they found were ghost villages, with no trace left of the people who had once lived there.

Dalstroy settlement fell under the jurisdiction of a notorious camp named Mamlin-Three on the other side of the valley. The twenty-odd inhabitants of Dalstroy-Seven were city folk, to judge from the mistakes they made – building the cabins too close to the river, not knowing it would flood in springtime, making their chimneys too short which meant the smoke would blow back into the cabins. With winter already descending, like a white tidal wave sweeping through the valley, the inmates of Dalstroy were as good as dead.

Pekkala saw himself as he was then, a barely human presence draped in the rags he had worn into the forest, staring at them from his hiding place: a rocky outcrop that looked down upon the valley where they had been abandoned with no instructions other than simply to survive until the spring.

He stepped back into the shadows, knowing there was nothing he could do for them. He did not dare to show himself, since he was well beyond the boundaries of the Borodok camp, of which he was officially an inmate. With the task of marking trees for cutting, he was allowed to roam within the borders of the Borodok sector, but never beyond. If news reached Borodok that he had been seen in an area designated for Mamlin-Three, on the other side of the valley, they would send in troops to execute him for the crime of trespassing.

Unlike the camp at Mamlin-Three, Borodok was a full-scale logging operation, processing trees from the moment they were cut until they emerged as kiln-dried boards, ready to be shipped to the west.

What went on at Mamlin-Three was kept a secret, but Pekkala had heard on his arrival at Borodok that to be a prisoner at Mamlin was considered worse than death. That was why convicts bound for that place were never told where they were going until the moment they arrived.

Pekkala's only company in this forbidden zone had been a man who had escaped from the Mamlin-Three camp. His name was Tatischev, and he had been a sergeant in one of the Tsar's Cossack regiments. After his escape, search parties had combed the forest but never found Tatischev, for the simple reason that he had hidden where they were least likely to search – within sight of the Mamlin-Three camp. Here, he had remained, scratching out an existence even more spartan than Pekkala's.

Pekkala and Tatischev met twice a year in a clearing on the border of the Borodok and Mamlin territorial boundaries. Tatischev was a cautious man, and judged it too dangerous to meet more often than that.

It was from Tatischev that Pekkala discovered exactly what was happening at Mamlin. He learned that the camp had been set aside as a research centre on human subjects. Low-pressure experiments were carried out in order to determine the effects on human tissue of high-altitude exposure. Men were submerged in ice water, revived and then submerged again to determine how long a downed pilot might survive after ditching in the arctic seas above Murmansk. Some prisoners had anti-freeze injected into their hearts. Others woke up on operating tables to find their limbs had been removed. It was a place of horrors, Tatischev told him, where the human race had sunk to its ultimate depths.

On the third year of their meetings, Pekkala showed up at the clearing to find Tatischev's marrowless and chamfered bones scattered about the clearing, and metal grommets from his boots among the droppings of the wolves who had devoured him.

Pekkala returned to Dalstroy-Seven at the end of winter. The snow had already begun to melt. Two nights before, he had awakened to what he thought was the sound of ice breaking in the river, but as the sharp cracking noise echoed through the forest, Pekkala realised that it was gunfire coming from the direction of the Dalstroy-Seven settlement.

The next day, Pekkala made his way there.

Seeing no smoke from the chimneys, he went down to the settlement. One after the other, he opened the doors and stepped into the dark.

Inside the cabins, people lay strewn around the room like dolls thrown by an angry child. A gauze of frost covered their bodies. They had all been shot. The cratered wounds of bullet holes stared like third eyes from the foreheads of the dead.

With hands rag-bound against the cold, Pekkala gathered up a few of the spent cartridges. All were army issue, all less than a year old, matching in year and make. Then Pekkala knew that guards from the Mamlin-Three camp must have carried out the killing. None of the nomad bands in this region would have had access to such recent stocks of ammunition. Pekkala wondered why the guards would have bothered to come all this way to liquidate the settlement when the winter would have killed them anyway.

He touched the emaciated and stone-hard cheek of a young woman who had died sitting by the stove. It seemed she had been too weak even to get up from the chair when the killers burst into the cabin. In the billowing heat of his breath, the white crystals melted from her hair, revealing red strands, like shreds of copper wire. It was as if, for one brief moment, life had returned to the corpse.

Two weeks later, when spring floods swept through the valley, the buildings and all they had contained were swept away.

'How did you manage to escape?' asked Pekkala.

'Just after we finished building our shelters,' replied Lysenkova, 'my father sat me down and made me write out a statement that he had killed two guards on our way out to the settlement. The truth was, two guards had gone missing, but they ran away on their own. No one in our group had killed them. We didn't have any paper or pencils. We used a piece of birch bark and the burned end of a stick. I was ten, old enough to know that none of what I was writing was true. I asked him if he wasn't going to get in trouble if somebody believed what I was writing and he said it didn't matter. "What are they going to do?" he asked. "Send me to Siberia?"'

'How well do you remember your father?' asked Pekkala.

Lysenkova shrugged. 'Some things are clearer than others. He had gold teeth. The front ones, top and bottom. I remember that. He had been kicked by a horse when he was young. Every time he smiled, it looked as if he had taken a bite out of the sun.'

'What happened after you wrote the letter?'

'He took me through the woods to the gates of the Borodok camp. We barely spoke on that journey, even though it took several hours to reach the camp. When we got to Borodok, he stuffed a knotted handkerchief in my pocket and then he knocked on the gate. By the time the guards opened up, he had disappeared back into the woods. I knew he wasn't coming back. When the guards asked me where I'd come from, I showed them the letter I'd written. Then they brought me into the camp.

'On my first night there, I took out the handkerchief he had given me. When I undid the knot, I saw what I first thought were kernels of corn. But then I realised they were teeth. His gold teeth. He had pulled them out. I could see the marks of pliers in the gold. They were the only things of value he had left. I used them to buy food in the camp in those first months. I would have starved to death without them.

'Eventually, I found a job delivering buckets of food to the workers who processed logs for the camp lumber mill. The job entitled me to rations and that is how I survived. After five years, they sent me back to Moscow to live in an orphanage. I don't know what happened to my parents, but I know now what my father knew back then, which was they had no chance of coming out alive.'

As her words sank in, Pekkala finally understood why the inhabitants of Dalstroy-Seven had been executed. Lysenkova's father had given his daughter a way out, but only at the cost of his own life. What Lysenkova's father had not reckoned on was that the camp authorities decided not only to punish him, but to obliterate the entire settlement. By the time the runaway guards were caught, the liquidations had already been carried out.

'So you see, Inspector,' said Lysenkova, 'I have learned what it takes to survive. That includes not caring about rumours. But I wanted you to know the truth.'

As he walked her to the door, Pekkala knew there was no point in telling the Major what he'd seen. She already knew what she needed to know, but he was glad they had chosen to help her.

A bell rang.

Pekkala sat up in bed, blinking the sleep from his eyes. He sat there, dazed and just as he had convinced himself that he had dreamed the sound of the bell, it came again, loud and clattering. Someone was down in the street. There were buzzers for each apartment. Every time this had happened in the past, the person pressing the bell had either pressed the wrong one or was looking to be let into the building after locking themselves out.

He grunted and lay back down, knowing that whoever it was would try another buzzer if they got no answer from him.

But the bell rang again and kept ringing, someone's thumb jammed against the buzzer. The spit dried up in Pekkala's mouth as he realised that there had been no mistake. The persistent ringing of a doorbell in the middle of the night could only mean one thing – that they had finally come to arrest him. Not even a Shadow Pass would save him now.

Pekkala dressed and hurried down the stairs. He thought about that suitcase Babayaga kept ready in the corner of her room and he wished he had packed one for himself. Reaching the dingy foyer, lit by a single naked bulb, he unlocked the main door. As he grasped the rattly brass door knob, a hazy calculation which had been forming in his mind now came into perfect focus.

He would probably never know what line he'd crossed to bring this down upon himself. Perhaps it was one too many questions that day he followed Stalin through the secret passageways. Perhaps Stalin had decided he should never have revealed what happened to the White Guild agents and was now in the process of covering all trace of his mistake.

The reason he would never know was because he knew he would not live long enough to find out. They had already exiled him to Siberia once. They would not do the same again. There was no doubt in Pekkala's mind that he would be shot against the wall of the Lubyanka prison, probably before the sun came up today. Suddenly, he realised that he had resigned himself to this a long time ago.

Pekkala opened the door. He did not hesitate. They would only have kicked it down.

But there was no squad of NKVD men, waiting to take him away. Instead, there was only Kirov. 'Good evening, Inspector,' he said cheerfully. 'Or should I say good morning? I thought this time I'd come and visit you.'

Before the expression could change on Kirov's face, Pekkala's fist swung out and knocked him in the head.

As if executing part of a complicated dance, Kirov took one step sideways, then one step backward and finally sprawled on the pavement.

A moment later, Kirov sat up, rubbing the side of his face. 'What was that for?' A thin thread of blood unravelled from his nose.

Pekkala was just as surprised as Kirov by what had happened. 'What are you doing here in the middle of the night?' he demanded in a hoarse whisper.

'Well, I'm sorry to have interrupted your sleep,' Kirov replied, climbing to his feet, 'but you told me . . .'

'I don't care about my sleep!' snarled Pekkala. 'You know what it means, coming to my door in the middle of the night!'

'You mean you thought . . .'

'Of course that's what I thought!'

'But Inspector, nobody's going to arrest you!'

'You don't know that, Kirov,' snapped Pekkala. 'I've tried to teach you how dangerous our job can be, and it's time you learned that we have as much to fear from those we're working for as from those we're working against. Now don't just stand there. Come in!'

Blotting his nose with a handkerchief, Kirov entered the building.

'Do you know this is the first time I've seen your apartment? I never understood why you chose to live on this side of town.'

'Hush!' whispered Pekkala. 'People are sleeping.'

When they finally reached the apartment, Pekkala put water on to boil for tea, cooking it on a small gas Primus stove which he lit with a cigarette lighter. The blue gas flame flickered beneath the battered aluminium pot. He sat down on the end of his bed and pointed to the only chair in the room, inviting Kirov to sit. 'Well, what have you come to tell me?'

'What I came to tell you,' replied Kirov, as he looked around the room with undisguised curiosity, 'is that I have found Zalka. At least I think I have.'

'Well, have you found him or haven't you?'

'I went to the address you gave me,' explained Kirov. 'He wasn't there. He moved out months ago. The caretaker said Zalka had gone to work at the swimming pool near Bolotnia square.'

'I didn't know there was a swimming pool there.'

'That's the thing, Inspector. There isn't one. There used to be. The pool was part of a large bathhouse which got closed down years ago. Then the building was taken over by the Institute of Clinical and Experimental Science.'

'So the caretaker must have been wrong.'

'Well, I put in a call to the Institute, just to be thorough. I asked if they had anyone named Zalka working there. The woman at the other end told me the names of all employees at the institute were classified and hung up on me. I tried calling them back but no one would answer the phone. But what would he be doing at a Medical Institute? He's an engineer, not a doctor.'

'We'll find out first thing in the morning,' said Pekkala.

Kirov stood and began to pace around the room. 'All right, Inspector, I give up. Why on earth are you living in this dump?'

'Have you considered that perhaps I choose to spend my money on other things?'

'Of course I've considered it, but I know you don't spend it on clothes or food or anything else I can think of, so if it doesn't go on rent, where does it go?'

It was a while before Pekkala answered.

In the silence, they could hear the rustle of water boiling in the pot.

'The money goes to Paris,' he said finally.

'Paris?' Kirov's eyes narrowed. 'You mean you're sending your wages to Ilya?'

Pekkala got up to make the tea.

'How did you even find out where she lives?'.

'That's what I do,' replied Pekkala. 'I find people.'

'But Ilya thinks you're dead! As far as she knows, you've been dead for years.'

'I realise that,' muttered Pekkala.

'So who does she think the money is coming from?'

'The funds are channelled through a bank in Helsinki. She believes they are being provided through the will of the headmistress of the school where she taught.'

'And what does the headmistress have to say about this?'

'Nothing,' replied Pekkala, as he sprinkled a pinch of black tea into the pot. 'She was shot by Red Guards the day before I left Tsarskoye Selo.'

'But why, Inspector? Ilya is married! She even has a child!'

Pekkala crashed the pot down on to the stove. Hot tea splashed on his shirt. 'Don't you think I know that, Kirov? Don't you realise I think about that all the time? But I do not love her out of hope. I do not love her out of possibility.'

'Then what is driving you to this madness?'

'I do not call it madness,' said Pekkala, his voice barely above a whisper.

'Well, I do!' Kirov told him. 'You might as well be throwing your money into the fire.'

'It is mine to throw,' replied Pekkala, 'and I don't care what she does with it.' He set about brewing a fresh pot of tea.

*

The two men stood outside the Institute of Clinical and Experimental Science. The windows of this old bathhouse had been bricked up and the bricks painted the same pale yellow colour as the rest of the building.

'Did you bring your gun this time?' asked Pekkala.

Kirov held open one flap of his coat, showing a pistol tucked into a shoulder holster.

'Good,' said Pekkala, 'because you might need to use it today.'

They had arrived at the Institute just after eight in the morning, only to find that it did not open until nine. In spite of the fact that the building was closed, they could hear noises inside. Kirov banged on the heavy wooden door, but no one answered. Eventually, they gave up and decided to wait.

To pass the time, they ordered breakfast in a café across the road from the Institute. The café had only just opened. Most of the chairs were still upside-down on top of the tables.

The waitress brought them hard-boiled eggs, black rye bread and slabs of ham, the edges still glistening with the salt used to cure the meat. They drank tea without milk from heavy white cups which had no handles.

'Waiting for the Monster Shop to open up?' asked the woman. She was tall and square-shouldered, with her hair pulled back in a knot and slightly arching eyebrows that gave her a look of critical appraisal.

'The what?' asked Kirov.

The woman nodded towards the Institute.

'Why do they call it that?' asked Pekkala.

'You'll see for yourself if you go in there,' said the woman as she headed back into the kitchen.

'The Monster Shop,' muttered Kirov. 'What kind of a place deserves a name like that?'

'I'd rather we didn't find out on an empty stomach,' replied Pekkala as he gathered up his knife and fork. 'Now eat.'

A few minutes later, Kirov set down his knife and fork loudly on the edges of his plate. 'There you go again,' he said.

'Mmm?' Pekkala looked up, mouth full.

'You're just . . . inhaling your food!'

Pekkala swallowed. 'What else am I supposed to do with it?'

'I've tried to educate you.' Kirov sighed loudly. 'But you just don't seem to take any notice. I've seen the way you eat those meals I cook for you. I've tried being subtle.'

Pekkala looked down at his plate. The food was almost gone. He was pleased with the job he had made of it. 'What's the problem, Kirov?'

'The problem, Inspector, is that you don't savour your food. You don't appreciate the miracle,' he picked up a boiled egg and held it up, 'of nourishment.'

'It's not a Fabergé egg,' said Pekkala. 'It's just a regular egg. And besides, what if someone hears you going on like that? You are a major of the NKVD. You have an image to uphold, which doesn't include the loud and public adoration of your breakfast!'

Kirov looked around. 'What do you mean, "if someone hears me"? So what if they can hear me? What are they going to think – that I can't shoot straight?'

220

'All right,' said Pekkala, 'I admit I owe you an apology for that but . . .'

'Forgive me for saying so, Inspector, but this talk about upholding an image – it's no wonder you never get any women.'

'What's that got to do with anything?'

'The fact that you are asking me this question . . .' he paused, 'is the answer to your question.'

Pekkala wagged his fork at Kirov. 'I'm going to eat my breakfast now, and you can just carry on being strange if you want. The miracle of nourishment!' he spluttered.

After their meal, they left the café and walked across the road to the Institute.

Kirov tried to open the door but it was still locked. Once more, he pounded on it with his fist.

Finally, the door opened just enough to let the head of an elderly woman appear. She had a big, square face and a blunt nose. A heavy, acrid smell, like sweat or ammonia, wafted out of the building. 'This is a government institute!' she told them. 'It is not open to the public.'

Kirov held out his NKVD pass book. 'We are not the public.'

'We are exempt from routine inspection,' protested the woman.

'This is not routine,' said Pekkala.

The door opened a little further, but the woman still blocked the entrance. 'What is this about?' she asked.

'We are investigating a murder,' said Pekkala.

The colour ran out of her face, what little had been there to begin with. 'Our cadavers are supplied to us by the Central Hospital! Every one of them is cleared before . . .'

'Cadavers?' interrupted Pekkala.

Kirov winced. 'Is that what the smell is?'

'We are looking for a man named Zalka,' continued Pekkala.

'Lev Zalka?' Her voice rose as she spoke his name. 'Well, why didn't you say so?'

Finally, she allowed them to come in and they stepped into what had once been the main foyer of the bathhouse. Tiles covered the floors and huge pillars supported the roof. To Pekkala, it looked more like an ancient temple than a place where people went to swim.

'I am Comrade Dr Dobriakova,' said the woman, nodding at each man in turn. She wore a starched white jacket, like those worn by doctors in the state hospitals, and thick, flesh coloured tights which made her legs look like wet clay. She did not ask the men their names, but wasted no time ushering them down the long main corridor. In rooms leading off on either side, the two inspectors saw animals in cages – monkeys, cats and dogs. From those rooms came the odour they had smelled in the street – the sour reek of animals in captivity.

'What happens to these animals?' asked Kirov.

'They are used for research,' replied Dr Dobriakova, without turning around.

'And afterwards?' asked Pekkala.

'There is no afterwards,' replied the doctor.

As she spoke, Pekkala glimpsed the pale hands of a chimpanzee gripping the bars of its prison.

At the end of the corridor, they arrived at a door, painted cornflower blue, on which Pekkala could still read the word

'Bath', painted in yellow. Here, Dr Dobriakova turned and faced them. 'It does not surprise me,' she said in a low voice, 'to learn that Comrade Zalka is involved in something illegal. I have always suspected him as a subversive. He is drunk most of the time.' She breathed in, ready to say more, but paused when she saw the two men draw their guns. 'Do you really think that's necessary?' she asked, staring at the weapons.

'We hope not,' replied Pekkala.

The woman cleared her throat. 'You should prepare yourself for what you see in here,' she said.

Before either of the men could ask why, Dr Dobriakova swung the door wide. 'Come along!' she ordered.

They entered a high-roofed chamber, in the centre of which was a swimming pool. Above it, supported by pillars like the ones they had seen when they first walked in, was a balcony that overlooked the pool. The warm, damp air smelled musty, like dead leaves in the autumn.

The water in the pool was almost black, not clear or glassy green, the way Pekkala had expected it to be. And in the middle of this pool was the head of a man, floating as if detached from its body.

The head spoke. 'I was wondering when you would show up.' Then he held up a bottle and, with the other hand, twisted out a cork. As he did so, the bottle's paper label, bearing the bright orange triangle of the State Vodka Monopoly, came unstuck from the glass and slithered back into the pool. The man took a long drink and smacked his lips with satisfaction.

'Disgraceful!' hissed Dr Dobriakova. 'It's not even lunchtime and you are already halfway through a bottle!'

'Leave me alone, you freak of nature,' said the man.

'You must be Professor Zalka,' said Pekkala.

Zalka lifted the bottle in a toast. 'And you must be the police.'

'What are you doing in there?' asked Kirov.

At that moment, the blue door opened and a woman in a white nurse's uniform walked in. She stopped, surprised to see two strangers in the bathhouse.

'These men are from the government,' explained Dr Dobriakova. 'They are investigating a murder, in which this imbecile,' she jabbed a finger towards Zalka, 'has been involved!'

'We merely want to speak with Professor Zalka,' said Kirov.

'You don't look as if you came to talk,' replied Zalka, nodding at the guns.

Pekkala turned to Kirov. 'I guess we can put these away.'

The two men holstered their weapons.

'Your time is up, Lev,' said the nurse.

'And I was just getting comfortable,' he grumbled, as he made his way towards the edge of the pool.

'Why is that pool so dark?' asked Kirov.

'The water is maintained with the correct balance of tannins for the research subjects.'

Kirov blinked at her. 'Subjects?'

Zalka had reached the edge of the pool, where the water was only knee deep. At first glance, his pale and naked body appeared to be covered with dozens of gaping wounds. From these wounds oozed thin trickles of blood. It took a moment for Pekkala to realise that these wounds were actually leeches, which had attached to his body and hung in bloated tassels from his arms and legs. As he floated in the shallow water, Zalka began plucking the leeches from his skin and throwing them back into the centre of the pool. They landed with a splat and vanished into the murky liquid.

'Careful!' warned the nurse. 'They are delicate creatures.'

'You are a delicate creature,' replied Zalka. 'These,' he snatched another leech from his chest and flung it into the pool, 'are the inventions of the same twisted god that invented Dr Dobriakova.'

'As I've told you many times already, Comrade Zalka,' replied Dr Dobriakova, going red in the face, 'leeches play a valuable role in medical science.'

'So will you when they lay you out on an autopsy slab.'

'I should dismiss you!' shouted the doctor, rising up on the tips of her toes. Her voice echoed around the pillars. 'And if I could find anyone else who would do this work, I certainly would!'

'But you won't dismiss me,' smirked Zalka, 'because you can't find anyone else.'

Dr Dobriakova's mouth was open, ready to carry on the fight, when Pekkala interrupted.

'Professor Zalka,' he said, 'we have a serious matter to discuss with you.'

'By all means,' replied Zalka.

Pekkala turned to see the nurse holding out a tangle of metal hoops and leather straps, which he realised was a leg brace.

'That's yours?' asked Kirov.

'Unfortunately, yes,' replied Zalka. 'The only time I don't think about it is when I'm floating in this pool.'

'How long have you worn a brace?' asked Pekkala.

'Since July 10th, 1914,' replied Zalka. 'So long ago that I can't even remember what it feels like to walk without it.'

Pekkala and Kirov looked at each other, realising that whoever they had chased through the forest on the day Nagorski died, it wasn't Lev Zalka.

'How do you remember the date so precisely?' asked Pekkala.

'Because the day I strapped on that contraption was exactly one month after a car lost control in the French Grand Prix, skidded off the track and right into the side of me.'

'The 1914 Grand Prix,' said Pekkala. 'Nagorski won that race.'

'Of course he did,' replied Zalka. 'I was his chief mechanic. I was standing at our pit stop when the car slammed into me.'

Now Pekkala remembered that Nagorski had mentioned the accident in which his chief mechanic had been badly hurt.

'If you wouldn't mind helping,' said Zalka, his arms still raised towards them.

While Pekkala and Kirov supported him, the nurse handed Zalka a towel, which the crippled man wrapped around his waist. Then, with Zalka's arms around their shoulders, they walked him to a chair. Once he was seated, the nurse gave him the brace, and he went through the process of strapping it to his left leg. Where the leather straps crossed over, the hair on Zalka's leg had been worn away, leaving pale stripes in the flesh. The muscles of his withered thigh and calf were barely half the size of those on his right leg.

Dobriakova stood back and watched, arms folded. Her face was set in a frown which seemed to be permanently carved into the corners of her mouth and eyes.

Where the leeches had been on Zalka's arms and chest, his skin showed grape-sized bull's-eye welts. In the centre of each one was a tiny red dot, where the leech had been attached. All over his body, like freckles, were the marks where other leeches had dug into his skin.

'Are you ready for your meal now?' asked the nurse.

Zalka looked up at her and smiled. 'Marry me,' he pleaded.

She gave him a swat on the head and went out through the blue doors.

'Inspectors,' said Dobriakova, scowling at Zalka, 'I'll leave you to question this criminal!'

When she had gone, Zalka sighed with relief. 'Better you with your guns than that woman with her moods.'

'Zalka,' asked Kirov, his voice a mixture of awe and disgust, 'how can you do this?'

'Do what, Inspector?' replied Zalka.

Kirov pointed at the dingy water. 'There! That!'

'Healthy leeches require a living host,' explained Zalka, 'although preferably one who's not intoxicated. As I tend to be, these days.'

'I'm not talking about them. I'm talking about you!'

'I don't have many options for employment, Inspector, but for one hour a day in the pool I make as much as I would in a nine-hour shift at a factory. That is, if I could get work at a factory. What I make here gives me enough time to carry on with my own research, a line of work for which I am, at the moment, tragically undercompensated.'

'Aren't you worried about catching some kind of disease?'

'Unlike humans,' said Zalka, 'leeches don't carry disease.' He reached around to the back of his head, where he discovered another leech buried in his hair. As he slid his thumbnail under the place where the leech had attached itself to his skin, the leech curled around his thumb. He held it up admiringly. 'They are very deliberate creatures. They drink blood and they have sex. You have to admire their sense of purpose.' Now his face became suddenly tense. 'But you did not come to talk about leeches. You came to talk about Nagorski.'

'That is correct,' said Pekkala, 'and until two minutes ago, you were our prime suspect for his murder.'

'I heard about what happened. I'd be lying if I told you I was sad to hear he's gone. After all, it's because of Nagorski that I have to bleed for a living, instead of designing engines, which is what I should be doing. But I'm better off now. The way Nagorski treated me was worse than anything those leeches ever did.'

'Why were you kicked off the Konstantin Project?' asked Pekkala. 'What happened between you and Nagorski?'

'We used to be friends,' he began. 'In our days of racing cars, we were together all the time. But then I was injured, and the war came along. After the armistice, Nagorski tracked me down in Paris. He told me about his idea, which eventually became the Konstantin Project. He said he needed help designing the engine. For a long time, we were a team. Designing the V2 engine was the best work I've ever done.'

'What went wrong?'

'What went wrong,' explained Zalka, 'is that Nagorski's facility had become like an island. There were bunk houses for us to sleep in, a mess hall, a machine shop so well equipped that there were tools in there which none of us could even identify. The idea was that we would be able to get on with the project undisturbed by government inspections, meddling bureaucrats or any of the daily concerns which might have eaten up our time. Nagorski dealt with the outside world, while we were left alone to work. What we didn't realise was that out there in the world, Nagorski was taking credit not only for his work but for ours as well.

'Was he always like that?' asked Pekkala.

Zalka shook his head. 'Nagorski was a good man before the Konstantin Project took over his life. He was generous. He loved his family. He didn't wrap himself in secrets. But once the project had begun, he turned into something else. I barely recognised him any more, and neither did his wife and son.'

'So what happened between you was an argument over the engine?' Pekkala was trying to understand.

'No,' replied Zalka. 'What happened was that Nagorski's design virtually guaranteed that the tank crew would be burnt alive if any kind of fire broke out in the main compartment or the engine.'

'I heard,' said Pekkala.

'I wanted to change that, even if it did weaken the hull by a small margin. But Nagorski would not even discuss it.' In frustration, Zalka raised his hands and let them fall again. 'How perfectly Russian – that the machine we build to defend ourselves becomes as dangerous to us as it is for our enemies!'

'Is this why Nagorski fired you from the project?' asked Pekkala.

'I wasn't fired. I quit. And there were other reasons, too.'

'Such as?' asked Kirov.

'I discovered that Nagorski was intending to steal the plans for the T-34 suspension system.'

'Steal them?'

'Yes,' Zalka nodded. 'From the Americans. The design for the suspension is known as a Christie Mechanism. The wheels are fitted on to trailing suspension arms with concentric double coil springs for the leading bogies . . .'

Pekkala held up his hand. 'I will take your word for it, Professor Zalka.'

'We had been working on a design of our own,' continued Zalka, 'but Nagorski's meddling had put us so far behind schedule that we weren't going to meet the deadline for going into production. Nagorski panicked. He decided we would go with the Christie Mechanism. He also decided we would say nothing about this to Stalin, figuring that by the time the design was approved, nobody would care, as long as it worked.'

'What did you do?' asked Pekkala.

'I confronted him. I said how dangerous it was to keep information from Stalin. He told me to keep my mouth shut. That was when I decided to quit and, in return, he saw to it that I couldn't find another place to do my work. No one would team up with me. No one would even come close! Except them,' he jerked his chin towards the leeches in the pool.

'But you said you still do research,' said Pekkala.

'That's right.'

'And what happens to your work?' asked Pekkala.

'It piles up on my desk,' replied Zalka bitterly, 'page after page, because there is nothing else I can do with it.'

'That reminds me,' said Pekkala, removing the equation from his coat pocket. 'We were wondering if you could tell us what this is. It may have something to do with Nagorski's death.'

Carefully, Zalka took the brittle paper from Pekkala's hand. He stared at it intently as the meaning unravelled in his head. At one point, he laughed sharply. 'Nagorski,' he muttered and kept reading. A moment later, Zalka raised his head. 'It is a recipe,' he told them.

'A recipe for what?'

'Oil.'

'That's it?' said Kirov. 'Just oil?'

'Oh, no,' replied Zalka, 'not just oil. Motor oil. And not just any motor oil, either. This is a special low-viscosity motor oil for use in the V2 engine.'

'And are you sure this is Nagorski's writing?'

Zalka nodded. 'Even if it wasn't, I could still tell this belonged to Nagorski.'

'Why?'

'Because of what's not there. See?' He pointed to a batch of figures. The numbers seemed to gather around his finger tip like iron filings around a magnet. 'The polymer sequence is interrupted at this point. He left it out on purpose. If you tried to recreate this formula in a lab, all you'd get would be sludge.'

'Where is the rest of the formula?'

Zalka tapped a finger against his temple. 'He kept it in his head. I told you he didn't trust anyone.'

'Could you complete these equations?' asked Pekkala.

'Of course,' replied Zalka, 'if you gave me a pencil and ten minutes to work out what's missing.'

'What's the point of low-viscosity motor oil?' asked Kirov.

Zalka smiled. 'At thirty degrees below zero, normal motor oil will begin to thicken. At fifty degrees below zero, it becomes useless. What that means, Inspectors, is that in the middle of a Russian winter, you can have an entire army of machines which suddenly comes to a stop.' He held up the piece of paper. 'But that wouldn't happen with this oil. I'll give Nagorski this much. He was certainly planning for the worst.'

'Is this formula valuable enough for someone to have killed him over it?' asked Pekkala.

Zalka narrowed his eyes. 'I don't think so,' he said. 'This simply represents a design decision. The recipe itself is not unknown.'

'Then why keep it a secret?'

'It's not the formula he was trying to keep secret. It's the decision to put it to use. Look,' sighed Zalka, 'I don't know why Nagorski was murdered, or who did it, but I can tell you that he must have known the person who killed him.'

'Why do you say that?'

'Because Nagorski never went anywhere without a gun in his pocket and that means he didn't just know the person who killed him. He must have trusted them to let the killer get that close.'

'Who did Nagorski trust?'

'As far as I know, there is only one person who fits that description, and that's his driver, Maximov. Nobody got to Nagorski without getting past Maximov, and believe me, nobody got past Maximov.'

'We have spoken with Maximov,' said Pekkala.

'Then you'll know Nagorski didn't hire him for his witty conversation. He hired Maximov because the man used to be an assassin.'

'A what?'

'He was an agent for the Tsar,' explained Zalka. 'Nagorski told me so himself.'

'That would explain why he didn't answer any of my questions,' said Pekkala, and suddenly he remembered something Rasputin had once told him, on that winter's night when he came knocking on the door.

'There are many others like us,' Rasputin had said, 'each one entrusted to a different task – investigators, lovers, assassins, each one a stranger to the other. Only the Tsar knows us all.' At the time, Pekkala had thought it was just the ramblings of a drunk, but now he realised that Rasputin had been telling the truth.

'It also explains why there was nothing on him in the old police records,' added Kirov.

The door opened and the nurse came in with a tray, on which sat a plate covered by a metal dome.

'Ah, good!' Zalka held out his arms.

The nurse handed him the tray. 'Just the way you like it,' she said.

Zalka set the tray carefully on his lap and removed the metal dome. A puff of steam wafted up into his face and he breathed it in as if it were perfume. On the plate was a slab of roasted meat, around which a few slices of boiled potato and carrot had been strewn like an afterthought. Zalka picked up a knife and fork from the tray and sawed off a slice of the meat. Beneath the surface, it was almost raw. 'They feed me here,' he told them, 'red meat every day. I have to get the blood back in me somehow.'

The investigators turned to leave.

'The T-34 will not save us, you know,' said Zalka.

Both men turned around.

'That's what this is about, isn't it?' asked Zalka, talking as he chewed. 'Nagorski has you all convinced that the T-34 is a miracle weapon. That it will practically win a war on its own. But it won't, gentlemen. The T-34 will kill hundreds. Thousands. Tens of thousands. What Nagorski or any of those insane scientists he's got working for him won't admit, is that it's just a machine. Its vulnerabilities will be found out. Better machines will be built. And the men who used it to kill will themselves, eventually, be killed. But you mustn't worry, detectives.' He busied himself sawing off another piece of meat.

'With a forecast like that,' muttered Kirov, 'why wouldn't we be worried?'

'Because the only people who can destroy the Russian people,' Zalka paused to pack another slab of meat into his mouth, 'are the Russian people.'

'You may be right,' said Pekkala. 'Unfortunately, we are experts at that.'

Pekkala breathed in deeply as they stepped outside the building, clearing the sour reek of the bathhouse from his lungs.

'I thought we had him,' said Kirov.

Pekkala nodded. 'So did I, until I saw that leg brace.'

'Trailing suspension arms,' muttered Kirov, 'concentric double coil springs, leading bogies. It all sounds like nonsense to me.'

'It's poetry to Zalka,' replied Pekkala, 'just as caviar blinis are poetry to you.'

Kirov stopped abruptly. 'You just reminded me of something.'

'Food?'

'Yes, as a matter of fact. The day I went into that restaurant to fetch Nagorski in for questioning, he was eating caviar blinis.'

'Well, that's very helpful, Kirov. Perhaps he was shot by a blini.'

'What I remembered,' continued Kirov, 'was a gun.'

Now Pekkala stopped. 'A gun?'

'Nagorski was carrying a pistol. He gave it to Maximov for safekeeping before he left the restaurant.' Kirov shrugged. 'It might mean nothing.'

'Unless Nagorski was shot with his own weapon, in which case it could mean everything.' He slapped Kirov on the arm. 'Time we paid Maximov a visit.'

Maximov's home was in the village of Mytishchi, north-east of the city.

They found him at a garage across the street from the boarding house where he lived by himself in a room on the top floor. The caretaker at the building, a skeletally thin, angry-looking man in a blue boiler suit, aimed one stiletto-finger at the garage. Then he held out his hand and said, 'Na tchay.' For tea.

Pekkala dropped a coin into his palm.

The caretaker folded the coin into his fist and smiled. Men like this had a reputation for being the most enthusiastic informants in the city. It was a running joke that more people had been sent to Siberia for failing to tip caretakers on their birthdays than ever went away for crimes against the state.

'Maximov is here,' said the manager at the garage, a broad-faced man with thick black hair and a moustache gone yellowy-grey. 'At least half of him is.'

'What do you mean?' asked Kirov.

'All we ever see of him is his legs. The rest of him is always under the hood of his car. Whenever he's not on the job, you'll find him working on that machine.'

The two investigators walked through the garage, whose floor was dingy black from years of spilled motor oil soaked into the concrete, and emerged into a graveyard of old motor parts, the husks of stripped down cars, cracked tyres driven bald and the cobra-like hoods of transmissions ripped from their engine compartments.

At the far end, just as the manager had said, stood half of Maximov.

He was naked to the waist and stooped over the engine of Nagorski's car. The hood angled above him like the jaws of a huge animal, and Pekkala was reminded of stories he'd heard about crocodiles which opened their mouths to let little birds clean their teeth.

'Maximov,' said Pekkala.

At the mention of his name, Maximov spun around sharply. Squinting into the bright light, it was a moment before he recognised Pekkala. 'Inspector,' he said. 'What brings you here?'

'I have been thinking about something you said to me the other day,' began Pekkala.

'It seems to me that I said many things,' replied Maximov, wiping an oily rag along the fuel relay hoses which curved like the arcs of seagull wings from the grey steel of the cylinder head.

'One thing in particular sticks in my mind,' continued Pekkala. 'You said that you had not been able to defend Nagorski on the day he was killed, but I'm wondering if he might have been able to defend himself. Isn't it true that Nagorski never went anywhere without a gun?'

'And where did you hear that, Pekkala?' Maximov worked the cloth in under his nails, digging out the dirt.

'From Professor Zalka.'

'Zalka! That troublemaker? Where did you dig up that bastard?'

'Did Nagorski carry a gun or not?' asked Pekkala. A coldness had entered his voice.

'Yes, he had a gun,' admitted Maximov. 'Some German thing called a PPK.'

'What calibre weapon is that?' asked Pekkala.

'It's a 7.62,' replied Maximov.

Kirov leaned over to Pekkala and whispered, 'The cartridge we found in the pit was 7.62.'

'What's this all about?' asked Maximov.

'On the day I brought Nagorski in for questioning,' said Kirov, 'he handed you a gun before he left the restaurant. Was that the PPK you just mentioned?'

'That's right. He gave it to me for safekeeping. He was afraid it would be confiscated if you put him under arrest.'

'Where is that gun now?' asked Kirov.

Maximov laughed and turned to face his interrogator. 'Let me ask you this,' he said. 'That day in the restaurant, did you see what he was eating?'

'Yes,' replied Kirov. 'What's that got to do with anything?'

'And did you see what I was eating?'

'A salad, I think. A small salad.'

'Exactly!' Maximov's voice had risen to a shout. 'Twice a week, Nagorski went to Chicherin's place for lunch and I had to sit there with him, because no one else would, not even his wife, and he didn't like to eat alone. But he wouldn't think to buy me lunch. I had to pay for it myself, and of course I can't afford Chicherin's prices. The cost of that one salad is more than I spend on all my food on an average day. And half the time Nagorski didn't even pay for what he ate. Now do you think a man like that would hand over something as expensive as an imported German gun and not ask for it back the first chance that he got?'

'Answer the question,' said Pekkala. 'Did you return Nagorski's gun to him or not?'

'After you had finished questioning Nagorski, he called and ordered me to meet him outside the Lubyanka. And the first words he spoke when he got inside the car were, "Give me back my gun." And that's exactly what I did.' Angrily, Maximov threw the dirty rag on to the engine. 'I know what you're asking me, Inspector. I know where your questions are going. It may be my fault Nagorski is dead, because I

238

wasn't there to help him when he needed me. If you want to arrest me for that, go ahead. But there's something you two don't seem to understand, which is that my responsibility was not just to Colonel Nagorski. It's to his wife and Konstantin as well. I tried to be a father to that boy when his own father was nowhere to be found and no matter how poorly the Colonel treated me, I would never have done anything to hurt him, because of what it would have done to the rest of his family.'

'All right, Maximov,' said Pekkala. 'Let's assume you gave him back the gun. Was Zalka correct when he said Nagorski never went anywhere without it?'

'As far as I know, that's the truth,' answered Maximov. 'Why are you asking me this?'

'The gun wasn't on Nagorski's body when we found him,' replied Pekkala.

'It might have fallen out of his pocket. It's probably still lying in the mud.'

'The pit was searched,' said Kirov. 'No gun was found.'

'Don't you see?' Maximov reached up, hooked his fingers over the end of the car hood and brought it down shut with a crash. 'This is all Zalka's doing! He's just trying to stir things up. Even though the Colonel is dead, Zalka's still jealous of the man.'

'There was one other thing he told us, Maximov. He said you were once an assassin for the Tsar.'

'Zalka can go to hell,' spat Maximov.

'Is it true?'

'What if it is?' he snapped. 'We've all done things we wouldn't mind forgetting.'

'And Nagorski knew about this when he hired you to be his bodyguard?'

'Of course he did,' said Maximov. 'That's the reason he hired me. If you want to stop a man from killing you, the best thing to do is find a killer of your own.'

'And you have no idea where Nagorski's gun could be now?' asked Pekkala.

Maximov grabbed his shirt, which was lying on top of an empty upturned fuel drum. He pulled it over his head. His big hands struggled with the little mother of pearl buttons. 'I have no idea, Inspector. Unless it's in the pocket of the man who murdered Nagorski, you'll probably find it at his house.'

'All right,' said Pekkala. 'I'll search the Nagorski residence later today. Until that gun turns up, Maximov, you are the last one known to have had it in his possession. You understand what that means?'

'I do,' replied the bodyguard. 'It means that unless you find that gun, I'm probably going to end up taking the blame for a murder I did not commit.' He turned to Kirov. 'That ought to make you happy, Major. You've been looking for an excuse to arrest me ever since the day Nagorski was killed. So why don't you just go ahead?' He thrust out his arms, hands placed side by side, palm up, ready for the handcuffs. 'Whatever happened, or didn't happen, you'll bend the truth to fit your version of events.'

Kirov stepped towards him, red in the face with anger. 'You realise, I could arrest you for what you just said?'

'Which proves my point!' shouted Maximov.

'Enough!' barked Pekkala. 'Both of you! Just stay where we can find you, Maximov.'

Pekkala went by himself to the Nagorski house.

The same guard let him in at the entrance gate of the facility.

Before turning down the road which led to Nagorski's dacha, Pekkala stopped his car outside the main facility building. Inside, he found Gorenko sitting on a bullet-riddled oil drum, thumbing through a magazine. The scientist's shoes were off and his bare feet rested in the sand which had poured out of the barrel.

When he saw Pekkala, Gorenko looked up and smiled. 'Hello, Inspector!'

'No work today?' asked Pekkala.

'Work is done!' replied Gorenko. 'Only two hours ago, a man arrived to transport our prototype T-34 to the factory at Stalingrad.'

'I didn't realise that the prototype was ready.'

'It's close enough,' replied Gorenko. 'It's like I said, Inspector. There's a difference between excellence and perfection. There will always be more things to do, but Moscow obviously felt it was time to begin mass production.'

'How did Ushinsky take it?'

'He hasn't come in yet,' replied Gorenko. 'Being the perfectionist that he is, I doubt he will be very pleased. If he starts talking crazy again, I'll send him straight to you, Inspector, and you can sort him out.'

'I'll see what I can do,' said Pekkala. 'In the meantime, Professor, the reason I'm here is that I'm trying to find out about a gun belonging to Colonel Nagorski. It was a small pistol of German manufacture. Apparently, he carried it with him all the time.'

'I know it,' said Gorenko. 'He didn't have a holster for the thing, so he used to keep the gun in the pocket of his tunic, rattling around with his spare change.'

'Do you know where it came from? Where he got it?'

'Yes,' replied Gorenko. 'It was a gift from a German general named Guderian. Guderian was a tank officer during the war. He wrote a book about tank warfare. Nagorski used to keep it by his bedside. The two of them met when the German Army put on a display of armour in 1936. Dignitaries from all over the world were invited to watch. Nagorski was very impressed. He met Guderian when he was there. Obviously, the two of them had plenty in common. Before Nagorski returned home, Guderian gave him that pistol as a gift. Nagorski always said he hoped we'd never have to fight them.'

'Thank you, Professor.' Pekkala walked to the door. Then he turned back to Gorenko. 'What will you do now?' he asked.

Gorenko gave him a sad smile. 'I don't know,' he said. 'I suppose this is what it is like when you have children and they grow up and leave the house. You just have to get used to the quiet.'

A few minutes later, Pekkala pulled up to the Nagorski house.

Mrs Nagorski was sitting on the porch. She wore a short brown corduroy jacket with the same Mandarin collar as a Russian soldier's tunic and a faded pair of blue canvas trousers of the type worn by factory workers. Her hair was covered by a white head scarf, decorated along the edges with red and blue flowers.

She looked as if she'd been expecting someone else.

Pekkala got out of the car and nodded hello. 'I am sorry to disturb you, Mrs Nagorski.'

'I thought you were the guards, come to throw me out of my house.'

'Why would they do that?'

'The question, Inspector, is why wouldn't they now that my husband is gone?'

'Well, I have not come to throw you out,' he tried to reassure her.

'Then what brings you here?' she asked. 'Have you brought me some answers?'

'No,' replied Pekkala. 'I have only brought questions for now.'

'Well,' she said, rising to her feet, 'you had better come inside and ask them, hadn't you?'

Once they were inside the dacha, she offered him a place in one of two chairs which faced the fireplace. Wedged under the iron grating was a bundle of twigs wrapped in newspaper and balanced on the blackened iron bars of the grate stood a tidy pyramid of logs.

'You can light that,' she said, and handed him a box of matches. 'I'll fetch us something to eat.'

As he struck a match and held it to the edges of the newspaper, Pekkala watched the blue glow spread and the printed words crumbled into darkness.

On the hearth she laid the plate with slices of bread fanned out like a deck of cards. Beside it, she placed a small bowl made of tin which was heaped with flakes of sea salt, like the scales of tiny fish. Then she sat down in the chair beside him.

'Well, Inspector,' she said, 'have you learned anything at all since we last spoke?'

Her bluntness did not surprise him and, at this moment, Pekkala was grateful for it. He reached down and picked up a piece of bread. He dipped a corner of it in the flakes of salt and took a bite. 'I believe that your husband was killed with his own gun.'

'That thing he carried in his pocket?'

'Yes,' he replied with his mouth full, 'and I am wondering if you know where it is.'

She shook her head. 'He used to put it on the bedside table at night. It was his most prized possession. It's not there now. He must have had it with him when he died.'

'There's nowhere else it could be?'

'My husband was precise in his habits, Inspector. The gun was either in his pocket or on that table. He didn't like not knowing where things were.'

'Did your husband have any meetings scheduled on the day he was killed?'

'I don't know. He wouldn't have told me if he did, unless it meant that he would be coming home late, and he didn't say anything about that.'

'So he did not talk about his work with you.'

She waved her hand towards the T-34 blueprints plastered across the walls. 'It was a combination of him not wanting to talk and me not wanting to listen.'

'When he left here on that day, was he alone?' asked Pekkala.

'Yes.'

'Maximov did not drive him?'

'My husband usually walked to the facility. It had started out sunny so he set off on foot. It's only about a twenty-minute walk and the only exercise he ever took.'

'Was there anything unusual about that day?'

'No. We had an argument, but there's nothing unusual about that.'

'What was it about, this argument?'

'It was Konstantin's birthday. The argument started when I told my husband that he shouldn't be spending the whole day at work when he should have stayed home with his son on his birthday. Once we started shouting at each other, Konstantin got up and left the house.'

'And where did your son go?'

'Fishing. That's where he usually goes to get away from us. He is old enough now that he does not have to tell us where he's going. I wasn't worried, and later I saw him out in his boat. That's where he was when you arrived with Maximov.'

'I assume he can't go into the forest because of the traps.'

'There are no traps here, only in the woods surrounding the facility. He's perfectly safe around the house.'

'Did Konstantin ever accompany his father to the facility?'

'No,' she replied. 'That was one of the few things my husband and I agreed upon. We did not want him playing around where there were weapons being built, guns being fired and so on.'

'This argument you had about the birthday. How did it resolve itself?'

'Resolve?' she laughed. 'Inspector, you are being far too optimistic. Our arguments were never resolved. They simply ended when one of us couldn't take it any more and got up to leave the room. In this case, it was my husband, after I had accused him of forgetting Konstantin's birthday altogether.'

'Did he deny it?'

'No. How could he? Even Maximov sent Konstantin a birthday card. What does that tell you, Inspector, when a bodyguard takes better care of a young man than his own father does?'

'This was the only thing you argued about?'

'The only thing in front of Konstantin.'

'You mean there was more?'

'The truth is,' she sighed, 'my husband and I were splitting up.' She looked at him, then looked away again. 'I was having an affair, you see.'

'Ah,' he said softly. 'And your husband found out about it.' She nodded.

'How long had the affair been going on?'

'For some time,' she replied. 'More than a year.'

'And how did your husband find out?'

She shrugged. 'I don't know. He refused to tell me. By then, it really didn't matter.'

'With whom did you have the affair?' asked Pekkala.

'Is this absolutely necessary, Inspector?'

'Yes, Mrs Nagorski. I'm afraid it is.'

'With a man named Lev Zalka.'

'Zalka!'

'That sounds as if you know him.'

'I spoke to him this morning,' replied Pekkala, 'and he didn't tell me anything about an affair.'

'Would you have mentioned it, Inspector, if you could have avoided the subject?'

'Is that why he stopped working on the project?'

'Yes. There were other reasons, small things which could have been put right, but this was the end of everything between them. Afterwards, my husband wouldn't even allow Zalka's name to be mentioned at the facility. The other technicians never knew what had happened. They just thought it was a difference of opinion about something to do with the project.'

'And what about Konstantin? Did he know about this?'

'No,' she replied. 'I begged my husband not to mention it until the project was completed. Then we would move back to the city and find different places to live. Konstantin would be going off to the Moscow Technical Institute to study engineering. He would live in the dormitory there, and he could come and see me or his father whenever he wanted.'

'And your husband agreed?'

'He did not tell me that he disagreed,' she replied, 'and that was as much as I had hoped for, under the circumstances.'

'This morning,' said Pekkala, 'my assistant and I ruled out Zalka as a suspect, but after what you've told me, I'm no longer sure what to think.'

'Are you asking me if I think Lev killed my husband?'

'Or that he ordered it, perhaps?'

'If you knew Lev Zalka, you would never think that.'

'Why not?'

'Because Lev never hated my husband. The person Lev hates is himself. From the first day we began seeing each other, I knew it was destroying him inside.'

'And yet you say this lasted for over a year.'

'Because he loved me, Inspector Pekkala. And, for what

it's worth, I loved him, too. A part of me still does. I was never strong enough to finish things with Lev. It was my great weakness and it was Lev's as well. I was almost relieved when my husband found out. And what Lev does to himself now, those medical experiments he endures, he does out of guilt. He will tell you that it is so he can carry on his research, but the man is just bleeding to death.'

'Are you still in contact with him?'

'No,' she said. 'We could never go back to just being acquaintances.'

There was the sound of a door opening at the back of the dacha. A moment later, it closed again.

Pekkala turned.

Konstantin stood in the kitchen. In his hand, he carried an iron ring on which three trout had been skewered through the gills.

'My dear,' said Mrs Nagorski. 'Inspector Pekkala is here.'

'I wish you would leave us alone, Inspector,' replied Konstantin, as he laid the fish upon the kitchen counter.

'I was just about to,' said Pekkala, rising to his feet.

'The Inspector is looking for your father's gun,' said Mrs Nagorski.

'Your mother says he kept it on his bedside table,' added Pekkala, 'or in the pocket of his coat. Did you ever see the gun anywhere else?'

'I hardly ever saw that gun,' replied the boy, 'because I hardly ever saw my father.'

Pekkala turned to Mrs Nagorski. 'I'll rely on you to search the house. If the gun turns up, please let me know immediately.'

Outside the house, she shook his hand. 'I'm sorry for the way Konstantin spoke to you,' she told Pekkala. 'I'm the one he's angry with. He just hasn't got around to admitting it yet.'

It was late in the day by the time Pekkala returned to the office. He had stopped to refuel the Emka, which took him out of his way, and the mechanic at the garage had persuaded Pekkala to change the oil and radiator fluid. He then discovered that the radiator needed replacing, by which time most of the day had gone.

'We should probably change the fuel gauge as well,' said the mechanic. 'It appears to be sticking.'

'How long will that take?' asked Pekkala, already at the end of his patience.

'We'd have to order the part from Moscow,' explained the mechanic. 'You'd need to leave it here overnight, but there's a cot we keep in the back . . .'

'No!' shouted Pekkala. 'Just get me back out on the road!'

When the repairs had finally been completed, Pekkala returned to the office. He was halfway up the stairs when he met Kirov coming down.

'There you are!' said Kirov.

'What's the matter?'

'You just had a call from the Kremlin.'

Pekkala felt his heart clench. 'Do you know what it's about?'

'They didn't tell me. All they said was to get you over there as soon as possible. Comrade Stalin is waiting.'

'He is waiting for me?' muttered Pekkala. 'Well, there's a change.'

Together, the two men returned to the street, where the Emka's engine was still warm.

'It's over!' shouted Stalin.

They were walking down a corridor towards Stalin's private study. Staff officers and clerks in military uniform stood to the side, backs against the wall and staring straight ahead, like people disguised as statues. As if taking part in this elaborate game, Stalin ignored their existence.

'What is over?' asked Pekkala.

'The case!' Stalin replied. 'We have the man who killed Nagorski.'

From offices on either side came the sounds of typewriters, the rustle of metal filing cabinets opening and closing and the murmur of indistinct voices.

'You do?' Pekkala was unable to hide his surprise. 'Who is he?'

'I don't know yet. I haven't received the final report. All I can tell you is that we have a man in custody and that he has confessed to killing Nagorski, as well as trying to sell information on the Konstantin Project to the Germans.'

As they reached the door to the waiting room, two guards, each armed with a sub machine gun, crashed their heels together. One guard opened the door with a flick of his hand so that Stalin passed through into his study without even breaking his stride.

The three clerks, including Poskrebyshev, rose sharply from their chairs as Stalin entered. Poskrebyshev moved towards the study door, in an attempt to open it for Stalin.

'Get out of the way,' barked Stalin.

Without any change of expression, Poskrebyshev stopped in mid stride, turned and went back to his desk.

Inside the study, Stalin closed the door and broke into a smile. 'I must say, Pekkala, I am taking some pleasure in the fact that this was one case you were unable to solve.'

'How did you catch this man?' asked Pekkala.

'That woman brought him in, that NKVD Major you thought might prove useful.'

'Lysenkova?'

'That's her. She got a call from someone at the Nagorski facility who was able to identify the killer.'

'I knew nothing about this,' said Pekkala. 'We had agreed that Major Lysenkova would keep me informed.'

Stalin made a vague grumble of surprise. 'None of that matters now, Pekkala. What matters is that we have the man who did it.'

'What about the White Guild and those agents who were killed?'

'It looks as if that might be a separate matter,' replied Stalin.

'May I speak to this man?' asked Pekkala.

Stalin shrugged. 'Of course. I don't know what kind of shape he is in, but I assume he can still talk.'

'Where is he being held?'

'At the Lubyanka, in one of the isolation cells. Come now,' Stalin rested his hand on Pekkala's shoulder and steered him towards the tall windows, which looked out over the empty parade ground below. Stalin stopped a few paces short of the window itself. He never took the risk of being seen by someone outside. 'Within a matter of months,' he said, 'you will see T-34 tanks parked end to end down there and it won't be a minute too soon. Germany is now openly preparing for war. I am doing everything I can to buy us time. Yesterday, I halted all patrols along the Polish border, in case of accidental incursions into their territory. Any movement by us beyond our own national boundaries will be interpreted by Germany as an act of aggression and Hitler is looking for any excuse to begin hostilities. These measures cannot prevent what is inevitable. They can only delay it, hopefully long enough that the T-34s will be waiting when our enemies decide to attack.'

Pekkala left Stalin staring out the window at the imaginary procession of armour.

Down on the street, Kirov was pacing back and forth beside the Emka.

Pekkala came running out of the building. 'Get us over to the Lubyanka as quickly as you can.'

Minutes later, the Emka roared around the corner of Dzerzhinsky square and into the main courtyard of the Lubyanka prison. Even though it had not snowed in weeks, piles of filthy snow left over from the winter were still ploughed up into the corners where the sunlight failed to reach. On three sides of the courtyard, walls rose up several storeys high. Windows stretched along the ground floor, but above that were rows of strange metal sheets, each one anchored with iron pins a hand's width from the wall, hiding whatever lay behind them.

A guard escorted them inside the prison. He wore a bulky greatcoat made of poor-quality wool dyed an irregular shade of purplish brown, and a bulky, fur-lined hat known as an ushanka. Pekkala and Kirov signed in at the front desk. They scrawled their names in a huge book containing thousands of pages. The book had a steel plate, covering everything except the space for them to write their names.

The man behind the desk picked up a phone. 'Pekkala is here,' he said.

Now another guard took over from the first. He led them down a series of long, windowless and dimly illuminated corridors. Hundreds of grey metal doors lined the way. All were closed. The place stank of ammonia, sweat, and the dampness of old stone. The floors were covered with brown industrial carpeting. The guard even wore felt-soled boots, as if sound itself was a crime. Except for the padding of their feet upon the carpet, the place was absolutely silent. No matter how many times Pekkala came here, the silence always unnerved him.

The guard stopped at one of the cells, rapped his knuckles on the iron, and opened it without waiting for a reply. He jerked his head, indicating that they were to go inside.

Pekkala and Kirov entered a room with a tall ceiling, roughly three paces long by four paces wide. The walls were painted brown up to chest height. Above that, everything was white. The light in the room came from a single bulb set back into the wall above the door and covered with a wire cage.

In the centre of the room was a table, on which lay a heap of old rags.

Between Pekkala and this table, with her back to them, stood Major Lysenkova. She wore the NKVD dress uniform: an olive-coloured tunic with polished brass buttons, and black knee-length boots tucked into dark blue trousers with a purplish-red stripe running down the side.

'I told you I was not to be disturbed!' she shouted as she turned around. Only then did she realise who had entered the room. 'Pekkala!' Her eyes widened with surprise. 'I was not expecting you.'

'Evidently.' Pekkala glanced at a figure huddled in the corner of the cell. It was a man, wearing the thin beige cotton pyjamas issued to all prisoners at Lubyanka. The man's knees were drawn up to his chest and his head lay on his knees. One of his arms hung limply at his side. The shoulder had been dislocated. The other arm was wrapped around his shins, as if he were trying to make himself as small as possible. Now, at the sound of Pekkala's voice, the man lifted his head.

The side of his face was so puffed with bruises that at first Pekkala could not identify him.

'Inspector,' croaked the man.

Now Pekkala recognised the voice. 'Ushinsky!' He gaped at the wreckage of the scientist.

Major Lysenkova lifted a sheet of paper from the desk. 'Here is his full confession, to the crime of murder and of intending to sell secrets to the enemy. He has signed it. The matter is closed.'

'Major,' said Pekkala. 'We agreed that you would take no action without informing me first.'

'Don't look so surprised, Inspector,' she replied. 'I told you I had learned what it takes to survive. I saw a chance to get myself out of that mess and I took it. Whatever agreement you and I had has been cancelled. Comrade Stalin does not care who solved this case, just that it has been solved. The only people who care are you,' she glanced at Kirov, 'and your assistant.'

Kirov did not reply. He stood against the wall, staring in disbelief at Lysenkova.

'Since the case is officially closed,' said Pekkala, 'you won't mind if I have a few words with the prisoner.'

Lysenkova glanced at the man in the corner. 'I suppose not.'

Finally, Kirov spoke. 'I can't believe you did this,' he said.

Lysenkova fixed him with a stare. 'I know you can't,' she said. Then she walked past him and stepped out into the hall. 'Take all the time you need, Inspectors,' she told them, before closing the door behind her.

In the cell, nobody spoke or moved.

It was Ushinsky who broke the silence. 'It was Gorenko,' he whispered hoarsely. 'He called her. He said I was planning to give the T-34 plans to the Germans.'

Pekkala crouched down before the injured man. 'And were you?'

'Of course not! When I showed up for work and found out that the prototype had been picked up, I exploded. I told Gorenko it wasn't ready yet. Those tanks might look all right. They will run. The guns will fire. They will perform adequately under controlled conditions like the ones we have at the facility, but once you put those machines to work out in the real world, it won't be long before you'll be looking at major failures in the engine and suspension systems. You must get in touch with the factory, Inspector. Tell them they cannot begin production. Too many pieces of the puzzle are missing.'

'What did Gorenko say when you told him this?' asked Pekkala.

'He said it was good enough. That's what he always says! Then I told him we might as well hand over the design to the Germans, since they wouldn't stop until they got it right. The next thing I knew, I was arrested by the NKVD.'

'And what about Nagorski?' asked Kirov. 'Did you have anything to do with his death?'

The prisoner shook his head. 'I would never have done anything to hurt him.'

'That confession says you did,' Kirov reminded him.

'Yes,' said Ushinsky, 'and I signed it right after they dislocated my arm.'

'Are you a member of the White Guild?' asked Pekkala.

'No! I've never even heard of them before. What's going to happen to me now, Inspector? The Major says I'm being sent out to a special location in Siberia, a camp called Mamlin-Three.'

At the mention of that place, Pekkala had to force himself to breathe. Suddenly, he turned to Kirov. 'Leave the room,' he said. 'Go out to the car. Do not wait for me. I will join you at the office later.'

Kirov watched him in confusion. 'Why?' he asked.

'Please,' Pekkala urged.

'You are going to try to get him out of here?' Slowly Kirov raised his hands, open palms towards Pekkala, as if to fend off what was coming. 'Oh, no, Inspector. You can't.'

'You have to go now, Kirov.'

'But you mustn't!' spluttered Kirov. 'This is completely irregular.'

Ushinsky no longer seemed aware of their presence. His one good hand wandered feebly over his body, as if by some miracle of touch he hoped to heal himself.

'This man is innocent,' said Pekkala. 'You know that as well as I do.'

'But it's too late,' protested Kirov, lifting the confession from the table. 'He signed!'

'You'd have signed, too, if they'd done the same thing to you.'

'Inspector, please. This isn't our problem any more.'

'I know where they're sending him,' replied Pekkala. 'I know what happens there.'

'You can't get him out of here,' Kirov pleaded. 'Not even a Shadow Pass will allow you to do that.'

'Leave now,' said Pekkala. 'Go back to the office. When you get there, put in a call to Major Lysenkova. Put it through the main switchboard.'

'Why would I want to speak to her?' asked Kirov.

'You don't,' replied Pekkala, 'but you need that switchboard operator to log in the time that you called. That way, it will show that you were not in the Lubyanka. Just find some excuse, talk to her for a minute, then hang up and wait for me to come back.'

'Do you really mean to go through with this?'

'I will not stand by and let an innocent man be sent to Mamlin-Three. Now, Kirov, my friend, do as I tell you and go.'

Without another word, the young man turned towards the door.

'Thank you,' whispered Pekkala.

Then suddenly Kirov spun around and this time he had a Tokarev aimed at Pekkala.

'What are you doing?' asked Pekkala.

'You will thank me later,' said Kirov, 'when you have come to your senses.'

Calmly, Pekkala stared down the barrel of the gun. 'I see you brought your weapon this time. At least I have taught you that much.'

'You also taught me that the law is the law,' said Kirov. 'You cannot pick and choose what to obey. There was a time when it seemed to me you knew the difference between right and wrong.'

'The older I get, Kirov, the harder it becomes to tell one from the other.'

For a long time, the two men stood there.

The barrel of the gun began to tremble in Kirov's hand. 'You know I can't shoot you,' he whispered.

'I know,' replied Pekkala in a kindly voice.

Kirov lowered the gun. Clumsily, he returned the pistol to its holster. Then he shook his head and left the room.

Pekkala and Ushinsky were alone now.

A hoarse rattling echoed from Ushinsky's throat.

It took Pekkala a moment to realise that Ushinsky was laughing.

'Major Kirov is right, isn't he? You can't get me out of here.'

'No, Ushinsky, I can't.'

'And the things that go on in this camp, are they as bad as you say?'

'Worse than anything you can imagine.'

A faint moan escaped his lips. 'Please, Inspector. Please, don't let them take me there.'

'You understand what we are talking about?' asked Pekkala.

'I do.' Ushinsky struggled to stand, but he could not manage on his own. 'Help me up,' he pleaded.

Pekkala hooked a hand under Ushinsky's good arm and raised him to his feet.

The scientist sagged back against the wall, breathing heavily. 'Gorenko thinks I hate him, but the truth is he's the only friend I've got. Don't tell him what happened to me.'

'I won't.'

'Which tank did they take?' asked Ushinsky.

'I don't know.'

'I always hoped it would be number 4.'

'Professor, we don't have much time.'

Ushinsky nodded. 'I understand. Goodbye, Inspector Pekkala.'

'Goodbye, Professor Ushinsky.' Pekkala reached into his coat and drew the Webley from its holster.

At the far end of the hallway, the guard on duty heard the shot. It sounded so muffled that at first he confused it with the clank of the vision slit plate moving back and forth as the guard in the next hallway inspected the other cells. But then, when the other guard stuck his head around the corner and asked, 'What was that?' he realised what had happened.

The guard ran to Ushinsky's cell, feet padding on the carpeted floor, threw back the locking bolt and flung open the door. The first thing he saw was a halo of blood on the wall.

Ushinsky lay in the corner, one leg bent under him and the other stretched out across the floor.

Pekkala stood in the centre of the room. The Webley was still in his hand. Gunsmoke swirled around the light bulb and the air smelled of burnt cordite.

'What the hell happened?' yelled the guard.

'Take me to the prison commandant,' Pekkala replied.

Five minutes later, Pekkala stood in the office of a bull-necked man with a shaved head named Maltsev. He was in charge of the Kommendatura, a special branch within the Lubyanka prison system, responsible for carrying out executions. In the past three years, Maltsev himself had liquidated over a thousand people. Now Maltsev sat at his desk. He looked stunned, as if he couldn't have stood up even if he'd wanted to.

Behind Pekkala stood two armed guards.

'Explain yourself,' Maltsev's balled fists rested on the desk top like two fleshy hand grenades. 'And you'd better make it good.'

Pekkala took out his NKVD ID book and handed it to Maltsev. 'Read this,' he said quietly.

Maltsev opened the red booklet. Immediately, his eyes fastened on the Classified Operations Permit. Maltsev looked up at the guards. 'You two,' he said, 'get out.'

Hurriedly, the guards abandoned the room.

Maltsev handed back the ID book. 'I should have known you'd have a Shadow Pass. I can't arrest you. I can't even ask why you did it, can I?' he said, looking even more annoyed than he had done a minute before.

'No,' replied Pekkala.

Maltsev sat back heavily in his chair and laced his fingers together. 'I suppose it doesn't matter. We have his confession.

His transfer paper to Mamlin had already been made out. One way or another, he was not long for this world.'

Fifteen minutes later, as the gates of the Lubyanka closed behind him, Pekkala glanced up and down the street. The Emka was gone. Kirov had followed his orders. Now Pekkala set off on foot towards the office.

But that wasn't where he ended up.

Frozen in his mind was the image of Kirov, staring at him down the barrel of a gun. Kirov had done the right thing. He had simply followed regulations, and if he had continued to follow them, Kirov would now be back at the office, writing up charges against Pekkala of professional misconduct.

The more Pekkala thought about this, the louder he heard Kropotkin's words from the last time they had met – that the day would come when he would have to choose between what his job required him to do and what his conscience would allow.

Perhaps the time has come at last to disappear, he told himself, and suddenly, it no longer seemed impossible.

He remembered the morning he had stood with the Tsar on the terrace of the Catherine Palace, watching Ilya lead her students on a walk to the Chinese Theatre just across the park. 'If you let her get away,' the Tsar said, 'you'll never forgive yourself. And neither will I, by the way.'

The Tsar had been telling the truth. Pekkala had not forgiven himself. We did not separate by choice, he thought. We were driven apart by circumstances which neither of us caused or wanted. Even if she is with someone else now, even if she has a child, what order of the universe demands that I be satisfied with living out my days as a ghost in her heart?

With his office building only two blocks away, Pekkala turned the corner and headed for the Café Tilsit. He didn't know if he would find Kropotkin there, but when Pekkala came within sight of the café, he saw Kropotkin standing on the pavement next to the triangular, double-sided board on which Bruno, the owner, wrote down the menu for the day. Kropotkin was smoking a cigarette. A short-brimmed cap obscured Kropotkin's face, but Pekkala recognised him by the way he stood – the legs slightly spread and firmly planted on the ground, one hand tucked behind the back. There was no mistaking the stance of a policeman, whether he had left the ranks or not.

Kropotkin noticed him and smiled. 'I wondered if I'd see you again,' he said, and flicked the cigarette into the street.

In the café, the two men found a place away from the crowded benches, sitting at a small table tucked away beneath the staircase to the second floor. Here, they knew no one would overhear them.

Bruno, the chef, had made borscht. He ladled the soup like torrents of blood into the wooden bowls in which all meals were served.

'I have thought a lot about our last conversation,' said Pekkala, as he spooned up the ruby-coloured soup.

'I hope you have forgiven me for speaking as bluntly as I did,' replied Kropotkin. 'It is in my nature, and I cannot help it.'

'There is nothing to forgive. You mentioned the possibility of disappearing.'

'Yes,' replied Kropotkin, 'and I realise I was wrong to have suggested it.'

The words struck Pekkala. It was the last thing he had expected Kropotkin to say.

'This is not a time for running,' continued Kropotkin. 'What good can we do if we simply allow ourselves to fade away?'

Pekkala gave no answer. His head was spinning.

Kropotkin ate as he spoke, slurping his soup off the spoon. 'The truth is, Pekkala, I had hoped we might find a way to work together, as we did back in Ekaterinburg.'

It took Pekkala a moment to understand that Kropotkin was asking for a job. All that talk about disappearing had been nothing more than words. He did not blame Kropotkin. Instead, Pekkala blamed himself for believing it. At the time, Kropotkin may have meant what he was saying. He might even have gone through with it, but that was then, and now he believed something else. The long days of driving back and forth across this country have caught up with him, decided Pekkala. He is looking back on his days in the police and wishing things could be the way they used to be. But the world he is remembering has gone for good. It may never have existed in the first place. Besides, Pekkala told himself, the reason he was dismissed from the force would prevent him from ever being reinstated, no matter how many strings I tried to pull. 'I can't,' said Pekkala. 'I'm sorry, Kropotkin. It is not possible.'

When Kropotkin heard this, the light went out of his eyes. 'I'm sorry to hear that.' He glanced around the room. 'I'll be back in a minute, Pekkala. I am due to pick up some cargo on the other side of town and I need to find out if it is ready for loading on to my truck.'

'Of course,' Pekkala assured him. 'I'll be here when you get back.'

While he waited for Kropotkin to return, Pekkala felt as if he were waking from a dream. Suddenly, he felt ashamed, deeply ashamed, that he had even considered abandoning his post and leaving Kirov to face the consequences. He thought about Ilya, and as her face shimmered into focus in his mind, he experienced a strange hallucination.

He was standing on the platform of the Imperial Station at Tsarskoye Selo. Ilya was with him. Winter sunlight on the plastered brickwork glowed like the flesh of apricots. It was her birthday. They were heading into Petrograd for dinner. He turned to speak to her and, suddenly, she disappeared.

Next, Pekkala found himself at an iron gate, an ornate bronze wreath bolted to the railings, just outside the Alexander Palace. It was a place he knew well. He often met Ilya here, after she had finished classes for the day. Then they would walk out across the grounds together. The following year, the Tsarina and her daughters would stand at this gate and plead with the palace guards to remain loyal as soldiers of the Revolutionary Guard advanced upon Tsarskoye Selo. But that was still to come. Now Pekkala saw Ilya walking towards him, still carrying her text books, feet crunching on the pale carpet of gravel. Pekkala reached out to open the gate and this time it was he who disappeared.

Now he stood at the dockside in Petrograd, watching the Tsar's yacht, the Standart, pulling up to the quay. Sailors threw their mooring lines, the ropes weighted at the ends with huge monkey-fist knots. Dozens of signal flags hung from the halyard lines, so gaudy that together they looked like the laundry of court jesters hung out to dry. Again, Ilya was with him, a breeze stirring her white summer dress about her knees. He wore his usual heavy black coat on the excuse that he'd heard some rumour of a cold front approaching. The truth was he wore the coat because, even in this weather, he did not feel comfortable in anything else. They had been invited on board for dinner, the first time the Romanovs had asked them as a couple. Ilya was very happy. Pekkala felt uneasy. He did not care for dinner parties, especially in the confines of a boat, even if it was the Royal Yacht. She knew what he was thinking. He felt her arm across the back of his waist.

'I don't want to leave,' he told her, but even as he said the words, his eyes opened and he found himself back in the café.

At first, Pekkala did not understand.

It was as if his memories of Ilya had all been thrown into the air like confetti and were flickering down around him. So often he had returned to these images, retreating from the world around him, their vividness erasing all the years between that world and this. But now time began to accelerate. All he could do was watch things going by, too fast to comprehend until, at last, the strands of memory in which he had cocooned himself began to snap. Finally, when the last strand had broken free, he realised that there could be no going back.

Kropotkin returned. 'My cargo is ready,' he said. 'I'm afraid I can't stay any longer.'

'I'll walk you out,' replied Pekkala, rising to his feet, back stooped against the staircase which loomed over their heads.

Outside the café, the two men shook hands.

The lunchtime crowd was leaving the café. People stood on the pavement, buttoning up their coats or lighting cigarettes to keep them company on the walk back to their jobs.

'Goodbye, old friend,' said Kropotkin.

Bruno, the chef, came out with a wet rag and a stub of chalk. 'Out of soup!' he announced to them as he passed. He crouched down in front of the menu board and began to erase the word 'Borscht'.

As he let go of Kropotkin's hand, Pekkala thought about the people who had drifted through his life. Their faces shuffled behind his eyes. Now, to that long line, as if fixing a photo into an album, he added the picture of Kropotkin.

'Goodbye,' said Pekkala, but his voice was drowned out by the thudding rumble of a large motorcycle coming up the road.

'Hey!' shouted Bruno.

Pekkala turned to see Bruno waving the wet rag at the motorcycle driver, who was riding his machine almost in the gutter as he swooped by. The rider wore a leather helmet and goggles. To Pekkala, he looked like the head of a giant insect with the body of a man. His arm reached out, as if to snatch the rag from Bruno's hand.

That's a stupid prank, thought Pekkala.

But then he realised that the rider was holding out a gun.

What happened next took only seconds, but it seemed to Pekkala that everything had slowed down to the point where he could almost see the bullets leaving the barrel.

The rider began to fire, steadily pulling the trigger as round after round left the gun. His arm swivelled as he aimed, but the pavement was so crowded with people leaving the restaurant that Pekkala had no idea who the man was aiming at.

He heard the crash of glass behind him as the window of the Café Tilsit shattered. Kropotkin sprang to the side. As Bruno lunged away from the motorcycle, he caught his leg on the menu board. The heavy board flew into the air, hinges spreading like a pair of wings.

Pekkala saw it coming towards him.

That was the last thing he remembered.

The next thing he knew, a man was bending down over him.

Pekkala grabbed him by the throat.

The man's face turned red. His eyes bulged.

'Stop!' shouted a woman's voice.

Now someone had hold of Pekkala's hand, trying to prise it off the man's throat.

Completely disoriented, Pekkala squinted at this pair of hands and followed them to the body of the woman. She was wearing the uniform of an ambulance nurse – grey skirt, white tunic and a white cap with a red cross on the forehead.

'Let go of him!' shouted the woman. 'He's only trying to help you!'

Pekkala released his grip.

The man tipped over backwards and lay gasping on the pavement.

Pekkala struggled upright. He realised he was outside the Café Tilsit. The pavement was covered with broken glass. A body lay under a black sheet, only an arm's length away. Further along the pavement, there were two more bodies. Those had been covered, too. Blood had seeped out from under one of the sheets, following the cracks in the pavement like a red lightning bolt.

The man Pekkala had been choking climbed unsteadily to his feet, still holding his throat. He was also wearing the uniform of an ambulance worker.

Now Pekkala remembered the gun. 'Have I been shot?' he asked.

'No,' replied the man, hoarsely. 'That's what hit you.'

Pekkala looked at where the man was pointing and saw Bruno's menu board.

'You're lucky,' said the man. 'You won't even need stitches.'

Pekkala put his hand to his face. He felt a ragged tear of skin just below the hairline. When he pulled his hand away, his fingertips were flecked with blood.

Uniformed men from the Moscow Police Department were milling about on the pavement. Their boots crunched on the broken glass. 'Can I talk to him now?' one of the officers asked the nurse as he pointed at Pekkala.

'In a minute,' she replied sharply. 'Let me bandage him first.'

'How long have I been lying here?' he asked.

It was the nurse who answered. 'About an hour,' replied the nurse, kneeling beside him and unwinding a roll of gauze to place upon the wound. 'We dealt with the most serious cases first. They have already been taken to hospital. You were lucky . . .'

She was still talking when Pekkala got up and went over to the black sheet lying beside him. He pulled it back. Bruno's eyes were glazed and open. Then he went over to the other two sheets and pulled them back as well. One was a man and the other was a woman, neither of whom he recognised. He felt a moment of relief that Kropotkin was not among the dead. 'I was standing with another man,' he said, as he turned to the nurse.

'Those not injured were sent away by the police,' she replied. 'Your friend probably just went home. Only the dead were covered up, so your friend must know you're still alive.'

Pekkala remembered that Kropotkin had been on his way to pick up cargo for his truck. It didn't surprise him that Kropotkin had not waited. When they said their goodbyes, there had been a finality in Kropotkin's voice which told Pekkala that the two of them would never meet again. Kropotkin was probably on the road by now, driving to Mongolia for all Pekkala knew. 'Do you have a description of the gunman?' he asked.

The officer shook his head. 'All we know is that it was a man on a motorcycle. He drove by so quickly that nobody got a good look at him.'

While the nurse was bandaging his head, Pekkala gave a statement to the policeman. He sat on the kerb, the soles of his shoes two islands in a puddle of Bruno's blood. There was not much he could tell them. It had all happened so quickly. He recalled the rider's face hidden behind the goggles and the leather helmet.

'What about the motorcycle?' asked the policeman.

'It was black,' he told the officer, 'and bigger than most I have seen on the streets of this city. There was some writing on the side of the fuel tank. It was silver. I couldn't tell what it said.'

The policeman scribbled down a few words on a notepad.

'Do you know who he was shooting at?' asked Pekkala.

'Hard to say,' replied the policeman. 'There were a lot of people standing here when he rode by. He might not have been aiming for anyone in particular.'

The nurse helped Pekkala to his feet. 'You should come with us to the hospital,' she said.

'No,' he replied. 'There's someplace else I need to be.'

She rested her thumb against the skin just under his right eyebrow. Then she opened his eye and shone a small pen-light against his pupil. 'All right,' she told him reluctantly, 'but if you have headaches, if you get dizzy, if your eyesight becomes blurred, you should get to a doctor immediately. Understand?'

Pekkala nodded. He turned to the ambulance man. 'I'm sorry,' he said.

The man smiled. 'Next time,' he said, 'I'll leave you to fix yourself.'

Pekkala walked the rest of the way to his office. His head hurt like a hangover and the smell of the gauze, as well as the disinfectant used to clean the wound, made him queasy. Once inside the building, he went into the ground-floor bathroom, removed the bandage, and washed his face in cold water. Then he climbed up the stairs to his office.

He found Kirov sweeping the floor. 'Inspector!' he said, when Pekkala had entered the room. 'What on earth happened to you?'

Pekkala explained.

'Do you think he was aiming for you?' asked Kirov, bewildered.

'Whether he was or not, he came pretty close to finishing me off. How many people have I put behind bars, Kirov?'

'Dozens.' He shrugged. 'More.'

'Exactly, and any one of them could have come after me, if they were even trying. The police are investigating it. They said they'd get in touch if they learn something.' Now Pekkala paused. 'There is something I need to tell you, Kirov.'

Without a word, Kirov set the broom against the wall and sat down at his desk. 'Inspector, I have been thinking . . .'

'I've been thinking as well,' replied Pekkala. 'About rules. At the Lubyanka today, I broke every one I ever taught you. If you need to file a report on my conduct, I will support your decision.'

Kirov smiled. 'Not every rule, Inspector. You once told me only to do what I can live with. That was what you did back at the prison, and it is what I'm doing now. Let's not speak of reports. Besides, if Nagorski's killer is still out there, there is plenty of work to be done.'

'I agree.' Pekkala walked to the window and looked out over the rooftops of the city. The grey slates gleamed like copper in the evening sunlight. 'They may have their confession, but they don't have the truth. Not yet.' Then he breathed in and sighed, and his breath bloomed grey against the glass. 'Thank you, Kirov,' he said.

'And Major Lysenkova won't be taking all the credit.' Kirov folded his arms and slumped in his chair. 'What a bitch.'

'Because she happened to take advantage of you more effectively than you took advantage of her?'

'It's not like that!' protested Kirov. 'I was really beginning to like her!'

'Then she really did take advantage of you,' said Pekkala.

'I don't see how you can be so jovial,' huffed Kirov. 'I almost shot you today.'

'But you didn't, and that is reason enough to celebrate.' Pekkala slid open a drawer of his desk, hauling out a strangely rounded bottle wrapped in wicker and plugged with a cork. It contained his supply of plum brandy, which he obtained in small quantities from a love-sick Ukrainian in the Sukharevka market. But as with many things in that market, he traded rather than paid. The Ukrainian had a girlfriend in Finland. He had met her when he worked on a trading ship in the Baltic. She wrote to him in her native language and Pekkala translated the letters in exchange. Then, while the Ukrainian poured out his heart, Pekkala wrote a translation for the Finnish girl. For this, and for his discretion, he received half a litre every month.

'The slivovitz!' exclaimed Kirov. 'Now that's more like it!' He picked two glasses off the shelf, blew the dust out and set them down before Pekkala.

Into each glass, Pekkala poured the greenish-yellow liquid. Then he slid one over to Kirov.

In a toast, they raised their glasses to the level of their foreheads.

As he drank, a taste of plums blossomed softly in Pekkala's head, filling his mind with the ripe fruit's dusty purpleness. 'You know,' he said, after the fire had left his breath, 'this was the only liquor the Tsar would touch.'

'It seems unpatriotic,' replied Kirov, his voice gone hoarse from the drink, 'to be Russian and not to like a drop of vodka now and then.'

'He had his reasons,' said Pekkala, and decided to leave it at that.

Pekkala stood out in the wide expanse of the Alexander Park.

It was an evening in late May. The days had grown longer, and the sky remained light long after the sun had gone down.

The pink and white petals of the dogwood trees had fallen, replaced by shiny, lime green leaves. Summer did not come gradually to this place. Instead, it seemed to explode across the landscape.

After a long day in the city of Petrograd, Pekkala would finish his supper and walk out on the grounds of the estate. He rarely encountered anyone else this time of night, but now Pekkala saw a rider coming towards him. The horse ambled lazily, its reins held slack, the rider slouched in his saddle. He knew instantly from the man's silhouette that it was the Tsar. His narrow shoulders. The way he held his head, as if the joints of his neck were too tight.

At last, the Tsar came up alongside him. 'What brings you out here, Pekkala?'

'I often walk in the evenings.'

'I could get you a horse, you know,' said the Tsar.

And then the two men laughed quietly, remembering that it was a matter of a horse which had first brought them together. In the course of Pekkala's training with the Finnish Legion, he had been ordered to jump his horse over a barricade on which the drill instructor had laced a coil of barbed wire. By the time the exercise was halfway through, most of the animals were bleeding from cuts to their legs and bellies. Blood, bright as rubies, speckled the sawdust floor. When Pekkala refused to jump his horse, the drill instructor first threatened, then humiliated him and finally attempted to reason with him. Pekkala had known before he said a word that a refusal to carry out an order would mean being thrown out of the cadets. He would be on the next train home to Finland. But it was at this point that the sergeant and cadets realised they were being watched. The Tsar had been standing in the shadows.

Later, as Pekkala led his horse back to the stables, the Tsar was waiting for him there. One hour later, he had been transferred out of the Finnish Legion and into a special course of study with the Imperial Police, the State Police and the Okhrana. Two years and two months from the day that he led his horse out of the ring, Pekkala pinned on the badge of the Emerald Eye. Since that time, he had always preferred, whenever possible, to travel on his own two feet.

That spring evening, the Tsar removed a pewter flask from the pocket of his tunic, unscrewed the cap, took a drink and handed the flask to Pekkala.

That was the first time he ever tasted slivovitz. At first, Pekkala did not know what it was. The aftertaste reminded him of a liquor his mother used to make from a distillation of cloudberries, which she gathered in the forest near their home. They were not easy to find. Cloudberries did not always grow in the same place year after year. Instead, they sprouted unexpectedly and, for most people, finding them was so much a matter of chance that they often did not bother. But Pekkala's mother always seemed to know from one glance at the undergrowth exactly where cloudberries would be growing. How she knew this *was as much a mystery to Pekkala as the Tsar's reasons for making him into the Emerald Eye.*

'It is my wedding anniversary tomorrow,' remarked the Tsar.

'Congratulations, Majesty,' replied Pekkala. 'Do you have plans to mark the occasion?'

'That is not a day I celebrate,' said the Tsar.

Pekkala did not have to ask why. On the day of the Tsar's coronation in May of 1896, the Tsar and Tsarina sat for five hours on gold and ivory thrones while the names of his dominion were read out – Moscow, Petrograd, Kiev, Poland, Bulgaria, Finland. Finally, after he had been proclaimed the Lord and Judge of Russia, bells rang out across the city and cannon fire echoed in the sky.

During this time, a crowd of half a million had gathered on the outskirts of the city, at a military staging area known as Khodynka field, with a promise of free food, beer and souvenir mugs. When a rumour spread that the beer was running out, the crowd surged forward. More than a thousand people, some said as many as three thousand, were trampled to death in the panic.

For hours afterwards, carts loaded with bodies raced through the streets of Moscow, while their drivers searched for places where the dead could be kept out of sight until the wedding cortege had passed. In the confusion, some of those carts, with the legs and arms of the dead lolling out from under their tarpaulin covers, found themselves both ahead and behind the royal procession.

'That afternoon,' the Tsar told Pekkala, 'before the wedding ceremony began, I drank a toast to the crowd on Khodynka field. That's the last time I ever touched vodka.' Now the Tsar smiled, trying to forget. He raised the flask. 'So what do you

think of my alternative? I have it sent to me from Belgrade. I own some orchards there.'

'I like it well enough, Majesty.'

'Well enough,' repeated the Tsar, and he took another drink.

'It wasn't your fault, Majesty,' said Pekkala, 'what happened on that field.'

The Tsar breathed in sharply. 'Wasn't it? I have never been sure about that.'

'Some things just happen.'

'I know that.'

But Pekkala could tell he was lying.

'The trouble is,' continued the Tsar, 'that either I am placed here by God to be the ruler of this land, in which case the day of my wedding is proof that we are living out the will of the Almighty, or else . . .' he paused . . . 'or else that is not so. Do you have any idea how much I would like to believe you are right – that those people died simply because of an accident? They haunt me. I cannot get away from their faces. But if I believe it was just an accident, Pekkala, then what about everything else which happened on that day? Either God has a hand in our affairs or he does not. I cannot pick and choose according to what suits me best.'

Pekkala saw the torment in his face. 'No more than the plum can choose its taste, Majesty.'

Now the Tsar smiled. 'I will remember that,' he said, and he tossed the flask down to Pekkala.

Pekkala had been carrying that flask five years later when Bolshevik guards arrested him at the border, when he tried to flee the country after the Revolution had begun. Although his badge and gun were eventually returned to him, the flask disappeared somewhere along the way.

Since that day out in the twilight in the Alexander Park, the glassy green of slivovitz had taken on a meaning almost sacred to Pekkala. In a world where a Shadow Pass allowed him to do almost anything he chose, the taste of ripe plums served as a reminder to Pekkala of how much he did not control.

Late that night, as Pekkala sat on the end of his bed, reading his copy of the *Kalevala*, the phone rang at the end of the hall. There was only one phone on each floor and the calls never came for him there, so he did not even look up from his book. He heard Babayaga's apartment door open and the patter of Talia's footsteps as she raced to grab the receiver.

Nobody liked to be the one who had to go out and answer the phone, especially when it was so late, so an unofficial arrangement had been made that Talia would pick up the call and notify whoever it was for. In exchange for this, the child would receive a small gift of some kind, preferably something made with sugar.

Then there was more pattering and Pekkala was surprised to hear Talia knocking on his door. 'Inspector,' she called. 'It's for you.'

The first thing Pekkala did when he heard this was to look around the room for something he could give Talia as a present. Spotting nothing, he stood up and rummaged in his pockets. He examined his handful of change.

'Inspector?' asked Talia. 'Are you in there?'

'Yes,' he answered hurriedly. 'I'll be right out.'

'Are you finding me a present?' she asked.

'That's right.'

'Then you can take your time.'

When he opened the door a moment later, she plucked the coin from his hand. 'Come along, Inspector!' she said.

It was only as Pekkala picked up the receiver that he had time to wonder who might be calling at this hour.

'Inspector?' said a woman's voice. 'Is that you?'

'This is Pekkala. Who am I speaking to?'

'It's Yelena Nagorski.'

'Oh!' he said, surprised. 'Is everything all right?'

'Well, no, Inspector, I'm afraid it isn't.'

'What is it, Yelena?'

'Konstantin has learned the reason why my husband and I were splitting up.'

'But how?'

'It was Maximov who told him.'

'Why would he do a thing like that?'

'I don't know. He showed up here this evening. Maximov had gotten the idea in his head that he and I should get married.'

'Married? Was he serious?'

'I think he was completely serious,' replied Yelena, 'but I also think he was completely drunk. I wouldn't let him in the house. I told him that if he did not go away I would report him to the guards at the facility.'

'And did he go away?'

'Not at first. Konstantin came out and ordered him to leave. That was when Maximov told him what had happened between me and Lev Zalka.'

'But how did Maximov know?'

'My husband might have told him, and even if he didn't,

Maximov might have figured it out on his own. I always suspected that he knew.'

'And where is Maximov now?' asked Pekkala.

'I don't know,' she replied. 'I think he drove back to the facility, assuming he didn't run off the road on his way there. Where he might have gone from there I have no idea. The reason I'm calling you, Inspector, is that I have no idea where my son is either. When I had finally persuaded Maximov to leave, I turned around and discovered that Konstantin was gone. He must be out there in the forest. There's nowhere else for him to go. Konstantin knows his way around those woods in daylight, but it's pitch black out there now. I'm worried that he'll get lost and wander too close to the facility. And you know what is out there, Inspector.'

An image flashed into Pekkala's mind of Captain Samarin, impaled upon that rusty metal pipe. 'All right, Yelena,' he said, 'I'm on my way. In the meantime, try not to worry. Konstantin is a capable young man. I'm sure he knows how to take care of himself.'

One hour later, as the headlights of the Emka bulldozed back the darkness on the long road that bordered the testing facility, Pekkala felt a sudden loss of power from the engine. While he was trying to figure out what might have caused it, the engine stumbled again.

He stared at the dials on the dashboard. Battery. Clock. Speedometer. Fuel. Pekkala muttered a curse. The fuel gauge, which had registered three-quarters full when he left the city, now slumped against empty. He remembered the mechanic who had told him the fuel gauge appeared to be sticking and should be changed. Pekkala wished now that he'd taken the man's advice. The engine seemed to groan. The headlights flickered. It was as if the car had swooned.

'Oh, no you don't,' snapped Pekkala.

As if to spite him, the engine chose that moment to die completely. Then there was only the sound of the tyres rolling to a standstill as Pekkala steered the car to the side of the road.

Pekkala got out and looked around. Then he cursed in Finnish, which was a language well-equipped for swearing. '*Jumalauta!*' he roared into the darkness.

The road stretched out ahead, shining dimly in the night mist. On either side, the forest rose black and impenetrable. Stars crowded down to the horizon, hanging like ornaments from the saw blade tips of the pine trees.

Pekkala buttoned up his coat and started walking.

Fifteen minutes later, he reached the main gate.

Outside the guard shack, the night watchman sat on a little wooden stool, stirring a stick in a fire. The orange light made his skin glow, as if he had been sculpted out of amber.

'Good evening,' said Pekkala.

The guard leaped to his feet. The stool tipped over backwards. 'Holy Mother of God!' he shouted.

'No,' said Pekkala quietly. 'It's me.'

Clumsily, the man regained his balance and immediately rushed into his shack. He reappeared a moment later, carrying a rifle. 'Who the hell is out there?' he shouted at the dark.

'Inspector Pekkala.'

The guard lowered his rifle and peered at Pekkala through the wire mesh. 'You scared me half to death!'

'My car broke down.'

This brought the guard to his senses. He set the rifle aside and opened the gate. The metal creaked as it opened.

'Is Maximov here?' asked Pekkala.

'He drove in just before sunset. He hasn't come out since and I've been on duty the whole time.'

'Thank you,' said Pekkala and he headed off down the road towards the facility. A moment later, when he looked back, Pekkala could see the guard back on his stool, sitting by the fire, poking the flames with a stick.

With only a couple of hours before sunrise, Pekkala arrived at the muddy central yard of the facility. He found Maximov's car parked outside the mess hut, where workers at the facility took their meals. The door was open. Inside, Pekkala discovered Maximov passed out on the floor, mouth open, breathing heavily. He nudged Maximov's foot with the toe of his boot.

'Stop it,' muttered Maximov. 'Leave me alone.'

'Wake up,' said Pekkala.

'I told you . . .' Maximov sat up. His head swung in a wobbly arc until he caught sight of Pekkala. 'You!' he said. 'What do you want?'

'Yelena Nagorski sent for me. She said you had been causing trouble.'

'I wasn't causing trouble,' protested Maximov. 'I love her. And I care for her son!'

'You have a strange way of showing it, Maximov.'

Maximov looked blearily around the room. 'I might have said some things I shouldn't have.'

Pekkala set his boot against Maximov's chest. Gently, he pushed the man over. 'Leave Mrs Nagorski alone.'

Maximov settled back with a soft thump on to the floor. 'I love her,' he muttered again.

'Go back to your dreams,' said Pekkala, 'while I borrow your car for a while.'

But Maximov had already fallen asleep.

Pekkala removed the keys from Maximov's pocket and had just settled himself in the driver's seat of Maximov's car, when a door opened in the Iron House and a man ran out towards him.

It was Gorenko. 'Inspector? Is that you? I must speak with you, Inspector! I've done a terrible thing! Ushinsky showed up for work just after you and I spoke the other day. When he found out that one of our T-34s had been sent to the factory for production, he practically went insane. It's just as I told you he would. He said the prototype wasn't ready, and that we might as well deliver it to the Germans! I tried calling you, Inspector. I wanted you to speak to him, just like we had discussed, but there was no answer at your office so I called Major Lysenkova instead. I told her what was happening. I said I just needed someone to talk some sense into him. Now I hear he's been arrested. They're holding him at the Lubyanka! Inspector. You've got to help him.'

Pekkala had been listening in teeth-clenched silence, but now he finally exploded. 'What did you think was going to happen when you called Major Lysenkova?' he shouted. 'Nagorski sheltered you from these people when he was alive, because he knew what they were capable of. You've been living in a bubble, Professor, out here at this facility. You don't understand. These people are dangerous, even more dangerous than the weapons you've been building for them!'

'I was at my wit's end with Ushinsky,' protested Gorenko, wringing his hands. 'I just wanted someone to talk to him.'

'Well, someone has,' said Pekkala, 'and now I've done all I can for your colleague.'

'There is something else, Inspector. Something I don't understand.'

Pekkala turned the key in the ignition. 'It will have to wait!' he shouted over the roar of the engine.

Gorenko raised his arms in a gesture of exasperation. Then he turned and walked back into the Iron House.

Pekkala wheeled the car around and drove towards the Nagorski house. As he raced along the muddy road, Pekkala wondered again what would become of Yelena and Konstantin now that the T-34 project was completed. Neither of them seemed prepared for the world beyond the gates of this facility. It's too bad Maximov made such a fool of himself this evening, thought Pekkala. From what he knew about the man, Maximov might have made a good companion for Yelena, and a decent father figure for the boy.

Pekkala was lost in these thoughts when suddenly he heard a loud snap and something struck the windshield. His first thought was that a bird had flown into it. This time of night, he told himself, it must have been an owl. Cool air whistled in through the cracked glass. Pekkala was just debating whether to drive on or to pull over when the entire windshield exploded. Glass blew all over the inside of the driving compartment. He felt shards bouncing off his coat and a sharp pain in his cheek as a sliver embedded itself in his skin.

He did not realise he was losing control of the car until it was too late. The back wheels slewed, and the whole car spun in a roar of kicked-up grit and mud. There was a stunning slam, his head struck the side window and then suddenly everything became quiet.

Pekkala realised he was in the ditch. The car was facing the opposite direction from which he had been driving. Opening the door, he fell out into the wet grass. For a moment, he remained there on his hands and knees, not sure if he could stand, trying to get clear in his head what had happened. He was dizzy from the knock to his head, but he did not think he had been badly hurt. Slowly, he clambered to his feet. Upright, but on shaky legs, he slumped back against the side of the car.

Then Pekkala noticed someone standing in the road. All he could see was the silhouette of a man. 'Who's there?' he asked.

'You should have left when you could,' said the silhouette.

The voice was familiar, but Pekkala could not place it.

Then, out of the black, came the flash of a gunshot.

In that same instant, Pekkala heard the clank of a bullet striking the car door beside him.

'I warned you, Maximov!'

'I'm not Maximov!' shouted Pekkala.

The shadow walked towards him. It stood at the edge of the ditch, looking down at Pekkala. 'Then who are you?'

Now Pekkala recognised the voice. 'Konstantin,' he said, 'it's me. Inspector Pekkala.'

The two were close enough now that Pekkala could make out the boy's face and the pistol aimed at his chest.

From the short barrel with its slightly rounded end and the angled trigger guard joining the barrel at the front like the web of a man's thumb, Pekkala recognised the weapon they'd been searching for. It was Nagorski's PPK. In that moment, the truth came crashing down upon Pekkala. 'What have you done, Konstantin?' he stammered as he climbed up out of the ditch.

'I thought you were Maximov. I saw his car . . .'

'I am talking about your father!' snarled Pekkala. He pointed at the PPK, still gripped in Konstantin's fist. 'We know that's the weapon which was used to kill Colonel Nagorski. Why did you do it, Konstantin?'

For what seemed like a long time, the boy did not reply.

Their breathing fogged the air between them.

Slowly, Pekkala held out his hand. 'My boy,' he said, 'there is nowhere you can go.'

Hearing these words, Konstantin's eyes filled with tears. After a moment's hesitation, he placed the PPK upon Pekkala's open hand.

Pekkala's fingers closed around the metal. 'Why did you do it?' he repeated.

'Because it was his fault,' said Konstantin. 'At least, I thought it was.'

'What happened on that day?'

'It was my birthday. The week before, when my father asked me what I wanted, I told him I would like a ride in the tank. At first, he said it was impossible. My mother would never allow it. But then he said that if I promised not to tell her, he would take me out in the machine, out into the proving ground. My mother thought he had forgotten about the birthday altogether. They started arguing. By then, I almost didn't care.'

'Why not?' asked Pekkala.

'Maximov sent me a letter. A letter in a birthday card.'

'What did the letter say?'

'He told me that my parents were splitting up. He said he thought I should know, because they weren't going to tell me themselves.'

'They were going to tell you,' said Pekkala, 'as soon as you moved back to Moscow. It was for the best, Konstantin. Besides, this was none of Maximov's business. And why would he tell you on your birthday?'

'I don't know,' replied Konstantin. 'For news like that, one day is as bad as another.'

'Do you still have that letter?'

Konstantin pulled a canvas wallet out of his pocket. From a jumble of crumpled banknotes and coins, he removed the folded letter. 'I must have read it a hundred times by now. I keep waiting for the words to tell me something different.'

Pekkala looked at the letter. He couldn't read it very well in the dark, but from what he could see, it was exactly as Konstantin described. 'May I keep this for a while?' he asked.

'I don't need it any more,' the boy whispered. He seemed close to tears. Everything seemed to be catching up with him at once.

'Did you tell your parents what was in the letter?' asked Pekkala, folding the page and placing it inside his ID book for safekeeping.

'What would be the point of that?' asked Konstantin. 'I was always afraid they would break up. When I read the letter, a part of me already knew. And I knew Maximov would never lie. He looked after me. More than my own parents.'

'So what did you do?'

'I met up with my father, just as we had planned. He brought me to the proving ground and let me drive the tank, through the puddles, over the bumps, sliding around in the mud. My father was enjoying himself. It was one of the few times I had ever seen him laughing. I should have been enjoying myself, too, but all I could think about was Maximov's letter. The more I thought about it, the more angry I became with my father; that he had chosen this damned machine over our family. I couldn't stand the thought of him hurting me and my mother any more than he'd already done. We stopped the tank out in the middle of the proving ground, in the middle of a muddy pit. We sank down into it. I thought the water would pour in at any moment. I was afraid we were going to drown inside that tank. But my father wasn't worried. He said this machine could drive through anything. We couldn't hear each other properly. It was too noisy in the driving compartment. So we kept the engine running, put the gears in neutral and climbed out on top of the turret.'

'And what happened then?' asked Pekkala.

'He turned to me, and suddenly he wasn't laughing any more. "Whatever happens," he said, "I want you to know that I love your mother very much." He started to climb back inside. That was when the gun fell out of his pocket. It landed on the back of the tank, just above the engine compartment. Because I was closest to it, my father asked me to fetch it, so I did. Until I picked up the pistol, I hadn't thought about hurting him, I swear it. But then I started thinking about what he had just said – about loving my mother. I couldn't bear to let him tell me such a lie and get away with it. He was standing on the turret with his back to me, looking out over that muddy field as if it was the most beautiful place on earth.'

'And that was when you shot him?'

The boy didn't answer his question. 'I had been so furious with him only a second before, but when I saw him fall into the water, all of that anger suddenly disappeared. I couldn't believe what I'd done. I don't know how to say this, Inspector, but even with the gun in my hand, I wasn't even sure I had done it. It was as if someone else had pulled the trigger. I don't know how long I stood there. It felt like a long time, but it may only have been a few seconds. Then I climbed back inside the tank, put it in gear and tried to drive it out of the pit.'

'Why?'

'I panicked. I thought maybe I could make it look like an accident. No one else knew I was with my father that day. Even my mother didn't know. But I didn't really understand how to work the engine. When I was halfway out of the pit, the motor stalled and the machine slid back into the water. My father's body was crushed under the tracks. Then I got out and ran to the supply building. I hid there for a long time. I was covered in mud. I was too scared to move. But then, when the soldiers arrived, I knew I had to get away, so I bolted into the woods. That was when you came after me, and when Captain Samarin was killed.'

'But how did you know the safe path through those woods? Weren't you afraid of the traps?'

'My father hammered little metal discs into the trees. There is a colour scheme. Red, blue, yellow. As long as you keep following that sequence of colours, you are on a safe path through the woods. He never told that to anyone else except me.'

Already, in his mind, Pekkala had begun to run through exactly what would happen to Konstantin now. He was old enough to be tried as an adult. Whatever the extenuating circumstances, he would almost certainly be executed for his crime. Pekkala thought back to his first conversation with Konstantin, when the boy had pleaded with him to track down his father's killers. 'Find them,' Konstantin had said. 'Find them and put them to death.' Hidden in those words, spoken to the man whom Konstantin must have known would one day track him down, was an acceptance of the penalty he realised he'd have to pay.

'Please believe me, Inspector,' pleaded Konstantin, 'I was not trying to harm you. I saw Maximov's car coming down the road and I thought it must be him. I don't even understand why you are here.'

'Your mother called me. She was worried about you, after Maximov's visit this evening. His car was the only one available. What I don't understand, Konstantin, is that if you trusted Maximov, why were you trying to kill him just now?'

'Because, after everything that's happened, I don't know who to trust any more. When he showed up this evening, he had gone wild. We yelled at him to go away and I believed that was the end of it, but when I saw his car coming back, I thought he was going to kill us.'

'For what it's worth,' said Pekkala, 'I don't think Maximov would ever try to hurt you. I do believe that, in his own way, he really loves your mother.' Pekkala's bruises were beginning to throb. 'Why did you run into the forest after he left?'

Konstantin shrugged with a gesture of helplessness. 'Maximov said my mother had been having an affair. I was afraid he might be telling the truth and I could not bear to hear my mother say the words.'

'He was telling the truth. I know he shouldn't have written that letter or said anything about your mother's affair, but people do some strange things when they are in love. Believe me, Konstantin, very strange things.'

Konstantin's voice cracked. 'So it wasn't my father's fault that he and my mother were splitting up.'

'I'm sure if your father were here,' said Pekkala, 'he would tell you they were both to blame.' He rested his hand on Konstantin's shoulder. 'I need you to come with me now.' One glance at Maximov's car told Pekkala that it wasn't going anywhere. 'We'll have to travel on foot.'

'Whatever you say, Inspector.' His voice sounded almost relieved.

Pekkala had seen this kind of thing before. For some people, the burden of waiting to be caught was far worse than whatever might happen to them afterwards. He had known men to walk briskly to their deaths, bounding up the gallows steps, impatient to be gone from this earth.

It was a January morning. Ice floes drifted down the Neva river into Petrograd, then drifted out again with the tide, heading for the Baltic Sea.

In a small motor launch, Pekkala, the Tsar and his son the Tsarevich Alexei, travelled out towards the grim ramparts of the prison island of St Peter and St Paul.

The three of them stood huddled in their coats, while the launch pilot manoeuvred around miniature icebergs, twisting like dancers in the current. Alexei wore a military uniform without insignia and a fur cap, exactly matching the clothes of his father.

They had set out before dawn from Tsarskoye Selo. Now, several hours later, the sun had risen, reflecting pale and milky off the huge stones which made up the outer walls of the prison.

'I want you to see this,' the Tsar had told Pekkala, after summoning him to his study.

'What is the nature of the visit, Majesty?'

'You'll know when we get there,' replied the Tsar.

As they arrived at the island, the fortress towering above them, its battlements like blunted teeth against the dirty winter sky. Leathery streamers of seaweed clung to the lower walls and the waves which slapped against the stone looked as thick and black as tar.

Alexei was lifted from the boat and the three of them walked up the concrete ramp to the main prison door.

Inside, a guard in a greatcoat which reached to his ankles escorted them down a series of stone steps to a level under ground. Here, frost rimed the walls and the damp chill seeped through their clothing. Pekkala had been here before, but never in winter. It did not seem possible that anyone could survive in these conditions for long. And he knew that in the spring, conditions in the dungeons were even worse, when the cells flooded knee-deep in water.

The only light in this stone corridor was an oil lamp carried by the guard, illuminating small wooden doors built into the walls. The guard's shadow teetered drunkenly ahead of him.

The guard led them to one cell and opened the door. Behind the door was a set of bars which formed a second door, so that those on the outside could see who'd been confined inside, without any risk of letting them escape.

When the guard held up the lamp Pekkala looked through the bars at a man strangely hunched on the ground. Only his knees and elbows and the tips of his toes touched the floor. His head rested in his hands and he appeared to be asleep.

Alexei turned to the guard. 'Why is he like that?'

'The prisoner is preserving his body heat, Excellency. That is the only way he will not freeze to death.'

'Tell him to get up,' said the Tsar.

'On your feet!' boomed the guard.

At first, the man did not move. Only when the guard jangled his keys, ready to burst into the cell and haul the man up, did the prisoner finally stand.

Pekkala recognised him now, although just barely. It was

the killer Grodek, convicted two months previously for leading an attempt on the life of the Tsar. The trial had been swift and held in secret. After the verdict, Grodek, who was barely older than Alexei himself, had disappeared into the catacombs of the Russian prison system. Pekkala assumed that Grodek had simply been executed. Even though he had failed to assassinate the Tsar, to attempt it, or even to speak of it, was a capital offence. In addition, Grodek had managed to kill several Okhrana agents before Pekkala caught up with him on the Potsuleyev bridge. It was more than enough to consign this young man to oblivion.

Now only the shape of Grodek's face looked familiar to Pekkala. His hair had been shaved off, and scabies sores patched the large dome of his scalp. Prison clothing hung in rags from his emaciated body and his skin bore the grey polished look of filth which was as old as his imprisonment. His sunken eyes, which had appeared so alert at the trial, stared huge and vacant from their bluish sockets.

Grodek backed against the wall, shivering uncontrollably, his arms crossed over his chest. To Pekkala, it was hard to believe that this was the same person who had shouted defiantly from the witness stand, cursing the monarchy and everything it stood for.

Grodek squinted at the light of the oil lamp. 'Who's there?' he asked. 'What do you want from me?'

'I have brought someone to see you,' said the guard.

Now the Tsar turned to the guard. 'Leave us,' he ordered.

'Yes, Majesty.' The guard set down the lantern and made his way back along the corridor, touching the walls with his hands to find his way.

Now that he was no longer blinded by the lantern light, Grodek could see his visitors. 'Mother of God,' he whispered.

The Tsar waited until the sound of the guard's footsteps had faded away before he spoke to Grodek. 'You know me,' he said.

'I do,' replied Grodek.

'And my son, Alexei,' said the Tsar, resting his hands on the young man's shoulders.

Grodek nodded but said nothing.

'This man,' the Tsar said to Alexei, 'is guilty of murder, and of attempted murder. He tried to kill me, but he failed.'

'Yes,' said Grodek. 'I failed, but I have set something in motion that will end in your death, and the termination of your way of life.'

'You see!' said the Tsar, raising his voice for the first time. 'You see how he is still defiant?'

'Yes, Father,' said Alexei.

'And what is to be done with him, Alexei? He is your own blood; a distant relative, but family all the same.'

'I don't know what should happen,' said the boy. His voice was trembling.

'Some day, Alexei,' said the Tsar, 'you will have to make decisions about whether men like this live or die.'

Grodek stepped forward to the middle of the cell, where the imprints of his knees and elbows dented the mud beneath his feet. 'It may come as a surprise that I have nothing against you or your son,' he said. 'My struggle is against what you stand for. You are a symbol of all that is wrong with the world. It is for this reason that I have fought against you.'

'You have also become a symbol,' replied the Tsar, 'which I suspect was what you wanted all along. And as for your noble reasons for attempting to shoot me in the back, they are nothing

but lies. But I did not come here to gloat over your current situation. I came here because, in a few moments, my son will decide what is to be done with you.'

Alexei turned to look at his father, as confused and frightened as the young man behind the bars.

'But I am to be executed,' said Grodek. 'The guards tell me that every day.'

'And that may still happen,' replied the Tsar, 'if my son decrees it.'

'I don't want to kill that man,' said Alexei.

The Tsar patted his son on the shoulder. 'You will not kill anyone, Alexei. That is not your task in life.'

'But you are asking me to say if he should die!' protested the boy.

'Yes,' replied the Tsar.

Grodek dropped to his knees, his hands resting palm-up on the floor. 'Excellency,' he addressed the Tsarevich. 'You and I are not so different. In another time and place, we might even have been friends. What separates us is only these bars and the things we have seen in this world.'

'Are you innocent?' asked Alexei. 'Did you try to kill my father?'

Grodek was silent.

Water dripped somewhere in the shadows. They heard waves break against the fortress walls, like thunder in the distance.

'Yes, I did,' said Grodek.

'And what would you do now,' asked the Tsarevich, 'if I opened this door and let you out?'

'I would go far away from here,' Grodek promised. 'You would never hear from me again.'

Already, the damp of this dungeon had worked its way into Pekkala's skin. Now he shuddered as it coiled around his bones.

Alexei turned to his father. 'Do not execute this man. Keep him here in this cell for the rest of his life.'

'Please, Excellency,' Grodek begged. 'I never see the sun. The food they give me is not fit even for a dog. Let me leave! Let me go away. I'll disappear. I'd rather die than stay any longer in this cell.'

Turning again, Alexei fixed Grodek with a stare. 'Then find a way to kill yourself,' he replied. The fear had gone from his eyes.

Before they left, the Tsar brought his face close to the bars. 'How dare you say you are the same as him? You are nothing like my son. Remember this. Alexei will rule my country when I'm gone, and if you live to see that day, it will be because he is merciful to animals like you.'

Heading back across the water, Pekkala stood beside the Tsar. He breathed in deeply, filling his lungs with the cold salt air and chasing the stench of that prison from his lungs.

'You think me cruel, Pekkala?' asked the Tsar. He faced straight ahead, scanning the shore.

'I don't know what to think,' Pekkala replied.

'He needs to learn the burden of command.'

'And why bring me to see it, Majesty?'

'One day he will rely on you, Pekkala, as I am relying on you now. You must know his strengths and weaknesses better than he knows them himself. Above all, his weaknesses.'

'What do you mean, Majesty?'

The Tsar glanced at him and looked away again. A layer of frost had formed where his breath touched the lapels of his coat. 'When I was young, my father brought me to that island. He took me to the dungeon and showed me a man who had conspired to murder him. I had to make the same choice as Alexei.'

'And what did you do, Majesty?'

'I shot the man myself.' The Tsar paused. 'My son has a gentle heart, Pekkala, and you and I both know that in this world all gentleness is crushed eventually.'

Less than five years later, having been released by Revolutionary guards from the prison of St Peter and St Paul, Grodek caught up with the Romanovs in the town of Ekaterinburg in western Siberia. It was there, in the basement of a house belonging to a merchant named Ipatiev, that Grodek shot the young Tsarevich, and all the other members of his family.

Pekkala and Konstantin made their way along the dark road, headed towards the facility.

As they walked, Pekkala tried to fathom what must have been going on in Konstantin's mind in that moment he picked up the gun to shoot his father. There were some crimes Pekkala understood. Even the motives for murder made sense to him sometimes. Unchecked fear or greed or jealousy could push anyone to the brink of their own sanity. What happened beyond that point, even the murderers themselves could not predict.

Pekkala remembered the last time he had seen his own father; that day on the train as it pulled out of the station. But now the image seemed strangely reversed. He stood, not on the train but on the platform, seeing through the eyes of his father. Almost out of sight, he glimpsed the young man he had been, arm raised in farewell as he leaned from the window of the carriage, bound for Petrograd and the ranks of the Tsar's Finnish Legion.

Then the train was gone, and he found himself alone. Sadness wrapped around his heart as he turned and walked out of the station. In that moment, Pekkala grasped something he had never understood before – that his father must have known they would not meet again. And if, in the end, the old man had not forgiven him for leaving, it was only because there had been nothing to forgive.

As the image stuttered into emptiness, like a reel of film clattering off its spool, Pekkala's thoughts returned to the present. And he wondered if Nagorski might also have forgiven his son, if he could have found the breath to do so.

By the time they arrived at the facility, the sky was already beginning to lighten.

Pekkala rapped on the door of the Iron House and stood back.

Konstantin waited beside him, resigned to whatever happened next.

The door opened. A waft of stuffy air blew past them, smelling of old tobacco and gun oil. Gorenko filled up the doorway. He had pulled on his dingy lab coat and was fastening its black metal buttons, like a man welcoming guests to his home. 'Inspector,' he said. 'I thought you had gone back to Moscow for the night.' Then he caught sight of Konstantin and smiled. 'Hello, young man! What brings you here so early in the morning?'

'Hello, Professor.' Konstantin could not return the smile. Instead, his face just seemed to crumple.

'I need you to watch him,' Pekkala told Gorenko. 'I regret he will need to be handcuffed.'

'Handcuffs?' Gorenko's eyes grew wide with astonishment. 'He's the Colonel's son. I can't do that!'

'This is not a request,' said Pekkala.

'Inspector,' said Konstantin, 'I give you my word I will not try to run away.'

'I know,' Pekkala answered quietly. 'Believe me, I do, Konstantin, but from now on, there are procedures we must follow.'

'I don't have any handcuffs!' protested Gorenko.

Pekkala reached into his pocket and brought out a set. A key was clipped on to the chain. He handed them to Gorenko. 'Now you do.'

Gorenko stared at the cuffs. 'But for how long?'

'A couple of hours, I expect. My car ran out of fuel on the road. I have to get out there with some petrol and then return to the facility. Then I will pick up Konstantin and we will travel back to Moscow. Until I tell you so myself, no one is to see him or to speak with him. Do you understand?'

Gorenko stared at Konstantin. 'My dear boy,' he said, 'what have you gone and done?' The old professor seemed so confused that it looked as if Konstantin might have to lock the handcuffs on himself.

'Where do you store your fuel, Professor?' asked Pekkala.

'There are five-litre cans on a pallet on the other side of this building. Two of those would be more than enough to get you back to Moscow.'

Pekkala put his hand on the boy's shoulder. 'I'll be back as soon as I can,' he said, as he turned to leave.

'Inspector,' Gorenko called after him, 'I must speak with you. It is a matter of great importance.'

'We can talk about Ushinsky later,' said Pekkala.

'It's not about him,' insisted Gorenko. 'Something has happened. Something I don't understand.'

Pekkala stared at him for a moment, then shook his head, walked into the building and handcuffed Konstantin to a table. Then he turned to Gorenko. 'Follow me,' he said.

Around the side of the building, Pekkala picked up two fuel cans from the pallet. 'What is it, Professor?' The cans were heavy and the liquid sloshed about in them. He hoped he had the strength to carry them all the way back to the Emka.

'It's about the tank,' Gorenko, lowered his voice. 'The one they sent to the factory in Stalingrad.'

'The prototype? What about it, Professor?'

'The tank has not arrived. I called to check. You know, in case there were questions.'

'It's a long way to Stalingrad from here. Perhaps the truck broke down.'

'No, Inspector. I'm afraid that's not it. You see, when I called them, they told me they had never put in a request for the tank.'

Slowly, Pekkala lowered the fuel cans to the ground. 'But they must have. You saw the requisition form, didn't you?'

'Yes. I have it here.' Gorenko rummaged in the pocket of his lab coat and produced a crumpled yellow paper. 'This is my copy. I was going to frame it.'

Holding up the page so that he could read it in the lights which illuminated the compound, Pekkala searched the form for anything out of the ordinary. It was a standard government requisition form, correctly filled out by someone at the Stalingrad Tractor Factory, which he knew had been converted to tank production. The factory designation code looked right – KhPZ 183/STZ. The signature was so hastily scrawled as to be illegible, as most of them were on these forms. There was nothing unusual at all.

'I received a call the day before the truck arrived,' continued Gorenko, 'from someone at the Stalingrad works, informing me about the requisition and telling me to prepare the tank for transport.'

'Did you mention that to the people in Stalingrad?'

'Yes.'

'And what did they say?'

'That they never telephoned me, Inspector.'

'This is probably just a miscommunication. Mistakes like this happen all the time. Was there anything suspicious about the truck or its driver?'

'No. It was just a big truck, like you see on the Moscow highway every day. The driver even knew Maximov.'

'Knew him?'

Gorenko nodded. 'I saw the two of them talking together after the tank had been loaded on board. It didn't seem unusual to me. They're both drivers of one sort or another. I assumed they must have got to know each other the same way that professors become acquainted through their work, even if they live at opposite ends of the country.'

'This truck,' said Pekkala, 'was it a flat bed or a container?'

'I don't know what you mean, Inspector.'

'Did the tank sit on a platform at the back or was it inside a cargo area?'

'Oh, I see. Yes. It was a container. A large metal container big enough to hold the tank.'

'How did the driver get the tank into the container?'

'He drove it in himself. I showed the man how to operate the T-34's gears and pedals. It only took him a minute to get the hang of it. Anyone who knows how to operate a tractor or a bulldozer is already familiar with the principles. Then he rolled the tank up a ramp and into the container.'

'And the container was sealed?'

'Yes, with two large metal doors.'

'What did this container look like?'

'It was painted red, with the State Transport Commission letters painted in green on the side.'

Like almost every other container on the highway, thought Pekkala. 'And the driver? What did he look like?'

'Short, heavyset. Moustache.' Gorenko shrugged. 'He seemed friendly enough.'

'Have you spoken to Maximov about this? Perhaps he knows how to reach the man.'

'I tried to, but he was too drunk to make any sense.'

'Fetch me a bucket of water,' said Pekkala.

For a moment, the ragged silver arc seemed to hang suspended over the sleeping Maximov. Then the water shattered on his face as if it were a pane of fragile glass. Maximov sat bolt upright, spewing a mouthful of water from between his puckered lips.

Pekkala tossed the bucket to the other side of the room where it rolled, clattering loudly into the corner.

'*Mudak!*' shouted Maximov. He doubled over, coughing, then swiped the water from his eyes and glared at Pekkala. 'I thought you were going to let me sleep!'

'I was,' replied Pekkala, 'but now I need you to tell me something.'

'What?'

'What is the name of the driver who picked up the tank from this facility?'

'How should I know?' groaned Maximov, smoothing the hair back on his head.

'You knew the driver. Gorenko saw you talking.'

'He was asking me directions. That's all. Why?'

'The tank has not arrived in Stalingrad.'

'Then perhaps he is a very slow driver.' Maximov ran his hand over his mouth. 'What's the matter, Pekkala? Has your sorcery failed you at last?'

'Sorcery?' Pekkala crouched down in front of the man. 'There never was any sorcery, Maximov, but I've been in this job long enough to know when I'm being lied to. I saw the way your back straightened when I mentioned that the tank had disappeared. I see your eyes drifting up and to the right when you are talking to me now. I see you covering your mouth, and I can read those signs like you can tell when it will rain by looking at the clouds. So tell me, Maximov. Who has that machine and where have they taken it? You don't want this on your conscience.'

'Conscience!' spat Maximov. 'You're the one who needs to search his conscience. You took an oath to serve the Tsar, and just because he's dead doesn't mean that oath no longer applies.'

'You're right,' agreed Pekkala. 'I did take an oath, and what I swore to do I'm doing now.'

'Then I pity you, Pekkala, because while you're wasting your time talking to me, an old friend of yours is deciding the fate of this country.'

'You must be mistaken,' said Pekkala. 'All of my old friends are dead.'

'Not this one!' laughed Maximov. 'Not Alexander Kropotkin.'

Pekkala saw again the wide jaw, the strong teeth clenched in a smile and shoulders hunched like a bear. 'No,' whispered Pekkala. 'That's impossible. He just asked me for a job in the police.'

'Asking for a job? No, Pekkala, he was offering you a chance to work with us. The White Guild could have used a man like you.'

It took a moment for Maximov's words to sink in. 'The Guild?'

'That's right, but he said the Communists had got to you. The incorruptible Emerald Eye had finally been corrupted!'

Now, as Pekkala recalled the words of his last conversation with Kropotkin, it all began to turn around inside his brain. He realised he had utterly misunderstood. 'How did you find Kropotkin?'

'I didn't,' replied Maximov. 'He found me. Kropotkin was the one who figured out that the White Guild was just a front for luring Stalin's enemies to their deaths. He decided to turn the White Guild against the Communists.'

'It was you who killed those agents, wasn't it?'

'Yes, and he ordered me to kill you as well. I would have, if Bruno hadn't got in the way.'

'That was you, outside the Café Tilsit . . . But why?'

'Kropotkin had decided to give you one more chance to join us. He waited at the café every day, knowing you'd show up eventually. When you turned him down, he made a call to me. I drove to the café on a motorcycle. When I saw you lying on the ground, I thought I'd killed you. It was only later that I found out you were still alive. From the apartments of the agents we killed, we managed to steal enough weapons and ammunition to keep us supplied for months. We even got our hands on a brand-new German motorcycle which one of the agents had parked in the middle of his living room! That's the one I was riding when I took a shot at you. Then Kropotkin came up with the idea of stealing a T-34. By the time you people figured out what happened, it would already be too late.'

'Too late for what?'

'To stop the war we are about to declare.'

Pekkala was wondering whether Maximov had gone completely insane. 'You might have been able to murder some government agents, but do you really think the White Guild can overthrow this country?'

'No,' replied Maximov, 'but Germany can. They are looking for any excuse to invade us. All we have to do is offer them a reason. And what better reason than an attack across the Polish border by the Soviet Union's newest, most devastating weapon? If we strike into Poland, the Germans will see it as an act of aggression against the West. That is all the reason they need.'

'How much damage do you think could be done by a single tank?'

'Kropotkin has chosen a place where the Poles have nothing but cavalry units on their border with us. One tank could wipe out an entire brigade.'

'But don't you realise what the Nazis will do to this country if they invade? We are not prepared to defend ourselves.'

'Kropotkin says that the quicker we are defeated, the less bloodshed there will be.'

'That's a lie, Maximov! You may have taken an oath to the Tsar, but do you honestly think this is what he would have wanted? You will have unleashed a thing you can't control. The Germans won't just overthrow the Communists. They will turn this place into a wasteland.'

'I don't believe you.'

'But Kropotkin does! You might think that you're both fighting for the same cause, but I have known Kropotkin for a long time and I have seen his kind before. His only cause is vengeance for a world that no longer exists. All he wants to do is see this country burn.'

'Then let it burn,' replied Maximov. 'I am not afraid.'

Hearing this, Pekkala was consumed by rage. He lunged at Maximov, grabbing him by the lapels of his jacket, and heaved him across the room.

Maximov crashed against the far wall of the mess hut and slumped down with a groan.

'Have you stopped to think that you are not the only one who will go down in flames?' shouted Pekkala. 'Kropotkin doesn't care who lives or dies! That's the difference between you and him. There are people you care about who will suffer even more than you. Yelena, for example. And Konstantin. He is already under arrest.'

'Listen, Pekkala,' growled Maximov, massaging the back of his head. 'He had nothing to do with the Guild. You had no right to arrest him for a thing he did not even know about.'

'I arrested him,' said Pekkala, 'because he murdered his father.'

Maximov froze. His face turned suddenly pale. 'What?'

'Who do you think killed Colonel Nagorski?'

'I don't know!' replied Maximov. 'It wasn't us. That's all I knew for sure. It might have been any number of people. Almost everyone who met Nagorski ended up hating the bastard. But it couldn't have been Konstantin!'

'How did you expect him to react after you wrote him that letter?'

'What letter? What the devil are you talking about?'

'The one you sent him on his birthday, telling him his parents were about to split up.'

'Have you lost your mind? I never wrote him any letter and even if I did, I wouldn't have told him such a thing. That poor boy was already close to a breaking point. Why would I want to make things any worse for him, especially on his birthday?'

'Then how do you explain this?' Pekkala unfolded the letter. He walked across to where Maximov was still slumped against the wall and held the page up in front of him.

Maximov squinted at the letter. 'That's not my writing.'

'Then whose is it? And why would they sign your name to the letter?'

'I . . .' Maximov's face was a mask of confusion. 'I don't know.'

'Who else knew about the break-up besides you and the Nagorskis?'

'What could be gained . . .?' asked Maximov. Then suddenly he shuddered. 'Let me see the letter again!'

Pekkala handed it to him.

Maximov stared at it. 'Oh, no,' he whispered. Slowly, he raised his head. 'This is Kropotkin's writing.'

'What did you tell him about the Nagorskis?'

'Only that I didn't want them involved. I knew that Nagorski and his wife were splitting up. They had been trying to keep it a secret. Konstantin was already on the edge. I knew that once he realised what was going on between his parents, it would destroy his whole world.'

'Did Kropotkin know about the affair with Lev Zalka?'

'No,' replied Maximov, 'only that Nagorski was divorcing his wife.'

'After what you told him, Kropotkin must have guessed that the boy might try something like this. That way, he could not only steal the T-34, but also get rid of the man who invented it.'

'But how did Konstantin get hold of a gun?'

'Nagorski's PPK was found in his possession. He fired it at me earlier this evening. The thing is, Maximov, the person he was trying to shoot was you.'

'Me? But why would he do that? He knows I would never do anything to harm him or his mother.'

'I believe that you care for them, Maximov, and if you hadn't shown up drunk, you might have been a little more convincing. Instead of that, all you managed to do was terrify them.'

'What will they do to him now?' asked Maximov, dazed by what he had heard.

'Konstantin is guilty of murder. You know what they will do to him.'

'Kropotkin swore to me he'd keep them out of it,' whispered Maximov.

'Then help me stop him,' said Pekkala. 'Kropotkin has betrayed you and, whatever you think of me, that's not a thing I ever did.'

It was a moment before Maximov replied. 'If I help you, Pekkala, you will see to it that Konstantin does not get sent to jail. Or worse.'

'I'll do what I can for the boy, but you are guilty of murder and treason, not to mention trying to blow my head off . . .'

'I need no help from you, Pekkala. Just do what you can for Konstantin.'

'I promise,' said Pekkala.

Maximov seemed about to speak, but then he paused, as if he could not bring himself to give up Kropotkin, no matter what the man had done to him.

'Maximov,' Pekkala said gently.

Hearing his name spoken seemed to snap him out of it.

'Kropotkin's heading for some place called Rusalka on the Polish border. It's in the middle of a forest. I could show you on a map. How do you plan on stopping him?'

'One tank can be stopped by another,' said Pekkala. 'Even if it is a T-34, we could send in a whole division to stop him.'

'That is exactly what Kropotkin would want you to do. The sudden arrival of troops in a quiet sector on the border is bound to be misinterpreted by the Poles. And if fighting breaks out, even if it is on our side of the border, Germany will have no trouble seeing that as an act of aggression.'

'Then we will have go in there alone,' said Pekkala.

'What? The two of us?' Maximov laughed. 'And supposing we do track him down? What then? Will you just knock on the side of the tank and order him to come out? Pekkala, I will help you, but I am not a miracle worker . . .'

'No,' interrupted Pekkala. 'You are an assassin and, for now, I am glad of that fact.'

Leaving a guard in charge of Maximov, Pekkala went to find Gorenko in the Iron House.

Gorenko and Konstantin sat side by side on a couple of ammunition crates, like two men waiting for a bus. The handcuffs hung so loosely on Konstantin's wrists that Pekkala knew the boy could have let them slip off without any effort at all if he had chosen to.

'Is there anything that can destroy a T-34?' asked Pekkala.

'Well,' said Gorenko. 'It all depends . . .'

'I need an answer now, Gorenko.'

'All right,' he replied reluctantly. 'There is a weapon we have been working on.' He led Pekkala to a corner of the building and pointed to something which had been covered with a sheet of canvas. 'Here it is.' Gorenko removed the canvas, revealing a long wooden crate with rope handles and a coat of fresh Russian Army paint, the colour of rotten apples. 'No one is supposed to know about this.'

'Open it,' said Pekkala.

Down on one knee, Gorenko flipped the latches of the crate and lifted the lid. Inside was a narrow iron tube. It took Pekkala a moment to realise that this was actually some kind of gun. A thick, curved pad at the end was designed to fit into the user's shoulder, and another pad had been attached to the side, presumably to shield the user's face when the gun was put to use. In front of these, he could see a large pistol grip, and a curved metal guard protecting the trigger. The weapon had a carrying handle about halfway up the tube, and a set of bipod legs for stabilising it. Attached to the end of the barrel was a squared-off piece of metal, which Pekkala assumed must be a muzzle-flash hider. The whole device looked crude and unreliable – a far cry from the neatly machined parts of his Webley revolver or the intricate assembly of Nagorski's PPK.

'What is it?' asked Pekkala.

'This,' replied Gorenko, unable to conceal his pride in the invention, 'is the PTRD, which stands for Protivo Tankovoye Ruzhyo Degtyaryova.'

'You have no imagination when it comes to names,' said Pekkala.

'I know,' replied Gorenko. 'I even have a cat named Cat.'

Pekkala pointed at the gun. 'That will stop a tank?'

Gorenko reached for a green metal box which had been fitted into the wooden case. 'To be precise, Inspector,' he replied, lifting the lid of the box and taking out one of the largest bullets Pekkala had ever seen, 'this is what will stop a tank.' Then he hesitated. 'Or it should. But it's not ready yet. The final product could be years away. And in the meantime, the whole thing is top secret!'

'Not any more,' said Pekkala.

From the telephone in Captain Samarin's office, Pekkala put in a call to Stalin's office at the Kremlin.

Poskrebyshev answered. He was always the one who answered the phone, even at night.

When he heard the man's voice, Pekkala found himself wondering if Poskrebyshev ever left the building.

'Put me through to Comrade Stalin,' Pekkala told the secretary.

'It is late,' replied Poskrebyshev.

'No,' said Pekkala, 'it is early.'

Poskrebyshev's voice disappeared with a click as he rerouted the call to Stalin's residence.

A moment later, a gruff voice came on the line. 'What is it, Pekkala?'

Pekkala explained what had happened.

'Konstantin Nagorski has confessed to killing his father?' asked Stalin, as if he could not understand what he'd been told.

'That is correct,' replied Pekkala. 'He will be transferred to Lubyanka first thing in the morning.'

'This confession, was it obtained in the same manner as the other?'

'No,' said Pekkala. 'It did not require force.' He looked at the mess of papers on Samarin's desk. It seemed as if no one had touched them since the Captain died. In one corner stood a small, framed picture of Samarin with a woman who must have been his wife.

'Do you believe,' asked Stalin, 'that this man Ushinsky really intended to hand over the T-34 to the Germans?'

'No, Comrade Stalin. I do not.'

'And yet you are telling me that one of the tanks has gone missing?'

'That is also correct, but Ushinsky had nothing to do with it.' Pekkala heard the rustle of a match as Stalin lit himself a cigarette.

'This is the second time,' growled Stalin, 'that Major Lysenkova has provided me with faulty information.'

'Comrade Stalin, I believe I can locate the missing T-34. I have narrowed the search to an area of dense woodland on the Polish border. It is a place called the forest of Rusalka.'

'The tank is armed?'

'Fully armed, Comrade Stalin.'

'But there's only one man! Is that what you are telling me? Can he operate it by himself?'

'The process of driving, loading, aiming and firing can be accomplished by a single person. The procedures take considerably more time, but . . .'

'But the tank is just as dangerous in the hands of one person as it is with an entire crew of . . . how many is it?'

'Four men, Comrade Stalin. And the answer is yes. One person who knows what he is doing can turn the T-34 into an extremely dangerous machine.'

There was a silence. Then Stalin exploded. 'I will send an entire infantry division to the area! The Fifth Rifles will do. I will also send the Third Armoured Division. They don't have T-34s but they can get in his way until he's run out of ammunition. I don't care how many men it takes to stop it. I don't care how many machines. I'll send the entire Soviet Army after the bastard if I need to!'

'Then you will give the Germans just the excuse they have been looking for.'

There was another pause.

'You may be right about that,' admitted Stalin, 'but whatever it costs, I will not allow that traitor to go free.'

Pekkala heard the sound of Stalin breathing out. He imagined the grey haze of tobacco smoke around Stalin's head.

'There is a detachment specialising in irregular warfare. It's run by a Major Derevenko. They are a small group. We could send them instead.'

'I am glad to hear it, Comrade Stalin.'

There was a clatter as Stalin put down the receiver and then picked up a second telephone. 'Get me Major Derevenko of the irregular warfare detachment in Kiev,' he commanded. 'Why not? When was that? Are you sure? I did?' Stalin slammed the phone down. A second later, he was back on the line with Pekkala. 'Derevenko has been liquidated. The irregular warfare detachment was disbanded. I can't send in the Army.'

'No, Comrade Stalin.'

'Then you are suggesting I simply allow the attack to go ahead?'

'My suggestion is that you allow me to go out there and stop him.'

'You, Pekkala?'

'I will not be completely alone,' he explained. 'My assistant will accompany me, and there is one other man. His name is Maximov.'

'You mean the one who helped Kropotkin steal the tank?'

'Yes. He has agreed to cooperate.'

'And you need this man?'

'I believe he is our best chance of negotiating with Kropotkin.'

'And what if Kropotkin won't negotiate?'

'Then there are other measures we can take.'

'Other measures?' asked Stalin. 'What sorcery have you got planned, Pekkala?'

'Not sorcery. Tungsten steel.'

'A new weapon?'

'Yes,' replied Pekkala. 'It is still in the experimental stage. We will be testing it out before we leave.'

'Why haven't I heard about this?'

'As with most things, Comrade Stalin, Nagorski ordered it to be kept secret.'

'But not from me!' Stalin roared into the phone. 'I am the keeper of secrets! There are no secrets kept from *me*! Do you remember what I told you about those rumours British Intelligence was spreading? That we are planning to attack Germany across the Polish border? The Germans believe those rumours, Pekkala, and that is exactly what they will think is happening if you don't stop this tank! Our country is not ready for a war! So this had better work, Pekkala! You have forty-eight hours to stop the machine. After that, I am sending in the Army.'

'I understand,' said Pekkala.

'Did you know,' asked Stalin, 'that I also have a son named Konstantin?'

'Yes, Comrade Stalin.'

Stalin sighed into the receiver, the sound like rain in Pekkala's ears. 'Imagine,' he whispered, 'to be killed by your own flesh and blood.'

Before Pekkala could reply, he heard the click of Stalin hanging up the phone.

As the sun rose above the trees, Pekkala squinted through a pair of binoculars at the far end of the muddy proving ground. Trapped like a fly in the filaments of the binoculars' ranging grid was the vast hulk of a T-34, a white number 5 painted on the side of its turret.

'Ready?' he asked.

'Ready,' replied Kirov. He lay on the ground, the stock of the PTRD tucked into his shoulder and the barrel balanced on its tripod. He had only just arrived from Moscow, having been summoned by Pekkala two hours before.

'Fire,' said Pekkala.

A stunning crash filled the air. Two bright red flashes spat from the side of the T-34's turret, followed by a puff of smoke. When the smoke had cleared, Pekkala could see a patch of bare metal where the bullet had struck, obliterating half of the white number. He lowered the binoculars. 'What happened?' he asked.

It was Gorenko who replied. 'The bullet struck at an angle and was deflected.'

Kirov still lay on the ground, his mouth open and eyes wide, stunned by the concussion of the gun. 'I think I broke my jaw,' he mumbled.

'You hit it, anyway,' replied Pekkala.

'It doesn't matter whether you hit it or not,' said Gorenko. 'The shot must be perfect in order to penetrate the hull. The armour at that point is seventy millimetres thick.'

'Look, Professor,' said Kirov, lifting another bullet from beside the gun. 'What happens to one of those machines if it is fired on in battle?'

'That depends,' Gorenko replied matter-of-factly, 'on what you're shooting at it. Bullets just bounce off. They won't leave any more of a dent than a fingerprint on a cold slab of butter. Even some artillery shells can't get through. It makes a hell of a noise, but that's better than what happens if a shell gets through the hull.'

'And what does happen if a shell gets through?'

Gorenko took the bullet from Kirov's hand and tapped the end of it with his finger. 'When this round hits a vehicle,' he explained, 'it is travelling at 1012 metres per second. If it gets inside, the bullet begins to bounce around.' He turned the bullet slowly, so that it seemed to cartwheel first one way and then another. 'It strikes a dozen times, a hundred, a thousand. Everyone inside will be torn to pieces, as thoroughly as if they had been cut apart with butcher knives. Or it will strike one of the cannon shells and the tank will explode from the inside out. Trust me, Inspector Kirov, you do not want to be in a tank when one of these comes crashing through the side. It shreds the metal of a hull compartment into something that looks like a giant bird's nest.'

'Try it again,' said Pekkala.

Once more, Kirov fitted the gun stock against his shoulder. He slid back the breech, ejected the empty cartridge and placed a new round into the chamber.

'This time,' said Gorenko, 'aim for the place where the turret joins the chassis of the tank.'

'But that gap can't be more than a couple of centimetres wide!' said Pekkala.

'We did not design this machine,' said Gorenko, 'so that what you are trying to do would be easy.'

Kirov nestled the side of his face against the cheek pad. He closed one eye, baring his teeth. His toes dug into the ground.

'Whenever you're ready,' said Pekkala.

The words were not even out of his mouth when a bolt of flame shot out of the end of the gun. The air around them seemed to shudder.

When the smoke cleared from around the tank, another stripe of silver showed at the base of the turret.

Gorenko shook his head.

In the distance, the squat shape of the T-34 seemed to mock them.

'It's useless,' muttered Pekkala. 'We will have to think of something else.'

Kirov climbed to his feet and slapped the dirt off his chest. 'Maybe it's time we called in the Army. We've done everything we can do.'

'Not everything,' said Gorenko.

Both men turned to look at him.

'Even Achilles had his heel,' said the Professor, reaching into his pocket and pulling out another cartridge for the PTRD. But this one was not like the others. Instead of the dull metal of tungsten steel, the bullet gleamed like mercury. 'This is a mixture of titanium tetrachloride and calcium,' explained Gorenko. 'It was invented by a man named William Kroll, only a few years ago, in Luxembourg. There is less than a kilo of the stuff in existence. Ushinsky and I obtained some for our experiments.' He tossed the bullet to Kirov. 'I have no idea what will happen. It has never been tested before.'

'Load the gun,' said Pekkala.

At the next shot, there was no red flash. Instead, a small, black spot appeared in the side of the turret. They heard a faint crackling sound, but that was all.

'Nothing,' muttered Kirov.

'Wait,' replied Gorenko.

A moment later, a strange bluish glow outlined the T-34. Then the turret of the tank rose into the air, hoisted on a pillar of flame. A wave of concussion spread out from the machine, flattening the grass. When the wall struck Pekkala, he felt as if he had been kicked in the chest.

The turret spun slowly in the air, as if it weighed nothing at all, then fell to earth with a crash that shook the ground beneath their feet. Thick black smoke billowed from the guts of the machine. Now more explosions sounded, some deep like thunder and others thin and snapping as the ammunition detonated in the blazing machine.

Kirov stood up and slapped Pekkala on the back. 'Now you've got to admit it!'

'Admit what?' Pekkala asked suspiciously.

'That I'm a good shot! A great shot!'

Pekkala made a quiet, grumbling noise.

Kirov turned to Gorenko, ready to congratulate him on the success of the titanium bullet.

But Gorenko's face was grim. He stared at the wreckage of the T-34. 'All this work bringing them to life,' he murmured. 'It's hard to see them killed that way.'

The smiles faded from their faces, as they heard the sadness in the old professor's voice.

'How many more of those titanium bullets have you got?' asked Pekkala.

'One.' Gorenko pulled the other bullet from his pocket and placed it in Pekkala's open hand.

'Can you make others?' said Pekkala.

'Impossible.' Gorenko shook his head. 'What you hold in your hand is all the titanium left in the country. If you miss with that, you will have to resort to something altogether more crude.'

'You mean you have something else?' asked Kirov.

'It is a last resort,' sighed Gorenko. 'Nothing more.' He disappeared back into the assembly building. A moment later, he reappeared carrying what looked like a wicker picnic basket. He set it down in front of the investigators and lifted the lid. Inside, separated by two wooden slats, were three wine bottles. The bottles had been sealed with pieces of cloth instead of corks. These hung down over the lip of each bottle and were held in place by black plumber's tape wound several times around the glass.

Gorenko removed one of the bottles and held it up. 'This is a mixture of paraffin, petrol, sugar, and tar. The cloth stopper on each bottle has been soaked in acetone and allowed to dry. To use this, you light the cloth, then throw the bottle at the tank. But your throw must be very precise. The bottle must land on the top of the engine grille compartment. There are vents on the grille, and the burning liquid will pour down on to the engine. It should set the engine on fire, but even if it doesn't it will melt the rubber hoses connected to the radiator, the fuel injection, and the air intake. It will stop the tank . . .'

'But only if I can get close enough to throw that bottle on to the engine,' said Kirov.

'Exactly,' replied Gorenko.

'For that, I practically have to be on top of the machine.'

'I told you it was a last resort,' said Gorenko, as he replaced the bottle in the wicker container.

Before they parted company, Gorenko pulled Pekkala aside.

'Can you get a message to Ushinsky?'

'Depending on how this mission goes,' replied Pekkala, 'that is a possibility.'

'Tell him I'm sorry we argued,' said Gorenko. 'Tell him I wish he was here.'

They had been driving for twenty-four hours. Kirov and Pekkala worked in three-hour shifts as they travelled towards the Polish border. Maximov sat in the back, his hands cuffed tightly together.

It was Kirov who had insisted on the cuffs.

'Are you sure that's necessary?' asked Pekkala.

'It's standard procedure,' replied Kirov, 'for the transportation of prisoners.'

'I don't blame him,' said Maximov. 'After all, I'm not helping you because I have decided that you're right. The only reason I'm here is to save the life of Konstantin Nagorski.'

'Whether I trust you or not,' said Kirov, 'is not the thing that's going to change Kropotkin's mind.'

It was spring now, a season which, at home in Moscow, Pekkala noticed only in the confined space of Kirov's window boxes, or stuffed into tall galvanised buckets in the open-air market in Bolotnia Square or when the Yeliseyev store set out their annual display of tulips arranged in the shape of a hammer and sickle. But here, it was all around him, like a gently spinning whirlwind, painting the black sides of the Emka with luminous yellow-green dust.

They were fortunate to have missed the time known as the Rasputitsa, when snow melted and roads became rivers of mud. But there were still places where their route disappeared into lakes, reappearing on the far bank and stubbornly unravelling across the countryside. Out in the middle of these ponds, tilting signposts seemed to point the way into a universe below the water's edge.

The detours cost them hours, following paths which did not exist on their maps and even those which did exist sometimes ended inexplicably, while according to the map they carried on like arteries inside a human body.

On their way, they flew through villages whose white-picket-fenced gardens flickered past them as if in the projection of a film.

They stopped for fuel at government depots, where the oil-soaked ground was tinted with rainbows. Half-hidden behind heaps of rubber tyres left to rot beside the depot, the milky purple blossoms of hyacinth cascaded from the hedges. The scent of them mingled with the reek of spilled diesel.

Depots on the Moscow highway were a hundred kilometres apart. The only way fuel could be obtained from them was with government-issued coupons. To prevent these coupons from being sold on the Black Market, each one was made out to the individual to whom they were issued. At each depot, Kirov and Pekkala checked to see whether Kropotkin had cashed in any of his coupons. They turned up nothing.

'What about depots off the highway?' Pekkala asked one depot manager, a man with a fuzz of stubble on his cheeks like a coating of mould on stale bread.

'There are none,' replied the manager, removing his false teeth and polishing them on his handkerchief before replacing them in his mouth. 'The only way to get fuel is from these depots or through the local commissariats, who issue it for use in farm machinery. If the driver of a heavy truck tried to requisition fuel from a commissariat, he would be turned down.'

Kirov held up the bundle of fuel coupons which the manager had given him to inspect. 'Could any of these have come from the Black Market?'

The manager shook his head. 'Either you have a pass book allowing you to requisition fuel for government use, as you do, or you have coupons, like everyone else. Now, if you have coupons, each one has to be matched up with the identity card and driving licence of the person requisitioning the fuel. I've been doing this job for fifteen years and, believe me, I know the difference between what's real and what is fake.'

While the manager filled up their car, Pekkala opened the Emka's boot and stared at the short-wave radio provided by Gorenko. It was the same type to be used in T-34s, enabling them to communicate with artillery and air support groups out of normal radio range at the front. If the mission was successful, they could use it to transmit a message to an emergency channel monitored by the Kremlin before the forty-eight-hour deadline was up. Otherwise, as Stalin had promised, thousands of motorised troops would be dispatched to the Polish border.

Beside this radio lay the ungainly shape of the PTRD. The more Pekkala stared at it, the less it looked to him like a weapon and more like a crutch for some lame giant. He kept the titanium bullet in the pocket of his waistcoat, fastened shut with a black safety pin.

'Leave it,' said Kirov, closing the lid of the boot. 'It will be there when we need it.'

'But will it be enough?' asked Pekkala. The thought that they might already be too late to prevent Kropotkin from driving the tank into Poland echoed through Pekkala's mind.

At some point in their eighteenth hour on the road, Kirov fell asleep at the wheel. The Emka slid off the highway and ended up in a field planted with sunflowers. Fortunately, there was no ditch, or the Emka would have been wrecked.

By the time the car had stopped moving, its side and windshield were coated with a spray of mud and the tiny pale green tongues of baby sunflower leaves. Without a word, Kirov got out of the car, went around to the back door and opened it. 'Get out,' he said to Maximov.

Maximov did as he was told.

Kirov unlocked the cuffs. Then he held out his hand towards the empty driver's seat.

With Maximov at the wheel and the two investigators pushing with their shoulders against the rear cowlings, they eased the Emka out of the mud and back on to the road.

High above them, vultures circled lazily on rising waves of heat. All around was the smell of this landlocked world, its dryness and its dustiness sifting through their blood, as spiced as nutmeg powder.

From then on, they drove in shifts of two hours each. By the time they arrived at the Rusalka, all three of them had reached the point of exhaustion where they could not have slept even if they'd wanted to.

On the map, the forest resembled a jagged shard of green glass, hemmed in by white expanses indicating cultivated fields. It straddled the Soviet and Polish border, marked only by a wavy dotted line.

The Rusalka lay approximately 200 kilometres due east of Warsaw. Only a handful of villages existed on the Russian end of the forest, but there were, according to Pekkala's map, several on the Polish side.

Pekkala had studied it so many times that by now the shape of it was branded on his mind. It was as if by knowing its outline he might be better prepared for whatever lay inside its boundaries.

It was late in the afternoon when they reached a tiny village called Zorovka, the last Russian settlement before the road disappeared into the forest. Zorovka consisted of half a dozen thatched-roof houses built closely together on either side of the road running into the Rusalka. Indignant-looking chickens wandered across the road, so unused to traffic that they barely seemed to notice the Emka until its wheels were almost on top of them.

The village seemed deserted except for a woman who was tilling the earth in her garden. When the Emka rolled into sight the woman did not even raise her head, but continued to chip away with a hoe at the muddy clumps of dirt.

The fact that she did not look up made Pekkala realise that she must have been expecting them. 'Stop the car,' he ordered.

Kirov hit the brakes.

Pekkala got out and walked over to the woman.

As he crossed the road towards her, the woman continued to ignore him.

Beneath the marks of wagon wheels and horses' hooves, Pekkala saw the tracks of heavy tyres. Now he knew they were on the right path. 'When did the truck pass through here?' he asked the woman, standing on the other side of her garden fence.

She stopped chipping at the earth. She raised her head. 'Who are you?' she asked.

'I am Inspector Pekkala, from the Bureau of Special Operations in Moscow.'

'Well, I don't know anything about a truck,' she said in a voice so loud that Pekkala wondered if she might be hard of hearing.

'I can see the tyre tracks in the road,' said Pekkala.

The woman came to the edge of her fence and looked out into the road. 'Yes,' she said, her voice almost a shout, 'I see them, too, but I still don't know anything about it.' Then she glanced at him and Pekkala knew from the look on her face that she was lying. And more than this – she wanted him to know she was lying.

A jolt passed through Pekkala's chest. He looked down at the ground, as if distracted by something. 'Is he here?' he whispered.

'He was,' whispered the woman.

'How long ago?'

'Yesterday, some time in the afternoon.'

'Was he alone?'

'I did not see anyone else.'

'If he is gone,' asked Pekkala, 'why are you still afraid?'

'The others in this town are hiding in their houses, watching us and listening at their doors. If anything happens, they will blame me for talking to you, but I will blame myself if I say nothing.'

'If anything happens?' asked Pekkala.

The woman stared at him for a moment. 'This man who drove the truck, he took somebody with him. Someone from this village. His name is Maklarsky; a forester here in the Rusalka.'

'Why would he kidnap somebody?' asked Pekkala.

'At first the driver said he only wanted some fuel for his truck. But the thing is we are only allowed so much every month from the local commissariat. We only have one tractor in this village and what they give us isn't even enough to keep it running. The amount of fuel he wanted was more than we draw in a month. So we told him no. Then he asked for someone to show him the way to the border. The Rusalka is patrolled by Polish cavalry. Our own soldiers come through here sometimes, once a month or so, but the Poles ride through that forest almost every day. The woods are full of trails. It's easy to get lost. We told him he should go back out to the Moscow highway and cross the border into Poland from there. That was when the driver pulled a gun.'

'What did he look like?' asked Pekkala.

'Broad shoulders, a big square face and a moustache. He had blond hair turning grey.'

'His name is Kropotkin,' said Pekkala, 'and he is very dangerous. It is very important that I stop this man before he crosses into Poland.'

'He may have done that already,' said the woman.

'If he had,' said Pekkala, 'we would know about it.'

'This man said that people would come looking for him. He said we should keep a look out for a man with a black coat, who wore a badge shaped like an eye on his lapel.'

Pekkala turned up the collar of his coat. 'He meant this.'

'Yes,' said the woman, staring at the emerald eye. 'He told us if we kept quiet, he would let his hostage go. But I didn't believe him. That is why I'm talking to you now. The others are too scared to speak with you. My name is Zoya Maklarskaya and that man I told you about is my father. The decision is mine whether talking to you now will do more harm than good.'

'We will do what we can to bring your father back,' said Pekkala.

The woman nodded at the churned-up road. 'Those tracks will lead you to him,' she said, 'and you had better leave now if you want to find him before nightfall. Once the dark has settled on that forest, even the wolves get lost in there.'

As Pekkala turned around, he saw a face in the window of a house, sliding back into the shadows like a drowned man sinking to the bottom of a lake.

In fading light, they followed Kropotkin's tracks into the forest. The ranks of trees closed around them. Sunset leaned in crooked pillars through the branches, lighting up clearings where blankets of grass gleamed as luminously as the emerald in Pekkala's gold-framed eye.

The road itself appeared to mark the border.

On one side, they passed wooden signs written in Polish, indicating that they were travelling right along the edge of the two countries. On the other side, nailed to trees, were metal plaques, showing the hammer and sickle emblem of the Soviet Union. From beneath the signs, where the nails had pierced the bark, white trickles of sap bled down to the ground.

From his hours of staring at the map, the Rusalka compressed in Pekkala's mind until he had convinced himself that such a monster of a tank could never hide for long.

But now that they were in it, bumping along over washboard roads, eyes straining to follow the snakeskin trail of Kropotkin's tyre tracks, Pekkala realised that a hundred of those tanks could vanish in here without trace.

Overwhelmed by the vastness of these woods, Pekkala's memories of the great cities of Leningrad, Moscow and Kiev all began to feel like a dream. It was as if the only thing that existed on this earth, and had ever existed, was the forest of Rusalka.

When the sunlight had finally gone, the darkness did not seem to settle from above as it did in the city. Instead, it rose up from the ground, like a black liquid flooding the earth.

They could no longer see the truck's wheel marks, and it was too dangerous to use the Emka's headlights when Kropotkin might be waiting for them around every bend in the road.

They steered the Emka off the road, cut the engine, and climbed stiff-legged from the car. The dew had settled. Wind blew through the tops of the trees.

'We'll start looking again as soon as it is light,' said Pekkala. 'As long as it's dark, Kropotkin can't risk moving either.'

'Can we make a fire?' asked Kirov.

'No,' replied Pekkala. 'Even if he couldn't see the flames, the smell of smoke would lead him right to us. We will all take it in turns standing guard. I'll take the first watch.'

While Pekkala stood guard, Maximov and Kirov lay down in the cramped space of the car, Maximov in the front seat and Kirov in the back.

Pekkala sat on the hood of the Emka, feeling the warmth of the engine, which sighed and clicked as it cooled, like the irregular ticking of a clock.

After years spent in the constant rolling thunder of underground trains snaking their way beneath the pavements of Moscow, the clunk of water pipes in his apartment, and the distant clattering of trains pulling into the Belorussian station, the stillness of this forest unnerved Pekkala. Old memories of his time in Siberia come back to haunt him as he stared helplessly into the dark, knowing that Kropotkin could come within a few paces before he'd be able to see him.

Beads of moisture gathered on his clothes, transforming the dull black of his coat into a cape of pearls which shimmered even in this darkness.

After a while, the back door of the Emka opened and Kirov climbed out. The windows of the car had turned opaque with condensation.

'Has it been three hours already?' asked Pekkala.

'No,' replied Kirov. 'I couldn't sleep.' He came and stood beside Pekkala, hugging his ribs against the cold. 'How much time do we have left?'

Pekkala checked his pocket watch. 'Fourteen hours. By the time the sun comes up, we'll only have a couple left.'

'Would it really be enough to start a war?' asked Kirov. 'One tank, driven by a lunatic? Even if he does manage to kill a few innocent people, surely the world would come to its senses in time . . .'

Pekkala cut him off. 'The last war was started by a lunatic named Gavrilo Princip. The only thing he used was a pistol, and all he had to do was kill one man, the Archduke Ferdinand.'

'An archduke sounds pretty high up.'

'He may have had an important title, but was Ferdinand important enough to bring about the deaths of over ten million people? You see, the war began, Kirov, because one side wanted it to begin. All that side needed was a big enough lie to convince its own people that their way of life was being threatened. The same is true today, and so the answer is yes. One lunatic is more than enough.'

The car door opened.

Pekkala felt a rush of cold brush across his face, sweeping away the stale air inside the Emka. He had been asleep, legs twisted down into the seat well and head resting on the passenger seat. The Emka's gear stick jabbed into his ribs. His neck felt like the bellows of a broken accordion.

Someone was shaking his foot.

It seemed to Pekkala as if he had only just closed his eyes. He couldn't believe it was time to go back out on watch again.

'Get up, Inspector,' whispered Kirov. 'Maximov is gone.'

Kirov's words jolted him awake. He scrambled out of the car. 'What do you mean he's gone?'

'I finished my watch,' explained Kirov. 'Then I woke up Maximov and told him it was his turn to go on. I got up a few minutes ago to take a piss. That's when I noticed he was gone.'

'Perhaps he's nearby.'

'Inspector, I searched for him and found nothing.'

Both men stared out into the dark.

'He's gone to warn Kropotkin,' muttered Kirov.

At first, Pekkala was too shocked to reply, stubbornly refusing to believe that Maximov had deserted them.

'What should we do?' asked Kirov.

'We won't find them in the dark,' replied Pekkala. 'Not out here. Until it gets light, we wait for them to come to us. But as soon as it is light enough to see, we will go looking for them.'

A short distance up the road from where the Emka had been parked, they set up the PTRD anti-tank rifle in the ditch and covered it with a camouflage of pine branches. In addition, each of them carried a bottle filled with the explosive mixture. The greasy liquid sloshed inside its glass containers.

They spent the rest of the night huddled in the ditch, watching the road. In the plunging darkness, their eyes played tricks on them. Phantoms drifted in among the trees. Voices whispered in the hissing of the wind, then suddenly were gone and had never been there at all.

In the first eel-green glimmer of dawn, they saw something coming towards them.

It did not seem human. The creature loped like a wolf, keeping to the edge of the road.

Slowly, Pekkala reached up to the edge of the ditch and eased his gun out of its holder.

Kirov did the same.

Now they could see it was a man, and a moment later, they recognised the bald head of Maximov. He ran with a long, steady stride, hunched over, his arms hanging down at his sides.

Arriving at the Emka, Maximov stopped and peered cautiously into the trees. 'Kirov,' he whispered, 'Pekkala, are you in there?'

Pekkala climbed out of the ditch and stood in the road, keeping the gun in his hand. 'What do you want, Maximov?' In spite of what his instincts told him about Maximov, Pekkala had made up his mind to shoot the man if he so much as made a sudden movement.

Maximov seemed confused that Pekkala was not by the car. But then he realised what the two inspectors must be thinking. 'I heard him!' said Maximov urgently, as he made his way towards Pekkala. 'I heard the sound of metal against metal. I followed. I had to move quickly.' He came to a stop. Only then did he notice Kirov in the ditch, and the PTRD laid out under its covering of pine. He stared at the two men in confusion. 'Did you think I had abandoned you?'

'What else were we supposed to think?' snapped Kirov.

'After what that man did to Konstantin,' Maximov answered, 'did you honestly believe I would go back to helping him?'

'You say you followed him?' Pekkala asked, before Kirov could respond.

Maximov nodded. He pointed down the road. 'He's only about fifteen minutes away. There's a clearing just off the road. The tank is already off the truck. It looks like he's getting ready to head out as soon as it is light enough to see.'

'Was he alone?' asked Pekkala. 'Did you see the man he took hostage?'

'The only person I saw was Kropotkin. We must go now if we're going to catch him. It will be much harder to stop that tank once he's on the move.'

Without another word, Kirov gathered up the PTRD. As he climbed out of the ditch, he handed his Tokarev to Maximov. 'You'd better have this,' he said, 'in case you can't talk him out of it.' Then he glanced into the sky and exclaimed softly, 'Look!'

Maximov and Pekkala turned. A plume of thick smoke rose above the trees in the distance.

'What is that?' asked Kirov. 'Is that the exhaust from the tank?'

'It looks more like he's trying to burn the forest down,' said Maximov.

At the car, each man took a bottle of the explosive mixture and as much extra ammunition as he could carry. Then they set off running, Maximov in the lead, wolf-striding ahead of the two inspectors.

As they ran, the black smoke spread across the sky.

Before long, they could smell it, and then they knew it wasn't wood smoke. The thick haze reeked of burning oil.

They moved as quickly as they could through the maze of trees, over spongy earth where mud sucked at their boot heels and strange insect-eating plants, their smell like rotting meat, reared their open mouths.

Kirov followed close behind Pekkala, cursing softly as he scraped his shins against the limbs of fallen trees. Spindly branches whipped their faces and snatched at the guns in their hands.

By the time Maximov held up his hand for them to stop, Pekkala was completely drenched in sweat. He still had on his coat and the bottle in his hand had made running even more difficult.

Burdened by the bulky PTRD, Kirov was also exhausted.

Only Maximov seemed to show no sign of exertion, as if he could have kept on running without a pause, until the waves of the Atlantic washed about his feet.

They stepped into the trees to take cover. It was quickly growing lighter now.

Ahead, Pekkala could make out the blazing skeleton of the truck.

'What's he doing, giving away his position like that?' whispered Kirov. 'The smoke must be visible halfway across Poland.'

They crawled forward until, through the shifting flames, they could make out the shape of the tank. In front of it, they saw Kropotkin. He was pouring fuel from a battered petrol container into the tank. Then, with a roar of anger, he flung the container across the clearing.

'That's why he didn't stop at the depots,' whispered Maximov. 'He's been draining fuel out of the T-34. Now he probably doesn't have enough to drive the tank all the way into Poland.'

'So he set fire to the truck,' said Pekkala. 'The woman I talked to in the village said that Polish cavalry run patrols through these woods all the time. He lit the fire so the Poles will to come to him.'

Kropotkin disappeared around the other side of the tank. When he reappeared, an old man was with him. He was short and bald, with narrow shoulders, wearing a collarless blue work shirt and heavy corduroy trousers. Pekkala knew it must be Zoya Maklarskaya's father. Kropotkin had tied Maklarsky's hands behind his back. Now he hauled the old man to the centre of the clearing.

'You swore there would be petrol here!' shouted Kropotkin.

'There was!' The old man pointed at the empty fuel can. 'I told you, they always leave some here for an emergency.'

'One fuel can is not enough!'

'It is if you're driving a tractor,' protested Maklarsky. 'You didn't tell me how much you needed. You just asked if there was fuel.'

'Well, I guess it doesn't matter now,' said Kropotkin, taking a knife from his pocket.

'What are you going to do with that?' Maklarsky's eyes were fixed on the blade.

'I'm letting you go, old man,' replied Kropotkin, 'just like I promised.' He cut through the ropes and they fell like dead snakes to the ground. 'Go on,' said Kropotkin, and gave him a shove.

But Maklarsky didn't run. Instead, he turned and looked back at Kropotkin, motionless.

'Go on!' bellowed Kropotkin, folding the knife shut with a click and returning it to his pocket. 'I don't need you any more.'

Slowly, Maklarsky began to walk out of the clearing, following the short path which led to the main road.

Then the three men watched helplessly as Kropotkin drew a gun from his coat. The dry snap of a pistol echoed through the trees.

Maklarsky staggered forward. He did not seem to realise what had happened. Crookedly, he walked on a few more paces.

Kropotkin strode across the clearing. With the barrel of the gun touching the back of Maklarsky's head, he pulled the trigger. This time, the old man dropped, so suddenly it looked as if the ground had swallowed him up.

Kropotkin returned to the tank. He climbed up on to the turret, whose hatch was already open, and dropped down inside the machine.

Pekkala realised that Kropotkin was preparing to move out, whether he had enough fuel or not. He nodded at Kirov.

Kirov unlocked the tripod from the barrel of the anti-tank rifle. He set it up and lay down behind the gun.

'Do you have a clear shot?' asked Pekkala.

'No,' replied Kirov, after he had squinted through the sights. 'Too many trees in the way.'

'We'll move around the side and stop him where the clearing meets the road,' said Pekkala.

Kirov picked up the gun and the three men set off down the road, keeping inside the cover of the trees. They reached the place where the wide path intersected with the road. Here, they realised that the path from the clearing did not run straight out to the road. It curved to the left, so that the tank was out of sight. The only way Kirov would have a clear shot was if the tank drove out to the road.

Knowing they had little time to spare, the three men dashed across the road and slid down into the ditch on the other side. With trembling hands Kirov set up the PTRD so that it was pointing directly down the path into the clearing.

If Kropotkin tried to drive the T-34 out on to the road, Kirov would have a clear shot.

'Do you still think you can talk him out of it?' Pekkala asked Maximov.

'I doubt it, but I can probably buy you some time.'

'All right,' said Pekkala. 'We'll both go. We'll have a better chance if we both try to reason with him, but if he won't listen to us, get out of his way as fast as you can. He's bound to head towards the road. He doesn't want to get trapped in that clearing and he's got nowhere else to go except down that path.'

'I don't see how you can walk out there to face a tank with nothing more than words to shield yourself,' said Kirov.

Pekkala held out the titanium bullet. 'If words don't convince him, then maybe this will. No matter what happens, if you see an opportunity to take the shot, take it. Do you understand?'

'It's a hell of a risk, Inspector.' Kirov took the bullet from his hand. 'If this thing hits you, it will blow you to pieces.'

'That's why I'm glad you're a good shot.'

'At least you finally admitted it,' said Kirov, as he settled himself behind the gun.

Maximov and Pekkala set out towards the clearing.

Pekkala felt the open space around him as if it were a field of electricity. He spotted the tank, hunched like a cornered animal at the edge of the clearing. With each step towards the iron monster, he felt his legs weaken. His breathing grew shallow and fast. He had never been so aware of the impossible fragility of his own body.

Leading away from the clearing, Pekkala saw woodsmen's trails, too narrow for trucks, which snaked into the darkness of the forest. On one of these, a glint of silver caught his eye. Just off the path, partially camouflaged with branches, a motorcycle stood propped against a tree. A pair of leather-padded goggles hung from the handlebars. The machine looked almost new and it was close enough that he could even see the maker's name – Zundapp – emblazoned in silver on the teardrop-shaped fuel tank. In that moment, he realised it was the same machine he had seen the day Maximov had tried to gun him down outside the Café Tilsit. This motor-cycle was the first indication Pekkala had seen that Kropotkin planned on surviving what he was about to do.

There was no sound except the crackle of the flames still rising from the wreckage of the truck. Smoke swirled through bolts of sunlight which made their way down through the trees.

They reached the clearing, which was littered with strips of old bark from the logs which had been piled there by the foresters. Between them and the tank lay the body of the old man, face down in the dirt, a red circle in the pale blue cloth of his shirt.

The two men halted.

Now that he was only a few paces from the T-34, it seemed to Pekkala that his quarrel was no longer with Kropotkin but with the machine itself. He tried to shake off the feeling that the monster had come to life, and was watching them through the hatred-narrowed eyes of its gun ports.

'Kropotkin!' shouted Maximov.

There was no reply. Instead, with a dreadful bellowing sound, the tank engine fired up. The noise was deafening. Two jets of smoke poured from its exhaust pipes. The T-34 lurched forward.

Instinctively, the two men stumbled back.

Suddenly the tank jerked to a stop, like a dog held by a chain.

'Kropotkin!' Pekkala called out. 'We know you're short of fuel. Just listen to us!'

But if his words reached through the layers of steel, Kropotkin gave no sign of having heard them.

The T-34 jolted towards them, spinning its tracks. Mud and twisted shreds of bark sprayed out behind the machine. This time it did not stop.

'Run!' shouted Pekkala.

But Maximov was already on the move.

As Pekkala turned and sprinted for the road the bottle fell out of his hands but he did not stop to pick it up. He could feel the machine right behind him.

One moment, Maximov was beside him and the next he was gone as he dived away into the trees.

Pekkala kept running. The tank was almost on top of him.

The weight of his coat held him back. His feet slipped on the muddy ground. With every gasp of breath, the acrid haze of burning rubber poured into his lungs. Pekkala saw the main road straight ahead. He spotted Kirov in the tall grass growing along the edge of the ditch and the PTRD aimed right at him.

The roaring grew louder as the tank gathered speed. Pekkala realised he would not make it to the road before the T-34 overtook him.

'Shoot!' he yelled.

The tank was closing on him, only a few paces behind.

'Shoot!' he screamed. And then Pekkala slipped. He barely had time to register that he had fallen before slamming into the ground.

A second later, the huge machine rolled over him, its tracks on either side of his body, their terrible clatter filling his ears. Pekkala was sure he would be crushed, like some animal run over by a car.

As the belly of the tank slid past above him, Pekkala saw a flash from the PTRD , and then there was a stunning crash of metal as the titanium round struck the turret.

The treads of the T-34 locked. The machine slid to a halt and the engine clanked into neutral.

The shot must not have penetrated the hull, thought Pekkala. Kropotkin is still alive.

Now the tearing rattle of the T-34's machine gun sounded above him. A line of bullets stitched across the ditch. The trees where Kirov had taken cover began to fly apart, revealing pale slashes as the bark was torn away.

Pekkala heard footsteps behind him. Turning his head, he saw Maximov running out of the woods, clumps of mud flicking up from his heels. Clasped in his hand was a bottle of the explosive mixture, the rag end already lit and spilling greasy flames as he sprinted towards the tank.

'Get away!' Maximov shouted. 'Damn it, Pekkala, get out while you can!' In a few more strides, he had reached the T-34 and immediately climbed up onto the engine grille.

Underneath the tank, Pekkala struggled though the mud, clawing at the ground to free himself before Maximov detonated the explosives. Scrambling clear, Pekkala heard a crash of glass as Maximov smashed the bottle. Then came a roar as burning liquid splashed through the engine grille and into the T-34's motor compartment.

Pekkala heard Kropotkin scream inside the tank.

He didn't look back. Pekkala had just raised himself up, ready to sprint towards the road, when a wall of concussion blew him off his feet. He landed heavily, face down, the wind knocked out of him. In the next instant, a wave of fire washed over him, spreading like fingers over the ground and setting it alight.

'Get up!' Kirov waved to him from the ditch. 'Inspector, it's going to explode!'

Pekkala climbed to his feet and ran. Behind him, he could hear the crackle of ammunition bursting inside the machine. He threw himself down beside Kirov just as the muffled thump of superheated cannon shells thundered out of the tank.

Still slapping the sparks from his clothes, Pekkala raised his head and watched as the machine tore itself apart.

The T-34 was now engulfed in flames. Its gun ports glittered red as fire consumed first the driver's, then the gunner's compartment.

A few seconds later, when the remaining ammunition exploded, the top turret hatch blew off with a shriek of tearing steel. It tumbled like a blazing wheel into the woods, leaving a spray of molten paint in its path. Now, from the ruptured hull of the tank, brilliant orange geysers, tinged with black, reared up into the sky.

The air was filled with the smell of burning diesel fuel and pine sap from branches cut down by the T-34's machine gun.

As smoke boiled from the wreckage, the T-34 no longer seemed like a machine to Pekkala. Instead, it looked more like a living thing writhing in agony.

When the explosions had finally died away, Pekkala and Kirov climbed cautiously out of the ditch, so mesmerised by the death throes of the T-34 that at first they did not see the line of men on horseback appearing from around a bend in the road.

The horses were moving at a canter, and the men had drawn rifles from the scabbards mounted on their saddles.

'Poles,' whispered Pekkala.

The squad of Polish cavalry rode up to them. The men carried their guns with barrels pointed upwards and the butt plates resting on their thighs. The officer of the troop, a pistol on his belt, sat on his horse and stared at the tank, which resembled the carapace of some huge and predatory insect, hostile even when the soul had been burned out of it. The officer looked at his men, all of whom were watching him for a sign of what to do next.

Pekkala and Kirov were completely surrounded by the horses. Not knowing what else to do, they raised their hands.

This drew the attention of the officer. He flapped his hand and grunted, to show that their gesture of surrender was not necessary.

Bewildered, Kirov and Pekkala lowered their hands.

Then one of the men, somewhere hidden in the ranks, began to laugh.

The officer's head snapped up. At first, he looked angry, but then a smile crept across his face. 'Machine bust!' he said.

The others started laughing now. 'Machine bust!' they all began to shout.

Bewildered, Kirov looked at Pekkala.

Pekkala shrugged.

Only when the laughter had died down did the cavalry men replace their rifles in the scabbards.

The officer nodded at Pekkala. He said something in Polish, which Pekkala could not understand. Then he shouted an order and spurred his horse. The troop of cavalry began to move. The men were talking in the ranks, joking loudly and glancing back at the two inspectors, but at a sharp command from their officer, they immediately fell silent. Then there was only the sound of horses' hooves as they passed on down the road.

The two men were alone again.

'What was that?' asked Kirov.

'I have no idea,' replied Pekkala.

They walked back to the tank. Scorched metal showed where the paint had been. The engine grille sagged down on to the ruined motor parts, and the tyres had melted into black puddles beside the tracks.

There was no sign of Maximov.

'I guess he didn't make it,' said Kirov.

Pekkala prepared himself for the sight of Maximov's shattered corpse. He wondered how much could be left of anyone caught in the path of such destruction. But there was no sign of Maximov. Bewildered, as Pekkala glanced around the clearing, it occurred to him that the fire must have consumed the man entirely. In that moment he realised that the Zundapp motorcycle was missing. He saw the line of motorcycle tracks, disappearing down one of the woods-men's trails. Then it dawned on Pekkala that Maximov was not dead at all. He had escaped, hidden by the wall of fire and the roar of exploding ammunition.

'I misjudged him,' said Kirov. 'He died very bravely.'

Pekkala did not reply. He glanced at Kirov, then glanced away again.

They started walking back towards the Emka.

'How much time do we have?' asked Kirov.

'About an hour,' replied Pekkala. 'I hope that radio works.' It was only now that he realised his coat was still smoulder-ing. He swatted at his sleeves, smoke lifting like dust from the charred cloth.

'Good thing you have those new clothes I bought you.'

'Yes,' said Pekkala. 'Lucky me.'

If there was a border checkpoint at the edge of the Rusalka forest, Maximov never saw it. The first indication he had that he was in a different country was when he rumbled through a village and saw a sign for a bakery written in Polish. Since then, he had not stopped. At fuel-ling stations in the eastern part of the country, he had been able to pay for petrol with the Russian money he was carrying in his wallet. But as he approached the border of Czechoslovakia, the locals stopped accepting Russian cur-rency and he was forced to barter his watch, then a gold ring. Finally, he siphoned it out of other vehicles using a piece of rubber hose.

Now it was the third day of Maximov's journey. As the Zundapp crested the hill, sunrise winked off his goggles. He had been riding all night, coat buttoned up to his throat to fend off the chill as he raced across the Polish countryside.

He pulled off the road and looked out over fields of newly sprouted barley, wheat and rye. Feathers of smoke rose from the chimneys of solitary farmhouses.

Maximov could see the little checkpoint at the bottom of the hill and knew that all the land beyond was Czechoslovakia.

Minutes later, Maximov arrived at the border. Like most of the crossings on these quiet, secondary roads, the checkpoint consisted of a hut which had been divided into two, with a red-and-white-striped boom across the road, that could be raised and lowered by the guards.

A bleary-eyed Czech border guard shuffled out to meet him. He held out his hand for Maximov's papers.

Maximov reached into his coat and pulled out his pass book.

The Czech flipped through it, glancing up at Maximov to check his face against the picture.

'The Polak is asleep,' he said, nodding towards the other half of the building, where beige blinds had been pulled down over the windows. 'Where are you going, Russian?'

'I am going to America,' he said.

The Czech raised his eyebrows. For a moment, the guard just stood there, as if he could not comprehend the idea of travelling that far. Now his gaze turned towards the motorcycle. 'Zundapp,' he said, pronouncing it 'Soondop'. He grunted with approval, resting his knuckles on the chrome fuel tank, as if it were a lucky talisman. At last, he handed Maximov his pass book and raised the boom across the road. 'Go on to America,' he said, 'you and your beautiful Soondop!'

It took Maximov another week to reach Le Havre. There, he sold the beautiful Zundapp and bought a ticket to New York. When the ship left port, he stood at the railing, watching the coast of France until it seemed to sink beneath the waves.

Pekkala stood in Stalin's office at the Kremlin, hands behind his back, waiting for the man to appear.

Finally, after half an hour, the trap door clicked and Stalin ducked into the room. 'Well, Pekkala,' he said as he settled himself into his red leather chair, 'I have taken your advice and placed the engineer named Zalka in charge of completing the T-34. He assures me that the final adjustments to the prototype design will be ready in a matter of weeks. Zalka has told me that he will be adding several safety features to the original design. Apparently, the test drivers had already started calling it . . .'

'I know,' said Pekkala.

'I happen to agree with Nagorski,' continued Stalin. 'The machine should come first, but we can't have them calling the T-34 a coffin before it's even started rolling off the production line, can we?'

'No, Comrade Stalin.'

'All mention of Colonel Nagorski in connection with the Konstantin Project has been erased. As far as the rest of the world is concerned, he had nothing to do with it. I have no wish for our enemies to gloat over the death of one of our most prominent inventors.'

'And what about the boy?' asked Pekkala.

'I have given it some thought.' Stalin reached for his pipe.

'It seems to me that can all be pushed to the edge, don't you agree, Pekkala?'

'Yes, Comrade Stalin.'

'The killer lurks in every one of us,' Stalin continued. 'If it didn't, our whole species would long ago have ceased to walk this earth. And it would be a waste to throw away a young man who might one day follow in the footsteps of his father.'

'He has potential,' said Pekkala.

'I agree, and that is why I have appointed the boy to be Zalka's apprentice until the Konstantin Project is completed. After that, he will be enrolled in the Moscow Technical Institute. But I am expecting results. I will be watching. And you, Pekkala, will keep your Emerald Eye on him.'

'I will indeed,' he said.

Stalin aimed the pipe at him. 'I see you have a nice new jacket.'

'Ah,' said Pekkala. He looked down at the clothes Kirov had bought him. 'This is just temporary. I'm having some made up at Linsky's.'

'Linsky's?' asked Stalin as he hunted in his desk drawer for a match. 'Over by the Bolshoi Theatre? You know what they say about the things he makes? Clothes for dead men! What do you think of that, Pekkala?'

'It gets more funny every time I hear it.'

'Anyway,' said Stalin, 'you won't be needing anything from Linsky.'

'I won't?'

Stalin had found a match. He struck it, the tiny stick positioned between his thumb and first two fingers. For the next few seconds, the only sound was the dry rustle of his breathing as he coaxed the tobacco to burn. The soft, sweet smell drifted towards Pekkala. Finally he spoke. 'I am sending you to Siberia.'

'What?' shouted Pekkala.

'You are going back to Borodok.'

The door opened. Stalin's secretary, Poskrebyshev, poked his head into the room. 'Is everything all right, Comrade Stalin?'

'Out!' snapped Stalin.

Poskrebyshev took a long and disapproving look at Pekkala. Then he closed the door behind him.

'You are sending me to prison?' asked Pekkala.

'Yes, although not as a prisoner. Not officially, at any rate. There has been a murder in the Borodok camp.'

'With respect, Comrade Stalin, there are murders in that camp every day of the week.'

'This one has caught my attention.'

'When am I leaving?'

'In two days. Until then, you may consider yourself on vacation.'

'What about Major Kirov?'

'Oh, the Major will be busy here in Moscow, handling his end of the investigation. I have already spoken to him, here in this office, earlier today. Which reminds me.' Stalin reached into his pocket and then, from his closed fist, dropped four kumquats upon the desk. 'He gave me these. What am I supposed to do with them?'

'Kirov didn't tell you?'

'He just said they were a gift.'

'You eat them, Comrade Stalin.'

'What?' He picked one up and stared at it. 'In little pieces?'

'No,' said Pekkala. 'All at once. All four of them. Just put them in your mouth and bite down. It's a real treat.'

'Hmm.' Stalin gathered the fruit back into his hand. 'Well, I suppose I could give it a try.'

'I should be going, Comrade Stalin, or my vacation will be over before I am out of the building.'

Stalin's attention was focused on the kumquats in his palm. 'Good,' he mumbled, staring at the tiny orange globes laid out on his palm. 'Goodbye, Pekkala.'

'Goodbye, Comrade Stalin.'

As he walked out through the waiting room, Pekkala heard Stalin roar as he bit down on the kumquats and then spat them across the room. 'Pekkala!'

Pekkala only smiled and kept on walking.

MA